# THE RISE OF THE
# HORNED RAT

The end of the world is coming, and few realise it. In the mountain realm of the dwarfs, even the stoutest longbeard is starting to doubt that they can weather the coming storm. Orcs, goblins and skaven swarm the Underway in ever-growing numbers. A vast exodus of all sorts of vile creatures from the barren lands to the east tests the defenders of the mountain passes, and allies are scarce as war and horror falls across the lands of man. And in the skaven Under-Empire, a new power is rising – the great rat-daemons known as vermin-lords walk the world in ever greater numbers, and they have a plan that will ensure the dominance of the skaven over all. The Rise of the Horned Rat has begun.

*Visit* blacklibrary.com *for the full range of Warhammer: The End Times novels and Quick Reads, as well as digital versions of the Warhammer: The End Times campaign books to use in your games of Warhammer.*

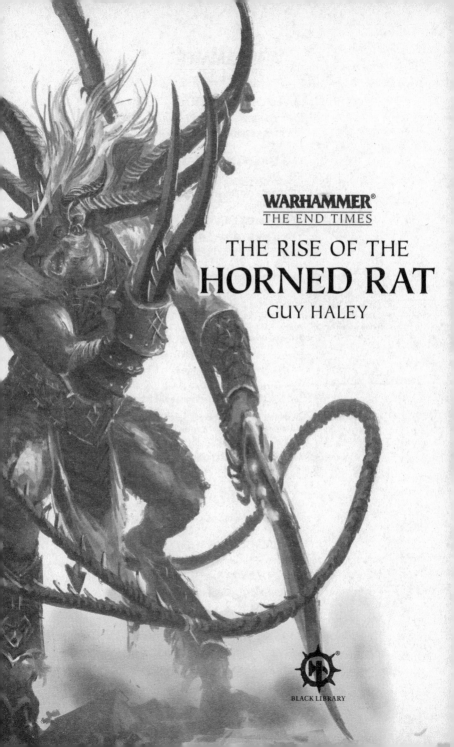

WARHAMMER®
THE END TIMES

# THE RISE OF THE
# HORNED RAT

## GUY HALEY

BLACK LIBRARY

## A BLACK LIBRARY PUBLICATION

First published in 2015.
This edition published in 2015 by
Black Library,
Games Workshop Ltd.,
Willow Road,
Nottingham, NG7 2WS, UK.

10 9 8 7 6 5 4 3 2 1

Cover artwork by Paul Dainton.
Internal artwork by Mark Holmes and Alex Boyd.
Map artwork by John Michelbach.

A CIP record for this book is available from the British Library.

UK ISBN: 978 1 84970 941 5
US ISBN: 978 1 84970 946 0

See Black Library on the internet at

# blacklibrary.com

Find out more about Games Workshop
and the world of Warhammer at

# games-workshop.com

Printed and bound by CPI Group (UK) Ltd, Croydon, CR0 4YY

The world is dying, but it has been so since the coming of the Chaos Gods.

For years beyond reckoning, the Ruinous Powers have coveted the mortal realm. They have made many attempts to seize it, their anointed champions leading vast hordes into the lands of men, elves and dwarfs. Each time, they have been defeated.

Until now.

In the frozen north, Archaon, a former templar of the warrior-god Sigmar, has been crowned the Everchosen of Chaos. He stands poised to march south and bring ruin to the lands he once fought to protect. Behind him amass all the forces of the Dark Gods, mortal and daemonic. When they come, they will bring with them a storm such as has never been seen.

And beneath the world, the ratlike skaven have united for the first time in many centuries. Their numbers are beyond counting and with the daemonic verminlords leading them to glory, their ascension is assured. In the western lands of Lustria, Clan Pestilens launch an all-out assault on their ancient foes, the lizardmen, an assault that the cold-blooded servants of the Old Ones cannot weather.

The southern countries of Tilea and Estalia have been devastated, and Skavenblight expands to create a capital city for the skaven from which they can rule the surface world as well as their Under-Empire. Further north, they swarm into Sigmar's Empire to finish what the hosts of the Glottkin began and drown the remaining cities of man beneath a tide of fur.

And in the Worlds Edge Mountains, the most hated foes of the skaven, the stalwart dwarfs, fortify their holds, preparing for the onslaught that they know is coming. Their time is coming to an end and the time of the skaven is at hand.

These are the End Times.

# PROLOGUE

*The Realm of Ruin*

In the darkest of places, in the most timeless of times, the twelve Shadow Lords of Decay convened in dire assembly.

They came swiftly on foot, scurrying through the rotting refuse that choked their domain. Their high horned heads bobbed furtively, now visible, now hidden by mounded rubbish: the wealth and wisdom of myriad ages taken, gnawed, despoiled, tasted and inevitably discarded. One could find all manner of treasure buried in the stinking filth, but it meant nothing to the creatures who possessed it. It was only to be coveted for the sake of having, ruined for the sake of ruination, and quickly forgotten.

Such was the way of this young race. Scavengers, usurpers, content to squat in the desolation of better peoples, their unnatural vitality and ingenuity nought but engines for entropy. The skaven were the true children of Chaos, and this place, this foetid reek under a glowering sky, was theirs alone – a nowhere realm nibbled out of the Realm of Chaos, given shape by the spirits of the ratmen that came to dwell there. A dismal place, the Realm of Ruin, a hell its inhabitants dearly desired to remake upon the mortal world.

A verminlord is a huge creature, tall as a giant, but in the wrack of the Realm of Ruin there is no scale a mortal mind can make sense of. Thus, although the Shadow Lords walked on two feet, although their heads were capped with mighty horns – and although all possessed some obvious, uncanny power – when seen from afar they appeared small and timorous, resembling nothing so much as the lowly creatures from whom they had descended. They moved like rats and they were cautious like rats, stopping every hundred paces to lift their noses and sniff at the air with a rat's sly mix of boldness and fear. Rats – rats cavorting in the rubbish of worlds.

In ones and threes, but never twos – for two lends itself too readily to betrayal – they came to the place of gathering. Verminhall, the great hall of the Realm of Ruin. The immortal lords of skavenkind converged upon the building. Once close, they broke into a scurrying run, when they were sure no others could see them scamper. They entered the portals of the vast edifice with unseemly haste, keen to clear the open space around its walls and the terrible things that hunted there.

A grandiose, overstated mirror to the Temple of the Horned Rat that stood in the living world, Verminhall was dominated by a tower that soared impossibly high. Sprouting from the uncertain centre of the building, thick and ugly, it disappeared into the churning purple clouds. Its top was lost to the sky, and its filth-encrusted walls flashed to the violence of emerald lightning. As with all things the children of Chaos possessed, it had doubtlessly been stolen from forgotten creatures – some race that had regarded itself as finer and worthier, only to fall in surprise to the vermintide. After all, this chain of events was set to repeat itself forever. In a sense, it already had. Time has no meaning in the Realm of Chaos.

The greater powers sneered at the Horned Rat, seeing him as one of the infinite array of petty godlings whose insignificant domains marred the purity of Chaos. They were wrong to do so. The Horned Rat was no longer some minor creature, for he had grown mighty. His children were legion. Long-fermented plans were at last coming to fruition.

If this terrible place taught any lesson at all – to those few able to survive here long enough to receive it – it would be this: one should not dismiss the offspring of the lowly.

The hour of the Horned Rat was at hand.

The daemonkind verminlords, first among the servants of the Horned Rat, were as numerous as their mortal counterparts, countless in their multitudes and ubiquitous in the culverts and gulleys of creation. But of them, only twelve were deemed truly great. The greatest of these twelve was Lord Skreech Verminking. He who had once been many, and was now one.

Causality had no meaning in the Realm of Ruin, not in any sense that a mortal would understand. But Verminking's intention was to arrive after his peers, in order to underscore his own importance, and he always performed as to his intent.

The interior of Verminhall was a cave, a monument, a howling void, a place of life and of death, a temple, a palace – all, none and many more of these things besides. The laws of nature were openly mocked. Braziers burned backwards, green light glinting from Verminking's multiple horns as warpstone condensed from the very air. Fumes pulled themselves into dented brass firebowls, adding second by second to the mass of the solid magic growing within them. The lump of warpstone embedded in the daemon's empty left eye socket flared with sympathy at its brothers' birth pangs as the verminlord passed.

There was no sense to the geometry of the great hall. Stairs went on infinitely to nowhere. Black rivers flowed along walls. Within round cages of iron, cats roasted eternally in green fire without being consumed. Windows opened in midair, looking upon places neither near nor far, but most definitely not within the bounds of the Realm of Ruin. The squeaking of a billion times a billion anguished skaven souls made a painful chittering that obliterated all other sound. Verminking moved through it as one long accustomed to visiting, taking unexpected turns and secret ways precipitately and without warning, the ultimate rat in the ultimate maze.

The other eleven great verminlords awaited their lord in the Chamber of the Shadow Council, a room that was at once endless in size and claustrophobically small. A hollow, thirteen-sided table, as wide as forever, dominated the floor. A pool of noisome liquid was at its centre, in whose oceans strange images stirred.

As they awaited their chief, the Shadow Lords of Decay bickered and schemed with one another, or sat grooming their remaining patches of fur with long tongues, content to listen to their peers, hate them, and secretly plot their undoing. All the others were present, and thus only two places were empty: Verminking's own, the first position; and that next to his, the thirteenth. The head of the table, in a sense, this was the seat of the Horned Rat himself – a massive throne carved of warpstone, big enough for a god. The likeness of its owner glared in baleful majesty from its canopy's apex.

It was said that the Great One could watch them from the unblinking, glowing eyes of his facsimile. Verminking suspected he watched them all the time; he was a god after all, the verminlord reasoned. Such was the burden of being the most favoured of the Horned Rat's many children.

Lord Verminking was not alone in his nervousness, although he hid it better than most. As was usual at such gatherings, each member of the assembled Shadow Council broke regularly from his bluster, blagging and threats to glance at the place of the Horned Rat. The god was known to attend the meetings himself – infrequently perhaps, but thus always unexpectedly. When he did attend, the musk of fear hung heavy on the air, and often as not a new opening became available upon the Council. In their own fear of the verminlords, no mortal skaven would have ever suspected that the rat-daemons felt terror for any reason, but they did. Their hearts were as craven as those of lesser ratkin.

'Lord, I have come!' announced Verminking. As he made for his chair, he kicked aside dozens of the blind white rats carpeting the floor. From the mouths of these pathetic vermin came the mewling excuses of fallen skaven lords, their souls condemned to recount their failures forever.

Verminking's musk glands clenched as he squeezed past the Horned Rat's throne to gain his own seat. When he reached his place, a lesser verminlord – one of the elite guard of the Shadow Council – appeared from the gloom and pulled Verminking's chair out for him. The daemon gave it a cursory examination before sitting. One could never be too careful in the domain of the Great Horned One. The verminlord guards in service to the Council had their tongues ripped out so that they could not relay what they heard, but that was no barrier to ambition – nor, in that place of sorcery, to speech.

'You are late, Lord Skreech,' hissed Lurklox, the shadow-shrouded Master of All Deceptions. He was Verminking's opposite number and, therefore, his second greatest rival. At least that was the case bar every third meeting, when Lurklox was replaced by Lord Verstirix of the fourth position in ceremonial opposition to Verminking. All this was enshrined on the Great Black Pillar growing in the tower. The rules governing the mortal Lords of Decay were maddeningly complex, but as nothing to those that dictated the politics of their hidden demigods. The Black Pillar in Skavenblight had been inscribed by the Horned Rat himself. The Great Black Pillar – the *real* sum of the Horned One's knowledge, the verminlords liked to think – was eternally updated. It grew constantly from the root like gnawing-teeth as more edicts were added to its hellishly contradictory catalogue. Rarely a day went by without some new ruling. The pillar was already over one hundred miles high, and the text upon it was very small. Only Verminking confidently claimed to know the full scope of the Horned Rat's teachings. He was lying.

'We are entitled to be late, yes-yes, Lurklox. It is our right!' insisted the lord of all verminlords. 'Many places we must go, many things we must see, so that you might see them too.'

'You dishonour us,' said Lurklox. One could never quite catch sight of the assassin, he was so swathed in shadow.

Vermalanx the Poxlord waved a diseased hand at Verminking. 'Yes-yes,' he said thickly. 'Mighty-exalted the great Skreech is, he of the many minds and many horns.'

Vermalanx dipped his head in a bow that could have been mocking, but so much of the Poxlord's face had rotted down to brown bone that it was impossible to tell. The more sycophantic members of the Council clapped politely. From lumps of warp rock, empty eye sockets and multiple eyes randomly arranged around malformed heads, they gave sidelong looks to their fellows, determined not to be out-fawned.

The shard of warpstone embedded in Verminking's face flared dangerously. 'Do not mock-mock, do not tease!' He slammed his hand-claw down on the table. 'We are the greatest of all of you. The Great Horned One himself whispers into our ear.' Among Verminking's many untruths, this statement had the distinction of being mostly true, even if it was disconcerting for him when the Horned Rat did actually whisper in his ear.

'Oh, most assuredly you are the greatest, O greatest great

one, most pusillanimous sage, O most malfeasant malefactor,' said Verminlord Skweevritch. The metal prosthetics covering the upper part of his body hissed green steam as he twitched submissively.

'Lickspittle,' chittered the Verminlord Basqueak.

'I say vote Skweevritch off-away! We have no time for such sycophancy,' said Lord Skrolvex, the fattest and most repugnant, to Verminking's eyes, of their number.

'Silence!' he shouted, his multiple voices covering all frequencies audible to skaven ears, to deeply unpleasant effect. 'Silence,' he said again for good measure. Long tails lashed. Ears quivered in discomfort. 'There is business afoot, yes. Business we must watch, oh so carefully, my lords. In the mortal lands, great Lords of Decay meet, great Lords of Decay plot-scheme. They meet, so we the Shadow Council, great *Vermin*lords of Decay, the *true* Council, must meet too-also.'

Chattering and insults were traded. Verminking silenced them with a hand-claw, and pointed his other at the pool. 'Listen! See-smell! Look-learn!' he said. Greasy bubbles popped on the surface as the pool became agitated. In slow circuit the liquid turned, swirling around and around, faster and faster, to form a whirlpool, whose funnel plunged deeper and deeper until it surely must have surpassed the limits of the water. A black circle appeared at its bottom, and the whirlpool went down forever. The other verminlords looked at it in askance, lest it drag them in, but Verminking had no such fear. He stared eagerly into the depths of eternity. Fumes rose from the liquid, sparking with warp-lightning, before settling down as a glowing mist. Within the mist, the following image formed.

A room not unlike the Shadow Council's, though not so grand. A table like the Shadow Council's, though not so ornate. Thrones around the table, like the Shadow Council's, though not so large. In the twelve thrones sat twelve skaven lords of great power, though not so powerful as the twelve who watched them unseen.

Verminking's skin twitched. The Verminlords of Decay watched the mortal Lords of Decay. Who watched them? Where did it stop? Were there conclaves of rats, squeaking in the sewers observed by gimlet-eyed beastmasters? Were there layer upon layer of ever greater rat-things plotting and interfering with those below? He chased the thought away, but it lingered at the back of his fractured mind, insistent as a flea in his ear.

The mortal skaven were in full debate. Things were not going well. Shouting and squeaking raised a clamour that shook the room. Many were standing to wave accusing forepaws at one another. Some squeaked privately to one another, or shot knowing looks across the table as deals were silently struck and as quickly broken.

Just as Verminking had silenced the Shadow Council, so Kritislik the Seerlord silenced the Council of Thirteen, although nowhere near as majestically. He was white-furred and horned, and that should have ensured him supremacy. He was chief of the grey seers, the wizard lords of the skaven, blessed by the Horned Rat himself, and nominal chief of the Council in his absence. But the others were in rebellious mood. Kritislik was agitated, squeaking rapidly and without authority. He had yet to squirt musk, but the look of fear was on him, in his twitching nose, widened eyes and bristling fur.

'Quiet-quiet! You blame, shout-squeak! All fault here. Great victories we have were in manlands of Estalia and Tilea.'

'Many slaves, much plunder-spoils,' said Kratch Doomclaw, warlord of Clan Rictus. 'All is going to plan. Soon the man-things will fall. Listen to the white-fur.'

'No!' said one, huge and deep voiced. He was black as night and unconquerable as the mountains. Lord Gnawdwell of Clan Mors. 'You take-steal too much, far beyond your scavenge rights. You test my patience, thief-thief, sneaker. I will not listen to your prattling one heartbeat longer.'

'My clanrats, my victory,' said Kratch, making an effort to

keep his voice low and slow. 'Where is Lord Gnawdwell's trophy-prize? I shall squeak you where – still in the hands of the dwarf-things, who you have not yet defeated.'

Squeaking laughter came from several of the others, including, most irksomely for Gnawdwell, Lord Paskrit, the obese warlord-general of all Skavendom.

The lords of the four greater clans scowled at this display of indiscipline among the warlord clans. Lord Morskittar of Clan Skryre, emperor of warlocks and tinkerer in chief, was not impressed.

'Many devices, many weapons, many warptokens' worth of new machines you of the warlord clans were given-granted in aid of the Great Uprising. What have we to show-see for it? Yes-yes, very good. Tilea-place and Estalia-place gone-destroyed.'

General noises of approval interrupted him. Morskittar held his paws up, palms flat, and bared his teeth in disapproval. 'Fools to cheer like stupid slave-meat! The weakest human-lands destroyed only. Frog-things still in their stone temple-homes. Dwarf-things still in the mountains. And Empire-place not yet destroyed!' He shook his head, his tail lashing back and forth behind him. 'Disappointing.'

'What you squeak-say? Where are your armies?' said Lord Griznekt Mancarver of Clan Skab. 'Guns no good without paw-fingers to pull triggers.'

More uproar and shouted accusations. All around the room, the elite Albino Guard of the Council stiffened, ready to intervene on the winning side should open conflict erupt.

'No! No!' said Morskittar. 'I will speak! I will speak!' He slammed a skull carved of pure warpstone down onto the table. It banged like a cannon, the report buying him silence. 'Why point-indicate me with paw of blame?' said Morskittar slyly. 'I say the grey seers are the ones who shoulder responsibility. Clan Scruten are those who bring everything to ruin.' He pointed at Kritislik.

'Yes-yes!' chittered the others immediately, all of whom had their own reasons for loathing the priest-magicians. 'The seers, Clan Scruten!'

'Outrage! Outrage!' squealed Kritislik. 'I have led this council long ages-time! I led great summoning many breedings ago! I speak for the Horned Rat!'

'You speak for yourself,' said Paskrit the Vast, gruffly. Sensing weakness, he heaved his bulk up to face Kritislik on his foot-paws. 'You speak for Clan Scruten. Always scheming, always plotting. Always say do this, do that! Why is it Clan Mors find itself fighting Clan Rictus? Why Clan Skurvy lose half of thrall clans the day before sea-battle of Sartosa-place?'

'Grey seer is why, Clan Scruten! Clan Scruten are to blame,' croaked Arch-Plaguelord Nurglitch.

They all shouted then, except for the inscrutable Night-lord Sneek, master of Clan Eshin, who watched it all with hooded eyes half hidden by his mask and no scent to betray his thoughts.

'It is not our fault! Your incompetence and greed-grasping stops the obeying of our rightful orders! We are the horned rats. We are the chosen-best of the Great Horned One! You fight-fight, scrapping like common rat-things on human middens. Listen to us, or suffer,' shouted Kritislik.

'No! Lies-deceit. You pit us against one another when all we wish to do is work in harmony for the betterment of all skavenkind!' said Lord Gnawdwell.

The others nodded solemnly. 'Truth-word!' they said. 'We would conquer, but for you. Grey seers make us fight-fight!' They would all happily have knifed each other in the back at the least provocation, whether a grey seer was pulling the strings or not. That the grey seers usually *were* pulling the strings complicated matters enormously.

The Council of Thirteen erupted into a cacophony of squeaked accusations. The scent of aggression grew strong.

The Shadow Lords looked on with growing disapproval.

'See-see,' said Verminking. 'Great victories they have, and now they fall to fighting.'

'They are what they are, and no more,' said Vermalanx disinterestedly. 'Children yet, but mastery shall come to them. Then true greatness we shall see-smell in due course. I care not for this – my Nurglitch's plans are well advanced.'

'Yes-yes,' said Throxstraggle, Vermalanx's ally and fellow plaguelord. 'What care we for these pup squeakings?'

'Your grave error to set aside Clan Pestilens from the doing-aims of the others. You are not apart from this, poxlords,' said Verminking. 'You and yours distance yourselves, but Clan Pestilens is nothing alone. You think-remember that.'

Vermalanx chirred angrily.

'No mastery will come. They fail! They fail!' spat Basqueak. 'Fool-things! Squabbling while the world slips from their paws. Always the same, civil war comes again. Skavenblight will ring to the sound of blade on blade. Man-things and dwarf-things will recover, and skaven stay in the shadows. Always the same.'

'Yes-yes,' said Verminking. 'They fail. But watch...'

In the mortal realm, Kritislik stood, waving a fist at the other Lords of Decay, admonishing them for their stupidity. From the look on his face, he thought it was working, for the others suddenly fell silent and shrank back in their seats, eyes wide. A few bared their throats in submission before they could catch themselves. Someone shamefully let spray the musk of fear. It hung heavy over the crowd, an accusation of cowardice.

Kritislik began to crow. The mightiest lords of Skavendom, and he had them in the palm of his paw. Now was his chance to stamp his authority all over this rabble again!

Or maybe not. Kritislik was so taken by his own oratory that he had completely failed to notice the shape growing behind him.

Black smoke jetted from the seat of the Horned Rat. The

wisps of shadow built into a cloud that writhed and began to take the form of something huge and malevolent.

'Ah! Now! Order, is good, yes! You listen-hear good, you...' Kritislik stopped mid-sentence. His nose twitched. 'You are not listening to me, are you? You do not hear-smell me good?' he said. He was answered by eleven shaking heads, the owners of which were all trying to look inconspicuous.

He turned around to see a horned head forming from darkness more complete than that found in the deepest places of the world.

Kritislik threw himself to the floor in outright obeisance as the manifested Horned Rat opened eyes that flooded the room with sickly green light. Words of power rumbled from some other place, the voice underpinned by hideous chittering – the deathsqueaks of every rat and skaven ever to have drawn breath.

*'Children of the Horned Rat,'* he said, his voice as final as a tunnel collapse, *'how you disappoint your father.'*

'O Great One! O Horned One! Once more I welcome you to the–'

*'No one summon-bids I, Kritislik. I come, I go, wherever I please. I have no master.'*

'I... I...'

*'You squabble pathetically. This will cease now. Your plans are sound, your alliances are not. I will not countenance another failure. Long have Clan Scruten had my blessing. I have given you my mark, great power, and long life.'* The head bore down on Kritislik, lips parting to show teeth made of crackling light. *'You have wasted my favour.'*

Without warning, a hand formed from the smoke, scrabbling as if seeking purchase on an unseen barrier. Fingers and claws pointed forwards. The air warped as the hand pushed against an unseen skin, then burst its way into common reality and reached down.

Kritislik squealed in terror as he was plucked from the floor by his tail. His fine robes dropped down to cover his head. The musk of fear sprayed without restraint, followed by a rich stream of droppings.

*'The others are right-correct, little Kritislik.'* A second hand reached out from the darkness, where now a muscular torso had also formed. A gentle claw-finger lifted the hem of Kritislik's upended robes to reveal his petrified face, and stroked along his horns. *'So much I have given you, and yet you scheme for more. Greedy, when there is enough for all to feast upon. Your avarice stops now.'*

The mouth of the Horned Rat gaped wide. Kritislik was hoisted high by the tail over a maw swirling with terrible possibilities. Kritislik stared down and gibbered at what he saw there.

'M-mercy! M-mercy, O Great One! We will double our efforts! Triple them! Quadrupl–' His pleas ended in a scream as his tail was released. The grey seer fell into the eternally hungry mouth of his god. The Horned Rat's jaws snapped shut. His eyes closed with pleasure, and when he opened them again they burned with a cold and terrible light.

*'Thirteen times thirteen passes of the Chaos moon I will give you. Thirteen times thirteen moons I will wait. Go to your legions and your workshops! Bring me victory. Bring me dominance over this mortal realm! You must be as one, work as one, as single-minded as a swarm pouring from a cracked sewer-pipe – all rats scurry-flood in same direction. Only then will you inherit the ruins of this world, only then will you rule. Thirteen times thirteen moons! Fail, and all will suffer the fate of the seer.'*

With a crackle of green lightning and the tolling of a bell so loud the room quaked, the Horned Rat vanished. Kritislik's bones lay black and smoking upon the floor.

The tolling bell faded and stopped. The Lords of Decay

uncovered their ears, picked themselves up off the floor and sniffed the air.

The ensuing silence lasted for all of fifteen swift skaven heartbeats.

'I move,' said Morskittar, swallowing to moisten his dry throat, 'to vote the grey seers from the Council. Clan Scruten will sit-rule no more!'

For only the fourth time in skaven history, a vote was passed unanimously. As soon as it was done, the clanlords immediately fell to arguing again: over what to do, and more importantly, over who should occupy the empty seat.

In the Realm of Ruin, the twelve Shadow Lords of Decay managed a shocked silence for a little longer.

Skweevritch broke it. 'But the Great Horned One has not gone abroad in the mortal realm for many-many years. Centuries!' he wailed.

'What-what? What?' squealed Soothgnawer, white-furred as the unfortunate Kritislik. He was the champion of Clan Scruten and was dismayed, but he did not voice his objections too loudly in case the Horned Rat became aware of them. 'No seer on the Council? No seer? Unthinkable.'

'And what of us, what do we do?' said Skrolvex. They all glanced nervously at the throne, in case their god should pay them a visit also. The Horned Rat's appetite was notoriously insatiable.

Verminking spoke, cunningly and persuasively. 'Pups need guidance. Who becomes slave, who becomes lord. The strongest decides. The Horned Rat! The Great Horned One has shown us the way. Is it not clear? We must follow his example. We must go to them, into the mortal realm. We will guide them.' He pointed at the bickering mortal skaven.

Lord Basqueak twitched. 'Mortal realm? We are vulnerable there! Danger! Much peril.' His tail twitched.

They were all immortal, chosen of the Horned Rat. And yet

certain rules applied to them, as they did to all inhabitants of the higher realms. To suffer death and banishment for a hundred years and a day back into the Realm of Chaos was not a terminal experience, but their places on the Shadow Council would be forfeit, and no verminlord could countenance such a loss of power.

'Coward!' squealed Kreeskuttle. He stood tall with a rattle of armour. Kreeskuttle was the mightiest of arm upon the Council, if not of intellect.

Basqueak hissed, jutting his head forwards. 'Then you, Lord Kreeskuttle, shall go to the mortal lands and take the risk! Show-tell how brave you are.'

Kreeskuttle growled, and sank back into his chair.

'I will go,' said Vermalanx arrogantly. 'I have no fear. I will go to the land of the frog-things, there to guide the great plagues.'

'Yes! Go-go!' burbled Throxstraggle enthusiastically, notably making no promise of his own to follow.

'I too,' said Soothgnawer. 'It wrong-bad no seer sits on the Council. I will help them win their place again. We must atone for our sins against the Horned Rat.'

They eyed each other with quick, suspicious eyes. Plots were forming, plans being drawn up. No doubt others would go without declaring their intentions. Outrageous risk for ephemeral gain wobbled yet again on the balance of the skaven soul.

'Soothgnawer is right,' said Verminking. 'The grey seers hold the key.'

The mist over the pool shivered, clearing away the bickering lords of the mortal skaven. The image wavered, and a narrow alleyway materialised, one of thousands within the crammed confines of Skavenblight. Noses twitched, teeth bared. The verminlords recognised it instinctively, although it changed daily. The home of all skaven.

'Here-here, valued lords. Here-here is our weapon!' said Verminking.

A white-furred figure scuttled along, constantly looking over his shoulder. A massive rat ogre paced along beside him, taking one step for every fifteen of the grey seer's.

'Is that...' asked Vermalanx.

'It isn't...' said Kreeskuttle.

'It is!' gasped Basqueak.

'Thanquol!' squeaked Poxparl.

'Why him-him?' said Grunsqueel, moved finally to speak. 'He is useless! Great power has been gifted-given to this horned one, and what has he done? He has squandered-wasted it. Of all of them, he is by far the worst.'

'Used it no good.'

'True-true. How many times has Thanquol, great grey seer, failed us?' said Lurklox. 'The Horned Rat should eat him too!'

'Many-many times!' chittered the others. 'Failure! Liability!'

'See-watch, how weak he is! He goes always tail down, the musk of fear never far from squirting. He is weak. Excuses, excuses and never success,' said Basqueak.

'He is a coward!' said Skweevritch, which was a little rich, as he was no hero himself.

'Fool-fool. The dwarf-thing and man-thing have thwarted him alone many-many times!' said Kreeskuttle.

'The disaster at Nuln.'

'The shame of his failed summoning!' said Basqueak. The others nodded in emphatic agreement. More than one of them had been ready to step into the mortal world that day, only for Thanquol to botch it.

Verminking held up a hand-claw and hissed. 'He is all these things and more. Failure! Dreg! It is in part because of him no grey seer sits upon the Council in the world below.'

'Failure!' the others squeaked.

'Fool-fool! He should be destroyed-killed, not aided,' said Throxstraggle.

'Yes, failure. Yes, fool-fool. But in him is our greatest tool.'

'What-what?'

'Lord Skreech squeaks madness,' said Verstirix. The warrior verminlord puffed up his chest. 'Enough! Veto right is mine.'

'Do you challenge us, the greatest of our number?' said Verminking.

Verstirix looked to his colleagues for support; they pointedly looked away.

'Grey Seer Thanquol has much service to render. Yes-yes,' said Soothgnawer.

'Too much faith you have in him,' said Basqueak. 'Fool-thing, Throxstraggle is correct. We should slay-kill very slowly. Then find another.'

Verminking stroked the surface of the foetid pool, his long black claw sending ripples across its surface and the image shimmering above it. 'No-no. It is he, it is he.'

'Who make you decide-determine? Vote! Vote!' screeched Verstirix.

'Yes, vote-vote. Ten against two. You lose, Soothgnawer, Skreech,' bubbled Vermalanx.

'Not two against ten, not that at all. You count bad.'

'Two! Two! I see only two, fool-things!'

'*Three* against ten,' said Verminking quietly. He looked meaningfully at the Horned Rat's throne. It could have been a trick of the light, but it appeared that the warpstone eyes of the effigy atop it glowed more brightly.

A silence fell over the Council. Tails twitched. Beady eyes darted beneath horns that shook, just a little, with fear.

'I say,' said Poxparl calculatingly, 'that we give Thanquol another chance. Mighty Lord Skreech has moved-touched my heart.'

'Yes-yes,' squeaked Basqueak very loudly, talking directly towards the vacant throne. 'I vote yes-yes.'

'I too,' said Throxstraggle.

'If it is so, it is so,' muttered Vermalanx.

One by one, the verminlords voted. The motion was passed by a narrow margin – there had never yet been a unanimous vote on the Shadow Council. Verminking looked to Verstirix, challenging him to use his veto. The ex-warlord looked at the empty throne, then found something on the surface of the table that needed his urgent attention.

'It is done, then,' said Lord Skreech Verminking triumphantly. 'Let us rip the veil between worlds. Let us stalk mortal lands again! Skitter-disperse, go to your favourites.' He peered hungrily into the pool. 'Go where you will, as quickly as you can. We shall go to Thanquol.'

Thanquol's nose twitched, his famous sixth sense giving him the itchy feeling that he was being watched. He looked around the stinking alley, into crooked windows, along the skyline, black against the foggy night, into alleyways where sagging duckboards crossed open sewers. He saw no threat, but shivered nonetheless. His musk gland clenched.

'Sssss! Jumping-fear at own shadow! At own shadow!' he scolded himself. He jerked an angry paw at his bodyguard. 'Boneripper, on-on!'

And so, unknowing of the attention focused upon him at that moment, Thanquol continued with his furtive passage through Skavenblight.

# PART ONE

The Lords of Ruin
Autumn–Winter 2523

# ONE

*Kingsmeet*

The kingsmeet was over, and Belegar was glad. Soon he could go home.

The dwarf kings met in Karaz-a-Karak, Everpeak, home of the dwarf High King. Everpeak was the last place in the world where the ancient glory of the dwarfs shone undimmed. No matter that only half its halls were occupied, or that the works of its forges could never recapture the skill of the ancestors. The place teemed with dwarfs in such multitudes that one could be forgiven for thinking that they were still a numerous people.

Being there made Belegar miserable. In the distant past his own realm had been Karaz-a-Karak's rival in riches and size. His inability to return it to glory filled him with shame.

He sat in an antechamber awaiting the High King, nursing a jewelled goblet of fine ale. He had been born and raised in Karaz-a-Karak, but half a century of dwelling in the dangerous ruins of Vala-Azrilungol had blunted his memory of its riches. The opulence on display was astounding – more value in gold and artefacts in this one, small waiting room than were in his own throne room. He felt decidedly shabby, as he had done all the way through the kingsmeet. Two months hard travelling and fighting to get here. He had to sneak out of his own hold, and he would have to sneak back in. Now here he was, kept behind like a naughty beardling after all the other kings had been sent to feast. Nothing Thorgrim would have to say to him would be good. The two of them had ceased to see eye to eye some time ago. Belegar steeled himself for another long rant about failed obligations and unpaid debt.

He rolled his eyes. What had he been thinking, telling the others he occupied a third of Karak Eight Peaks? From a strictly technical point of view, it could be deemed truthful. He had opened up mines, captured a good part of the upper deeps, and held a strong corridor between the surface city and the East Gate. But in reality his holdings were far less. The East Gate itself, the citadel, the mountain halls of Kvinn-wyr. Everything else had to be visited in strength. And he had promised military aid. With what?

Not for the first time, he cursed his pride.

The doors to the far end of the chamber opened wide. A dwarf in the livery of Thorgrim's personal household bowed low, sweeping his hood from his head.

'Majesty, the King of Kings is ready for you.'

Belegar slid from the rich coverings of the bench. A second servant appeared from nowhere, a fresh mug of ale on his silver tray. Belegar downed his first, until that moment untouched, and took the second.

'This way,' said the first dwarf, holding out his hand.

Belegar was shown into a chamber he knew only too well. One of Thorgrim's private rooms high in the palace, it was large and impressive, and consequently used by the High King when he was going to dress down others of royal blood. It had grand views of the approach to Karaz-a-Karak, seven hundred feet below. Summer sunlight streamed in through the tall windows. A fire of logs burned in the huge hearth. A clock ticked on the wall.

'Belegar,' said Thorgrim levelly. The king wore his armour and his crown. Belegar tried to think of a time he had seen him without it, and failed. The latest volume of the Great Book of Grudges sat open on a lectern. A bleeding-knife and a quill rested in specially cut spaces by it. 'Please, take a seat.'

Thorgrim gestured to one of a number of smartly dressed servants. They disappeared, returning moments later with a tall jug of beer and a platter piled high with roast meats.

Belegar sat down opposite the High King with resignation. 'I do not mean to keep you from the feast. Please, help yourself, sharpen your appetite for when you join the others,' he said.

Belegar did as asked. The kingsmeet had been long, and he was hungry. Both food and ale were delicious.

'We'll wait a moment before we get started,' said Thorgrim. 'There's another I wish to speak with.'

The door opened again then. Belegar turned in his seat, his eyebrows rising in surprise at the sight of Ungrim Ironfist. The Slayer King strode in and took up a seat. He nodded at Belegar as he sat. His face was stony. Ungrim always had been angry. Belegar had no idea how he managed to survive caught between two oaths so contradictory. And he had just lost his son. Belegar felt a stab of sympathy for Ungrim. The safety of his own boy was never far from his thoughts.

Thorgrim pressed his hands on the desk before speaking, formulating his words with care. 'All this business with the elgi and the walking dead has got me unsettled,' said Thorgrim. 'Things are happening of great portent, things that speak to me that...' He shook his head. He looked even more tired than he had in the meeting. 'We discussed all that. I am grateful for your support.'

'Of course, my king,' said Belegar.

'Why wouldn't I want to march out and destroy our enemies? You've heard all I have to say on this matter,' said Ungrim.

'I have,' agreed Thorgrim. 'Summoning the throngs will not be easy. You have heard Kazador and Thorek's objections. They are not alone. The argument between attack and defence is one I have had all my life, and I fear it is too late to win it.' Thorgrim paused. 'I have asked you both here as you are, in your own ways, special cases. Ungrim,' he said to the Slayer King, 'to you I urge a little caution. Do not throw away your throng in the quest for vengeance for your son's death, or in order to fulfil your Slayer's oath.

Ungrim's face creased with anger. 'Thorgrim–'

Thorgrim held up his hand. 'That is all I will say on the matter. I do not criticise you, it is a plea for aid. We will need you before the end. Should you fall marching out to bring war upon our enemies, the others will follow Kazador's advice and lock themselves away. That way, we shall all fall one by one. By all means fight, old friend. But use a little caution. Without you, my case is weakened.'

Ungrim nodded curtly. 'Aye.'

'And you, Belegar,' said Thorgrim. His face hardened a little, but not so much as Belegar might rightfully have expected. 'Long have you struggled to keep your oaths. Loans have gone unpaid, warriors have been unforthcoming, and your hold swallows dawi lives and dawi gold as if it were a bottomless pit without any noticeable gain.' Thorgrim stared hard at him. 'But you are a great warrior, and the proudest of all the kings here. You and I have our differences to be sure, but of all the others, I think our hearts are most similar. Of them all, only you have set out to reconquer what was once ours. I respect you for that far more than you realise. So what I am going to ask of you will cut hard and deep. Nevertheless, it must be asked.'

'My king?' said Belegar.

Thorgrim sighed. 'Against all my own oaths and desires, and against yours, I must ask you to consider abandoning Karak Eight Peaks. Take your warriors to Karak Azul. Aid Kazador. If you do, I will consider all your debts repaid.'

It was a generous offer, and sensible advice. Karak Eight Peaks was weak, besieged, a drain on the other holds.

Belegar did not see it that way. All his misery at his plight flashed at once into anger. When he stood, which he did quickly, his words were spoken in haste and fuelled by more than a little shame at his failure to secure all of Vala-Azrilungol.

When he had finally stopped shouting and stormed out of the room, his path was set. That very day, he left Karaz-a-Karak for the final time. He brooded on the High King's words all the way to Karak Eight Peaks.

They would haunt him to his grave.

# TWO

*Lord Gnawdwell*

In the underbelly of the mortal world, a flurry of activity was set in motion. Rarely had the ancient Lords of Decay moved so quickly. A febrile energy gripped Skavenblight. Messengers scurried from place to place, carrying missives that were, in the main, far from truthful. Conspirators struggled in vain to find a quiet spot to talk that was not already full of plotters. Assassinations were up, and a good killer became hard to find.

The doings of the Council were supposed to be of the utmost secrecy, but on all lips, squeak-talked on every corner, were tidings of the death of Kritislik, and of who would inherit the vacant seat on the Council of Thirteen.

Into this stewing pit of intrigue Warlord Queek, the Head-taker, came, thronged by red-armoured guards. Through the underway, into the seeping bowels of Skavenblight, he marched to see his master, Lord Gnawdwell.

Queek avoided the streets, coming to Gnawdwell's burrows without once having a whisker stirred by Skavenblight's dank mists. This suited Queek, who was no lover of the surface world or the crowded lanes of the capital.

Gnawdwell's palace was a tall tower rising over multiple layers of cellars and burrows at the heart of the Clan Mors quarter of the city. That he had summoned Queek to the underground portion of his estates was a subtle reminder of power, an accommodation to Queek. Gnawdwell was saying he knew Queek was more at home under the earth than on it. Gnawdwell was highlighting weakness.

Queek knew this. Queek was no fool.

Queek and his guards took many twisting lanes from the main underways to reach the underpalace. Great doors of wutroth barred the way to Gnawdwell's domain. At either side were two times thirteen black stormvermin. Their champions crossed their halberds over the door. Not the usual rabble, these. They were bigger than and outnumbered Queek's Red Guard.

Queek's nose twitched. There was no scent of fear from the guards. Nothing – not even in the presence of mighty Queek! Was he not the finest warrior the skaven had ever pupped? Was his murderous temper not the stuff of nightmare? But they did not fidget. They stood still in perfect imitation of statues, glinting black eyes staring at the warlord without dismay.

'State-squeak business and rank-name,' one said.

Queek paced back and forth. 'How stupid-meat not know Queek! Warlord of Clan Mors, Lord of the City of Pillars?' His trophies rattled upon the rack he wore on his back, a structure of wood akin to half a wheel, every spoke topped by a grisly memento mori. His forepaws twitched over the hilts of his weapons, a serrated sword and the infamous war-pick Dwarf Gouger.

'We know you, Queek,' responded the guard, unmoved. 'But all must state-squeak name and business. Is Lord Gnawdwell's orders. As Lord Gnawdwell commands, so we obey.'

'Stupid-meat!' spat Queek. A quiver of irritation troubled his fur. 'Very well. I Queek,' he said with sing-song sarcasm. 'Let me in!'

The corridor was so quiet Queek could hear water dripping, the constant seepage of the marshwaters above the undercity into the tunnels. Machines churned night and day to keep them dry. Their thunder reverberated throughout the labyrinth and the streets above, and their heat made the tunnels uncomfortable. They were Skavenblight's beating heart.

'Good-good,' said the guard. 'Great Warlord Queek, mightiest warrior in all the Under-Empire, slaughterer of–'

'Yes-yes!' squeaked Queek, who had no time for platitudes. 'In! In! Let me in!'

The guard appeared slightly deflated. He cleared his throat, and began again. 'Queek may enter. No one else.'

Chains rattled and the doors cracked with a long creak, revealing a gang of panting slaves pushing upon a windlass. Queek darted towards the gap as soon as it was wide enough.

The guard champions crossed their halberds to block the way.

'No, Queek. Queek leave trophy rack at door-entry. No one is more glorious than great Lord Gnawdwell. No insult. Be humble. Arrogance in the face of his brilliance is not to be tolerated.'

Queek bared his incisors at the guards aggressively, but they did not react. He wished greatly to release his pent up aggression on them. Spitting, he undid the fastenings and handed his trophies over to the stormvermin. He growled to hide his own disquiet. He would miss the counsel of the dead things when he spoke to Lord Gnawdwell. Did Gnawdwell know? Stupid Queek, he thought. Gnawdwell know *everything*.

The guards also demanded his weapons, and this made Queek snarl all the more. Once divested of them, Queek was allowed entrance to the first hall of Gnawdwell's burrow. A fat and sleek-furred major-domo with a weak mouse face came to receive Queek. He bowed and scraped pathetically, exposing his neck submissively. The scent of fear was strong around him.

'Greetings, O most violent and magnificent Queek! Red-clawed and deadly, warrior-killer, best of all Clan Mors. O mighty–'

'Yes-yes,' squeaked Queek. 'Very good. I best. All know. Why-why squeak-whine about it all day? You new or you know this,' said Queek. 'Guards new too.' He looked the little skaven up and down contemptuously. 'You fat.'

'Yes, Lord Queek. Lord Gnawdwell gain many scavenge rights in Tilea-place and Estalia-place. War is good.'

Queek bared his teeth in a hideous smile. He rushed forwards, a blur in scarlet armour, taking the majordomo by surprise. He grabbed the front of the slow-thing's robes in his paws and jerked him forwards. 'Yes-yes, mouse-face. War good, but what mouse-face know of war? Mouse-face stupid-meat!'

The musk of fear enveloped them both. Queek drooled at the smell of it.

'Mouse-face fear Queek. Mouse-face right about that, at least.'

The fat skaven raised a hand and pointed. 'Th-this way, O greatest and most marvellous–'

'Queek know way,' said Queek haughtily, shoving the other to the floor. 'Queek been here many times. Stupid mouse-face.'

Many years had passed since Queek was last in Skavenblight, but scent and memory took him to Gnawdwell's private burrow quickly. There were no other skaven about. So much space! Nowhere else in all of Skavenblight would you be further from another skaven. Queek sniffed: fine food and well-fed slaves, fresh air pumping from somewhere. Gnawdwell's palace disgusted him with its luxury.

Queek waited a long time before he realised no servant was coming and that he would have to open Gnawdwell's door himself. He found the Lord of Decay in the chamber on the other side.

Books. That was the first thing he saw every time. Lots and lots of stupid books. Books everywhere, and paper, all piled high on finely made man-thing and dwarf-thing furniture. Queek saw no use for such things. Why have books? Why have tables? If Queek wanted to know something, someone told him. If he wanted to put something down, he dropped it on the floor. Not bothering about such things left more time for Queek to fight. A big table occupied a large part of the room. On it was a map quill-scratched onto a piece of vellum, made from a single rat ogre skin, and covered in models of wood and metal. Poring over this, an open book in one brawny paw, was Lord Gnawdwell.

There was nothing to betray Gnawdwell's vast age. He was physically imposing, strongly muscled and barrel-chested. He might have lived like a seer, surrounded by his stolen knowledge. He might be dressed in robes of the finest-quality cloth scavenged from the world above, fitted to his form by expert slave-tailors in the warrens of Skavenblight. But he still moved like a warrior.

Gnawdwell put down the book he was holding and gestured at Queek to come closer. 'Ah, Queek,' said Gnawdwell, as if the warlord's arrival were a pleasant surprise. 'Come, let me see-examine you. It is a long time since I have seen-smelt Clan Mors's favoured general.' He beckoned with hands whose quickness belied their age. Gnawdwell was immeasurably ancient to Queek's mind. He had a slight grizzling of grey upon his black fur, the sign of a skaven past his youth. The same had recently begun to mark Queek. They could have been littermates, but Gnawdwell was twenty times Queek's age.

'Yes-yes, my lord. Queek come quick.'

Queek walked across the room. He was fast, his body moving with a rodentine fluidity that carried him from one place to the other without him seeming to truly occupy the space in between, as if he were a liquid poured around it. Gnawdwell smiled at Queek's grace, his red eyes bright with hard humour.

Awkwardly, hesitantly, Queek exposed his throat to the ancient rat lord. Submission did not come easily to him, and he hated himself for doing it, but to Gnawdwell he owed his absolute, fanatical loyalty. He could have killed Gnawdwell, despite the other's great strength and experience. He was confident enough to believe that. Part of him wanted to, very much. What stories the old lord might tell him, mounted on Queek's trophy rack, adding his whispers to the other dead-things who advised him.

But he did not. Something stopped him from trying. A caution that told Queek he might be wrong, and that Gnawdwell would slaughter him as easily as he would a man-thing whelp.

'Mighty-mighty Gnawdwell!' squeaked Queek.

Gnawdwell laughed. They were both large for skaven, Gnawdwell somewhat bigger than Queek. Ska Bloodtail was the only skaven that Queek had met who was larger.

Both Queek and Gnawdwell were black-furred. Both were of the same stock ultimately, drawn from the Clan Mors breeder-line, but they were as unalike as alike. Where Queek was fast and jittery, Gnawdwell was slow and contemplative. If Queek were rain dancing on water, Gnawdwell was the lake.

'Always to the point, always so quick and impatient,' said Gnawdwell. Old skaven stank of urine, loose glands, dry skin, and, if they were rich enough, oil, brass, warpstone, paper and soft straw. That is not what Lord Gnawdwell smelt of. Lord Gnawdwell smelt vital. Lord Gnawdwell smelt of power.

'I, Gnawdwell, have summoned you. You, Queek, have obeyed. You are still a loyal skaven of Clan Mors?' Gnawdwell's words were deeply pitched, unusually so for a skaven.

'Yes-yes!' said Queek.

'Yes-yes, Queek says, but does he mean it?' Gnawdwell tilted his head. He grabbed Queek's muzzle and moved Queek's head from side to side. Queek trembled with anger, not at Gnawdwell's touch, but at the meekness with which he accepted it.

'I have lived a long time. A very long time. Did you know, Queek, that I am over two hundred years old? That is ancient by the terms of our fast-live, die-quick race, yes-yes? Already, Queek, you age. I see white fur coming in black fur. Here, on your muzzle.' Gnawdwell patted Queek with a sharp-clawed hand-paw. 'You are... how old now? Nine summers? Ten? Do you feel the slowness creep into your limbs, the ache in your joints? It will only get worse. You are fast now, but I wonder, do you already slow? You will get slower. Your whiskers will droop, your eyes will dim. Your smell will weaken and your glands slacken. The great Queek!' Gnawdwell threw up a hand-paw, as if to evoke Queek's glory in the air. 'So big and so strong now, but for how much longer?' Gnawdwell shrugged. 'Two years or four? Who knows? Who do you think cares? Hmm? Let me tell you, Queek. No one will care.' Gnawdwell went to his cluttered table and picked up a haunch of meat from a platter. He bit into it, chewed slowly, and swallowed before speaking again. 'Tell me, Queek, do you remember Sleek Sharpwit? My servant I sent to you to aid in the taking of Karak Azul?'

The question surprised Queek; that had been a long time ago. 'Old-thing?'

Gnawdwell gave him a long, uncomfortable look. 'Is that what you called him? Yes then, Old-thing. He was a great warlord in his day, Queek.'

'Old-thing tell Queek many, many times.'

'Did you believe him?' said Gnawdwell.

Queek did not reply. Old-thing's head had kept on telling

Queek how great he had been since Queek had killed him and mounted him on the rack. Skaven lie.

'He was not lying,' said Gnawdwell, as if he could read Queek's thoughts. A shiver of disquiet rippled Queek's fur under his armour. 'When Queek is old, Queek's enemies will laugh at him too because Queek will be too weak to kill them. They will mock and disbelieve, because the memories of skaven are short. They will call you Old-thing. I, Lord Gnawdwell, have seen it many times before. Great warlord, master of steel, undefeated in battle, so arrogant, so sure, brought low by creeping time. Slower, sicker, until he is too old to fight, devoured by his slaves, or slain by the young.'

Gnawdwell smiled a smile of unblemished ivory teeth. 'I am much older than Sleek was. Why am I so old yet I do not die? Why you do think-wonder? Do you know, Queek?'

'Everyone know,' Queek said quietly. He looked at the small cylinder strapped to Gnawdwell's back. Bronze tubes snaked discreetly over his left shoulder and buried themselves in Gnawdwell's neck. A number of glass windows in the tube allowed observation of a gluey white liquid within, dripping into Gnawdwell's veins.

'Yes!' Gnawdwell nodded. 'The life elixir, the prolonger of being. Each drop the essence of one thousand slaves, distilled in the forge-furnaces of Clan Skryre at ridiculous cost. It is this that allows me to live now, to stay strong. That and the favour of the Horned Rat. For many generations I have been strong and fit. Perhaps you would like to be the same, Queek? Perhaps you would like to live longer and be young forever, so that you might kill-kill more?'

Queek's eyes strayed again to the cylinder.

Gnawdwell chuckled with triumph. 'I smell-sense a yes! And why would you not? Listen then, Queek. Serve me well now, and you may win the chance to serve me well for hundreds of years.'

'What must I do, great one?'

Gnawdwell gestured at the map. 'The Great Uprising goes on. Tilea is destroyed!' He swept aside a collection of model towns carved from wood. 'Estalia followed, then Bretonnia.' He nodded in approval. 'All man-lands, all dead. All ready to accept their new masters.' Many other castles, fleets and cities clattered onto the floor.

'Queek know this.'

'Of course Queek knows,' scoffed Gnawdwell. 'But mighty though Queek is, Queek does not know everything. So Queek will shut up and Queek will listen,' he said with avuncular menace. 'The Great Uprising has been many generations in the planning, and soon the war will at last be over. Clan Pestilens fights to the south, in the jungles of the slann. But the Council is full of fools. All fight at first sign of success. They do not listen to I, Gnawdwell of Clan Mors, even though I make claim to being the wisest.'

'Yes-yes!' agreed Queek. 'Wiser than the wisest.'

'Do you think so?' Gnawdwell said. 'Listen more carefully, Queek. I make claim to be wise, I said. But I am not so foolish as to believe it. As soon as one completely believes in his ability, Queek, then he is dead.' He scrutinised the warlord. 'Over-confidence is ever the downfall of our kind. Even the wise may overreach themselves. This was Sleek's greatest error. His self-belief.'

'Lord Gnawdwell believes in himself,' said Queek.

'I am one of the Thirteen Lords of Decay, Queek. I am entitled to believe in myself.' He spread his paw fingers and looked at his well-tended claws. 'But I always leave a little room for doubt. Think on the current status of Clan Scruten. The grey seers never doubted themselves. Then the Great Horned One himself came and devoured the fool-squeaker Kritislik.' He tittered, a surprising noise from one so burly. 'It was quite the sight, Queek. Amusing, too. Now no white-furs are meddling in our affairs. They are gone from the Council with their sticky, interfering paws. The Lords are united. For a short while there is an empty seat on the Council, free for the first time in ages. It will not be empty for very long. I intend to put one of our clan allies in that seat.'

'How-how?' said Queek. He struggled to concentrate on all this. He understood all right, but he found intrigue tedious compared to the simple joys of warfare.

'Why do you think you are here, most noted of all skaven generals? Even Paskrit the Vast is an amateur by comparison. Through war, Queek! War on the dwarf-things. We have let them live for too long. They died twenty thousand generations ago, but are too stubborn to admit it. Now is the time to inform them of their demise. We will kill them all. See-look! Learn-fear how deadly skaven are when united!' he squeaked excitedly, his careful mode of speech deserting him momentarily.

'Here.' Lord Gnawdwell pointed at a set of models, these made from iron, sitting on the map. 'Clan Rictus and Clan Skryre have deal-pledged, and attack together the holdfast of Karak Azul.' He gave Queek a penetrating look. 'I think they will be more successful than you. You remember-recall Azul-place, yes, Queek?'

'Queek remembers.'

'Here, Clan Kreepus attacks Kadrin-place. They have raised many-many warptokens in trading man-thing food-slaves. So now Clan Moulder brings much strength to their paws. Many beasts, great and horrible. There, at Zhufbar-place, the dwarf-things have Clan Ferrik to fight.' Gnawdwell's long muzzle twitched dismissively. 'Weak they be, but many rabble clans flock to them, so their numbers are great. Enough to occupy them, if not prevail. Finally, at Barak Varr sea-place, Clan Krepid joined with Clan Skurvy.'

Queek's eyes widened, his expression settling into an

appreciative smile. 'All dwarf-things die at same time. They not reinforce each other. They not come-hurry to each other's aid. They all die, all alone.'

'Very good. Tell me, what do you think? Is this good, Queek? Is this bad?'

Queek shuddered. This was so boring! Queek would gladly go to war! Why did Gnawdwell tell him these pointless things? Why? But Queek had wisdom, Queek was canny. Gnawdwell was one of the few living beings he feared to anger, and Gnawdwell would be angry at his thoughts. So he kept his words back. Only his swishing tail gave away his impatience. 'Good-good that we attack everywhere at once. Then all the beard-things sure to die. Bad that Queek not get all the glory. Queek want to kill all the fur-face king-things himself! Queek the best. It not right that other, lesser skaven take trophies that rightfully belong to Queek!'

'You have half the answer, Queek.'

*Half?* thought Queek. There was no component to his thinking other than Queek.

Gnawdwell sucked his teeth in disappointment. 'It is not only you who matters, but our clan, Queek! Clan Rictus wants to discredit us, yes-yes! Take our glory, take our new seat from our allies. And Clan Skryre and Clan Moulder and Clan Rictus, and all the rest. It was Clan Mors that brought the dwarf-things down first. This is our war to finish!' Gnawdwell slammed his paw onto the table, making his models jump. He gestured at various positions on the map. 'This will not happen. I have taken precautions to ensure our glory. And many of our loyal troops wait with the others. To help, you understand.'

Queek didn't see. Queek didn't really care. Queek nodded anyway. 'Yes-yes, of course.' When could he go? The skin of his legs crawled with irritation.

'They wear the colours of our comrade-friend clans. We do not wish them to be confused, to think, "Why Clan Mors here, when they should not be?"' Gnawdwell mimicked the piping voice of a lesser skaven.

'No. No! That would be most bad.'

Gnawdwell glanced at Queek's thrashing tail. He bared his teeth in a skaven smile.

'You are bored, yes-no? You want to be away, my Queek. You never change.' Gnawdwell walked back to his general and stroked Queek's fur. Queek hissed, but leaned into his master's caress. His eyes shut. 'You wish to kill, hurry-scurry! Stab-stab!'

Queek nodded, a sharp, involuntary movement. Calmness of a type he felt nowhere else came upon him as his master groomed his sleek black fur. The needles of impatience jabbing at his flesh prickled less.

'And you shall!'

Queek's eyes snapped open. He jerked his head back.

'Queek is the best! Queek wish to kill green-things and beard-things! Queek wish to drink their blood and rip their flesh!' He gnashed his incisors. 'Queek do this for Gnawdwell. This is what Gnawdwell wants, yes-yes?'

Gnawdwell turned back to the map. 'You disappoint me, Queek. To be a Lord of Decay is not to stab and kill and smash all things aside. You lack circumspection. You are a killer, nothing more.' Gnawdwell's lips peeled back in disappointment. He stared at his protege a long time, far too long for Queek's thrumming nerves to stand. 'You were so magnificent when I found you, the biggest in your litter, and they were all large before you ate them. I raised you, I fed you the best dwarf-meat and man-flesh. And you have become even more magnificent. Such courage. There is none other like you, Queek. You are unnaturally brave. Others think you freakish for leading from the front, not the back. But I do not. I am proud of my Queek.'

Queek chirred with pride.

Sadness suffused Gnawdwell's face. 'But you are a blunt tool, Queek. A blunt and dangerous tool. I always hoped you would become Lord of Decay after me, because with one so big and so deadly as you as master of Clan Mors, all the others would be afraid, and the air would thicken with their musk.' He sighed deeply, the threads of his clothes creaking as his massive chest expanded. 'But it is not to be. Gnawdwell will remain head of Clan Mors.' He paused meaningfully. 'But maybe Queek can prove me wrong? Perhaps you might change my mind?'

'How-how?' wheedled Queek. He desperately wanted to impress Gnawdwell. Disappointing the Lord of Decay was the only thing Queek truly feared.

'Go to Karak Eight Peaks. Smash the beard-things. But not in Queek's way. Queek has brains – use them! We will bring down their decaying empire and the children of the Horned Rat shall inherit the ruins. I will see that it is Clan Mors that emerges pre-eminent from this extermination. Finish them quickly. Go to help the others complete the tasks they will not be able to finish on their own. Clan Mors must look strong. Clan Mors must be victorious! Bring me the greatest victory of all, Queek. March on Big Mountain-place. It may take years, but if you are successful there… Well, we shall see if you shall age as other lesser skaven must.'

Queek cared nothing for councils. Queek cared nothing for plots and ploys. What Queek cared for was war. Now Gnawdwell spoke a language he could understand. 'Much glory for Queek!'

'Do-accomplish what you do so well, my Queek. Finish the beard-things, and we will shame-embarrass the others when you bring me the head of their white-fur High King and the keys to their greatest city. Clan Mors will be unopposed. We will deliver the final Council seat to our favoured thrall-clan, and then Clan Mors rule all the Under-Empire, all the world!'

said Gnawdwell viciously, his speech picking up speed, losing its sophistication, falling into the rapid chitter-chatter used by other skaven. He clenched his fists and rose up. All vestiges of the thoughtful skaven disappeared. A great warrior stood before Queek.

'Queek is the best!' Queek slammed his fist against his armour. 'Queek kill the most-much beard-things! And then,' said Queek, becoming wily, 'Queek get elixir, so Queek not get old-fast and Queek kill-slay more for Lord Gnawdwell?'

Gnawdwell sank back into himself, the fires going out of him. His face reassumed its expression of arrogant calm. 'That is all, Queek. Go-go now. Return to the City of Pillars and finish the war there once and for all. Then you will march upon many-beard-thing Big Mountain-place.'

'But-but,' said Queek. 'Gnawdwell say...'

'Go, Queek. Go now and slay for Clan Mors. You are right – Queek is the greatest. Now show it to the world.' He retreated into the shadows away from the map, towards an exit at the back of the room. A troop of giant, albino skaven, even bigger than the guards of the outer gate and clad in black-lacquered armour, thundered out of garrison burrows either side of Gnawdwell's exit, forming a living wall between Queek and his master. They came to a halt, breathing hard, stinking of hostility.

Queek scurried over to them. They lowered their halberds. Queek vaulted over the weapons and landed right in front of the white-furs.

'Queek is the greatest,' he hissed in their faces. 'I kill white-fur guards before. How many white-fur guards Queek kill before white-furs kill Queek?' whispered Queek. He was gratified by a faint whiff of fear. 'But Queek not kill white-furs. Queek busy! Queek will do as Lord Gnawdwell commands.' He screech-squeaked over the heads of the unmoving guards, turned upon his heels and strode out.

\* \* \*

'Silence be!' screeched Lord Thaumkrittle.

The coven of grey seers stopped arguing and turned to look at their new leader.

'This is not the place to argue and fight. It is much-very bad that Clan Scruten is no longer on the Council, worse that our god has shown his disapproval. We must work to regain the favour of the Horned Rat.'

More than one emission of fear's musk misted the air. The grey seers chittered nervously.

'We are his chosen! We bear his horns and have his powers!' said Jilkin the Twisted, his horns painted red and carved with spell-wards. 'This all a trick by Clan Mors, or Clan Skryre! Tinker-rats want all our magic for themselves.'

'No. That was the Horned Rat himself, not some machine-born conjuring trick,' said another, Felltwitch. He was older than many, tall and rangy. One of his horns was missing, reduced to a stump by a sword swing long ago. 'And we have disappointed him.'

'It not our fault,' said Kranskritt, once favoured among the other clans, now as despised as the rest. 'Other clans plot and scheme against us, make us look bad to the master.'

'Yes-yes!' squeaked others. 'Traitors everywhere. Not our fault!'

'No,' said the old Felltwitch. 'It is our fault, and only our fault.' He stepped around in a slow circle, leaning on his blackwood staff. 'If we blame-curse other clans, we not learn anything.'

'What to do? What to do?' said Kreekwik, marked out by his deep-red robes. 'Grey Seer Felltwitch squeak-says we have failed? How to *unfail* the Great Horned One? Will any more grey seers be born? Are we the last?'

Panic rushed through the room, forest-fire quick, taking hold of each grey seer's limbs and sending them into a storm of tail lashing and twitching. Pent up magic added its own peculiar smell to the thick scent of the room.

'We should pray,' said Kranskritt. 'We are his priests and his prophets. Pray for forgiveness.'

'We should act,' said Felltwitch.

'Let us wait them out!' said Scritchmaw. 'We live much longer than they.'

'It is not possible. Clan Skryre has the secret of longevity-life elixir. Lords of Decay live too long – no one lives longer than they. No waiting, no waiting!' said Thaumkrittle. He too was nervous. It was one thing to become chief of Clan Scruten, another to become chief immediately after their god had eaten the previous incumbent. Thaumkrittle was on edge, his emotional state veering between great pride at his elevation and a suspicion that he had only got the job because no one else dared to take it.

'We have lost-squandered the favour of the Great Horned One! What are we to do?' said Kranskritt, the many bells on his arms, wrists, ankles and horns rattling.

'Win it back! Win it back!'

'How do you propose to do that?' A familiar voice came from the back of the room. The entire assembly turned to look. There, at the back, Boneripper hulking behind him, was Thanquol.

'Grey Seer Thanquol!' shrieked Kreekwik.

'It is him! All this is his fault!' said Kranskritt.

A hiss of hatred went up from every seer present. Magical auras fizzed into life. Eyes glowed.

'How my fault-guilt?' said Thanquol, as calmly as he could. 'Many times I am this close to victory.' He held his fingers a hair's-breadth apart. 'But treachery of other clans stop my winning. They are all at fault. It is not me, friends-colleagues. Not me at all!'

Thaumkrittle shook his head, sending the copper triskeles

depending from his horn tips swinging. 'You clever-squeaker, Thanquol. Always it is the same. Always it is the lies. Always we believe. Not this time. The Horned Rat himself came forth at the meeting and devoured our leader.' Thaumkrittle pointed his staff directly at Thanquol. 'Fool-thing! We no longer pay listen-heed to your squeak-talk. Go from here! Go!'

'Yes-yes, go-go!' the others chittered.

'You will listen to me,' said Thanquol. 'Listen to my speakings. I have a way!'

'No!' shouted Kreekwik. 'Squeak-talk of Thanquol grandiose lies.'

'Cast him out!' said Felltwitch. 'Cast him out! Banish him!'

Light fled and shadows deepened as each and every grey seer began to cast a spell, bringing a taste of rot and brimstone.

'No-no!' said Thanquol. He backed up to the door, only to find it inexplicably locked. He cursed the guards he'd bribed to let him in. Cornered, he summoned his own magic.

Boneripper. Boneripper was there. Sensing his master's peril, the rat ogre snarled out a thunderous roar and ran at the other seers, chisel-incisors bared.

A dozen beams of warp-lightning intersected on his powerfully muscled body. They flayed the skin from his chest, but Boneripper kept on coming. The muscle underneath smoked. Still he kept on coming. He reached the first grey seer and reached forwards with a mighty claw. Green fire blazed from the seer's eyes, reducing the rat ogre's hand to ash. He roared in anger, not in pain, for Boneripper was incapable of feeling pain. He punched forwards with one of his remaining fists, but this was snared in a rope of shadow and teeth that fastened themselves into his flesh.

'No-no!' Thanquol shrieked. He countered as many spells as he could, draining magic away from his peers, but there were too many. His glands clenched.

With a mighty howl, Boneripper was dragged to his knees.

Magic writhed all over him, burning and tearing pieces from him. Jilkin the Twisted, a particularly spiteful seer, reached the end of his convoluted incantation. He hurled an orb of purple fire at the injured construct, engulfing its wounded arm. The fire burned bright, then collapsed inwards into warp-black with a sucking noise.

Boneripper roared, his arm turning into a slurry of oily goo, which fountained over the other seers. A deafening thunderclap of magical feedback had them squeaking in agony. Many were blasted to the floor by the sudden interruption of their own sorcery.

When they got up, horned heads shaking out the ringing in their sensitive ears, they were grinning evilly.

'No-no! Wait-wait!' chittered Thanquol as they advanced on him. 'Listen-hear my idea!' He looked to them imploringly. 'I am your friend. I was master to many of you. Please! Listen!'

Thaumkrittle drew himself up. 'Grey Seer Thanquol, you are expelled-exiled from Clan Scruten. You will scurry from this place and never return.'

The other rats fell on him, sharp claws tearing, teeth working at his clothes, ripping his robes and charms from his body. Thanquol panicked. Drowning in a sea of hateful fur, he felt his glands betray him, drenching him in the shame of his own fear.

'No-no, listen! We must... Argh! We must summon a verminlord, ask them what to do! We are the prophets of the Horned Rat! Let us ask-query his daemons how to pass this trial-test he has set us.'

The seers hoisted Thanquol onto their shoulders and bore him from the room. The door's sorcerous locks clanked and whirred at their approach, the great bars rattling back into their housings.

The night of Skavenblight greeted Thanquol indifferently as he was hurled bodily into it, followed shortly after by the embrace of the mud of the street.

Thanquol groaned and rolled over. Unspeakable filth caked him.

'Please!' he shouted, raising a hand to the closing doors.

They stopped. Thanquol's tail swished hopefully.

Thaumkrittle's head poked out of the crack, the head of his staff protruding below his chin. At least, thought Thanquol, they were still wary of him.

'If you return, once-seer Thanquol, we will take-saw your horns,' Thaumkrittle said.

The large, messy figure of Boneripper was flung out magically after him. Thanquol barely dodged aside as the unconscious rat ogre slapped into the mud.

The door clanged shut. Thanquol snivelled, but his self-pity lasted only seconds before self-preservation kicked in. Interested red eyes already watched from the shadows. To show any sign of weakness in Skavenblight was to invite death.

'What you look-see?' he snapped, getting to his feet unsteadily. 'I Thanquol! I great seer. You better watch it, or I cook you from inside.'

He set off a shower of sparks from his paws, then stopped. The light showed his beaten, dishevelled state all too clearly. The shadows drew nearer.

Clutching the remains of his robes to preserve his modesty, Thanquol checked over his bodyguard. Boneripper had lost two of his arms and much flesh, but his heart still beat. He could be repaired. Thanquol spent some time rousing the construct, his head twitching with intense paranoia this way and that. But though his glands were slack, his heart hardened. Eventually, the rat ogre hauled itself to its feet. To Thanquol's relief, there suddenly appeared to be a lot fewer shadows in the street.

'If Clan Scruten does not want me, then maybe Clan Skryre will,' he said to himself. With all the haste he could manage, he headed off to their clan hall.

\* \* \*

Inside the Temple of the Grey Seers, dull-eyed skaven and human slaves mopped at the mess that had been part of Boneripper. The grey seers resumed their places and recommenced their debate.

'I have an idea,' said Jilkin. 'Let us summon a verminlord.'

'That great idea,' said Kreekwik. 'Ask-beg the great ones from beyond the veil.'

'Yes-yes,' said Thaumkrittle up on his platform. 'A great idea of mine. I am very clever. That why I your new leader-lord, yes? So, who want to follow my great idea and speak-pray to the Horned Rat for one of his servants?'

The grey seers looked at one another. Such blatant claiming of Jilkin's suggestion was majestic. They could respect that.

'Of course, O most mighty and powerful caller of magics,' Kranskritt said. He bowed.

The others followed.

# THREE

*Karak Eight Peaks*

Skarsnik, the King under the Mountains, looked out over the greenskin shanty town filling the dwarf surface city. In ruined streets, between ramshackle huts of wood and hide, raucous orcs drank and fought one another. Goblins squealed and tittered. On the slopes of scree studded with broken statuary, snotlings gambolled, throwing stones at passing greenskins, oblivious to the cold that turned their noses pink.

Autumn was halfway through, and the first flakes of the year's snow already drifted on the wind.

Skarsnik shivered and pulled his wolf pelt closer about him. He was old now – how old he wasn't quite sure, for goblins took less care in reckoning the years than men or dwarfs did. But he felt age as surely as he felt the grip of Gork and Mork on his destiny. He felt it in his bandy legs, in his creaking knees and hips. His skin was gnarled and scabbed, thick as tree bark, and he leaned more often on his famous prodder for support than he would have liked. His giant cave squig,

Gobbla, snuffled about around his feet, equally aged. Patches of his skin had turned a pinkish-grey, for he was almost as old as his master.

Skarsnik wondered how long he had left. It was ironic, he thought, that after years of wondering whether it would be a skaven blade or dwarf axe that finished him, it would be neither. Time was the enemy no one could fight.

In truth, no one knew how old a goblin could get because they did not usually last that long. Most of them would not even consider dying of old age. Skarsnik considered lots of unusual things because Skarsnik was no ordinary goblin, and what went on in his head would have been entirely alien to other greenskins. Lately, old age had occupied Skarsnik's thoughts a lot.

'Must be fifty winters and more I seen. Fifty!' he cackled. 'And here's another come on again. Still, stunty, I reckon I got another few to come.' Skarsnik was all alone on the balcony, save for a couple of mangy skaven skins and several dwarf heads in various states of decay, spiked along the broken balustrade. It was to his favourite, its eyes long ago pecked out, skin desiccated black in the dry mountain air, nose rotted away, that he addressed his words. A sorry-looking head, but even in death it had a magnificent beard. Skarsnik liked to stroke it when no one was looking. 'Duffskul's still knocking about, and he's well older than me.'

He grumbled and spat, muttering thoughts that not one of his underlings would understand, and drew his long chin into his stinking furs.

'What a bleeding mess, eh, stunty? Them zogging ratties done driven me out of me stunty-house. I am not happy about that, no, not one little bitty bit.'

He looked forlornly at the ruinous gatehouse marking the grand entry to the Hall of a Thousand Pillars, heart of the first of Karak Eight Peaks's many deeps. 'Once upon a time, stunty, that was mine. And everything under it. Not any more. On the other side of the great doors I won one of me greatest victories, and the stunty-house was me kingdom for dozens of levels down. Think about that, eh? Kept hold of it longer than your lot did, I reckon!' His laugh turned into a hacking cough. He wiped his mouth with the back of his hand. His next words came out all raspy. 'Gobboes, beat them all and sorted them out. Ratties. Beat them, and then I beat them, and then I blew them up, drowned them and beat 'em some more. Stunties came back. Beat them too,' said Skarsnik wistfully, looking across at the citadel that dominated the heart of the city. 'Look at that will you, stunty! That's all your king's got. Nuffink. I'm the king around here. I am. Right?'

He paused. The dwarf's beard stirred in the wind. Fat, wet flakes of snow splatted against its taut skin. It was coming down thicker, and the temperature was dropping.

'Well, I'm glad you agree.'

Not that that changed anything. Skarsnik was still dispossessed, and he was not happy about it. He watched another tribe of greenskins straggling into orctown from the west gate. His eyes narrowed, calculating. They were weedy little 'uns, worn by hard travels. Within seconds of coming into the gate they were rapidly set upon by orcs and bigger goblins, who stole everything they had, leaving them naked and shivering in the cold. 'Always more where they came from,' whispered Skarsnik. 'Always more.'

'Ahem!' A high-pitched cough demanded Skarsnik's attention. Behind him, standing ramrod straight, was his herald, pointy hood standing as diligently to attention as its owner.

'What you want, Grazbok?' said Skarsnik, squinting at the small goblin. The sky was overcast, brilliant grey with pending snow, and the glare of it hurt his eyes. 'You keep sneaking up on me like that, I'll have to send you out scouting for ratties. And you,' he said, kicking Gobbla in the side with a leathery *thwap*, 'are losing your touch.'

Gobbla snuffled and waddled off, the chain connecting him to Skarsnik's leg rattling as he licked scraps of dried dwarf flesh from the floor. Grazbok gave Skarsnik a sidelong look that suggested he was going to make more noise next time.

'Your highnessness,' the herald squeaked, 'I have da great Griff Kruggler here to sees ya!'

Skarsnik's lips split in a wide grin, yellow as the moon talismans dangling from his pointy hat. 'Kruggs, eh? Send him up! Send him up!'

Kruggler was a long time coming up the steps from the halls under the Howlpeak. A pained wheezing came first, followed by the click of unsteady claws on stone.

Skarsnik's eyes widened as Kruggler came out into the pale day upon the back of a staggering wolf. He had become fat. Enormously, disgustingly fat. His wolf mount gasped under him as it heaved itself up onto the balcony. Kruggler swung his leg over its back – with some difficulty – and slid to the flagstones. The wolf let out a huff of relief, dragged itself off into a corner and collapsed.

'Been a long time, boss,' said Kruggler.

Skarsnik took in the rolls of flab, the massive hat and the greasy gold trinkets festooning his underling.

'What the zog happened to you?'

Kruggler was abashed. 'Well, you know, living's been good...'

'You is almost as fat as that... what was he called? That boss. That one I killed of yours?'

'Makiki, the Great Grizzler-Griff.'

'Yeah! Only thing great about him was his size.' Skarsnik laughed at his own joke. Kruggler just looked puzzled. Skarsnik scowled at his confusion. Trouble was, Skarsnik was a lot brighter than every other greenskin he'd ever met. It was depressing. 'Gah, suit yerself. How you been?'

Kruggler pulled a face. 'Not good, boss, to tell da truth.'

'And there you was saying living was good.'

Kruggler looked confused. 'Well, I did, er – well, it was, boss, it was. But things... well, they is not no good no more.'

'What do you mean? Look at all these greenies come to join the Waaagh! Good times, Kruggs, good times. Soon there'll be enough to kick the ratties out and take back the upper halls!'

Kruggs gave him a puzzled look.

'Stop looking so zogging thick, Kruggs! Did I make an idiot king of all the Badlands wolf tribes?'

'Well, er, no, boss, but...'

'Go on, go on, spit it out!'

'Well, I said things is no good,' said Kruggler anguishedly. 'I mean it! Dead things everywhere, fighting each other. Dwarfs on the march, fire mountains spitting fire and such. And the ratties, boss. The ratties is all over the place! I ain't see so many, not ever. They's taking over the stunty-houses, all of 'em, and not just a few. They's slaughtering the tribes wherever they find 'em. Something big's happening, something–'

Skarsnik was nose to nose with Kruggler before the plains goblin realised he'd moved. Skarsnik's sour breath washed over his face.

'Careful there, Kruggs. Don't want you starting to bang on about the end of the world. Had a bit too much of that kind of talk lately from a few too many of the lads. Everything's going on as normal here. We fight the rats, the rats fight the stunties, the stunties fight us, got it?'

Kruggler made a funny noise in his throat. 'Got it, boss.'

'Good.' Skarsnik turned away from his vassal. 'So what's you saying then, Kruggs? You think they's going to come here too? Better not, because they'll have old Skarsnik to deal with and I–' He coughed mightily. The fit held him for a minute, his hunchback shoulders shaking with it. Kruggler looked around, his tiny goblin mind torn between helping his boss, stabbing him, and wondering if there was anyone that could see him do either. Paralysed by indecision, he just stood and watched.

Skarsnik hawked up a gob of stringy phlegm and spat it onto a skaven hide rotting on a frame. 'Because if they do, they'll have me to deal with, and I ain't no bleeding stunty! Anyways, look at all them. They's come here to help *me*. They hears I'm the baddest and the bestest. Old Belegar and his mates up there in his stupid tower might have done for old Rotgut, but he can't get me, can he? No zogging ratty or stunty is kicking me out of these mountains, you hear? You hear!'

He shouted loudly, his nasal voice echoing from the ruins of the dwarf surface city. Orcs and goblins looked up at him. Some cheered, some jeered. Some wandered off, uncaring.

'See, with this lot coming to join da Waaagh! I'll kick them ratties out and take it all back for good.'

Skarsnik had, of course, said this many, many times before. But it never happened. The balance of power between the greenskins and skaven swung backwards and forwards viciously; sometimes the goblins had the upper hand, some-times the skaven – sometimes the stunties stuck their beards in for good measure. So it had been for time immemorial. But lately that had been changing. Skarsnik would never have admitted it to anyone but Gobbla, but each time he was vic-torious, he was able to hold less of the city, and for shorter periods of time.

'But, boss! Boss!' said a dismayed Kruggler. Cowardice nearly made him stop, but his loyalty to Skarsnik ran deep. He was one of the few who could tell the warlord what he didn't want to hear. At least that's how it'd been in the old days, and he really hoped it was that way still because he couldn't stop him-self. He plunged on, gabbling faster as his panic built. 'They're not here to help you, boss. They ain't here for no Waaagh! That's what I'm trying to tell you, boss.'

Skarsnik's prodder swung round and was pointed at Krug-gler's face. Green light glinted along its three prongs. His expression became vicious. 'There you go again! What do you mean? End of the world is it, Kruggs, because if you keeps it up, it will be for you.'

Kruggler held his hands up. He leaned back from the prodder so far his boss helmet slipped from his head to clang on the floor. 'I means, boss, they is coming here because they knows you is here and you is da best.'

'Exactly, exactly!' said Skarsnik. He put the prodder up and nodded with satisfaction.

'Yeah, boss. Yeah,' said Kruggler with relief. 'You is the cleverest. I knew you'd be clever and see.' He came to stand next to Skarsnik and looked out. He smiled idiotically. 'They isn't coming here to fight. They think you can protect them! They is running away.'

Kruggler realised what he had said and clapped his hands over his mouth, but the fight had gone out of Skarsnik. He was staring out into the thickening snow at something Kruggler could not see.

'We'll see about that, we'll see,' he said sullenly.

A couple of miles away over the orc-infested ruins, King Belegar, the *other* king of Karak Eight Peaks, looked out into the gathering storm, engaged in his own contemplation. Abandon the hold indeed. Thorgrim's request dogged his thoughts still. But now, six months later, a small part of him feared that the High King might have been right...

Like Skarsnik, Belegar was troubled by what he saw. Something dreadful was afoot.

He pounded his mailed fist on the rampart of the citadel, causing his sentries to turn to look at him. He huffed into his beard, shaking his head at their concerns, although he was secretly pleased at their vigilance.

'Something dreadful is afoot,' he said to his companion, his first cousin once removed and banner bearer, Thane Notrigar.

'How do you know, my liege?'

'You can stop it with that "my liege" business, Notrigar. You're my cousin's son and an Angrund. Even if you weren't, we've fought back to back more times than I care to recall. Besides,' he added gloomily, 'a dawi has to be a real king to get the full "my liege" treatment.'

'But you are a real king, my liege!' said Notrigar, taken aback.

'Am I?' said Belegar. He gestured into the snowstorm, now so thick it had whited out everything further away than one hundred paces from the citadel walls. 'King Lunn was the last real king of this place. History will remember that it was he, not I.'

'There will be many more after you, my liege,' said Notrigar. 'A long and glorious line! Thorgrim is a grand lad. He is coming into his own with every day. You could not wish for a finer son, and he'll be a fine king, when the time comes.'

Belegar was mollified for a moment. 'A fine king, but one of rubble and ruination. And he needs to wed, and sire his own heir. Who will have him, the beggar king of Eight Peaks?'

'But my liege! You are a hero to every dawi lass and lad. Send him back to Everpeak and there you shall have dawi rinn of every clan begging for his hand.'

'What did I say to you? Belegar will do, lad. Or cousin, if you must.'

Notrigar, although now many years in the Eight Peaks, did not feel he knew his cousin well at all, raised as he had been in distant Karaz-a-Karak. Belegar was a legend to him, a hero. He could not countenance calling him by his name, cousin or not. He settled on 'my lord'.

'Yes, my lord,' he said.

Belegar rolled his eyes. 'Beardlings today,' he said, although Notrigar was well past his majority and a thane in his own right. 'All right, all right, "my lord" if it makes you feel better.'

'Thank you, my lord.'

'Don't mention it. What you said, just then. That's the problem, isn't it? He'd have to go back. He'd have to risk the journey. It took me nigh on four months to get to Karaz-a-Karak for the kingsmeet and back, and that in the summer. Things are worse now, mark my words. What if he's taken by grobi or urk? What if the thaggoraki steal him away. Then that'll be that, won't it? What we've all fought so hard for gone. A kingdom of ruins with no king. Fifty years! Fifty years! Gah!' He punched the stone again. His Iron Hammers had more sense and honour than to mutter, but they exchanged dark looks. 'When Lunn was king, this was still the finest city in all of the Karak Ankor. What is it now, Notrigar? Ruins. Ruins swarming with grobi and thaggoraki, with more coming every day.'

'But you have been here for fifty years, my lord. You are successful.' Notrigar had never dreamed to see his lord and kin in such poor temper, or to confide in him in such an open and upsetting manner. He did not know quite what to say. Reassurance did not come naturally to a dwarf.

'Right. Here I am in my glorious castle,' Belegar said sarcastically. 'I came here hoping to take it all back. I came hoping to look upon the far deeps, on the ancestor statues of the Abyss of Iron's Dream. I dreamed of opening up the Ungdrin again, so that armies might freely march between my, Kazador's and Thorgrim's realms. I dreamed of reopening the mines, of filling the coffers of our clan with gold and jewels.'

They both became a little misty-eyed at this image.

'But no. A few weapons hordes, a few treasure rooms and a lot of failure. We can't even keep our master brewer safe,' he said, referring to one of the more recent entries in Karak Eight Peaks's Book of Grudges. 'Six months since the damn furskins took Yorrik and I've not had a decent pint since.'

'We have the will and the resolve, my–'

'You've not read the reports, have you?' said Belegar. 'Not

seen what the rangers are saying, or what those new-fangled machines of Brakki Barakarson are saying.'

'The seismic indicators, my lord?'

'Aye, that's them. Scratchy needles. Thought it was all a lot of modern rubbish, to tell you the truth. But he's been right more than he's been wrong. There's a lot going on underground, down in the lower deeps. Never did get very far on the way to the bottom. Grungni alone knows how many tunnels the thaggoraki have chiselled out down there. Gyrocopters coming in, telling me every inch of Mad Dog Pass is crawling with ogres, grobi and urk. No message from half the holds in months, no safe road out, and no safe road in. I'll bet that little green kruti Skarsnik is out there right now too, standing on the parapets of Karag Zilfin looking over at us as we look over at him. It's been that way for far too long. If it only weren't for that little bloody...' He trailed off into a guttural collection of strong dwarfish oaths. 'One enemy,' he said, holding up a finger. 'I think I could have handled one. If it weren't for him I'd have driven the grobi off years ago and cleared the skaven out of the top deeps. Trust me to get saddled with the sneakiest little green bozdok who ever walked the earth.' He sighed, pursing his lips so that his beard and moustaches bristled. 'And now it's all gone quiet. Too bloody quiet. I'll tell you what this silence is, Notrigar.'

'What is it, my lord?' said Notrigar, for Belegar was waiting to be prompted.

'It's the beginning of the end, that's what it is. Or so those thaggoraki probably think.'

Notrigar looked around for help. The ironbreakers, hammerers and thunderers manning the ramparts were staring studiously off into the middle distance. He raised a hand, started to speak, then thought better of it. To Notrigar's dismay, the king began to hiccup, his chest heaving.

'My lord?' said Notrigar. Oh Grungni, thought the thane,

please don't let him be... crying? Belegar's shoulders heaved, and he turned away. Notrigar reached an uncertain hand out for his kinsman.

He leapt back as Belegar burst out laughing, a sound as sudden and surprising as an avalanche, and to the unnerved Notrigar, just as terrifying. The king's mirth rolled out from the ramparts, wildly bellicose, as if it could retake Vala-Azrilungol all on its own.

'That's right, you green bozdoks! King Belegar is laughing at you, and you, you vicious thaggoraki! I am laughing at you too!' he bellowed. His shout was blunted by the snow, the lack of echo unsettling to Notrigar, but Belegar did not care. The king wiped a tear of mirth from his eye, flicking it and a finger's worth of snow crystals away from his moustache. He clapped his arm around his cousin, his face creased with a grim smile. 'Oh don't look so glum, lad. I've always been a sucker for a lost cause, me. We'll show them, eh? We can hold out. We always have, keeping our heads down until more reinforcements come and the bloody fun can start all over again. They'll never get through the fortifications we're planning, no matter how many of the little furry grunkati come – there'll be a trap for each and every one of them, eh, lad? Don't worry, I haven't gone zaki. You see, lad, you have to know what you're fighting, and be certain you're not underestimating it before you can crush it. Once you know what's what, nothing is impossible, and you can shout your cries of victory right in the face of your enemy. Furry or green, or in our case both, it doesn't matter, lad. This is the Eternal Realm. We'll never fall.'

'Yes, my lord.' The other dwarfs were chuckling at their king's good humour, laughing at Notrigar for not seeing the joke. Belegar's arm was like a stone lintel on his shoulders. Notrigar had a sudden urge for an ale. A strong one.

'That's right!' Belegar bawled, making Notrigar's ears ring. 'I'll be ready for you, Skarsnik! Send everything you've got.

# FOUR

*The City of Pillars*

The upper deeps of Karak Eight Peaks were heaving with warm fur. Every corner, every cranny, from the Trench at the very bottom to the Hall of a Thousand Pillars once inhabited by Skarsnik and his lackeys. The noise of so many ratmen's squeaks and pattering feet close together merged into a sussuration so pervasive the very rocks seemed to be speaking with skaven voices.

Within the Hall of a Thousand Pillars, atop the pinnacle that had once housed the dwarf king's throne, and for fifty years until recently that of Skarsnik, Queek inspected the first clawpack of the warhost of Clan Mors, and he was not happy about it.

Queek paced up and down as block after block after block of skaven marched out of the tunnels around the base of the soaring throne pinnacle, wove their way through the forest of pillars and went back out again, banners waving, their leaders proudly bringing up the rear.

'How long this going to take? Queek bored,' said Queek. 'This boring!'

Thaxx Redclaw twitched his armoured neck, briefly exposing a patch of fur at his throat. He was the leader of the first clawpack, and appointed ruler of the City of Pillars in Queek's absence. With such overlap between their roles, Thaxx felt especially vulnerable. 'Great and deadly Queek, you are best and most perspicacious general! A cunning and mighty war-leader such as the incomparable Queek would want to inspect-smell troops?' Thaxx nodded eagerly, inviting agreement. He received a cold stare.

'There are many,' added Warlord Skrikk, Queek's supposed right claw. 'How glorious for your gloriousness to feast nose and eye on such an army, all gathered solely for you, O great and deadly, violent Queek!'

'Dull! Boring! Queek see hundreds of thousands of millions of skaven in his life,' snapped Queek. 'They all the same. Furry faces, pink noses. Some die, all die. There are always more. What need mighty Queek see all rat-faces?'

Thaxx snickered and bobbed his head, a poor attempt to hide his fear. The other clanlords atop the dais, out of Queek's sight, backed away until they ran into Queek's Red Guard and the massive body of Queek's chief lieutenant, Ska Bloodtail. He stared down at them and shook his head.

'But mighty Queek, O most cunning and stabby of all rat-kin, how will stupid warrior-things know how to follow mighty Queek's orders if glorious warlord is not there? See how their faces look upon your most awesome countenance with fear and, er, awe,' said Thaxx.

'You speak-squeak badly, Thaxx. Too long running this city without mighty Queek to keep you in your place. All things scared of Queek! Why is this useful for Queek to see-smell what he already knows?'

Skrikk and Thaxx glanced at each other.

'There are questions of strategy and disposition, great fierce one,' ventured Warlord Skrikk.

'Oh? Oh? Strategy and disposition for Queek. Forgive ignorant Queek for asking, what use is there for you in this case?' said Queek. 'Gnawdwell say you Queek's right claw.' Queek narrowed his eyes. 'Gnawdwell write-say "Take Skrikk! He your right claw!" Queek says he already has right claw. It good for holding Dwarf Gouger!' He held up his paw and clenched it. 'And Queek has Ska! Loyal, good Ska! So, Queek has two right claws. One for Dwarf Gouger, one for punching enemies. But Gnawdwell order Queek needs *another* right claw, so Queek obey. Queek think, maybe Skrikk good! Maybe Skrikk good for boring things, boring things that tire Queek and make him angry. Boring things like counting skaven clan-rats.' He leaned in close to the clanlords and twisted his head to regard them one at a time, causing them both to flinch. 'But now Skrikk squeak-says, "Queek must think strategy!" What? Queek fight. Queek command. Queek does not count stupid-meat.'

Skrikk hunched over, looking sideways at Queek nervously.

'Who Skrikk think he is? Queek does think strategy, stupid-meat. Queek greatest warlord there is! Queek think-scheme peerless battle plans. Queek the best strategist you will ever meet, weak-meat. You will see. But what does Queek need to know colours of every stupid-meat rat-flag for if he has Skrikk? Too much pointless knowing clouds Queek's mind.' He leaned back with a dangerous look in his eyes. He greatly relished the fear in Skrikk's. 'If Skrikk can't count or Skrikk can't see-smell clan banners and tell Queek how many rats, how many slaves, how many clan-things and Moulder-things left before Queek run out of battle-meat for victory, perhaps Queek not need Skrikk after all? Queek be very unhappy if Queek has to do all counting and scritch-scratching himself.'

'O mighty one is correct!' squeaked Skrikk, far more shrilly than he had intended. 'Skrikk count. Skrikk has counted very well! I have noted all banners and numbers. See-read!' He beckoned a slave bearing a pile of dwarf-skin scrolls forward. The warlords at least had the will to clench their musk glands, terrified of Queek as they were. But the slave shook uncontrollably, and the fear-stink was heavy on his fur. 'See-look. Skrikk make all these himself. All is in order. I have everything written down so I know, mighty Queek. And what humble, unworthy Skrikk knows, most cunning Queek can know too! By asking! By asking!' he added in a panic. 'Of course you should not weary your piercing eyes reading such dull-tedious reports.' He shooed the skavenslave away and bowed repeatedly.

Something big in the parade let out a long, mournful low. There were many Moulder-things in the army.

'Battle-meat, battle-meat to get Queek close to the beard-things. Five thousand, ten thousand, one hundred thousand, it not matter to Queek,' Queek muttered. He stared at the skaven tramping by and became suddenly still. He no longer saw the troops. In his mind, he watched images of past slaughter.

The others cringed, each subtly trying to be the rat at the back of the crowd, but not too close to the giant Ska. When Queek's constant twitching stilled, someone usually died.

Queek clenched his fists and rounded on them all. 'Bah! This place still stink-smell of goblin-thing. Queek hate it. Queek still smell Skarsnik-thing squatting on his throne.' He pointed to where Skarsnik's throne had once been. 'It so strong, Queek see him!' His quick red eyes darted about, taking in the goblin's defacement of the giant statues lining the walls of the Hall of a Thousand Pillars. The goblins' shanty had been cleared, but signs of the greenskins were everywhere. What wreckage had not already been scavenged was still piled along the walls. Every inch of the place stank of goblin. He longed to kill green-things. He stared at the great dwarf gates to the surface city, opening mechanisms improved with skaven engines by the tinker-rats. On the other side of the doors were thousands and thousands of greenskins. One word would open the gates and the relief of battle could be his. Somewhere out there was Skarsnik, and he hated Skarsnik more than anything else in the world. Killing dwarfs was business, but his feud with the green-thing king was personal. His muzzle quivered with temptation.

'Gnawdwell's orders, remember Gnawdwell's orders!' squeaked the voice of Ikit Scratch from his skeleton impaled upon Queek's back. 'Kill beard-things first, green-things later.'

'Queek go now,' he said quietly, 'before he choke on Skarsnik stink. What new boring thing has Thaxx and Skrikk to show mighty Queek?'

They had more of the same to show him, but neither dared say. 'To the fourth and fifth deeps, O wicked and savage Queek,' said Thaxx, spreading his arms and bowing low. 'To the second and third clawpacks, who await your merciless majesty with much fear and anticipation.'

'Yes-yes,' added Skrikk, not to be outdone. 'They are rightwise awestruck.' The three-week journey here from Skavenblight had been somewhat detrimental to his nerves, and he jumped every time he thought Thaxx bettered him in flattery.

Three days it took to see the next two clawpacks. Queek only stopped to eat – which he did savagely and messily – or to sleep, which he did in short, rapid-breathed bursts. The finest burrows were set aside for him, the best flesh-meat. He did not care.

Much to his annoyance, nobody tried to kill him. His legs spasmed with impatience when he lay down. His hands itched to hold Dwarf Gouger. Everyone around him feared his fury. Murder was imminent, they were sure. Each warlord and clan chief he greeted showed their necks and squeaked in most pitiable homage. Each one half expected to die. Thaxx and Skrikk had it worst by far, for they had to accompany Queek everywhere. They were both sure it was only a matter of time before Queek killed one or the other, and their attempts to outdo each other in their obsequiousness became more outrageous by the hour. Their wheedling only angered Queek more.

But no one did die. They could all see-smell Queek was bursting with the need to kill, but he raised a paw against no one.

'Steady, steady,' said the dead beard-thing Krug to Queek. 'You muff this up, lad, and you'll not be getting Gnawdwell's potion.'

'The beard-thing is correct, mad-thing,' added Sleek Sharp-wit's annoying voice. 'Be careful, or you will perish.'

Queek shot Sleek's fleshless skull a murderous glare. 'Do not call Queek mad-thing, dead Old-thing!'

'Steady!' said Krug. 'Steady.'

'Yes-yes,' mumbled Queek, cradling the dwarf king's skull to his chest one sleep. 'Krug right, Krug wise! Time only enemy Queek cannot kill. Only Gnawdwell help with that.'

'And so the mad-thing listens to the dead dwarf, but not to the wisdom of the living. You are a poor warlord, Queek, no match for me at my peak,' said Sleek.

'I alive, you dead. I better,' said Queek acidly.

And so Queek set all his will to restraining his considerable temper, resolving to add Thaxx and Skrikk's heads to his trophy rack in due course.

Clawpacks two and three were led by Skrak and Ikk Hackflay, ex-lieutenants from Queek's Red Guard. These stormvermin were known to him, and respected by him as much as he could respect any skaven. They were braver than most, and Queek was almost civil to them, bringing much prestige to their names. For all his hatred of machination, he changed the status of skaven simply by looking at them wherever he went. This in turn upset alliances and friendships, led to back-stabbings and new pledge-bonds. His passage through the ancient dwarf city rippled outwards, rewriting the architecture of treachery and false promises that underpinned any skaven society.

He was aware of it, but tried his best not to think about it. It only made him angrier.

Clawpacks two and three were much like the first. The second bigger than the third, half of each made up of Clan Mors warriors, the rest a selection of scruffy rabble clans.

'Queek not see-smell slaves. Where slaves?' he demanded shortly after visiting the third clawpack.

'This way, O most terrible one!' said Thaxx.

They cut across the city in the fourth deep, emerging below the stone-pile the beard-things called Karag Rhyn, and the goblins White Fang. There were many long tubular caves deep below this mountain, each carpeted with bones, some full to the ceiling with brittle skeletons. Queek looked repeatedly to the curved roof. Up there, somewhere, was Skarsnik. The imp had taken refuge in the northern range after finally, *finally* being chased out from the deeps. Queek sighed happily as he imagined gnawing his way up through the rock, to emerge in the imp-thing's own room, where he would bite him to death. He tittered to himself, but his amusement turned to anger as the scenario's impossibility rudely intruded. Queek's tail flicked in agitation.

Laired in the bone caves were so many skavenslaves that Queek could not count them. He was dizzy on their scent. They shrank back into side tunnels at his approach, tripping over their chains to get out of his way, their eyes downcast.

'There is many-many slave-meat?' he asked, peering into a tunnel packed full of eyes glinting as they looked away.

Thaxx and Skrikk fought to be the one to deliver the information.

'Over one hundred thousand, O lordly Queek!' said Thaxx, cutting Skrikk dead. 'We have bred them especially quickly, raising them in unprecedented time with black–'

'Many are from Thaxx's breeding pits, masterful Queek,' butted in Skrikk. 'He must be so proud, to make so many weak-meat for Queek. Poor, lowly Skrikk only provide clanrat warriors and stormvermin for Queek's armies. Skrikk sorry!'

Thaxx scowled at his colleague. Skrikk returned a cocky smile.

'Many weak-meat?'

'Many-many!' said Thaxx through gritted chisel-teeth.

'Good-good!' said Queek. 'Then Thaxx not miss these.'

Queek could restrain himself no longer. He leaped into the tunnel, drew his weapons, and vanished into the gloom.

'But they my slaves...' said Thaxx.

'If you like,' said Ska, lounging on a rock and picking his claws, 'you go stop him. I sure-certain that work out just fine for clever Warlord Thaxx.' Queek's Red Guards tittered.

The squeal of panicked ratmen blasted from the tube. They blundered out into the dimly lit corridor, but could not go far, caught by their chains.

One tripped and fell at Skrikk's feet. He looked up at the clanlords pleadingly.

'You go quick-quick now,' said Skrikk. 'Back in there so mighty Queek may kill-slay.'

'He very bored,' said Ska. 'You be good and make him happy.'

The skavenslave stared at them piteously as he was dragged back into the cave, knocking a pile of bones out of the way. He grabbed a skull, but it did not arrest his progress and he disappeared into the dark still clutching it.

A short and noisy time later, during which the cave's stale air ripened with the reek of blood, bowels and musk, Queek emerged from the tunnel, dripping with gore. He panted lightly.

'That no fun,' he said. He licked his lips free of blood and smiled with cruel joy nevertheless. 'No challenge for Queek to slaughter slaves.' He looked speculatively at Thaxx. Skrikk nodded enthusiastically behind his back, jiggling his eyebrows at Thaxx and making a pantomime of how formidable a warrior Skrikk was.

'Skrikk greater warrior!' said Thaxx in a tumble.

'Not so great as mighty Queek!' said Skrikk, his tail twitched nervously.

'Who is?' said Queek with a shrug. 'Now, where final claw-pack? If it far, Queek not happy. Maybe we see how good Skrikk and Thaxx are...'

'Not far! Not far, mighty Queek!' said Thaxx, bowing low. 'A half day, then all inspections done.'

Skrikk shot Thaxx a warning look. Thaxx caught it.

'Er, but Warlord Queek must be tired, so much travelling. He should go rest-sleep to increase his strength so that he might kill-slay beard-things and green-things better.'

'You say Queek is sleepy-tired, less-brilliant-than-Queek Warlord Thaxx?' said Queek.

'Oh no, your deadliness, of course not. All know that Queek could kill all things half asleep and with a small feeding spoon. It is just that you are right...' Thaxx took a step backwards as Queek reared up over him.

'You say sometimes Queek not-right?'

'No! No! Queek is always right! Every time! Everyone knows!' squealed Thaxx.

'Yes-yes, Queek the mightiest. Queek also the most correct and cleverest,' said Skrikk. Queek was mollified.

Thaxx relaxed a little. 'You say boring. It boring looking at so many rat-things.' He flapped his paw dismissively. 'They look all the same. Perhaps we go back now? Meet fifth claw-pack later?'

Queek's eyes narrowed. 'What Thaxx hide? What Thaxx think Queek not like about fifth clawpack?'

'Hide?' said Thaxx, his eyes wide with wounded innocence.

'Never,' said Skrikk.

'You quite insistent, both of you, that Queek see boring rats. And now, all of a sudden, you not want Queek to see boring rats. Queek not stupid. You think Queek stupid?'

'No,' wailed Thaxx.

'You better tell Queek now,' said Ska.

Thaxx abased himself upon the floor. 'It is not Thaxx's fault. Stupid-meat minions make mistake. He told by great lords to do it.'

'Do what?' said Queek. He hefted Dwarf Gouger and gave it a pleased lick.

'It better,' said Skrikk with a resigned expression, 'if Queek see-smells with his own eyes and nose.'

They went downwards from the bone caves into old skaven ways, gnawed by teeth long before the invention of tunnelling machines. These cut a slope across the outermost edges of the dwarf deeps under the Great Vale. Innumerable shafts and stairways joined the halls carved into the mountains to the undercity proper. The skaven tunnels cut across them all. They came to a winding stair, and went down this for many thousands of paces – round and round, until Queek felt dizzy. He had lived most of his life in Karak Eight Peaks, but this stair was new to him. The Eight Peaks was so vast that it was impossible to know it all, although the hated green-imp claimed to.

Down and down, passing into areas of the city that had collapsed. Some skaven, like Sleek Sharpwit, heretically said that beard-things were not stupid and built well. Queek laughed. Here was proof it was not so! There were many cave-ins and collapses that had sealed off whole sections of the beard-things' burrows before quicker minds had rejoined them.

'Earthquakes, poor skaven engineering undermining good dwarf work,' said Sleek's dead voice sulkily.

'Stupid beard-things,' said Queek.

His underlings, as always, pretended not to notice Queek's one-sided conversations with his trophies.

They skirted the edges of the City of Pillars, the main part of the skaven domain in the Eight Peaks, where the last of the dwarfish deeps gave way to broken mines and endlessly convoluted warrens of skaven burrows. The journey took three feedings before they emerged at the very bottom of the world.

Deep in the deepest reaches of the City of Pillars, hundreds of fathoms below the lowest of the old dwarf deeps, was the Trench.

Who knew what cataclysm had torn this gap into the bowels of the earth? Nearly a mile deep and half a mile across, it went further into the living rock than even the skaven wished to go, and they were the children of the underworld. Along its base were dozens of cave mouths. These were not natural formations. They were carved by living creatures, but only a portion of them by the skaven. Down there were strange things, blindwyrms, deep trolls, scumbloids, mad-things and worse. Skaven who went into those tunnels often did not come out again.

Not today. The tunnels had been pressed into use as barrack burrows and every one crawled with armed skaven. Nothing that did not squeak or bear fur would dare come into the Trench. From end to end and wall to wall, the floor of the canyon was a seething mass of ratkin bodies.

'The fifth clawpack, your most mightiness,' said Skrikk, bowing.

Queek's mouth opened. He shut it with a click. He was reluctantly impressed. There were dozens of warrior clans – none of the greater ones, admittedly, but some of the more respected names among the rabble clans were present. More arresting were the large numbers of Moulder-beasts, far more than in the other formations. He spotted a great number of rat ogres, thousands of giant rats and, most impressively, a pair of caged abominations. Far more monsters than Queek had seen in the rest of the city.

'Who lead-bring such an endless rat sea to the City of Pillars?' asked Queek quietly. Both his lieutenants ducked their heads submissively.

'It hard to say, most subtle and dangerous–' began Thaxx.

'That is, it not easy to put into words, great and–' interrupted Skrikk.

'I do,' said a voice from the shadows. A shape was there, lurking where the dark was too thick even for skaven eyes to see through. Queek smelt the identity of the squeaker before he threw back his hood to reveal the silhouette of horns.

'White-fur!' said Queek, his sword hissing free from its scabbard.

'O mighty, terrible and great warrior Queek! I am Kranskritt, servant of the Horned Rat and emissary of Clan Scruten.' Kranskritt stepped out of the dark and bowed to the jingle of small bells. A bunch of flunkeys came skulking out behind their master. They had precisely none of his poise and threw themselves down to the stone hurriedly for fear of Queek.

Thaxx and Skrikk scuttled backwards, banging into Ska.

'Where you go?' said Ska mildly. He arched an eyebrow. He enjoyed the effect Queek had on the warlords.

Queek laughed horribly. 'White-fur, white-fur! What you squeak-say?' He pointed the rusted blade of his sword at the grey seer, but Kranskritt walked directly towards Queek, his back straight, muzzle smooth and glands closed.

'I say I am the chosen of the Horned Rat, his emissary here in the City of Pillars, and master of the fifth clawpack.' He looked at Queek's swordpoint, hovering inches from his nose. 'I am not frightened of your sword.'

'Oh? Why-tell? You have few heartbeats before I kill-slay. Give me entertainment with last pathetic breaths, stupid-meat. Scruten no longer have favour of Horned Rat. Horned Rat say so himself. I hear he squeak-say it very forcefully to white-fur Kritislik.' Queek giggled a rapid, twittering series of squeaks.

The grey seer came fully into what little light there was. His eyes glowed a dull warpstone-green. He wore purple robes embroidered with arcane sigils. Bells were round his ankles, his horns and his wrists. They tocked and clonked with his every movement. Strangely, none of the skaven present had heard him approach.

'I am not frightened, because we work together for greater quick-death of beard-things. Allies not be frightened of each other, foolish, yes?' said the seer mildly. 'And Gnawdwell, he tell you to work with all, to make quick work of beard-thing pathetic fort-place? It would be a big shame if you kill me for supposed insult and all Kranskritt's warriors go home. Queek's job is then so much harder.' He shook his head sadly, rattling his ornaments.

'Gnawdwell a long way away from here, white-fur. I chop-kill and no one know.'

'Oh everyone will know, most indubitably dangerous and most martial Queek. I doubt-think you care much. But I will tell you a secret.' Kranskritt leaned in close. 'I not care either. You kill-slay me, I go to Horned Rat quick-fast. There perhaps I can explain why Clan Scruten has been wronged, and why Queek is a big danger to all his children. And then you can come too and tell him yourself, because without my clawpack, Queek not get what Gnawdwell promise. Big, big shame and sorrow for mighty Queek as age and time make him weak. And dead. Yes! Dead-dead!' He laughed weirdly.

Queek was outraged. His eyes bulged and veins stood out on his neck. His heart hammered so quickly its beats blurred into one constant note. Equally swiftly, Dwarf Gouger was in his hand. Kranskritt's lackeys shrank back on their bellies. But not Kranskritt.

Kranskritt tilted his head. 'Ah, the real Queek. Kill me then, I do not care.'

Queek squeaked. A paw held back his arm.

'Who dares touch Queek?' said Queek, trembling with fury.

'He is right,' hissed Skrikk. 'Gnawdwell. Remember what Gnawdwell said!'

Skrikk was shaking. Queek wondered what inducements their lord had given him to be so bold as to touch Queek's fur! But this other, he was even more troubling. He exhibited no sign of fear at all, and in the face of the mighty Queek. Queek let his weapons drop and paced around the grey seer, examining and sniffing the stranger from every angle. The seer's servants backed away, still on their bellies.

'You very brave, white-fur. I respect that. But there are no seers on the Council now.'

'We are being tested by the Horned One,' said Kranskritt. 'That is all. You will see. Observe the might I bring to your army!' He swept his paw behind him at the masses in the Trench.

'No power, no influence.' Queek sniffed suspiciously. Warp-stone, yes, name scent, yes. Food, old filth and fresh-licked fur. But no fear! No fear at all. 'You are not scared! Why you not scared of Queek?'

'Come and see. I will show you what I have brought, yes? Then Queek know why I know you will not kill-slay Kranskritt, and so Queek will know why I am not scared. Simple, yes?'

Kranskritt gestured to the skaven waiting in the canyon. 'No seat on the Council for Clan Scruten, no-yes. But still have power and influence we do, yes? See! I have warriors from thirty-eight clans, and many-much Moulder-beasts.'

Queek looked sidelong at the grey seer. Still he was unafraid.

He held up a delicate white paw and gongs sounded. The skaven below began to march in procession. The hubbub of their gathering became a roaring, the tramp of soft feet and rattle of weapons overwhelming, and the skaven lords struggled to be heard over it. Surely even Belegar high up above could hear this doom that approached him. Queek hid a smile under his scowl.

The fifth clawpack was vast. Kranskritt rattled off the names of units and clans as they went past and into their garrison-burrows, their leaders coming nervously forward from the back of the shelf to be introduced. Despite his avowed disinterest in military minutiae, Queek recognised most of the banners. Some of them were far from home: Clan Krizzor from the Dark Lands, Clan Volkn from the Fire Mountains, for example. He snarled as the banners of traitor-Clan Gritus wobbled past. Only recently they had turned on their Clan Mors masters. Their appearance there was a slight.

'How white-fur get so many warriors?' demanded Queek.

'Have power! Have influence, many-mighty horde of ratkin, yes? See! Many-much veterans, scavenge-armed from sack of Tilea-place and Estalia-place,' shouted Kranskritt.

Queek sneered. 'Stupid man weapons. Stupid man armour. This boring! Ska Bloodtail!'

'Yes, O Queek?'

'We go-depart now. Skrikk will stay. He write down all clanthings. Thaxx stay-listen to stupid white-fur boast-squeaks too. Punishment for not say-squeaking about white-fur.' Queek stepped in close. Thaxx stood his ground as best he could, quailing at the stench of old blood and death coming from Queek's armour. 'Queek bored. Queek go think.'

Skrikk and Thaxx bowed repeatedly.

As Queek swept irritably from the Trench, Kranskritt smiled at his back.

# FIVE

*Treachery in the Deeps*

Queek, Ska and Queek's Red Guard jogged upwards. The din of the fifth clawpack mustering in the Trench was amplified by the tunnel, hurting their sensitive ears. Time and distance diminished it, until the trumpets and stamping of feet joined with all the other mysterious echoes that haunted the City of Pillars, and they found they could talk again.

'This not good-good,' said Queek to Ska. The latter ran as fast as his master, but his great size – for he was a giant among his kind, as tall as a tall man, and bigger than the mighty Gnawdwell himself – made him seem plodding next to Queek's swift movements.

'No, great Queek,' said Ska.

'Thaxx and Skrikk sneaky-sneaks. Not like good and loyal Ska.'

'Thank you, great Queek.' Ska had fought by Queek's side for many years and was of a similar age. Where his arms were visible between his plates of scavenged gromril, his black fur was spotted with patches of brilliant white. Many battles had left their mark upon his face in a pattern of pink scars. One of his ears had been torn off. Already intimidating, he was made fearsome by his war wounds.

They passed onto a wide dwarf-built way. Once a feeder road for the lower mines, it led directly back to the lower levels of the skaven stronghold. Even there, there was little space left, most of the width of the road taken up by sleeping clan-rats atop unfolded nesting rolls. From top to bottom, Karak Eight Peaks heaved with vermin. They ran along this for a quarter of a mile, kicking skaven out of the way, then turned into a lesser-used tunnel.

'If white-fur here, much scheming. Queek hate tittle-tattle squeak plots! Queek only wish to fight.' He gnawed at his lower lip as he thought. 'Send-bring me Grotoose, leader of Clan Moulder here, and master assassin Gritch of Clan Eshin. Queek question them both. I find out who behind this, who try to trick Queek.' He squeaked with annoyance. 'Queek happier if Queek bury Dwarf Gouger in Kranskritt's stupid horned head.'

'That is not a good idea, great Queek,' said Ska cautiously.

'Stupid giant-meat Ska! Queek know this! Queek make joke! Queek only wish for sim–'

A tremendous rumble cut their conversation dead. The roof caved in, and a tumble of boulders rushed from the ceiling, clacking one atop the other until they filled the way. Ska pushed Queek aside, but his Red Guard were not so lucky. They squealed in pain and fear as three of them were crushed, and the rest cut off from their master.

Queek rolled with Ska's shove and was back on his footpaws instantly, sniffing the air. Fear musk, blood, the sharp scent of rock dust, registered on his sensitive nose.

'Where Ska?'

'Here, mighty Queek!' said his henchman from the ground. He lay with his feet trapped by rocks.

'Ska better not be hurt – big rat with crushed feet no good to Queek!'

Ska grunted. 'I am not hurt, only trapped. I will dig myself– Queek! Look out!'

Queek was moving before Ska had finished squeaking. He somersaulted backwards as three razored blurs sliced through the air where he had been standing – throwing stars, which clanged from the rock fall leaving smears of bitter-smelling poison on the raw stone.

Queek landed sure-footedly on a boulder. He drew his weapons as he leapt, pushing himself off with his back paws and tail. Ahead of him, a black shape detached itself from the tunnel wall. Its cloak was patterned to match the stone and no name-scent came from it. An assassin. They had their glands removed as part of their initiation. Only they among the skaven carried no smell.

'Die-die!' squealed Queek. He landed in front of the assassin, who promptly flipped backwards, hurling two more stars from quick paws at the apex of his jump. Queek's sword moved left then right, sparking as it deflected the missiles. Queek jumped after his attacker, bounding on all fours, the knuckles of his clenched fists hitting the floor painfully. The assassin turned to face him, brandishing a pair of daggers that wept a deadly venom.

Queek lashed his tail from side to side, aiming to wrap it around the assassin's ankle, but the killer stepped over it as easily as if it were a jumping rope and came in, daggers weaving. Queek parried rapidly, his and the assassin's blades making a network of steel between the skaven. Ska watched his master helplessly, moaning and tugging desperately at his feet. Metal sparked and rang. Suddenly, it stopped.

The assassin's arms sagged, his blades fell to the tunnel floor. Queek dropped Dwarf Gouger and grabbed the assassin by the throat. He struggled feebly in Queek's grip, his pathetic choking noises making Queek smile until they stopped.

The assassin's body followed his daggers to the floor as Queek withdrew his sword from his chest.

'Stupid-meat! No one beat Queek! Queek the best!' He licked his sword clean with a long pink tongue, working out chunks of gore from its serrated edge with his gnawing teeth. He smacked his lips and frowned at his friend. 'What Ska doing there, lying around? Lazy Ska! Come-come! Help Red Guard dig through. Hurry-scurry.'

'Yes, great Queek,' said Ska resignedly, and recommenced tugging at the lumps of rock trapping his legs.

Queek waited in his trophy den for his minions to arrive. Racks where runic axes and dwarf mail coats had once hung displayed skulls and battered armour. Piles of smashed objects and trinkets were heaped all over the floor, a chieftain's spoils gathered over a lifetime of war. He was ten! Ten years! He could not believe it. Time had gone so fast. His muscles twitched, setting his fur quivering. Not from fear, no, never that. But soon he would be old, and he did not like to think about it.

Queek had not been in his trophy room for over thirteen moons. He was gratified that it remained untouched. 'Queek the best,' whispered Ikit Scratch in the back of his head. 'Everyone fear Queek!'

'Yes-yes!' Queek said. 'No one dare touch Queek's trophies.' He ran his hands over a manticore skull, enjoying the memory of the beast's death. 'No one touch Queek's trophies but Queek.' He licked the skull and chirred with delight.

Krug Ironhand, Sleek Sharpwit and Ikit Scratch's eyeless skulls looked on from their shelf of honour. The pickled hands of Baron Albrecht Kraus of Averland had joined his head next to them. This had not been preserved and had mummified in the chamber's dry air, its browned flesh dried into a perpetual, lopsided grin.

'I must say that it is good to have my hands with me,' the baron said. 'You know, I always say that you should have my head with you. Do I not say that, chaps? When the mighty Queek is not here?'

A chorus of ghostly groans came from Queek's trophy collection.

'Yes-yes! Others right! It because you always say "I always say" that your head stays here and is not with Queek and hands are!' snapped Queek. '"I must say this," and "did you know" and "I suggest"! Very boring. Hands not talk. Hands come with Queek, head stay here.'

'My dear fellow...'

'Silence!' Queek was more irritable than ever. He rapidly read the source of his annoyance again, a parchment lately arrived from Skavenblight. On it were direct orders from Gnawdwell. Here he said that Queek should engage the dwarfs in a war of attrition, wear them out with the slave legions of Thaxx Redclaw.

He bared his teeth at it. The hand looked to be that of Gnawdwell, but it made no mention of their earlier conversation and Gnawdwell's orders to finish the beard-things quickly. He held it up to his nose. The scent mark was right too.

'This not right,' he said for the third time. 'Forgery. Must be trick.'

'Trick-trap!' suggested Ikit.

'Maybe,' Queek shrugged. 'Maybe Gnawdwell change his mind, not want Queek to go to other clans.' He sniffed the parchment again. 'Name-smell is Gnawdwell's,' he reassured himself.

'Your kind are traitorous vermin,' suggested Krug. 'Anything is possible. I'd watch out if I were you.'

'Yes-yes, true,' said Queek. 'Maybe Gnawdwell sick of Queek. Maybe Gnawdwell send white-fur to check my power.'

'Yes-yes!' agreed the ghost of Ikit Scratch. 'White-furs have no power. Someone else is behind this happening. Why not Gnawdwell?'

Queek stopped pacing, his tail swishing back and forth metronomically as he thought. The orders were contradictory, but in contradiction was latitude, freedom to act as he saw fit.

'Very useful. Very useful indeed. Queek...' He stopped and raised his nose into the air. 'Shhh,' said Queek, holding up his paw. 'Everyone silent! Someone coming.'

Even with his back turned, Queek knew who it was. He smelt them before they came. One of the reasons he had chosen this old armoury was that the prevailing air currents blew in, not out. One of the approaching skaven had a heavy reek of beasts and skalm, the other very little scent at all. Their footsteps gave them away in any case – the light pad of a stabber-killer from Clan Eshin and the heavier tread of a hulking beast-handler.

'Greetings, O most malevolent of potentates, O sovereign of mighty Mors. I have hurried quick-quick at your summons,' said Gritch, his cloak whispering as he bowed. 'My watch-spies have already told me much-much. So sorry for cave-in. Assassin not one of mine.'

'Hail, great Headtaker,' said Grotoose.

Queek smiled. Grotoose was gruff, to the point, and a deadly fighter – the qualities Queek admired the most. He almost trusted him. Gritch was a useful spy, but as with any Clan Eshin member, he favoured intrigue and was likely to be playing more angles than he had claws. Queek pointedly kept his back to them for a moment, showing he had no fear of a dagger between the shoulder blades. Besides, he could rely on the dead-things to warn him.

Queek placed the manticore skull upon the floor in front of him and stepped around it, acknowledging his minions by turning to face them. Without greetings or preamble, he went to the heart of the matter. 'A grey seer! What is the meaning of this? Did Queek not squeak-tell Lord Gnawdwell about the grey ones' interfering ways? Did either of you know that the fifth clawpack is led by a horned one?'

Grotoose looked Queek in the eyes and bared his fangs. 'I not know,' he said. 'My Moulder-brothers tell me nothing. Big secret.'

Gritch drummed his nervous, twitchy fingers against themselves, scratched his whiskers, and looked at his shuffling feet.

'Gritch? Speak-squeak,' coaxed Queek.

'Yes, yes-yes. I knew. Not for certain, O terrible one,' he said, looking up quickly. 'I hear rumours, I hear whispers. I wait-wait to tell Queek, when next we met.'

'You come see Queek earlier next time!'

'We meet-greet now,' said Gritch with a shrug.

With a swift flick of his wrist, Queek sent Dwarf Gouger to split the manticore skull before him.

'Ska!' shouted Queek.

'Yes, great one,' said Ska from the mouth of the tunnel.

'Fetch Skrikk! Queek want to know what he has to say about this. One look from Queek's eye and he squirt musk and tell all!'

'Yes, great one.'

'And send for Clan Skryre tinker-rats. Time for them to report to Queek. Much-much needs finishing before great signal.'

Queek snarled. He hated all this, hated, hated, hated.

'Queek want to bury Dwarf Gouger in beard-thing's head!' he said.

'Patience!' said Ikit Scratch. 'Soon the time come for death-slay and end of all dwarfs.'

Queek tittered. 'Yes-yes. You right. You clever warlord. But not so clever to kill Queek! Now be quiet, others here.'

Grotoose gave Queek a concerned look. His tail twitched. 'My lord?'

'Nothing! Nothing squeaking for your ears, beastmaster. No! You return to your beasts, Grotoose,' snapped the Headtaker. 'Gritch tell Queek everything he knows about this. This is the Council's doing. But,' he added thoughtfully, 'was Gnawdwell the paw behind it? That is the big question.' He let this last statement hang a moment, knowing full well it would reach eager ears. If they thought the rat was out of the bag, then his opponents might panic. Gritch's face stayed studiously neutral. 'Tell Queek about Kranskritt. Squeak-tell me everything.'

Kranskritt leaned hard against the burrow wall, his head pounding to the merciless beat of his heart. Every sphincter he had twitched, threatening to flood his robes with urine and musk. He shook all over and his paw-pads sweated. The potion was wearing off. Soothgnawer had warned him that the after-effects were unpleasant. Naturally, he expected the verminlord to lie to him, or not tell him the whole truth at least, but in this one thing he had been truthful – the sensations of withdrawal were awful.

It was horrible down there in the Trench. He hated being at the bottom of the pit. Every sleep he had he was woken by the screams of half-mad Clan Moulder-things. Every time it happened he thought they were coming from him. He was too hot and shook, as if all the fear he should have felt while under the potion's influence were merely delayed, and afflicted him all at once.

With palsied hands he pulled a soft man-skin pouch from under his robes, fished out a piece of dully glowing warpstone and nibbled at it. A surge of wellbeing coursed through him, driven on by his racing heart. Frantically, he dabbed at the crumbs on his front and licked them from his fingers.

Kranskritt closed his eyes and pressed his back and palms

against the cool rock, letting the rush of the warpstone chase away his discomfort. He stayed like that until his heart slowed and his glands gave one last twitch. Feeling weak but better, he staggered the remaining way into his burrow, using the wall as a support.

Crates and boxes, some opened and their contents half spilling into the room, filled his chambers. He had not known how much to bring, not knowing how long he would be in the City of Pillars. In the end, he had packed everything, worried he might leave something important behind. But the crammed state of his burrow meant he couldn't lay a paw on anything, and it made him anxious.

He sought a reason other than his own weakness – or Queek, for he was so frightened of him he didn't want to think about it – for his disquiet.

'Soothgnawer, yes-yes. He is too strong!' chittered Kranskritt. 'It is him! So tricksy and sneaky. Never a straight word for poor, honest Kranskritt.'

He paced back and forth. 'A binding, a binding. That must be it. Make him my servant, not the other way around. I am too strong for him!' he snickered. 'Guards!' he called. An unacceptable number of heartbeats later, three mangy stormvermin sloped into the room. Kranskritt missed the elite white-fur guard that usually accompanied seers of his rank, but all that had gone with Kritislik's death and Clan Scruten's disgrace. At least these, being of Clan Gritus, were unlikely to betray him to Queek and Clan Mors.

Probably.

'Clear the floor,' he squeaked imperiously. 'Make me a space! And carefully! No more breakages.'

The stormvermin rolled their eyes but did as they were bid, working until the floor was clear and the crates were stacked more or less safely along the burrow walls. Kranskritt dismissed the stormvermin and hunted about for his warpstone stylus. He couldn't find it. Forgetting his admonishment to the guards, he lost his temper and upended three crates before he seized upon it with a screech of triumph.

'Now,' he said, kicking packing straw and broken possessions to the edge of the room. 'Where to begin?'

Kranskritt spent a happy bell scuttling around his chamber, sketching out his circle in chalk then filling in the design with his stylus. Where the lines met, they glowed with the non-light of warpstone. The atmosphere of the room changed, growing pregnant with power. And then he was interrupted.

'Greetings, Grey Seer Kranskritt, O most wise and malign. I gather-bring news of the Headtaker.'

Turning from the writhing runes he was scratching into the chamber floor, Kranskritt glowered at his messenger.

Bowing profusely, the skaven gave his report to the floor, not daring to look upon the seer. 'A boulder trap missed Queek. Three of his Red Guard were smashed-slain, but the Headtaker leapt aside.'

Kranskritt's muzzle twitched. 'He will know it was a set-trap, yes-yes,' said the grey seer. 'Who will he suspect-blame? Tell me who has he questioned about my presence?'

'Grotoose of Clan Moulder, Gritch of Clan Eshin and Warlord Skrikk, my lord,' responded the messenger without raising his eyes.

'Hmmm, but not Gnarlfang?' said the grey seer, musing to himself. 'Strange-odd. Send Gritch to me immediately.'

Twitching his head to listen, Kranskritt waited until the sound of the messenger's footsteps had receded before returning to his circle.

'Your circle will not work,' said a whisper from the shadows. 'You are inscribing it wrong.'

Kranskritt froze. 'Why don't we tell-explain to the Headtaker that it is not us? Clearly he will come after me soon,' said Kranskritt to the darkness.

A soft and altogether evil laughter filled the room, a sound as palatable as nails scratching on polished slate. 'Of course he suspects you, but it would be no good to tell him that the one behind the attempts is Lord Gnawdwell. He suspects this to be the case, but he would not believe you. And yes, his agents are already on their way.'

After a long pause, the voice spoke again. 'I could protect you, little Kranskritt, but there must be no more attempts to bind me.'

Kranskritt stamped his footpaw in frustration and threw down his stylus. 'You tell me not to be scared of Queek. I not scared of Queek, but Queek almost kill this poor, stupid-meat. Then potion wear off and I am plenty-scared! Why did you not tell me how bad I would feel?'

'But I did,' which was true, 'and you were not scared, little horned one,' which was also true.

Kranskritt drew a breath in to whine and dissemble, but he stopped, puzzled. 'No. I was not scared.'

'And so you are still alive. My potion worked. Stop-Fear! No gland will betray you. Fear is weakness. When will you learn-understand that what I say is truth?'

Whenever you start telling the truth consistently, and not only when it suits you, thought Kranskritt, though he did not say it. He cringed. How did he know the verminlord could not read his mind? He hurriedly composed a fawning apology in his head.

A mist gathered in the centre of the circle, coalescing into the form of a verminlord with white fur and many horns sprouting from its bare skull. Soothgnawer stepped daintily over the bounds of the binding circle, eliciting a squeak of annoyance from the grey seer. 'I did say you were doing it wrong.'

Kranskritt slumped into a sulk, arms crossed. The first time he had seen the verminlord, taking shape in the magical fumes of the Temple of the Grey Seers in Skavenblight, he had collapsed in fear and adulation. He had been even more frightened when Soothgnawer had chosen him as the catspaw for his schemes. Not any more. Familiarity really did breed contempt. Now what he felt mostly was petulant, the verminlord treated him like a favourite slave. From under its impressive rack of horns, it gazed down at him with a wholly infuriating mixture of indulgence and smugness, like it knew it knew far more than Kranskritt ever could, and although it kept most of its knowledge to itself, it was secretly pleased when Kranskritt figured out a part of the greater picture. Most patronising, most infuriating!

'Queek is angry, little seer,' the verminlord said. 'He travels repeatedly from clan to clan, despite his irritation with the role. Soon he will visit you – you cannot hide from him forever.'

Kranskritt's tail twitched. His glands clenched. 'Queek has his paws full. Many clans, all together. Bad recipe for big trouble. He is a mad-thing, always talking to himself.'

'His name is enough to quell any revolt, little seer. He is not as mad-crazed as he pretends to be. When he talks, voices answer him.'

'Whose? Who speak-squeaks to Queek?'

Soothgnawer laughed, a velvety evil sound. 'That I will not tell you, for you do not need to know.'

'Then what do I need to know?' whined Kranskritt, and he threw himself flat on the floor, his forehead and the full length of his muzzle flat against the stone. 'O great and powerful malicious one! Give-tell humble servant of the Horned Rat instructions so he might further great verminlord's master's schemings.'

'Hush! Hush!' said the verminlord. It reached out a massive claw. Kranskritt forbore to be tickled between the horns. 'Be calm, little seer. You must keep Queek on your side, for now. Do as he says until I instruct-command otherwise.'

Kranskritt looked up into the currently skeletal face of

THE END TIMES | THE RISE OF THE HORNED RAT

Soothgnawer. His appearance was inconstant, and changed worryingly.

'Do not fear, little seer. Soon there will be opportunity for Clan Scruten to regain influence. That is what we both want-desire, yes-yes?'

'Of course, of course,' said Kranskritt.

'Your fellows labour upon the Great Spell in Skavenblight. Already they draw the Chaos moon nearer to this world. This has been revealed to the remaining eleven Lords of Decay. The disturbance its presence will have upon the earth will be the signal to attack.'

'But the tinker-rats? What if they are successful with their rocket and our spell is not?'

'Clan Skryre attempt the construction of their rocket to destroy the moon. This contest between the clans becomes heated. Much turmoil in Skavenblight, many assassinations.' Soothgnawer paused. 'And Grey Seer Thanquol helps Clan Skryre.'

'Thanquol?' said Kranskritt in surprise.

Soothgnawer nodded. 'It is not my doing. He has proven his lack of worth time and again. He is deservedly outcast. You are my preferred instrument to restore the fortunes of Clan Scruten.'

Kranskritt grovelled in appreciation.

'The head of our Council has plans for him, as I have plans for you, little seer. Thanquol will succeed in his venture, but Clan Skryre will fail. The Great Spell must succeed!'

'Why cannot Kranskritt join in this most holy of sorceries, great one?' said Kranskritt, who really would have been any-where else but near Queek.

'Because, little seer, there is more than one task to be done. The beard-things must die. All of them.'

Kranskritt, still abased on the floor, felt the air stir the fur on his neck as Soothgnawer bent low. 'And do you really think,' the verminlord said, his hot breath washing over the seer, 'that we can trust a mad-thing like Queek to accomplish that? No.' Soothgnawer often answered his own questions. 'Without you, he will fail. And without you, he might survive.' Soothgnawer's fleshless smile grew wider on his skull. 'And we can't have that, can we, little seer?'

# SIX

*The Breaking of the Mountains*

Morrslieb loomed, bigger than it had ever been, peering over Karag Nar like a glutton eyeing a honey cake. Sickly light shed from its mournful face reflected from the snow, painting the world a disturbing green.

'As you see,' said Drakki Throngton, loremaster of Vala-Azrilungol, 'the Chaos moon waxes huge, my lord.'

'What does this all mean?' whispered Belegar. 'Other than it's got bigger,' he said sharply, remembering Drakki's endless lectures on precise speech during his youth.

'I do not know,' admitted Drakki sorrowfully. His breath misted his half-moon spectacles in the cold night air. 'All I can do is check the measurements of our ancestors against our own observations.'

'And?' said Belegar.

'Technically, my lord?'

'Aye! Technically. I'm no beardling.'

'I apologise, my lord,' said Drakki. 'Well, see here.' He flopped open a book over his forearm. The moonlight, cursed though it was, was ample illumination for a dwarf to read by. 'The Chaos moon waxes and wanes according to its own whim. Sometimes there is a pattern, often there is not. It has grown larger and smaller in the past.' He licked an ink-stained finger and flicked back a couple of hundred pages, two centuries' worth of measurements. The handwriting was the same as in the recent pages. Drakki was old. 'Such as here. That was when it was at its largest.'

Belegar glanced up from the page. 'The years of the Great War Against Chaos.'

'Indeed, my king.'

'And the numbers?'

'Well, my liege. There we have the most troubling news. These indicate that this is the largest it has ever been. Diameter, illumination, frequency of transit…' His voice trailed away. 'All higher numbers even than during the Great War.'

'Hmph,' said Belegar. He leaned against the parapet. In the city in the Great Vale, greenskin campfires burned insolently. 'And what if I were to request the non-technical version?'

Drakki shut the book with finality. 'Then I would say we were in a great deal of trouble, my liege. And not just us. Everybody.'

'Now that's putting it mildly,' said Belegar. He drummed his fingers on the stone. 'I've had requests, from the other holds, asking for their warriors back. Even, would you credit it, from High King Thorgrim.'

'Yes, my liege.'

'What kind of world is it, where even a dwarf can't keep his word any more? A few weeks ago I was up here with Notrigar, winding him up.'

'Oh, he is a little on the sparse-chinned side when it comes to recognising a good joshing, sire,' said Drakki, his aged face crinkling with mirth.

'That he is,' said Belegar, no humour in his voice at all. 'But

I don't feel it now. I look out at this place, Drakki, and all I can see is my dream slipping through my fingers.'

'We will prevail, sire.'

'That's what I told Notrigar.' Belegar huffed. The breath strained through his frosty beard to break free in clouds. 'We do what we can. We're as fortified as we can be. All we can do is wait for them, because as sure as gold is in the ground and khazukan crave it, they are coming. The only question is *when*.'

They looked out over the vale for a while, until a rumbling from the earth had them both casting their eyes downwards. Fragments of stone jumped like frogs from shelf to shelf on the outside of the citadel, click-clacking all the way down. A louder grumble took up with the first, then another and another, all eight mountains ringing the city protesting the failures of the world, sorrowful as longbeards deep in their ale. The ground convulsed, once, then again. The grating of stone on stone from the city told of ruins collapsing.

Belegar and Drakki swayed, their flat dwarfish feet keeping them upright. Alarms went off up and down the citadel, horns and clanging triangles.

'Earthquake! Earthquake!' dwarfs shouted.

The citadel's masonry ground block on block, sending showers of ancient mortar down on the dwarf king, but the dwarfs were wise to the ways of the earth and built accordingly. The citadel did not fall. Hammerers ran to his side, pitched across the wavering battlements like sailors on a stone ship. 'Protect the king! Protect the king!' their leader, Brok Gandsson, bellowed. Shield rims clacked into one another as the dwarfs formed a barrier of gromril and steel to shelter their lord, half of them angling their shields upwards over his head. Fragments of masonry bounced off them.

'Get back! I'm no beardling frightened by a little shiver,' Belegar shouted, shoving at his protectors. They stood solid as the stones themselves.

'Not until this is over, my king,' said Brok.

The earthquake went on for long minutes, dying only gradually. Belegar waited under the shield roof while the earth gave one more heave. No more aftershocks came, and he shoved his men aside. Drakki followed him from the knot of hammerers.

A wind, unnaturally hot, stirred their beards, the runes on their weapons pulsing with blue light as it ran over them. Out in the ruins came the clamour of panicking orcs and goblins.

'My lord, look!' Drakki was pointing south. The winter skies were stained orange by distant fire. 'Karag Haraz is erupting most fiercely.'

A distant boom rolled over the mountains, reflected from every rock face, until it seemed they clamoured in despair. Far to the north, more flamelight tainted the sky, colouring the high vaults of night.

'And Karag Dronn,' said Belegar.

'They have been spouting fire for long months now, but these latest eruptions must be immense, if we can see them from here,' said Drakki, unconsciously reaching for a notepad to mark the phenomenon down. 'Karag Dronn is over one hundred leagues away.'

'If they both speak, then doubtless Karag Orrud and the Karag Dum do.'

'And east,' said Drakki quietly. A gentle aftershock shook the ground, causing the hammerers to tense again. Drakki nodded to the eastern night sky. A haze of red coloured it as far as they could see from north to south.

'Grungni's beard,' Belegar said. 'All of them?' The others remained silent. Such troubles from deep in the earth had brought the Karaz Ankor to its knees in the distant past and heralded the beginning of the dwarfs' long decline. Nobody needed reminding of that.

'Is it over, loremaster?' asked Brok.

'There will be further small earthquakes, but I expect the strongest have passed, for now.' He looked to the Chaos moon, crowding its once larger brother from the sky. 'There must be some connection. And if it continues to grow, there may be worse to come.'

Belegar nodded curtly. 'Messengers!' he called. Several lightly armoured dwarfs appeared from inside. 'Get yourselves down into the first deep. I want to know of every stone out of place, do you understand?'

'Yes, my liege,' they all said.

'It would be our bloody luck if that lot brought down some of our defences. If there are any casualties, Valaya forfend, you let me know.'

The messengers ran off, heavy boots clumping down the winding stairs leading down from the parapet into the citadel.

'Something's coming, very soon. If this doesn't–'

A sky-shattering explosion tore through the night. The face of Karag Nar leapt outwards with surreal slowness, long cloudy trails of rock dust puffing up like flour from a burst sack. The ruined fortress upon its shoulder tumbled down like a town made of model bricks pushed over by a child, the finely cut dwarf masonry becoming one with the tumble of broken rock racing down the mountain's flanks. Belegar watched open-mouthed as debris arced towards him.

Belegar was unceremoniously shoved to the flagstones of the wall-walk by his guards. This time he did not order them back. Pebbles rattled off gromril armour, the heavier stones that came tumbling soon after eliciting grunts from the hammerers covering the king. More explosions boomed, these muffled by depth.

A rain of boulders slammed down into the city, levelling whole districts. Avalanches of rock poured off the flanks of the mountains, burying further sections.

Silence was a long time coming.

Belegar's hammerers jumped up, hauling the dazed king to his feet. They attempted to hustle him back inside, calling for more of his bodyguard. Belegar was filled with rage and shoved their hands away. He went to the edge of the parapet to see what had been done to his kingdom, ignoring their cries for him to be careful, to get inside.

A choking mist of pulverised rock hung over the Great Vale, biting the throats of everyone who breathed of it. Caught by the wind, it drifted away like rain, to reveal a scene of utter devastation presided over by the grinning moon.

Three of the eight mountains bore wounds in their sides. Karag Nar's eastern face had slumped inwards, while Karag Rhyn had collapsed into a broad fan of rubble, its height reduced by a half.

Belegar stared out in disbelief. Behind him, his hammerers formed up, but none dared approach the king.

When he turned to face them, a tear tracked down one dusty cheek.

'The mountains. They have killed the mountains.'

'That was no earthquake,' said Drakki, blood from a cut on his forehead making red tracks in his dust-whitened face.

Horns sounded again, this time from inside the citadel, answering others blown in the first deep. Belegar clenched his fist.

'Thaggoraki,' he said. 'It is starting.'

'Another war,' said Drakki.

'No,' said Belegar, pitching his voice low enough that only Drakki and Brok could hear. 'The beginning of the end.'

# SEVEN

*The Hall of Reckoning*

Horns sang all over the dwarf-held part of Karak Eight Peaks, echoing down corridors and up forgotten shafts, so that it was impossible to tell where they were coming from.

'That's the signal! Here they come, lads!' cried Borrik Norrgrimsson. His ironbreakers, Norrgrimlings all, held their shields up and locked them together, awaiting the arrival of the ratmen.

'It's about time the thaggoraki got here,' growled Hafnir Hafnirsson, Borrik's second cousin. 'I'm eager to split a few heads.'

'We've been standing in this hall for two months waiting for this lot. I'm sure we can hang on for a few more minutes,' said the Norrgrimlings' notoriously miserable Ironbeard, Gromley. 'Now shut up, or you'll put the thane off. He's on to something.'

Borrik kept a careful eye on all three entrances to the Hall of Reckoning. Two dwarf-made stairwells leading down into the enemy-infested second deep, and a massive pit, gnawed by some unspeakable thing, gaped in the middle of the floor. Not goblin work, or Borrik was an umgi. Other places gave him cause for concern. He had a keen eye for tunnelling, Borrik, and had spent a goodly amount of time tapping at the walls with variously sized hammers. There were more tunnels behind the walls, some of them worryingly new. And if there was one thing 'new' meant to dwarfs, it was trouble.

When Belegar assigned him to the hall, he had examined every inch thoroughly. Four hundred and one half-dwarf paces long, part of a broad thoroughfare that once ran east-west through the first deep to join with the Ungdrin Ankor. Blocked at both ends by rock falls, it would have been of little concern, save one thing. The fall at Borrik's end was pierced by a narrow gap, shored up by a failed expedition many centuries ago. At the other end, in a chamber hacked out of the loose rubble, was a steel-bound door that led into another passageway. This in turn led to the lower parts of the citadel. The door of Bar-Undak was its name, a messenger's access way to the Ungdrin in happier days. Now, in Borrik's seasoned opinion, a bloody liability. Belegar had been determined to keep the hall open, it being one of the more easily defensible ways into the deeps. So it stayed open, as did thirty-nine other ways, thought Borrik grimly. Thirty-nine. Sometimes the king was a real wazzok.

In this tunnel, the Axes of Norr were arranged, two dozen in all, their front rank of ten flush with the low entrance. Seven irondrakes – the Forgefuries – were ranged in front of them.

'If Belegar has one fault, it's optimism,' he grumbled to his banner bearer, Grunnir Stonemaster.

'Aye,' said Grunnir, his eyes fixed like Borrik's on the arched stairwells leading into the hall. 'Like you, my lord, I find anything other than healthy cynicism in a dwarf entirely unnatural. But I'll say this, what other trait would lead a dwarf to try to retake Karak Eight Peaks? There's a lot to be said for bloody-mindedness. I thought you of all people could respect that.'

'If it had been down to me, I would have blocked off this tunnel long since. As I've said to the king a dozen times...'

Grunnir rolled his eyes. He'd heard this opinion a lot recently. Borrik wasn't one to let a point lie.

'...ever since Skarsnik's grobi got pushed out of the upper levels two years gone–'

'It's been obvious the thaggoraki are planning something,' said Grunnir, finishing his thane's words for him, so often had he heard them before. 'You're not the king, Borrik. And you and me and all the rest of us followed him here, didn't we, you grumbaki?'

'So? I've every right to grumble.'

'As has every dwarf with a beard as long as yours, cousin. My point is that we all share Belegar's fault – if it is a fault – in being here at all. So it's not really his fault, is it?'

Borrik sniffed. There was no arguing with that. He was quiet a moment. 'I'd still have sealed this tunnel off, mind.'

'Oh, give it a rest, would you?' said Grunnir. Borrik raised his eyebrows. 'Thane,' added Grunnir.

'That's better,' said Borrik.

There was so much history around them. Ancestor faces at the top of the stairways told of Vala-Azrilungol's glory days. The rock falls recalled its weakening and downfall, the marks of the mason who had chiselled out the tunnel they now defended harked back to one of the many doomed attempts to reclaim it, while the gaping, tooth-gnawed pit before them told them all who Karak Eight Peaks's real masters were now.

A hideous chittering echoed up out of the dark.

'Right, that's it, here they come,' said Borrik. 'Ready, lads!'

A musty draught blew up from the tunnels.

'By Grimnir's axe, there must be a lot of them,' said Grunnir, flapping his hand in front of his face. 'I can smell them from here!'

Hafnir grinned. 'There's always a lot of them, but it doesn't matter how many, because we're here. One hundred or a million of them, they'll not get past!'

'Aye!' shouted the lads.

Stone-deadened explosions sounded down the stairs, sending a brief, fiercer breeze washing over the dwarfs that smelt of gun smoke, sundered rock and blood.

'That'll be the traps, then,' said Hafnir. Grim chuckles echoed from gromril helms.

More explosions sounded, closer now. Any other attacking army might have been discouraged, but the skaven were numberless and were never put off. Borrik hoped they'd killed a lot anyway.

The first skaven spilled into the room, eyes wild with fear. They were scrawny, badly armed if at all, mouths foaming. They saw the dwarfs in their corner. The front rank hesitated but were pushed on, those attempting to go against the tide falling under the paws of their fellows.

'Typical,' said Borrik, indicating the rusted manacles and trailing chains of the lead skaven with a nod of his head. 'Slave rats. They're going to try and wear us down.'

'Don't they always?' said Grunnir.

'Just once, it'd be nice to go straight to the main course,' moaned Gromley.

'In your own time, lads,' said Borrik, nodding at Tordrek Firespite, the Norrgrimlings' Ironwarden leader. The Forgefuries levelled their weapons. The skaven scurried forwards, forced on by the mass of ratkin boiling up out of the depths. The far side of the chamber was a mass of mangy fur, crazed eyes, twitching noses and yellow chisel teeth.

'Fire!' said Tordrek.

Thick blasts of searing energy shot out of the Forgefuries' guns, punching through skaven and sending them sprawling back into the mob. The fallen disappeared under their scurrying colleagues. Many fell into the hole in the centre, forced over the edge by the surging press; others stumbled and were crushed underfoot.

'Fire!' cried Tordrek again. Once more the irondrakes spoke, misting the air with gunsmoke.

'Fire!' he said one more time. The entire front rank of the skaven horde had been smashed, but thousands more came on behind them.

'That's close enough. Part ranks!' shouted Borrik. The dwarf ironbreaker's formation opened up like a clockwork automaton, allowing the Forgefuries to slip through to the back. They went unhurriedly into the small chamber around the door of Bar-Undak, as if there weren't a numberless pack of crazed thaggoraki snapping at their heels.

'Close ranks!' bellowed Borrik. The gromril-clad dwarfs slid back together, presenting their shields as the first skaven hit home.

The skavenslaves were slight creatures, no bigger than grobi and less heavily built. The wave of them crashed feebly upon the shield wall. Rusty blades and rotten spears broke on impenetrable gromril. More and more skaven piled in from behind, pinning the arms of the foremost, crushing the air out of their lungs. The dwarfs stolidly pushed back, unmoved by the immense pressure. The skaven trapped at the front snapped at the dwarfs, shattering their teeth on armour. The dwarfs responded by swinging their axes, chopping the foe down with every swing. They could not miss. Behind the shield wall it was surprisingly peaceful, as if the dwarfs waited out a storm battering the windows of a comfortable tavern.

'This is too easy,' grunted Kaggi Blackbeard, hewing down his fourteenth skaven.

'Aye, but how long can we keep it up?' said Hafnir. 'How long will your muscles hold? This is not a contest of arms, but one of arms!' he laughed.

'I'm just getting warmed up,' said Kaggi. 'And save your puns for when you've a better one, Hafnir.'

Desperate claws scrabbled over the shields held over the front rank by those in the back, as a slave forced itself through the narrow gap between shields and tunnel ceiling.

'Oi! Oi! Up top!' shouted Grunnir. The skavenslave dropped down behind the back rank. It brandished a knife, realised where it was, vented the foulest stink and was promptly chopped down for its troubles.

'Woohoo! Smell that! It's like Albok's been at the chuf again!' said Kardak Kardaksandrison.

'You want to be up front,' said Hafnir. 'Fear stink. It's all over me shield.'

'It'll take an age to clean off,' said Gromley miserably. 'You mark my words. Don't get any of that muck in your beard or you'll run out of water before you ever get it out.'

'Here comes another!' warned Hafnir.

A second and third skaven scrambled over the shields, more intent on getting away from the crush than fighting. They found no escape. One was hewed down in midair, the other gut-barged by Tordrek and stamped to death by the Forgefuries.

The floor became slippery with spilt blood, but the sure-footed dwarfs barely noticed. The skaven were not so lucky, skidding over in the viscera of their slaughtered littermates.

'Pressure's easing off!' shouted Hafnir. The proof of his words came as more rotting spears and rusting blades battered against the shield wall as the skaven found room to move.

'Ready,' ordered Borrik. 'Prepare to advance!'

The dwarfs in the front pulled their shields in tighter, while those at the back lowered them from over the front rank's heads.

'Forward!' said Borrik. 'Deep formation!'

Swinging their axes, the Axes of Norr stepped forwards, mowing down skaven. As they advanced, they smoothly rearranged their formation, so that they were arranged into a block four dwarfs deep and five wide, the thane at the front in the middle. Shields overlapped to the fronts and sides, making them a walking fortress of gromril and thickset dwarfish limbs.

'Charge!' yelled Borrik.

'Gand dammaz! Az baraz! Norrgrimsson-za!' The dwarfs shouted the ancient war cry of their clan, and broke into a stately jog. They were not fast, but when they hit they were unstoppable. The skaven parted in front of them, scrabbling over each other to get out of the way. The Axes of Norr ploughed on. The stink of terrified skaven became overpowering, that sweet, old-straw smell of rodent urine mixed with something stronger and far more acrid.

Almost as one, the remaining rats broke and fled. Borrik and his ironbreakers pursued them, still in formation, as far as the pit in the centre of the chamber.

'Halt!' cried Borrik. 'Forgefuries!'

Blazing bolts of energy seared past the dwarfish block, cutting down fleeing ratmen. The skaven tore at each other in their haste to escape, ripping their comrades to pieces. Many were pushed into the hole, or leapt into its fathomless depths in blind panic. Another volley went booming past. The skaven poured back down the stairwells.

And shortly came running back out again, the fleeing, terrified rats who had just exited the room driven back into it by a fresh legion of skavenslaves.

'They're coming again,' shouted Hafnir.

'They always come again, lad,' said Kaggi.

'Pull back, lads. Back to the tunnel!'

The dwarf formation halted and reversed, faces always to the enemy, pulping the corpses of their foes under weighty dwarf boots. Once in the tunnel mouth, they held their ground again.

One more time the dwarfs rushed out. One more time the skaven were cast back. The fighting went on for hours, until the last assault broke, and the skaven fled. Borrik had his panting ironbreakers rest, ordering Tordrek forward with his irondrakes.

That time, the skaven did not come again. The ironbreakers rotated their shoulders and worked aching muscles, complaining loudly that they had not enjoyed proper exercise before the skaven fled. They broke out pieces of stonebread and chuf – the hard survival cheese of their kind. A keg of ale stored by the door of Bar-Undak was broached and leather flagons passed around thirsty lips.

'Oh look at that,' spat Gromley. 'Look at that!' He ran his finger along a tiny scratch in his shield. 'Ruined! Absolutely ruined.'

'Shut up and drink your ale,' said Grunnir.

Gromley stared mournfully from the depths of his helm. 'It's all right for you to say that. Nobody's scratched your shield, have they?' He shook his head. 'No respect for good craft, you youngsters. Happy with umgak work, you are. Now, in my day I'd have got a bit of sympathy. But is one of you reaching for your polish to help an old longbeard grind out the damage? No. And we wonder why we're in this mess!'

'Show some respect, shortbeards,' said Uli the Elder, the oldest of their number. 'Let's not let our standards slip.'

Good natured jeers vied with heartfelt grumbles.

At the front, Borrik conferred quietly with Tordrek.

'When will they come again?' Tordrek asked.

'Too soon. We've been lucky. I reckon we've accounted for about four hundred of their lot, for not a single one of the lads.' He sucked deeply on his pipe. 'Good work, and greater fortune, but it can't last.' He called back over his shoulder.

'Hafnir! Gromley! Get me some blackpowder.' He pointed the stem of his pipe at the doors. 'I reckon it's time to get ready to stop up some mouseholes. The rest of you, we need some clear space to fight. I want these corpses shifted to one hundred paces out.' The others gulped their ale and moved out from the tunnel, wiping suds from their beards with the backs of bloodied hands. 'And be clever about it,' said Borrik. 'Don't stack 'em – we don't want to give the thaggoraki anything to hide behind, do we?' He pointed the stem of his pipe at a young dwarf, barely sixty years old, who was doing just that. 'Call yourself a Norrgrimling, Albok? Think, lad! What would your old dad say?'

'Sorry, thane.' Albok pushed over the pile he'd made with a boot. 'Where do we put them then?'

Borrik grinned and jabbed with his pipe stem. 'Chuck them down that there hole.'

Albok heaved a skaven corpse into the black, his thick arms tossing it as easily as a wet fur blanket. No sound came. Albok cocked his head appreciatively, and began to throw them in quickly.

'That's right, lads, don't tarry. We're not going to have long before the little furry kruti come back for another go.'

Queek paced back and forth angrily. He struck down the messenger, drawing blood from his muzzle.

'Still standing! Still standing! What squeak-nonsense Clan Skryre tinker-speaker bring to Queek? Four mountains were bombed-targeted. Only one collapse! What news of Skarsnik?'

'No sign of him, O most undefeated and puissant of overfiends,' said the messenger. 'The other tall-rock, it also nearly gone. White Mountain-place, half size it was. My masters...'

Queek glared at him so hard the skaven pulled his head all

the way back into his shoulders. The sight of it was so pathetic that Queek laughed madly.

'Stupid-meat, or brave-meat, hrn?' Queek bounded over and flipped the Clan Skryre skaven onto his back with a footpaw. He leaned in and sniffed. 'Stupid-meat.'

The skaven squealed in terror, exposing his neck and spreading his arms. Queek had lost interest and walked away. 'And you, rest of you! Why beard-things not dead?'

'It stupid beard-things fault!' said Skrikk. 'Not mine, oh no. Seventy thousand slaves we sent...'

'Thaxx say one hundred thousand!' said Thaxx.

Skrikk shrugged. 'Skrikk count, Thaxx lie. Terrible, terrible shame. And I thought him so loyal. No doubt great and fiercely intelligent Queek can see to the traitor-meat squirming beneath loyal-fur.'

'Thaxx Redclaw the most loyal–' began Thaxx.

'No squeak-tellings! Beard-things!' snapped Queek so loudly Skrikk flinched.

'They are not killing the slaves quickly enough, grand one,' said Grotoose. 'They have chosen good spots for defence and cannot be dislodged. Our slave legions can attack on narrow fronts where they are easily slain. This is not the way to beat them.'

'You tell Queek that stupid-meat beard-things, with their slow and stupid minds, are outwitting the swiftest thinker-tinkers in all of the Under-Empire?'

The assembled skaven looked at one another and pointed fingers. Queek squeaked loudly, stopping the accusations and counter-charges of incompetence before they could begin.

'Enough, enough! Enough with slaves and weak-meat! Send in the clanrats. Call in the stormvermin. Kill the beard-things. Kill them all dead-dead!'

'What of orders?' said Thaxx. 'What of Lord Gnawdwell's commands?'

'I do not care. Queek general here – where is Gnawdwell?'

'In Skavenblight?' ventured one.

'Yes-yes, whereas Queek the Mighty here. We will win. Nothing else is important. We will destroy. Queek will show the whole world that Queek is the mightiest, the best, the most deadly! We will see what Gnawdwell says about orders then.'

The messengers bowed several times and rushed away. The clanlords and potentates of the City of Pillars attempted a more dignified exit. Queek's long mouth split in a hideous grin and he waved his paws at them. 'You too, hurry-scurry! Queek not like sluggards. Loyal Ska tell sluggards what Queek thinks of slow-meat.'

'Queek does not like them,' said the giant stormvermin, 'and I don't like them either.'

'Boo!' shouted Queek, making as if to leap into their midst, and away they fled spraying fear musk, much to Queek's amusement.

The chamber was empty bar the patter of retreating paws and the smell of fear. Queek snickered to himself.

'You see, Ska? This is why Queek is so great.'

There came no reply. Ska was thankfully brief in his praise of Queek. All the bowing and scraping and insincere flattery that characterised skaven social interaction the warlord found tiresome, but Ska usually said *something*.

Queek's nose twitched. Something was wrong. A smell of old fires, rubbish and hot warpstone made him sneeze. The light leached from his surroundings, leaving everything grey. Ska was unmoving, frozen in position. He called for his guards, but they did not come.

Movement in the unmoving world caught his eye. He did not turn to it, not immediately. Something big was in the corner.

He spun around, leaping into the air and twisting his entire body. Dwarf Gouger leapt into his hand, and moved in a blurred arc impelled by all his weight and speed. His serrated sword came up next, aimed directly at the vitals of his giant ambusher.

Queek crashed into the stone. The creature was not there.

'Oh ho! You are as good as they say. But mighty Queek could be the mightiest of all mortal skaven, and he still would not catch me.'

Shadows boiled all around him, darting like swarms of flies over the marshes. Queek hissed and made feints and jabs, but the darkness moved away from him, slipping around his weapons like water.

'Who-you?' he cried. His fur bristled with a fear he would not allow himself to feel. For the first time in years, his glands clenched. 'What you want with Queek?'

The darkness ran together and parted for an instant, affording the warlord a glimpse of a masked, rodent face, ten feet in the air, topped with three sets of horns, two straight, one curved. The ends of them were twisted into the runic claw-mark of Clan Eshin.

'I am Lurklox, Shadow Lord of Decay, one of the twelve above the twelve. And what I want with you, strutting warlord, is your victory.'

# EIGHT

## The Hall of Pillared Iron

In the Hall of Pillared Iron, King Belegar took counsel. Between the thick iron columns that gave the place its name, venerable dwarfs of many clans crowded around low tables layered with maps. The hall had been built with the same attention to detail and pride with which the ancestors had built everything. Each of the room's sixty-four column capitals had been wrought in red iron to resemble four straining longbeards holding up the roof. The remainder of the columns were inscribed with runes inlaid with precious minerals, most picked out by rapacious greenskins, but in the more inaccessible places electrum, silver, polished coal and agate still glittered, a reminder of the hall's former glory.

Despite the care and craft of its making, the Hall of Pillared Iron was a foundation, a utilitarian room intended to support the finer citadel halls above. The metal in its walls and pillars allowed the citadel to reach its great and graceful height without compromising its efficacy as a fortress.

That had been then. The upper chambers were mostly toppled by centuries of war and earthquakes, among them the magnificent Upper Throne Room, whose wide windows and fine art made it the mirror to the Great Throne Pinnacle in the Hall of a Thousand Pillars in the first deep. Unique in all the dwarf realms, at the height of the Karaz Ankor the twinned thrones had represented Karak Eight Peaks's mastery of the worlds under sky and under stone. Of these two hearts, one was rubble and the other had been occupied by a succession of foul creatures.

So low had the dwarfs of Karak Eight Peaks sunk that the Hall of Pillared Iron was their greatest hall. Magnificent though it was, as grand as Belegar's throne looked when viewed down its aisles, the Hall of Pillared Iron was a support. Might as well call a single stone block all the temple. Belegar had refused to have it completely restored, lest the dwarfs of Karak Eight Peaks forget why they were there, and become content with scraps.

Drakki was speaking, addressing his king and his advisors. Brunkaz Whitehair, the oldest dwarf in the hold, was beside him. His beard was so long it looped three times in a complicated plait about his thick gold belt.

'At Bar-Undak the Norrgrimlings are taking casualties. The endless stair is being overrun, half the Zhorrak Blue Caps are dead. Valaya's quay has fallen, our warriors there falling back to the base of the citadel.'

'The Undak?'

'Still running clear,' said Drakki. 'But how long will that continue? The thaggoraki poisoned the river once – now we've lost the quays at the headwater, they could easily do it again.'

'Buzkar,' swore Belegar. He looked from map to map, searching for a sign of hope, some weakness in the enemy he could exploit, some dawi strength he could call upon.

He spread his hands over a portion of the map, caging it

protectively in his fingers. 'Kvinn-wyr still holds strong. So long as we hold the mountain, our people will have somewhere safe to stand. We've got the gyrocopter eyries at Tor Rudrum. As long as we have them, we can stay in touch with the other holds. Above all, the citadel is safe. Perhaps it is time to abandon the first line of defence and make our next stand at the Hall of Clan Skalfdon,' said Belegar. He pointed to a great hall in the first deep below the citadel, three quarters of a mile from the collapsed east halls, where many lines of communication intersected. 'Beat them back there and they'll think twice about trying to crack the hold.'

'There's not time to fortify it,' said Brunkaz. 'We need to dig in there, or it'll be a slaughter.'

Belegar laughed. 'The only slaughter I've seen in recent weeks is that of the ratkin! We've slain so many I could carpet the east road all the way to the Uzkul Kadrin in vermin fur.'

'Aye, true enough,' conceded Brunkaz, although his expression made clear his distaste at covering good dawi stone with ratskin. 'But these aren't dregs we're facing – that part's done with. Belegar, you know how they work. The Headtaker is sending in his clan warriors and stormvermin. Our lads are worn down, and we've lost a good number. They'll not last until the defences are ready.'

'They'll have to,' said Belegar firmly.

'There's no time, my king,' said Brunkaz.

'There'll have to be time, or we'll not get the other lines finished!' snapped Belegar.

Drakki cleared his throat, politely interrupting before grudges began to sprout like grobi in a damp cave. 'And what of the way into Kvinn-wyr?'

'That at least is in hand,' said Belegar. 'Dokki,' he called over to an engineer hard at work over his own maps.

'My king?'

'How're the preparations at the Arch of Kings going?'

'Give me three weeks and the dawi I've got, or sixty more engineers and two days and I'll have the fort back in dawr order. Before that...' He sucked in his breath and clucked his tongue. 'You'll be lucky if it's before the end of the month.'

'This is the Eternal Realm! Surely we have time,' said Belegar. 'What about Kolbron Feklisson's miners?'

'Ah! Here we have less dire tidings,' said Drakki, brightening a little.

'We've retaken the western foundries?' said Belegar hopefully.

'Er, no. The miners have lost the foundries, but are still holding the eastern entrance.'

'That's good news,' said Belegar hesitantly, fully expecting the worst. He was rewarded with it.

'For now, my lord. They're going to be encircled here and here – it's only a matter of time,' said Drakki, tracing a series of halls on the map. 'We've rumour of thaggoraki tunnelling teams at work behind them.'

'From who?' said Brunkaz. 'Half our number are sparsely bearded hill dwarfs or umgdawi.'

'Sadly not from them, my lord,' said Drakki. 'From Kolbron himself. No one knows stone better. If he says there's something going on in the rock, you can bet your last coin there is.'

Belegar shook his head from side to side, his beard whispering against the parchment. 'Tell them to withdraw.'

'They won't retreat, Belegar,' said Drakki, a note of pleading in his voice.

'Tell them it's a direct command from me. I'll write it on a bit of paper if it makes them happy. Get them back up here. I want them reporting to Durggan Stoutbelly and helping him fortify the Hall of Clan Skalfdon before sunrise or I'll be writing grudges against the lot of them, is that clear? With their stonecraft under Stoutbelly's direction, we've a fighting chance of establishing the next perimeter.'

'It'll be a hard task,' said Brunkaz. 'Not like the old days.'

'Yes, yes, yes!' said Belegar tersely, only just reining in his temper and maintaining the appropriate level of respect due to the living ancestor. 'It never is like the old days, and it never will be again if we don't give good account of ourselves here. We're in a tough spot, aye, but we'll all be dead if we grumble about it.'

Brunkaz's wrinkled face paled under his beard at Belegar's lack of deference. Belegar regretted his tone. 'Have the messengers set out?' he said, more softly.

'This morning, my lord,' said Drakki. 'Six for each of Zhufbar, Karak Kadrin, Karaz-a-Karak and Karak Azul. No gyrocopters, as you commanded.'

'We need them here.' Belegar ground his broad teeth. Going cap in hand to the High King grated on his honour. What choice did he have? 'The other kings will understand we cannot send their warriors back. They've not failed us yet. We'll just have to dig in. Get Clan Zhudak to the gates of Bar-Kragaz, hold them back at the west tunnel. They'll be coming through from the foundries that way as soon as they discover the miners have gone.'

'Aye, my lord.' Drakki hesitated, words that would not be spoken keen on his lips.

Brunkaz curled his lip at Drakki and made a rumble of disapproval that started deep in his gut and travelled upwards, quivering his moustaches as it came out of his mouth. 'Drakki's too good a dwarf to say it, but I will. We've got no chance. Half of us are dead already. The skaven are numberless. They've never attempted anything like this before. We'd be better off fighting our way out and leaving them to the greenskins.'

'It's a bigger attack, I'll grant you. Nothing we can't handle,' said Belegar, his voice stiffening.

'They've blown up Karag Nar! The sunset mountain, gone! Karag Rhyn's a shadow of itself – half the old farmlands to the south are buried in its rubble. Can't you see? Has pride blinded you so much? The mountains, Belegar, the mountains themselves are in pieces! If they can't endure, what chance do we have?' Belegar stared at his advisor, but Brunkaz had gone too far to stop. 'There's only one reason the Headtaker's done that, and that's to keep the greenskins off his back while he comes to finish us off. Or have you considered, it may not be long before they do the same to us? The thaggoraki have changed. We are not fighting against rats with sticks any more. Some of their machines make the creations of the Dawi-Zharr seem like toys! Why do you think they've left the surface camps alone? Why has Lord Duregar not had so much as a whiff of rat round the East Gate these last months while we're knee deep in them? The answer's simple – they're coming to wipe us out! They don't care. They're massing for a final blow right at our heart, right into Kvinn-wyr.'

Belegar's face grew purple, and his words when they came were quiet, the hiss of rain before the first thunder crack of a storm. 'You will not mention the eastern kindreds in these halls again.'

'All your life you've asked me for my counsel, from beardling to the king I love and serve gladly. I'll give you the truth and aye, unvarnished,' said Brunkaz. 'This is my sooth, king of Karak Eight Peaks. Leave now, before we're all dead. We tried our best. Sometimes we have to retreat a little further than we wish. Let the grobi and thaggoraki fight over the scraps. When the world's troubles die down again, we can come back and take our lands from whoever wins. They'll be weaker for their victory. More importantly, we'll still be alive.'

'Is that all, Brunkaz?'

'Think of your *son,* Belegar.'

'*Is that all, Brunkaz?*' Belegar's shout cut through the quiet muttering of dwarfs at council, so loud the candles and torches lighting the hall wavered before its fury. Only the glimlight of the glowstones was unperturbed.

Brunkaz could not meet his king's eyes. He worked his cheeks, causing his beard and moustache to move around like a live thing. 'Aye. That should just about cover it.'

'Thank you. I suppose you'll be wanting to leave, then? If you do, I'll release you from your oaths, but the others'll not thank you for it.'

Brunkaz went bright red. 'I'll not abandon my oaths! Course I'm staying. Why, if you were a few decades younger I'd put you over my knee and–'

'Very well,' interrupted Belegar. 'If you're staying, I'd appreciate you keeping your words tucked up behind your beard unless they're something to do with defending the hold. Do you have anything useful to add in that regard?'

Brunkaz buried his chin in his chest, considering his next words. 'There are ogres in the pass, my lord,' he said slowly.

'There are always ogres in the pass,' said Drakki dismissively.

'More than usual, Drakki Throngton. Golgfag Maneater leads a great host of them,' said Brunkaz, still not looking at his king.

'The Maneater is in the Uzkul Kadrin?' said Belegar, brightening. He reached his hand, richly gloved, up to his mouth, as if he would hide the smile spreading under his beard.

'You can't be thinking on hiring him, my king? Ungrim nearly killed him. He's a thug, a pirate, a... a... mercenary,' said Drakki, taking his turn to be outraged.

'That's exactly what he is,' said Belegar. 'A mighty one.'

'I beg you, my king, recall Duregar from the East Gate,' said Drakki.

'What, and let Skarsnik have it? And how do we get out then, if it should come to that?' The king shot Brunkaz a warning look not to take up his cause again. 'The East Gate garrison stays where it is, for now. Golgfag is what we need. He's fought many times for the dawi.'

'And just as often against us. And he doesn't come cheap,' said Brunkaz.

'You'd beggar the kingdom for an ogre's sword?' Drakki shook his head so vigorously that he dislodged his spectacles. He pushed them back into place with an ink-stained finger, and squinted expectantly at his king.

'Better a beggared kingdom than a fallen one. I'll promise him the pick of the treasury.'

'There's precious little in the treasury,' grumbled Drakki.

'He doesn't know that, does he?' said Belegar. 'Get a messenger out to him.'

'There's a blizzard rising.'

'Then no one will be able to see him, will they?' said Belegar. 'Do it now, Grungni scowl at you!'

Now both longbeards were taken aback by Belegar's attitude. Belegar supposed he should feel guilty, snapping at these honoured elders like they were callow beardlings, but he didn't. They knew his temper well enough.

The longbeards walked away from the table, chins wagging like fishwives. Belegar ignored the pointed looks they gave him. To keep others from approaching him, he affected an air of bristling bad temper. He didn't have to try very hard. Those dwarfs waiting to petition him – priests, merchants, umgdawi and hill dwarfs – were discouraged, if not by his manner then by his hammerers, who ushered them out of the hall. He heard their complaints well enough; the hall wasn't that big. Fair enough, some of them had been waiting a day or so, but he wasn't in the mood to dispense the king's justice. He feigned deafness and returned to his maps, staring hard at them until his eyes swam. As if that would be enough to turn the red and green parts of the map blue again.

If only it were so simple.

One dwarf, somehow, got through.

'Perhaps now your majesty might consider our request?'

The smell of rancid pig fat and lime was unmistakeable. Belegar looked up from his maps into the magnificently crested face of Unfer, nominally the leader of the Cult of Grimnir in the hold. When the Slayers wanted something, it was Unfer who asked. Belegar assumed he must be their leader, but in truth he did not know. Their ways were closed and mysterious to all who had not taken the oath.

The king tried to look away, but was arrested by the Slayer's eyes. Beautiful eyes, set into a face scarred by cuts and inner pain. They were out of place, clear blue as ice, and as devoid of emotion.

Belegar tugged at his beard and cleared his throat. He waved his hand over his maps.

'I'm loath to let such fine warriors go out. I need every axe we have here.'

Unfer glanced at the maps like they were a carpet he had no interest in buying, and Belegar an overeager merchant. 'That is not the nature of our oath, my lord. We have no desire to retreat until there is nowhere left to retreat to, to find our doom backed into some corner, or worse, to be taken alive. There is no hope in this defence. Let us go, and kill as many of them as we can for you. It is a service we gladly offer you.'

Unfer's glacial gaze bored into Belegar's eyes. The insult to the king's ability as a general was implicit.

'There is always hope,' said Belegar. 'Help might come yet.' He heard the desperation in his own voice; he was afraid that the Slayer was right.

'There is no hope left in all the Karaz Ankor. No one is coming. The Eternal Realm is finished. Best we all shave our heads and take the oath so that we might die with a song on our lips and our shame washed away in blood.'

'Shame?' said Belegar. Unfer shrugged shoulders craggy with muscle. Blue tattoos writhed over them. In hands like boulders, he carried paired rune axes – royal weapons. Belegar often wondered who he'd been. Unfer would never tell.

'The shame of all our kind,' said Unfer. 'That we have failed to restore the glory of our ancestors. Better to fight. Better to wish for a good death than a ragged hope.'

Belegar was tempted. To sally out with his remaining few folk, and kill the thaggoraki until they themselves were killed. Let them taste dawi steel and remember them forever!

He blinked visions of a glorious end away. He could not. He was a king. He had responsibilities. He had a son, the first heir born to the king of Karak Eight Peaks since its fall two thousand years ago. He would not retreat. He would not abandon the legacy of his ancestors, so much dearer now it was the heritage of another.

'No,' he said. 'We wait here. We will defend, and retreat, and defend. And we shall prevail.'

Disappointment flickered over Unfer's face. 'As you wish. It is your kingdom.' The Slayer put one axe over each shoulder and turned away.

'I have not finished,' said Belegar sternly. 'You have my permission to go,' he added with understanding. 'I cannot keep you from your oaths. What manner of king would I be if I did? I wish you would reconsider, but if you must, you have my leave. Fight well, and find the doom you deserve, Unfer.'

Unfer nodded once. 'It is all any of us can hope for any more. Grimnir go with you, King Belegar. If we meet again, may it be in happier times for all dawi.'

'You'll not go yet,' said Belegar. Unfer cast a weary look over his shoulder. The Slayer moved in the way those with deep depression do: slowly, as if through a treacle of despair. 'I may be a poor king, but I'm still a king. You'll get a proper send off. I'll open my cellars to you, we'll say the right words, drink to your deaths.' He smiled awkwardly. 'The old way.'

Unfer gave an appreciative bow. 'Let no dawi say that King Belegar is ungenerous. It is good to hold to the old ways while we still can.'

'Aye,' said Belegar. 'Aye, it is.' He meant it as a good thing, but his troubled face said otherwise. All they had was the past, he thought, and even that was running away from them.

He didn't notice Unfer leave. A commotion at the gates drew his tired eyes. One of the Iron Brotherhood, Skallguz the Short, was pushing his way through. He jogged up to his lord, red faced and out of breath.

'My king!' he said, and dropped to his knees.

'What is it?' said Belegar.

'It is the queen, my lord. The prince...' The dwarf stammered to a halt.

'Spit it out!' Belegar's face went pale with terrible presentiment.

'My lord,' the dwarf said. 'I don't know how to say it... They've both gone!'

# NINE

*Kemma's Way*

Wind sang sadly through the teeth of the broken window, set in the dairy, high up in the side of Kvinn-wyr. A sheer drop of four thousand feet fell away down the mountain outside, ending in broad fans of scree covered by snow. Gromvarl pulled his head back in through mullions worn edgeless by the wind and rain, and leaned against a cracked milk trough. He shook the snow from his shaggy mane of hair and filled his pipe.

He winced at the taste of the tobacco. Once the dwarfs had produced the world's finest smoking weed in the Great Vale, along with much else. The soil of the bowl cupped between the eight mountains was so rich they called it Brungal – brown gold. In Belegar's pocket kingdom there had been plans, and much talk in ale cups, of how the dwarfs were going to clear the farmlands and raise great crops to end Vala-Azrilungol's reliance on the other holds. Of course, like so much Belegar said, it remained an unattainable dream.

A stealthy tread sounded in the old goat way outside.

Gromvarl brought his crossbow up one-handed, wincing as he rested the stock in the crook of his broken arm.

He narrowed his eyes, finger on the trigger lever, then relaxed. No skaven or grobi whistled like that.

A deeply tanned dwarf with an expression so cheerful it belonged on the face of no real dawi came in through the door. He doffed his wide-brimmed hat, showing the scarf tied tightly over his ears and under his chin. His name was Douric Grimlander, a dwarf reckoner, a calculator of debts and grudges. Little better than a mercenary, to Gromvarl's eyes.

'Gromvarl! What happened to you?' Douric said, his eyes lighting on Gromvarl's splinted arm.

'An urk happened to it. And then I happened to the urk.'

Douric peered about the small dairy. 'You alone then?'

'What does it look like?' said Gromvarl through teeth gripping his pipe. He had always found Douric insufferable, even at the best of times.

'I told you he'd say no,' said Douric breezily. 'I suppose it's all off then. Belegar's a fool to turn your offer down, but that's that.'

'Listen to me, you scraggle-bearded wazzok,' said Gromvarl. 'Why do you think he said no? This is his hold. Thorgrim is his son and heir.' Gromvarl fixed the shorter dwarf with a beady eye and poked him in the chest with his pipe stem. 'I wonder if you're a real dwarf at all. You've no honour.'

Douric took the insult as a compliment, or so his broad smile suggested. 'I like money. You like money. Who doesn't like money? I have honour, but like my money, I'm just a little more careful than you where I spend it, that's all.'

Gromvarl grunted, wiped the mouthpiece of his pipe on his bearskin, which was no cleaner than Douric's jerkin, and replaced it in his mouth with the clack of ivory on teeth. 'Oaths are worth more than gold, reckoner.'

'I keep mine, unlike your king,' said the reckoner mildly. 'If I combine honour with payment, does it make me all that bad? Besides,' he said, hitching his hands into his wide belt. 'You're the one who suggested to the king we should steal the queen out of the city against all tradition. So where's *your* honour?'

Gromvarl adjusted the sling holding his broken arm, sliding thick fingers between the fabric and his neck. 'My oath has always been to protect the queen, ever since she was a child. I'm doing that now.'

'Doing that...?' Douric's eyes widened. 'Oh ho ho! Gromvarl! I didn't think you had it in you. She is here isn't she?'

'Not yet,' said Gromvarl grudgingly. 'Soon.'

'Handing her over to me! A mere mercenary. Tut tut, Gromvarl. You'll be coming with us now, I'll warrant. It'll be a mite uncomfortable down there once Belegar finds you've kidnapped his son.' Douric jerked his thumb over his shoulder, back down the passageway in the exact direction of the citadel. Douric always had had a fine sense of direction, even for a dwarf.

Gromvarl grumbled, levered himself up from the tub and took a heavy step forwards, until he was nose to nose with Douric. 'I've other oaths, oaths of service to the king. I'll not break either. I need a dwarf of your... moral flexibility.' He looked the reckoner up and down, his grubby clothes, his odd umgak gear garnered from who knew where. He was right, this was no true dwarf.

'So you're in a bind, then? Who's the more fortunate here – you, all thick with responsibility, or me, who tends to the more cautious side–'

'Self-serving more like,' interjected Gromvarl.

'–of things?' continued Douric, undeterred. 'A philosophy that enables me to help you out now. Who else would, Gromvarl? Who's the better?' He waggled his eyebrows in almost lewd fashion.

'You little krutwanaz...'

'Will you two stop arguing? The pair of you, thicker-headed than trolls!' A sharp female voice speared out of the corridor. Queen Kemma of Karak Eight Peaks emerged into the dairy. She was followed by a very young dwarf, no older than ten or twelve, whose chin was covered in the straggly hairs of first bearding, and a hammerer, who nervously glanced behind them. Both the queen and youngster wore travelling cloaks and the rough clothes favoured by the kruti and foresters who worked overground. When the queen pushed past Gromvarl, her fastenings parted slightly, revealing rich gromril mail beneath. Both of them too had a royal bearing. Gromvarl sighed. No matter how they dressed up, there was no hiding who they were. He just hoped they had not been seen sneaking away.

'I am sorry, vala,' said Gromvarl, who at least had the decency to look abashed. He cast his eyes downwards. Douric, on the other hand, arched his back, and clasped his hands behind his back, an exceptionally self-satisfied look on his face.

The hammerer rubbed at his bulbous nose. 'Here they are. I better get back.'

'Another oath-bender!' said Douric. 'They're popping up like mushrooms.'

'Guard the queen as long as she is in Karak Eight Peaks, that was my oath. Well now she's not,' said the hammerer. 'Nearly.'

'You're a good dawi, Bronk Coppermaster,' said Gromvarl. He held up a small purse, distastefully pinched between finger and thumb, as if it were soiled. 'For your trouble.'

Bronk looked at it in horror. 'You've been hanging around with these here reckoners too long. Just see her safe, that's all I want. If this ends well, then I'll take my chances with Belegar, and we'll still have our prince. If it doesn't end well... Well,' he shrugged, his gromril rattling musically, 'then it's not going to matter very much what Belegar thinks.'

Gromvarl nodded. 'I look forward to fighting alongside you, Bronk.'

Bronk nodded and hurried off back up the passageway.

Meanwhile, Douric was attempting his charm upon the queen. 'Vala Kemma! It has been too long. With every passing year your beauty grows greater.' He bowed his head and reached for her hand.

'Don't even think about it, reckoner,' said Kemma, snatching her fingers back from his puckered lips. 'We have to be away now.'

'Mother, are we sure this is the right thing to do?' said Thorgrim. 'I am the prince of Karak Eight Peaks, my place should be here. Father will be furious.'

Kemma placed her hands on his shoulders, and looked up into his face. Not yet full grown, he was already turning into a fine figure of a dwarf. He was already three feet tall; chances were he was going to be bigger than his father, and certainly as strong. Bryndalmoraz Karakal they called him – the bright hope of the mountains.

'I am taking you to be safe, my son. Is it not your first responsibility to preserve the royal bloodline?'

Prince Thorgrim's young face twisted with inner conflict. 'But I am the prince, mother. I will not be an oathbreaker.'

'You have taken no oaths,' soothed his mother, stroking the lines on his face. 'If you did not believe us to be doing the right thing, then you would have stayed behind. We have already come so far.'

The prince looked doubtful and bit his lip, causing the fuzz of growing beard to puff up. He nodded in what was intended to be a decisive manner, but Gromvarl saw he was still unsure. He was brave for a boy of his age.

'Very well,' said Thorgrim.

'King Belegar for a father and that one there for his mother, I don't envy that youngster,' said Douric quietly.

'You're not wrong there,' Gromvarl replied as the queen and prince talked. 'But he's almost past all that. He'll be his own master soon, mark my words. He's got a strong head, that boy, but with her temperament, thank Valaya. The last thing Karak Eight Peaks needs is another Belegar.'

'I'm not sure the queen's temperament is necessarily an improvement,' said Douric.

Gromvarl snorted.

Strange noises sounded from deep in the mountain.

'We best be away, vala. These tunnels were much fractured in the time of Great Cataclysm. They are unsafe. No one knows where they go,' said Douric.

Kemma's face crinkled with bitterness. 'There is nowhere safe in Karak Eight Peaks – there never has been. I should have left as soon as Thorgrim was born.' She reached into her robes. Douric held up his hand.

'Payment upon safe delivery, or my word is not my bond,' he said. 'Best say your farewells.' Douric tactfully withdrew, drawing the prince after him to leave Kemma alone with her guardian.

Gromvarl gave his queen a bow. He huffed on his pipe like a steam engine building power, filling the dairy with smoke.

'Well, I suppose this is goodbye.'

'Brave Gromvarl. Are you sure you will not come with us?'

'Not with this, vala,' said Gromvarl, lifting his broken arm. 'And even without, I'd have to stay. You know why.'

Kemma smiled her understanding. 'I lack the words to thank you for all that you've done for me.' She leaned through the clouds around him and laid a gentle kiss on his old cheek.

'It's not necessary! Get on with you now, young lady,' said Gromvarl, his voice inexplicably warbly. He coughed. 'Damned tobacco making my eyes water! I'd give my other arm for a pouch of Everpeak Goldleaf.'

\* \* \*

Douric led on up the passage, a krut ungdrin, where in better days herds of goats had been driven from their pastures to be milked and overwintered. They went through ways long forgotten, winding up the secret stair to a door high up on the shoulders of Kvinn-wyr.

'Be careful, my lady, my prince,' said Douric. 'It's cold and mighty windy out.'

This proved to be something of an understatement. The three of them were buffeted by a howling gale that drove needles of snow into their faces. The path they found themselves on went down steadily towards alpine pastures arrayed on the mountain's shoulders. Rusted spikes of ancient iron in the rock showed where a safety line had once been anchored, but it was a distant memory. The three of them clung on to the stone for dear life until they turned a corner onto the southern flank of the mountain, where the wind dropped to strong gusts that plucked at their clothes, petulant at its lost power.

'That's the worst bit, for now,' said Douric.

'You know this way well?' said Kemma.

'I know all ways well, my lady. A reckoner's not a reckoner if he can't get in or out of a place where reckoning needs doing. Those with debts are generally shy, retiring sorts. They can be a little tricky to dig out,' he said with a grin.

They went through high fields well above the tree line. Subject to the caprices of the wind, much of the snow had been blown from them, gathering in huge drifts against broken dry-stone walls and the cairns of piled rocks cleared from the fields by the ancestors. Tumbledown shacks marked the refuges of goatherds, and in one place the walls of a ruined village made straight, soft lines in the snow. All was abandoned, as everything was in the Eight Peaks. Here, however, there had recently been dwarfs tending flocks. The signs of recent occupation were visible in places, especially near other krut ungdrin. Once again, the pastures were empty.

Kemma found it hard to believe, but not so long ago there was an optimism to Karak Eight Peaks, a sense that things were turning for the better. Another cruel joke, and one she had never fallen for herself. This had always been a fool's errand, and in Belegar the errand had found its fool. Nevertheless, she was a dwarf, and the ruination upset her as much as any other. She had never told anyone, but this was why she hated Vala-Azrilungol so much. Every inch of it was a shameful reminder of what her people had lost.

Douric hadn't looked back at them the whole time they'd been outside; if he did she hoped he'd think her tears were brought forth by the biting wind and not from sorrow.

At one corner, they passed a collection of dwarf beard scalps, frozen stiff in the wind and rattling against their posts. 'Thorgrim! Look away!' she said. Her son did not heed her, and gawped at them. Anguish pulsed in her breast that he had to see such things, but it hardened her resolve. This was why they had to leave.

As they threaded their way through a series of terraced fields, the air grew thicker and it became easier to breathe. The tall white finger of Kvinn-wyr, cloaked in winter snow from peak to skirts, raised itself behind them. They were hidden from the feeble sun, trudging through a world of shadow and ice.

'Soon we must go back inside,' said Douric. 'Through another way. We can rest a while at its head before we press on.' He said this for the benefit of Thorgrim, who had a long way yet to go before he developed the full width of his thighs. He was trying his hardest to hide his discomfort like a good dawi, but his pale face and trembling lips told another story.

Kemma went to her son, and fussed over him as mothers do. He was proud enough to shoo her away, and Douric smiled at that. Kemma frowned, which he thought a little extreme, but then she held up her hand. 'Shhh!' she said. 'What's that?'

Douric cocked his head. His eyes widened in concern. 'Curse my ears, I'm getting old!'

Kemma drew her hammer and put herself in front of her son.

'Off the path! To that hut down there, and stay on the rocks. Leave no tracks!' Douric pointed to a sorry ruin thirty yards away. Too late. A party of Belegar's hammerers came around the corner from below, lining up three abreast to block their way down the rocky path.

'Brok Gandsson,' said Kemma. 'Belegar has you chasing mothers who love their sons, has he? Your beard thickens with honour day by day.' She spoke haughtily. There was no point in pretence. There was only one reason he could be here.

'Halt! Halt in the name of the king!' said Brok Gandsson, leader of the Iron Brotherhood. He stood athwart the path, puffing clouds of cold breath. Dressed in full armour, he wore no extra garb in concession to the temperature, and his nose was red and dripping as a result. His expression made it clear that he meant business.

'I'll do no such thing. You'll let me by, Brok Gandsson. The future of the Angrund clan and all of the Eight Peaks is here by my side. Take him back, and you will doom him. Let me take him away from here.'

Brok stood his ground, his face set. Tension showed in the line of his jaw, bunching muscles under beard. He was not enjoying this role. That was something, thought Kemma.

'The mountains are full of grobi and urk, and the tunnels heave with vermin. If I let him off this mountain, it is you who will be killing him, not I. I will not let your mistake weigh on my conscience.'

'It'll be your mistake, not mine. I've made my mind up.'

'She's coming with us,' said Brok to his warriors in an unnecessary display of authority. 'If her highness complains, clap her in irons.'

'I am your queen!' said Kemma, outraged.

'No dwarf is to leave Vala-Azrilungol without the say of King Belegar. Queen or not, Vala Kemma, you'll not be among those who disobey him.'

Douric stepped forwards, hands held in front of him as if they were full of reason, and they would all go away content if only they would look into his palms to see. He wore his habitual grin openly, like they were all sharing a joke that needed a punch line. 'Wait a minute here, Brok. Can we not see our way through to some other solution? The lady only wants what's best for her son, and the Angrund clan.'

But Brok was in no mood for amity. He looked upon the reckoner with undisguised hatred. 'What do you know of the honour of the Iron Brotherhood? Long have you been a thorn in our king's side! Always you reckoners taking a peck of this here, a pick of that there, when you have no right.'

Douric's good humour fell away from his face in an avalanche, showing the cold hard stone beneath. 'I have every right. I am a lawmaster of the High King, my lad – a petty one, I grant you, but I bear his seal and his authority.'

'Then go back to Thorgrim in Everpeak, and steal your ale from his cup for a change!'

Douric took another step forwards. 'You should let them go.'

Brok raised his hammer. 'Do not come another step closer, wanaz. I'm warning you.'

'Let's just talk this out...'

Brok swung his hammer to smack into the side of Douric's head with a final crack. The reckoner spun on his feet and went down hard, falling limp to the ground, where broad red flowers bloomed in the snow. His hat blew away on the wind.

Brok stepped from foot to foot, horrified at what he had done. His dawi murmured. Brok's face hardened. 'A pox on all reckoners and their dishonourable dealings! Gazul judge you harshly, oath worrier, grudge doubter!' He spat on the rock. 'You dawi! Stop your grumbling. Help the queen and the prince here back into the mountain. It's cold up here and there are grobi about.'

Two hammerers came forward, reaching for Kemma.

'Unhand me! I command you to let me by!'

Their hands dropped.

Some of the fury went out of Brok, and he sagged, unmanned by what he had done. 'Belegar gives me my orders, vala,' said Brok. 'I had no choice. I am oath-given.'

'Dawi killing dawi. Oaths or not, that's a fine sight, not that my husband would care. He's wanted Douric gone a long time. Too stupid to see a good dwarf in front of his nose, like a wattock can't tell fool's gold from gold.'

'For what it's worth, I am sorry.'

'Not sorry enough to take the Slayer's oath.'

Brok stared at her with a peculiar mix of emotions, all strong.

'The reckoner's body?' asked one of his followers. 'We can't just leave it here.'

Brok stared at the dead dwarf. The wind teased his hair and beard, his hands were still open in a display of peace. He looked asleep, but for his caved-in skull. Self-hatred got the better of Brok, and he turned it outwards. 'Yes we can, and we will. He was a traitor. Umgdawi to the core and gold-hungrier than a dragon. Leave him for the grobi and the stormcrows.'

'Thane...'

'I said leave him!' bellowed Brok.

'Shame on you, Brok Gandsson, shame on you,' hissed Kemma.

'We should all be ashamed, vala. We've taken a few wrong tunnels on the way, and now it's too late for all of us,' he said, grabbing her by the elbow and pulling her forwards. Two other hammerers gently helped Prince Thorgrim away with encouraging words and swigs of ale. 'Each and every one.'

# TEN

*An Oath Fulfilled*

Borrik hewed down the last of the stormvermin still facing him, his runic axe pulsing with power. The pure blue of its magic, clear as brynduraz in the sun, radiated more than light. The axe's blessings brought relief to his burning muscles, drove the tiredness from leaden limbs. This was good, for Borrik could not remember the last time he had slept.

Once the Norrgrimlings had been renowned for sleeping upright while standing guard, taking turns in the centre where they might be held up by their brothers. Borrik yearned for those days as much as he yearned for sleep. Neither would come again. There were not enough Axes of Norr left to attempt their famed feat, and he feared they would never rebuild their numbers enough to do so again. It was a point of pride to his ironbreakers that they never had nor ever would abandon a post given them to guard. Pride had ever been the undoing of dwarfs. Soon it would be the end of them.

'They're falling back,' he said. His strong, proud voice reduced to a hoarse wheeze. 'Forgefuries, forward!'

With a stoicism that would shame a mountain, the remaining four Forgefuries set off with the same skill and speed they had possessed two months ago. Only their faces betrayed their fatigue, pale skin and brown smears under eyes grown small and gritty.

'Fire!' said Tordrek. His dawi reloaded and fired with breathtaking skill, pumping round after round of blazing energy into the back of the skaven, incinerating them as they fled.

The squeaking panic of the ratmen receded down the tunnels. Borrik stared at the near-invisible drill holes packed with powder around each stairwell mouth. If Belegar would only let him blow them... But the king would not. His name was a byword for stubbornness, even among the dwarfs. He cursed the king under his breath.

'Right, lads,' said Borrik. 'You know the drill.'

'Aye aye,' said Albok tiredly. 'Rats in the hole. Come on!'

The remaining Axes of Norr lumbered forward, clenching and unclenching fists that were moulded into claws suited only to holding axes. They betrayed no sign of weariness as they heaved up dead skaven from the floor, save perhaps a certain slowness as they tossed the corpses into the hole at the centre of the chamber. Not scrawny rat slaves these, but skaven elites, black-furred stormvermin equipped with hefty halberds and close-fitting armour. Some of this was dwarf-made. For the first days of the battle against the better skaven troops, the dwarfs had diligently stripped the work of their ancestors from the ratmen and stockpiled it in the chamber fronting the door of Bar-Undak. But there was so much of it, so very much, that they had given up. Now the defiled armour went into the hole like everything else, swallowed up along with their grief at seeing the craft of their ancestors so abused.

What cheer the Norrgrimlings had was gone. Weeks of hard

fighting had worn them down, stone-hard though they were, as centuries of rain will wear down a mountain. Their eyes were red with lack of sleep, their beards stiff with blood they had neither the time nor the strength to comb out. Seven of them had gone to the halls of their ancestors, among them Hafnir and Kaggi Blackbeard. Their voices were as missed as their axes. Uli the Elder had lost an eye to a lucky spear-thrust, but refused to retire. Gromley had several missing links from his hauberk to add to the scratch on his shield, and complained bitterly about it. No one teased him for his grumbling any longer.

'Is there any more ale?' asked Borrik. 'My throat's dryer than an engine-stoker's dongliz.'

'There's another delivery due soon, but they're getting tardy,' said Grunnir Stonemaster. There was no way of telling the time in the dark underground, but the dwarfs had an unerring knack for it. 'It's past midday or I'm a grobi's dung collector.'

Borrik managed a grin that hurt his face. 'That you certainly are not. Not only are they late, but the barrels are getting lighter.'

Grunnir shrugged. 'Back in the glory days that would never have happened. Proper brewmasters then, and proper brew.'

Borrik looked at the devastation around him. Nothing was like it was, not any more. 'You're sounding like a longbeard.'

Grunnir tugged his beard. 'It's been well watered with blood these last weeks. It's growing as quickly as my tally of grudges.'

Distant drums sounded. Borrik stood. 'All right, lads! Back in formation – they're coming for another go!'

The ironbreakers tossed another few corpses into the pit and trudged wearily back to their stations. Skaven began filing out into the Hall of Reckoning in organised lines that spread into calm ranks, a far cry from the panicking thralls they had first faced.

'Look at them,' said Gromley, taking in the number of stolen dwarf items in the hands of their enemies. 'Thieving vermin. They're so intent on killing us, they never stop to think who'll they'll steal off when we're gone.'

'Less of that,' said Uli. 'We're not going anywhere.'

'Well,' said Grunnir, settling his standard into a more comfortable position. 'If they do win, I hope the little furry beggars choke on their victory.'

'Borrik! Borrik!' A hand tugged at the mail shirt of the thane. Tordrek had come forward. 'There's someone at the door.'

'Ale?' said Borrik brightening.

Tordrek shook his head. Borrik cast an annoyed look at the marshalling skaven and followed his friend through the thin back rank of the Axes of Norr. There remained a single full line of ten to block the way.

The sound from the skaven was muted in the chamber at the rear. A steady tap-tapping came from the door. Borrik pressed his ear against it.

Borrik counted three different hammer sizes beating out the code, the notes they made identical to anyone but a dwarf.

'Aye, that's the right signal. Open the door,' he said. 'Quickly now, we don't want this gate gaping wide when the skaven come to attack.'

'We're all right for a minute,' came Gromley's sour voice from the front of the ironbreakers. 'They're still trying to get themselves in order.'

Tordrek's remaining Forgefuries, guarding the door, opened it.

What emerged was not ale. A spike of orange hair came around the door. Borrik took a step back, face grim. 'It's come to that, has it?' he said. 'Make way, lads!' he called. 'We've got company.'

Silently, the Slayers came out, more than twenty of them, all stony-faced killers. Their leader, an emotionless dwarf who made Borrik look the size of a beardling, nodded a greeting to the thane. The rest filed out without looking. Borrik didn't look them in the eye, because behind the flinty light that burned there you could catch the darkness of shame. A broken oath, a grandfather's mistake uncovered, a romantic advance rebuffed... Whatever crimes these dwarfs had committed or shames they had suffered, trivial or gross, they all felt the same. They were all broken by their experiences. Through the narrow passage they went. At the far end, the Norrgrimlings parted to let them past.

The skaven were working themselves up into a frenzy, biting at their shields, their leaders squeaking orders from the back, their soldiers squeaking together in response.

'Quickly now, quickly,' said Borrik. 'Close ranks as soon as they're through.'

Gromley gave him a hard stare that suggested that wasn't going to be necessary, but prodded his tired warriors into place with his axe haft.

The Slayers spread out once in the hall, not in a disciplined line but each finding a spot that suited him best. That meant as far away from the others as possible. They said nothing as they waited for the skaven to attack. The ratmen did so cautiously, their eagerness for the fight seeming to desert them when they saw these fresh opponents.

Driven on by furious squeaking and the clang of cymbals, the skaven charged, flowing over the broken, bloodied floor of the Hall of Reckoning as one.

When the enemy were close, the Slayers counter-charged. Some shouted out to Grimnir, some sang, others howled with the pain of whatever shame had driven them to take the oath. Yet others made no noise, but set to with voiceless determination.

They were engulfed by the vermintide like bright rocks in a dark sea. Like rocks, they were not overcome.

'Look at them,' muttered Gromley. The Slayer leader leapt

and whirled, his paired rune axes trailing light and blood in equal part.

'This is a rare sight. I'm glad I have one eye left to see it with,' said Uli.

'Look at that one! The big one with the scars!' Albok pointed to a dwarf who was wider than he was tall, his body covered in tattoos, his tattoos scratched through by scars. He wielded a single, double-handed axe with a head as big as his own torso.

'That's the Dragonslayer Aldrik the Scarred, if I'm not mistaken,' said Gromley. He blew out his cheeks and shook his head. 'If you live to be five hundred, you'll be half the warrior he is.'

Aldrik was a solid presence amid the churning mass of skaven. They were far quicker than him, but he moved aside from every blow. His axe strokes were deliberate. Not a single one missed. Every swipe cut a skaven in half.

The Norrgrimlings relaxed. It was plain to them all that they were not going to be needed in this engagement. The Slayers were butchering the skaven, and the ratmen were close to breaking. Already, their back ranks were becoming strung out from the mass at the front.

Of a sudden, the skaven had had enough. They fled, squealing frantically. The Slayers let out a shout and chased after them. Surrounded by piled bodies were three orange-haired dwarf corpses. The remainder disappeared down the stairheads after the fleeing skaven.

The Axes of Norr let their guard drop.

'That's that, then. Time for a rest,' said Grunnir.

'Aye, and more besides,' said Thane Borrik, pushing his way to the front with a metal message scroll in his hand. 'We've got new orders from the king. Time to pull back to the Hall of Clan Skalfdon.' He pointed over his shoulder with his thumb. 'Got a herald back there, so it's as official as it gets. Tordrek, blow those doors up before we go.'

'What about the Slayers, Thane?' asked Albok.

'Three groups of them have gone out,' said Borrik. 'It's shameful to say, but we won't see the likes of this for a long time. They've got their wish. Let's take their dead back. The least we can do is lay their axes on the shrine of Grimnir, and let him know they fulfilled their oaths.'

As the Norrgrimlings tenderly retrieved the dead Slayers, Tordrek stepped up with his dawi and headed for the centre of the room. Once there, they opened fire and ignited the charges packed around each stairhead. The explosion in the Hall of Reckoning sounded like the end of everything. Dust blew out, coating the surviving members of the Axes of Norr so they appeared like the ancestors, freshly awoken at the roots of the world. Bright eyes peered out from grey faces.

'That should keep them back a bit,' said Borrik, when the last rock had clattered to a standstill. 'Come on, lads, let's see if there's any ale left in the citadel. This has been a thirsty couple of weeks.'

# ELEVEN

*A Confrontation*

'A messenger is coming,' said Soothgnawer's voice, as yet unattached to a body.

Kranskritt startled. It was unnerving how the verminlord came from nowhere. He looked around for Soothgnawer, nose working frantically. He caught a whiff of the otherwordly creature, but the scent was faint and all around him, and Kranskritt could not see him.

'There is always a messenger coming. Who? What-what?' responded the grey seer testily.

'One of the Red Guard,' came the reply. Soothgnawer had still not manifested. Kranskritt saw a darkening against the wall, a shadow out of place. He stared fixedly at it, determined not to be surprised.

'Queek will give the orders I foresaw,' said Soothgnawer smugly. 'Queek has guessed the deception. It is to the peaks you will go, hunting goblins. He wishes your clawpack to engage Skarsnik and keep him away from the main assault upon the beard-things.'

'Pah! Mad-thing does great insult to me,' Kranskritt said. 'I should be with him, I should whisper-command in his ear! He is mad and foolish-stupid.' Kranskritt shivered. The bells on his ankles, wrists and horns tinkled with fury.

'Hush, little seer! Do you remember our plans? You will have what you wish.' Soothgnawer's voice was poison-perfumed velvet, smooth against the senses, beguiling, yet smothering.

Kranskritt bridled. They were most assuredly not his plans. He did not like this situation. It was typically he who had fore-knowledge and he who did the manipulating. This creature was always two scurryings ahead of him, possibly more.

'Not our plans!' he said, wringing the hem of his robe. 'Yours! What happens if Queek discovers? What if he say-accuses me? He has no fear of the Horned Rat. He has no fear of me!'

'Patience!' said the voice, now from right behind him.

With a yelp, Kranskritt spun on the spot. From the shadows between unpacked crates, a space far too small to accommo-date the verminlord, large eyes full of an ancient malevolence regarded him. Half concealed in this too-small space, yet there nonetheless, the creature's triple rack of horns seemed to grow and twist sinuously. At that moment skin and fur clothed his skull, and he looked like a grey seer grown vast on magic and evil. A clawed hand thrust out, holding an enormous gazing globe.

'You are right to fear the future, Kranskritt. If Queek sus-pects, then die long and horribly you will, and lower the status of Clan Scruten becomes. Look-look! There are many paths to follow. All bad but one. In life I too walked as a grey seer. Now I am more. Much more. I scry beyond space and time – the future is downwind. And I tell you, there is no other way.'

The voice left the room, burrowed directly into Kranskritt's mind. It was at once compelling and threatening. Sooth-gnawer had a way of posing questions that provided their own answers, which, when examined later, posed more questions.

The endless conundrums this generated in Kranskritt's agile mind was threatening to drive him as mad as Queek. He turned an involuntary blow at his own head into a scratch of his ear so furious it drew blood, and glanced into the ball.

'Yes-yes, I see-scry that now.' He saw nothing, but wished to appear wise before this creature. He instantly regretted the hesitancy in his voice. Verminlords could smell deception.

'You see nothing.'

Kranskritt wailed. 'I cannot see!'

'Look harder.'

The grey seer turned away, shaking his head, but the voice would not be dislodged. 'Tell me, why-why is my clawpack not ordered into the fight?' demanded Kranskritt. 'Why must I chase the green-thing? I have the largest clawpack.'

'Patience, little seer. Queek was confounded. Two sets of orders from his master demand his action in opposing manner.'

Kranskritt tittered. 'A good trick-treachery on the arrogant mad-thing! Who is behind it? Is it your doing, horned master? Such a trick is worthy of your unsurpassed intellect,' he said, remembering his manners under the verminlord's gaze.

Soothgnawer emerged a little further into the material world, huge and terrifying. 'Little seer must learn to listen more closely. Both sets of orders come from Lord Gnawdwell. The lord of Clan Mors tires of his general.'

Kranskritt wrinkled his muzzle. 'Then why two orders? Why not bad orders, or simple kill-slay? It makes no sense!'

Soothgnawer eased himself out of whatever hellish realm he inhabited and into Kranskritt's burrow. The laws of space-time asserted themselves, and he popped into existence. Fully manifested, he filled the room, his horns scraping fragments of stone from the ceiling. He pushed crates over and sat down on one. Still he towered over Kranskritt. 'Is this the level of the grey seers' intelligence in these times? So sad. No mystery to me why the Great Horned One punished Clan Scruten.' Soothgnawer spoke with infinite paternal patience to the seer. 'Gnawdwell wants to see what Queek will do. He is too attached-fond to the warlord. In his head, here,' the verminlord tapped between his eyes, 'he thinks that he confuses Queek to make him hesitate, to anger his underlings so that they will kill-slay him and replace him. But in his heart Gnawdwell has become too sentimental. His attempts on Queek's life are poorly planned and half-hearted, and so is this scheme-plan. He does not admit it, but he gives Queek another chance, a way from death. If Queek is successful here, Gnawdwell will not kill him. He knows Queek is unworthy as his successor, that a creature as insane as Queek can never sit upon the Council of Thirteen, but he has deluded himself that the Headtaker might change, and so Gnawdwell's heart wars with his mind.'

Kranskritt spat. 'The heart is quick and treacherous. Great thinkings only come from the mind. Is it not established that the skaven are the most intelligent of all races? We grey seers do not listen to our traitor-hearts.'

'This is so. This is right. Make sure you stay that way, little seer.'

'Tell-squeak me, how you know what Gnawdwell think-feels, great and wise Soothgnawer?' asked Kranskritt, half afraid of the answer, for if the verminlord could read minds as he suspected, Kranskritt would have a lot of grovelling to perform. His glands twitched.

'To be a master of our kind, as I am, little seer, you must look beyond what each ratkin does to another, and into the mind behind the scheme. Within all of you there are many reasons and many desires, and these vie and plot one against the other as surely as you fight one another.' The creature paused. Its white-furred face lost all flesh and skin to appear as an eyeless skull, turning back into a grey seer's face without appearing to change, even to Kranskritt's magic-sight. Kranskritt felt very weak indeed and flinched from him. 'Now Queek reacts with open violence. It is what Queek does. He is as unsubtle as his Dwarf Gouger. Look-look into the ball and see.'

Reluctantly, Kranskritt stared into the verminlord's over-sized gazing glass. If he had put his arms around it, his paws would not have met. Now he saw. In its uncertain depths were crystal-clear images of skaven marching all over the City of Pillars, all going upwards. The burrowing machines of Clan Skryre worked tirelessly to bore them new routes. Massed ranks of skaven confronted lines of glowering dwarf-things, the long-fur on their faces bristling. Skaven war machines opened up on them, killing the stupid creatures by the score.

'The dwarfs will soon retreat. The future is changing. We come to a nexus in the way. At the right moment, you must be in place to act and seize the right path. See why, little seer. Watch now and witness a fate that will be yours and all grey seers' if you are not successful,' said Soothgnawer, his voice lodged still in the space behind Kranskritt's eyes, more irritating than a tick. 'Watch-watch.'

Kranskritt gave a startled squeak. He was no longer in his burrow, but in a hall choked with many skaven dead. A large hole was in the centre, and two piles of shattered stone were to either side. Rock dust drifted on air currents, the smell of freshly broken rock and blackpowder was choking, but although he could smell it, although he felt he should be coughing hard, he breathed easily. He looked about for Sooth-gnawer. He could not see him, but could feel his presence.

'You are here and not-here, little seer. This is the Hall of Reckoning, as the dwarf-things call it. Great things happen here very soon. Be calm and watch.'

Kranskritt tried his best not to think about where he was or how he was there. On the edge of his perception was the endless, anguished squeaking of millions of voices that he did not care to hear.

Fortunately for him, the burring noise of heavy machinery soon troubled the chamber and drowned out the squeals of the damned. The ground shook. A short distance from the leftmost blocked tunnel, a fall of dust sheeted away from the rock. Small stones skittered from their position on the rock falls as the vibrations grew louder, until with the crack of broken stone, a giant drill head breached the wall, multiple toothed grinding heads all turning in separate directions. The Clan Skryre machine jolted as it drove out of the tunnel and dropped six inches to the floor of the hall. A platform on tracked wheels followed the drill head, two goggled and masked warlocks tending the mass of sorcerous machinery mounted atop it. They pulled levers, flicked switches. Lightning burst from the tops of brass orbs. Fluids bubbled in long glass tubes protected by copper latticework. The drilling machine drove off to one side, pulping skaven corpses under its truckles. The drill ceased spinning and the machine came to a halt, powering down with a teeth-wounding whine.

A score of heavily built stormvermin came from the new corridor, a thunder of pounding, muscular legs and thick armour. Stones pattered from their shoulders as they emerged, but the tunnel held. They fanned out, forming a solid square in the middle of the chamber. Kranskritt drew back into the shadows.

'Foolish little seer, they cannot see you,' laughed Soothgnawer in his mind. 'Do not fear!'

Their leader, a mid-ranking member of Clan Mors whose name-smell was Frizloq, came next, entering the Hall of Reckoning as warily as a common rat might dare a night-time kitchen. He sniffed the air, stepping delicately down the spilled rock to survey the room. Whatever he expected to find there was gone, and he grinned widely at its absence. He prodded one of his minions with the butt of his polearm, gesturing that he should enter the tunnel in one corner. The skaven cringed at being separated from the warmth and protection of his littermates, but obeyed. He disappeared into the tunnel with a wary backward glance.

A second passed. The stormvermin re-emerged.

'Empty!' he squeaked triumphantly. 'Broken beer keg. Slain skaven, but beard-things gone!'

'The door?' asked the leader.

'Locked-barred. No traps,' reported the scout.

The clawleader rubbed his hands together. 'Locked, you say? Barred, you squeak? We shall see-see. We shall see! Get it open! Get it open for the glory of Clan Mors! We shall be first into the citadel!'

A flurry of activity followed. At first the skaven tried to beat the door down themselves, but the gate of Bar-Undak was too strong and they were too feeble to breach its steel.

The leader pulled his warriors back, generously rewarding them for their efforts with the battle corpses littering the floor. As they settled down to eat, he conferred sharply with the warlocks, pointing and chittering something lost under the noise of the idling machine. The engine roared, black smoke tinged by green flecks puffed from its chimney, and it ground around to face the tunnel to the chamber. The drill picked up speed and the machine chewed through the thirty feet to the door chamber in short order, widening the original tunnel considerably. As soon as it backed up, Clan Moulder packmasters brought in two monstrously built rat ogres. Their masters gestured to the stones on the floor by the rock falls. The rat ogres understood, taking up a hefty lump of rock in each fist. They loped then into the widened tunnel and thence the chamber. There, under the direction of their masters, they battered at the doors, snarling as they grazed their knuckles and banged their heads on the ceiling in the cramped space. Their handlers goaded them with sparking prods and the rat ogres squeal-roared, bashing harder with their improvised tools. The door shook on its deep-set hinges.

For an hour, during which time Kranskritt continued to watch from his shadow-place, the door refused to give. The rocks scarred the steel, little else. But slowly the strength of the rat ogres began to tell, and the door became loose. They pounded out a bowl in the middle and a rent appeared. The rat ogres cast aside their stones to work their claws into the gaps and tug and pull at it.

At this juncture, Warlord Thaxx Redclaw arrived at the front, stepping imperiously from the tunnel mouth with an honour guard of equally arrogant stormvermin.

'Masterfully canny Thaxx arrives at the most opportune moment, as no doubt his incomparable planning intended,' squeak-greeted the skaven leader. 'Humble Frizloq has great news. This door is soon to be destroyed. Come-see!' He beckoned to his lord excitedly. 'You are just in time to witness the opening of the way!'

'You have done well, Frizloq,' said Thaxx coolly, looking down his muzzle at the clawleader. 'Four-score weak-meat I will pledge-give you for your adequate efforts on my behalf.'

Frizloq dipped his head in gratitude.

A bellow came from the door chamber, then a crash as the door was torn from its hinges and cast down.

Frizloq called out to his warriors, all of whom were feasting or sleeping, grabbing the opportunity to rest while the rat ogres worked. 'To arms! To arms!' he squeaked. 'To the beard-thing citadel, and there to victory!'

Thaxx Redclaw grabbed his underling's arm and shook his head. 'No-no! Wait-wait.'

Frizloq became confused. 'Why-why? The door is broken, the door so many died to breach. Why we not press on? Catch the beard-things unawares? If we hurry-scurry, we might disrupt them. Surely they fortify-build as we squeak? That is their way.'

'No-no,' repeated Thaxx. 'Warlord Queek's orders. All attacks on this front must halt. He does not wish Clan Mors warriors to die-die in dwarf-thing traps. First clawpack will wait, wait for slaves, for weak-meat.'

Frizloq opened his mouth, for Thaxx's command directly contradicted his earlier orders from Queek himself, but he thought better of it. He twitched meekly and exposed his throat as a display of his utmost subservience. 'As great Thaxx demands, so shall it be!'

'Not humble I, but mighty Queek,' corrected Thaxx. 'We must thank to his strategic pre-eminence for this clever-smart move. Thaxx is but his worthy message-bearer.'

As if in direct challenge to Thaxx's statement, a clanking came up the corridor. Frizloq's skaven were shoved aside. Red-armoured stormvermin burst into the room, their mouths twisted into snarls, tails swiping with pent-up aggression. At their head came the biggest skaven in the City of Pillars, Ska Bloodtail. Thaxx's nose quivered. He swallowed rapidly and blinked. Where Ska went, Queek was close behind.

The Headtaker bowed low to enter the Hall of Reckoning, saving his precious trophies from damage on the ceiling.

'Who speak-squeaks on my authority?' he demanded. 'Why this front not press on? Mighty Queek say all stormvermin attack! All clanrats to move forward! The time for weak-meat is done. Why Thaxx say otherwise?'

Thaxx curled his lips, exposing his teeth all along his muzzle. In his shadow-space, Kranskritt shrank back, terrified by the murderous glare burning in Queek's red eyes. The Headtaker bullied his way through the crowd, skaven scrambling over each other to get out of the way. He confronted Thaxx. Redclaw stood tall and held his ground.

'What bribe-gift you take to betray Clan Mors?' asked the Headtaker, tail swishing back and forth.

Those around the two powerful war-leaders spread out, forming a large challenge ring. Fear musk sprayed from the lesser members of the crowd. The stormvermin watched intently, but others were desperate to find elsewhere to be. Walking sideways, the two combatants began to circle each other, their muscles tensing to spring.

Excuses, denials and renewed pledges were the tried and true ways of skaven avoiding, or at least delaying, such confrontations. Thaxx Redclaw had known Queek Headtaker too long to attempt such pretence. He knew what was coming next, had planned for it. He had not expected it to happen now, necessarily, but no scheme was mad-thing proof, and he was ready. Baring his teeth in a hissing grimace, the warlord of the first clawpack drew his sword, its cruelly serrated edge glistening with warp venom. Yet how did Queek know? Thaxx had told no one of his dealings with Clan Skryre. And how did the Headtaker get here so quickly? Both things were impossible – but now was not the time to think upon it.

The Headtaker sneered. 'You wonder how I know? Mighty Queek has informants you could never dream of, fool-thing... No one bests Queek!' He drew his sword and weighed Dwarf Gouger carefully in his other hand, his gaze fixed on Thaxx's head. Thaxx glanced nervously at the new spike of pale wood lashed to the Headtaker's trophy rack. 'Now, tell Queek, Thaxx traitor-rat, what was the promise-pact? No warptokens or breeders – you have too many of those already,' said Queek. 'Yes-yes, don't look surprised. Queek knows what you hide in your under-warrens. No, the great Thaxx would not be tempted by what he already has. The offer was to be first warlord of Clan Mors, wasn't it? Yes-yes? Replace great and mighty Queek in City of Pillars? Delay long enough until Queek failed and a replacement was in order, unless there was an accident first?' Queek tutted. 'Queek say Thaxx has been left alone for too long in City of Pillars. Now Thaxx learn highly unpleasant lesson from good teacher Queek.'

Thaxx leapt forwards, his sword hissing down at Queek.

Queek dodged out of range with ease, and Thaxx went right past him. But Thaxx's attack was merely a feint, giving him space to draw a hidden warplock pistol with his free hand. He spun past the Headtaker, turning his failed lunge into a graceful turn.

'Die-die!' shrieked Thaxx, squeezing the trigger over and over.

Queek laughed. Thaxx should never have reached for another weapon. Without that, he stood more of a chance. Against the mighty Queek, Queek thought, that was still less than no chance, but he might have died with dignity.

With the agility of a warrior born, Queek leapt aside. Knowing he would never close the distance in time, he hurled his sword.

Thaxx had time to fire off three quick shots from his repeater pistol. Two of them dented Queek's armour, sending showers of warpstone-impregnated dust from it. The third missed, and then Queek's blade slammed into his pistol. The sword severed one of Thaxx's fingers, the digit still locked upon the trigger as the pistol clattered to the floor. Thaxx squealed with pain. In shock, the wounded warlord looked down first upon his bleeding hand, and then to the fallen pistol, to find his missing finger. This was his final mistake.

Queek crossed the gap between them in a single bound. He brought Dwarf Gouger down and then up, catching Thaxx under the chin with the blunt side.

Thaxx's jaw shattered, and he was sent sprawling onto his back. Queek pounced so that his feet were spread either side of Thaxx's chest. He thrust his yellow incisors close to Thaxx's face.

'Tsk tsk, foolish Thaxx. Queek knows a bribe from Clan Skryre when it is fired at Queek,' hissed Queek. 'But tell-say, who else is involved? That venom on your sword-blade smells like Clan Eshin good stuff. Tell-squeal and Queek will end it quick-quick.'

Queek leaned in, so that Thaxx's burbling, blood-choked words were audible to him alone. But Kranskritt, aided by Soothgnawer's magic, heard them too, mangled though they were through the Redclaw's wounded jaw.

'The Horned Rat skin you forevermore, mad-thing.'

To Kranskritt's surprise Queek laughed and nodded with satisfaction. He drove Dwarf Gouger down point first into Thaxx's belly, and ripped upwards, disembowelling Thaxx.

Straightening up, the Grand Warlord of the Eight Peaks surveyed the skaven gathered around him in the Hall of Reckoning. 'First clawpack,' rang out Queek's voice. 'Thaxx betrayed Clan Mors. I will lead you now.'

'Queek! Queek! Queek!' the others shouted. Frizloq prostrated himself with admirable alacrity. His officers, then the lesser rats, did the same, all chanting the Headtaker's name.

'Loyal Ska!' yelled Queek over the adulation.

'Yes, O mighty Queek?'

'This not over. Bring me Skrikk, bring me Kranskritt, bring me Gritch.' He snickered evilly. 'It is time all traitor-things dance with Queek!'

'See now?' said Soothgnawer to Kranskritt. 'This is what you face.'

Kranskritt nodded.

'Good. Back we go!'

The Hall of Reckoning faded from view, and Kranskritt found himself in his burrow once more.

The grey seer gathered what little courage he had and thrust out his horns. He closed his eyes – a skaven show of confidence. This time he spoke more boldly. 'Yes-yes. How could perfect Soothgnawer be anything but correct?'

'Indeed,' said Soothgnawer.

'I will find the goblin and make the offer. Goblin kill first clawpack, Kranskritt save the day with fifth clawpack. Grey seers look like heroes.'

And so, Kranskritt dearly hoped, Kranskritt could avoid his meeting with Queek.

When he opened his eyes once more, he was alone. Sooth-gnawer was gone, but the verminlord's voice rang still in the secret spaces of his skull. 'I know,' it said.

Kranskritt threw together a variety of magical ingredients. He called in his servants. 'Gather fifth clawpack! Into the mountains! Send-scurry message to mighty Queek.' Kranskritt smiled as his scribe fetched quill and man-skin parchment. 'Tell him unworthy Kranskritt follow mighty Queek's orders to the letter, loyally and without question.'

# TWELVE

*Skarsnik's Big Deal*

The halls under Karag Zilfin had once belonged to a powerful dwarf merchant family. In the glory days of the Eternal Realm, the place was plaqued with gold, its dark ways lit with glimlight glowstones and runic lamps whose oil never ran dry. Not that Skarsnik, the current occupant, knew that. Vala-Azrilungol had been stripped thousands of years before Skarsnik had sprouted. He had to contend with walls that ran black with mould, water that dripped from the ceiling all the time, and the constant blast of the mountain winds whistling in through glassless windows and empty door frames.

'I hates this. It's rubbish,' he muttered as he walked to his chambers. He passed through his audience room, which was embarrassingly tiny compared to the Hall of a Thousand Pillars he'd once called his own. Tribute lay heaped chaotically everywhere. 'Really rubbish. Nowhere near enough room for all me presents. I miss it in the proper underground, Gobbla. Nice and warm.' He cut down a long corridor, perfectly carved in the stunty way with not a curve or kink to halt the wind blasting in from outside. Treasuries, store rooms and steps leading down opened up either side of him. At the end were his private quarters. He wasn't too happy when he got there and came upon the moonhat guards and phalanx of little big 'uns trusted with his safety, all of whom were sprawled about the place snoring and not at all doing a good job of guarding. He was too annoyed to kick them awake. Instead, he let Gobbla eat one. His screams woke the others and they ran, mismatched armour rattling, to their posts.

'Zogging idiots!' he shouted. 'There's a bleeding war on!'

He muttered darkly and scowled at them. Gobbla burped. The goblin elite shook so hard their knees knocked.

There was, at least, a door across the entrance to his rooms. He went in and shut it behind him with a sigh. A fire of big-shroom stalks burned in a long stone trough in the fireplace. He looked at the filthy furs heaped on his bed, and thought of sleeping.

He shook his head. 'Nah, never no time for sleeping. Sleep when you's dead, eh, Gobbla?' He chuckled. 'Got work to do. First mind, I reckon it's time for a little drinky.' On a table piled high with parchment covered in his spidery handwriting were numerous bottles. He shook them until he found one that was full. He held it up critically, grumbling that he had to tilt it this way and that to read the label. His eyes weren't as good as they used to be.

'*Produzzi di Castello di Rugazzi,*' he said. He shrugged at it. Castello di Rugazzi had been burned down along with the rest of Tilea a couple of years before. He wouldn't have cared had he known, but what Skarsnik held in his hands was quite probably the last bottle of wine from that vineyard, if not from Tilea. Skarsnik's stash had once had brews from all across the Old World, purloined from caravans braving the trek over to the Far East. But once Gorfang was killed and the rats infested

Black Crag, there was no one to police Death Pass. Then the wars had started. No one had come that way he could bully or rob for a long while, and Skarsnik's cellars were running dry.

'Gotta be better than Duffskul's brew,' he said sourly. He found his goblet on the floor, groaning as he stood up straight and his back cracked. He tipped a spider out and peered in. The goblet was filthy, so he spat in it and cleaned it with his ink-stained thumb until he was satisfied.

He bit the top off the bottle with his needle-teeth and poured. As it glugged into the goblet, Skarsnik smacked his lips in anticipation. He pulled a snotling out of a cage and made it drink some. He watched it for a moment. It smiled stupidly, and obligingly did not die, so he shoved it back into its prison.

'Cheers, snotties,' he toasted his tasters, and slurped down a mouthful of wine. Then he lit a candle of dwarf fat and sat down to his work. 'Now then, now then,' he said, rubbing his hands. He was determined to update his list of tribes currently squatting in the surface city and the Great Vale. 'Got to be organised, eh, Gobbla? Where are you if you's not organised?'

Gobbla growled. That was not the correct response. Skarsnik stiffened. His ears prickled.

A ball of black lightning burst into being behind Skarsnik, caused him to spin round so fast he lost his face in the back of his hood.

'Not this again! Ratties, they never learn!' he said, wrestling with his bosshat. 'You've tried this fifteen times before, ya dumb gits! Garn! Get some new ideas!' He stood up violently, sending his papers onto the floor. His goblet he caught deftly in one hand as the table toppled from underneath it. With the other hand he snatched up his prodder, and pointed it at the fizzing orb.

Black energy throbbed, sending arcs of greenish-black sparks earthing in his possessions. Much to his annoyance, his papers caught fire. 'Oi! Oi! Oi!' he yelled. 'You want to come and talk to me, use the zogging front door like everyone else! You's burning all me stuff up! Bleeding ratties! Got no manners!'

The whirling energies settled down. Through a dark portal, an arrogant horned rat-thing, fur white as snow, robes suspiciously clean, stepped into Skarsnik's bedroom. The grey seer surveyed the room as if it owned it, and that really annoyed Skarsnik. Actually, that was kind of the entire problem with the Eight Peaks. When would they learn that the place was his!

The rat sniffed the air and pulled a face at what it found. 'I great Grey Seer Kranskritt. I come-skitter with deal-tidings, green-thing.' It spoke in accented orcish, higher than a gobbo, but perfectly intelligible. Skarsnik was used to that.

'Well, well, well – a horny rat!' said Skarsnik back in Queek-ish, the language of the skaven, and that took the grey seer by surprise, to Skarsnik's delight. 'Tinkle-tankle little bells too. Very nice, very pretty. Learn that off an elf? Cut above the average squeaker, ain't ya? But it's not like your lot to turn up yerselves. Usually get some poor rodent to do your dirty. You can't be that important.'

'I very-very much-important, green-thing!' said Kranskritt, eyes boiling with outrage. 'You show me respect!'

Skarsnik leered a yellow grin and slurped upon his wine. 'Yeah? Or what? I'll tell you what, you goat-rat... fing, whatever you is. You'll get angry and then I'll blow you up with me prodder, that's what'll happen. It's happened before. It's getting late and I've got a lot on, so be my guest. Tempt me, and then I can gets on with me work.'

Kranskritt clashed his incisors together, eyeing the prodder nervously. Its power was well known by his kind, and feared.

'I suppose you want to make a deal, then? Your lot don't do well in deals with me, you realise that?' said Skarsnik.

'You very annoying-pain, green-thing,' admitted Kranskritt. 'You could have just sent me a messenger.'

'We did. His skin-pelt now your new bedding,' said Kran-skritt, pointing disdainfully at Skarsnik's bed.

Skarsnik looked sidelong at the fresh rat pelt serving as a coverlet. 'Oh. Right. Yeah. He did try to tell us something, to be fair. If it makes you feel better, he was very tasty. Right then. I got things to be doing. Stuff to write. Plans to make. You know, you burneded all me papers up. Took me ages to do that. I'm not happy.'

'Pah! Green-thing plans little plans. I know-know much more.'

'So you said.' Skarsnik had another drink. The wine wasn't too bad. 'Actually, you haven't said much of anyfink apart from how important you is.'

The grey seer hissed and clenched its fists. This meeting was obviously paining it. 'Tomorrow, Lord Queek of Clan Mors begins the next stage of the great war of extermination against the beard-things. He attacks in the Hall of Many Beard-Things.'

'In the citadel?'

'Big beard-thing fortress, yes-yes!' snapped Kranskritt. His tail lashed.

'Funny really, don't know the citadel well. Even before the stunties came back, didn't really go there. Full of traps. Nasty little stunties. I quite like being alive, y'see. No idea what you're talking about.'

'I show-show!' snapped Kranskritt.

'All right, all right, keep your horns on.' Skarsnik giggled at the skaven as it bristled. 'What's the point?'

'It would be good-proper if Lord Queek is not successful. Tunnel teams dig-melt their way upwards. I show. You take them, good quick-fast, yes? You come up into citadel. You kill many dwarf-things, many, er, stunties, you stop Queek's easy victory.'

Skarsnik set his drink down. 'Why? I ain't no patsy for rat-sies.' He laughed again. He was on form today.

Kranskritt clawed his hands. 'Foolish green-thing! Now your time is done, but still you making stupid joke-laughs! The children of Chaos rise! The Under-Empire will rule over all! You be destroyed, swept-aside like leaves in storm! You do it, and you live. Not enough for you, green-thing? You die now, if you prefer.'

'Yeah, right. Blah, blah, blah. Squeak, squeak, squeak.' With his teeth on his lips, Skarsnik mimed a little rat mouth jabbering. 'I have heard it all before!' he said, suddenly angry. 'Year in, zogging year out! It's always the same with your lot! Ooh, we is so clever. Ooh, we is the best. If that's the bleeding case, how comes I'm the king of Karak Eight Peaks?'

Skarsnik stood tall. He was very large for a night goblin, bigger than the seer. The prodder thrummed with orcy power. 'I ain't no idiot. If you are so powerful, you don't need me, does you?'

Kranskritt growled in irritation. He and his kind were used to skaven grovelling before them, squirting the musk of fear as soon as a seer showed its face. This goblin's cool insolence was deeply disrespectful. 'Very well! You help my faction, you help yourself. Hand-claw to hand-claw. Friends-alliance! No war! You take back upper deeps when beard-things dead.'

'That's more like it,' said Skarsnik. 'All the deeps to the third, and no poking yer little pink noses out of yer burrows for four winters.'

'Skweee! Done-done,' said Kranskritt.

'All right then. Yeah. I'll do it.'

'Tomorrow! Third bell.'

Skarsnik shrugged. 'Sorry?'

Kranskritt squealed. 'New-day sunrise! Be in the west foundry, fifteen scurryings down-up-down-north of the Hall of a Thousand Pillars!'

'Lots of ratties down there. In my house, I might add,' said Skarsnik. 'I'll bet you know some of them. They'll probably try to kill me. I'm not all that popular with your lot.'

'I know you know-have ways in. Be there!'

Kranskritt disappeared with a squeak of annoyance and a burst of purplish light.

Skarsnik let out a long breath and shook his head. After a moment, he went to refill his goblet and gathered up the remains of his work. He frowned as he stared at the still-smouldering edges. 'So then, Gobbla, rats is fighting rats again. Always the way. And when they is fighting, there's some space for the likes of me to make something of it. Get me house back, get me halls back. Get some of them green-boys from up top down there to keep it, and for good this time! Be warm again!'

He flopped into a chair. The chamber rumbled with yet another tremor. They had never really stopped since the days the mountains had exploded. Gravel pattered onto his head. Gobbla waddled up and snuffled for a scratch. Skarsnik obliged, massaging Gobbla's favourite spot between his eyes. 'Of course, boy, it's all a big trap. It always is.' He slurped his wine. 'But,' he added thoughtfully, 'why does I have this feeling this time things is a teeny bit different? And not in a good way...'

He sat there a long time rubbing Gobbla's leathery skin, thinking thoughts no other goblin could, alone as always.

# THIRTEEN

*Payment for Services Rendered*

Duffskul flapped his sleeves manically until his grubby green hand was free to press the stunty face. The fist-sized carving made a click, and the secret door it activated rumbled back into the wall. Duffskul puffed on his pipe and clucked his tongue with appreciation. It never ceased to amaze him how long the stunty-stuff kept on working.

Cold wind keened through the crack of the door, became a moan as the gap widened, and then a blast of winter that put out his pipe. Duffskul frowned and tapped the ashes from the bowl. He tucked the pipe into his belt, muttered some words to Mork and Gork, and waved his hands around desultorily. It was a poor effort, but lately the world had been so heavy with the essence of the Twin Gods, he barely had to try any more. The spell came on quickly, flattening him out, deepening the darkness of his robes. Soon all that was visible of him was a shadow like all the other shadows, excepting perhaps a greenish smear that might have been a face until you looked right at it.

The door finished its grinding recession, leaving the shaman's way clear. Duffskul stuck his head out into the day. He was a night goblin and therefore not at all fond of daylight, but what little effort the sun put forth through the winter sky, choked as it was with ash and magic, was weak and unimposing.

He hopped out of the door. The odd flake of dirty snow splatted against his hood. Snow had been falling for weeks in the mountains, and Duffskul squinted at all the brightness of it, but wrapped up in his shadow cloak he felt safe enough from the Evil Sun. Besides, he couldn't see it through all that cloud, so it couldn't see him, could it? The thickest runt knew that. Even if the ground shone like silver. Humming tunelessly for courage, Duffskul tottered off, out onto the flanks of the Silverhorn.

Seventeen treacherous switchbacks later, a quick dart past a fresh skaven tunnel, and a hairy moment when a dozen rocks the size of cave squigs bounded inches past Duffskul's nose, the aged shaman reached the bottom of the mountain. There the path joined a wider dwarf way, its cobbles much split by tree roots, which in turn descended through scrubby pine woods to join the main old road that ran through Death Pass.

Duffskul came out in a place not far from the Tight Spot, where the road went through high moorland. The dwarf road was heaving with greenskins of every kind, passing in long scrap trains out of the Dark Lands. They had started coming a few years ago, fleeing some upheaval out there and heading into the Badlands. Goblins first by the thousand, because they don't like fighting. But lately there had been many orcs also. They had their fiercest faces on, but Duffskul was canny, almost as canny as Skarsnik, and he could see they were afraid. Duffskul wondered what was happening in the wider world. He had tried staring out through Gork and Mork's eyes, but there was so much magic bleeding into everything that it made him dizzy just to try. Most troubling was that on the western side of the pass, where most of this lot were heading, the greenskins were coming back again. Life in the Badlands wasn't too good either, Kruggler kept saying. All fine news for Skarsnik, thought Duffskul, as the majority of the greenskins, having nowhere else to go, were ending up in the Eight Peaks. But what did it mean? Through his persistent fug of intoxication, the old shaman couldn't help but be concerned.

The ground rumbled. Rocks pitter-pattered down from the heights. It was not, reflected Duffskul, a question that needed answering. Earthquakes were frequent. They'd always had a bit of the old heave-ho coming from the ground, but nothing like this. Over the eastern peaks of the mountains the sky was black as night, and the sun never, ever shone there any more. The Dark Lands had become a whole lot darker.

'The world is changing, that's what,' he muttered to himself. 'A sorry sight, and no mistake, oh yus.' A group of wolf riders bolted as his shadow popped, turning him back into his usual solid self. He giggled at the sight of the riders struggling to control their mounts, causing chaos in the already fractious crowds of greenskins marching west. It took his mind off being exposed to the light.

'Can't be helped,' he muttered. 'Get trod on if I is a shadow.'

He plopped himself down on a dwarf milestone. From under his filthy robes he produced a puffball flask. He guzzled down the contents, some of his own special brew. Courage fortified, he refilled his pipe with shroom-smoke fungus, and took in the view.

At this point past the Tight Spot, Death Pass opened up. Here it stretched ten miles wide, the far side blued by distance. Much of it thereabouts was inhospitable moorland, broken by humps of rock, little streams and the grey stumps of pines hacked down by the greenskins for their fires and rickety constructions. Only the old dwarf road offered good travel, and that's where the traffic was.

In a state of disrepair, the road of Death Pass still held the power to impress. It went dead straight as much as possible, burrowing through such minor inconveniences as mountain spurs without stopping. There were ditches to either side, deep and lined with stone, although all that was visible this time of year were indentations in the snow and hairy yellow grass poking through. Every eight hundred yards, paired statues of stunty gods stood guard over it. Most had been broken aeons ago by orcs, but a few were more or less whole, glaring at the usurpers marching under their noses. Duffskul scuttled by these intact ones whenever he encountered them, because they gave him the creeps.

The pass had long been the domain of the orcs. The way had been tightly controlled for years by Gorfang Rotgut down in Black Crag. But the Troll-Eater was gone, killed by the king of all the stunties, so they said, and no one collected his tolls any more. Duffskul supposed sudden freedom of passage hadn't helped the traffic levels.

He watched the endless caravans groan past. Most of the greenskins were wolf tribes, not much use for Skarsnik's battles underground, but they had at least a number of ferocious beasts in their rickety cages. He even saw a group of much-battered hobgoblins chained up in one.

What is the world coming to, he thought, if even them treacherous backstabbers aren't being stabbed first chance? They don't even taste very nice. Why keep 'em?

He scowled at them. Cowardly at the best of times, they were beaten and downcast, and did not return his gaze.

He smoked awhile with his eyes closed to shut out the horrid glare of the sun until he felt suitably fortified by smoke and brew. He opened one eye, then the other, hiccupped and slid off the rock.

'Suppose I better be getting on,' he said. He let his finger rise up of its own accord, snaking around in the clouds of pungent shroomsmoke until it had found the right direction. 'Ah,' he said, 'that way.'

He headed east, and the crowds parted for him. Now he was far from the ratties and stunties, he could trust to his status as a shaman of Mork and Gork to keep him safe. It wasn't just a matter of respect due him for his ability to commune with the Great Twins, but one of fear. Not even the biggest black orc wanted turning into a squig, a magic that was well within Duffskul's considerable capabilities.

When Skarsnik had called Duffskul in, he hadn't needed to ask what had happened; Skarsnik's rooms still stank of magic and rat.

'You had a visitor, boss?' he'd said.

'Them ratties are trying to make a deal,' Skarsnik said. And then he had told Duffskul what the deal was, and who had made the offer.

Duffskul wasn't fazed – the ratties were always trying some-such nonsense or other. 'Yus, boss,' Duffskul said. 'They is always trying to do that, isn't they, boss? Do deals and that, oh yus.'

'Yes, yes, they are. But I'm not having any of it. Not this time!'

'You not going to do it, then? Not make the deal?'

'Of course I'm going to do it!' Skarsnik said. He had paced up and down his room with his hands behind his back, head bowed in thought. Gobbla waddled faithfully behind him, the chain that connected them clinking. 'There's always more to it with them furry little zoggers. There'll be some nasty surprise for us in there. And the chances of them giving us back the upper stunty-house like what they said they would are about as big as Kruggler's brain.'

They both laughed, Duffskul's eyes spinning madly in his ancient face.

'What we need is a plan of our own. I says we do what that magic ratfing says. We go in and take these burrowing gizmos off of them rats, burst up through the floor as planned. But...' Skarsnik held up a finger. There was always a 'but' with the king of Eight Peaks, you had to hand it to him. 'But, we have a few alterations. Make a plan of our own, so to speak. They have a plan, and so I has a plan.'

'Oh yus, boss, right you are, boss,' said Duffskul, leaning on his staff. He'd never known Skarsnik not to have a plan. 'What plan would that be then, boss?'

Skarsnik grinned slyly. He pulled out a heavy-looking sack from under his bed and dropped it on one of his many work desks. It hit the wood with that kind of rich clunk only solid gold makes. He whipped back the filthy material to reveal a battered but still impressive crown. Five types of gold, stunty runes, some really finickity chasing work and an awful lot of big gemstones.

'Ooh, that's nice, that's lovely that is.' Duffskul reached out a hand; he couldn't help himself, but snatched it back when Gobbla fixed him with his one good eye and growled.

'Ogres, Duffskul! Ogres is me plan. Been saving this for a special occasion,' the boss said. 'Now's as good a time as any.' He nodded at the sack. 'I've heard Golgfag is nearby.'

'What, Golgfag the incredibly large and famous ogre chieftain, boss?'

'That's the one. Golgfag the incredibly large and famous ogre chieftain, Duffskul.'

'And what do we wants with this incredibly large and famous ogre chieftain? He's known for not playing it straight, if you gets me, and he often fights for the stunties.'

Skarsnik smiled broadly, Duffskul smiled back. 'And those two reasons, me old mate, is exactly why we want him, isn't it?'

'Oh yus, boss! Oh yus! I gets ya!'

The pair of them had laughed long and hard together. Skarsnik's snotling food tasters joined in from their cages, not a single idea as to what they were laughing at in their empty little heads.

Now Duffskul pushed on to where his finger told him Golgfag could be found – a trick he'd learned long ago, from the somewhat mad Tarkit Fing-Finga, back in the... Well, there was no telling how long ago it was now. Greenskins swore and cursed as he went against the tide of the migration, moving their wagons aside just the same. Wolves snapped at each other as they were whipped out of the way. The road got progressively narrower as he approached the Tight Spot, where the pass was squeezed hard between two mountains.

Then a wolf was before him, snarling and drooling. Duffskul squeaked with shock, but it yelped as reins tugged its head back. A wall of mangy fur and stinking, bandy-legged goblin raiders flowed into being in front of him.

'Shaman! Which way to the Eight Peaks?' a goblin warchief with gold teeth shouted at him, his accent all funny. Duffskul giggled at him, he sounded so stupid. 'Where do we find Skarsnik the Great?'

The Great? thought Duffskul. He'll like that. 'That way!' he said. 'Follow the big road up into the mountains. Big city, huge stunty-house. You really can't miss it, to tell the truth, oh yus.'

The goblin chief wheeled his steed around and let out an ululation, waving his hand around his head. He shot forwards and his band followed, leaping over the ditch, over the uneven ground at the roadside, and scrambling onto the loose rocks and snow that lined the pass. They must have been from the mountains somewhere, because they were quickly away on the rough ground, drawing annoyed shouts from the other goblins forced to trudge along.

A scrapwagon pushed by grumbling stone trolls creaked by next, the slave-cage atop it empty of prisoners but heaped with ragged possessions. A fat goblin on the top waved a couple of snotlings on a stick in front of the trolls to make them move. He looked unspeakably glum, as did the tribe behind. They were all injured, some seriously, many with burns and blackened faces.

There came a blast of brazen horns resounding off the pass's sides. Gruff orc voices shouted, huge black orcs moving forward in the crowd, shoving lesser greenskins out of the road. 'Make way! Make way for Drilla Gitsmash! Make way, yer lousy runts!' They backed their words with slaps and worse, spilling dark red blood on the setts. They stamped forward, until one was right in front of Duffskul, staring down at him with furious eyes. It snorted plumes of steam into the chill mountain air.

'Get out da way, wizlevard, or you'll be sorry.'

'Will I now?' said Duffskul. He cocked an eyebrow over one mad eye. The black orc roared and hammered its axe against its breastplate, but moved on just the same.

Around the corner came the biggest orc Duffskul had ever seen. That would have been enough to make him shift, but the contraption the orc rode decided it. Duffskul lifted the skirts of his dark robes and hopped over the ditch like he was a hundred years younger. He took up position well out of the way at the foot of a fan of scree.

Drilla Gitsmash's mount was a clanking, mechanical boar, its black iron spell-marked with the runes of the curly bearded tusk-stunties of the Dark Lands. Steam hissed from its pistons as it trotted by, hooves cracking the slabs. Four banner bearers came after him, holding high icons fashioned from steel. Further along the pass, the black orc heralds were shouting at the goblins and their troll cart, cursing them off the road. Trolls moaned, goblins wailed. A snap cracked off the mountainside, and the cart sagged on a broken axle. Shouting angrily, the black orcs cut the traces of the trolls, put their shoulders to the wagon bed and heaved it over, ignoring the shrill protests of its owners. It toppled into the ditch and broke apart.

Drilla's brigade of black orcs marched past Duffskul in perfect step. They held their heads high, the tusks of their visors jutting towards the sky. They were disgustingly clean, their armour immaculate. On and on they went. There must have been over three hundred of them. Screams sounded from further up the pass as they ran into the thick press of greenskin refugees, but they did not slow, they did not stop.

The last rank of black orcs went by. A final blast of brazen horns resounded off the pass's sides, and the black orcs disappeared round a shoulder of the mountain.

For a few minutes the pass was clear. Duffskul scrambled back onto the roadway to take advantage of the lull, and jogged as fast as his old legs would carry him. The crowds thickened soon enough, but when they caught sight of the shaman, his dirty robes held high over his knees, face determined, they got out of the way no matter how cramped the road was.

The ogres were camped at the Tight Spot. There were two old stunty-houses there, both forts, on knolls either side of the road. One was so tumbledown it looked like part of the mountain, the other was whole and, consequently, full of ogres. On the other side of the Tight Spot the pass rapidly widened again, becoming heavily wooded and sloping steeply down towards the Dark Lands. Duffskul left the road and puffed his way up the broken track to the gates, flanked by large ogre banners depicting that big gob of theirs. He paused in his ascent for a look out east. The line of greenskins went on forever. He tried counting them – and he could count, properly; not quite as well as his boss, but not far off. He had to give up. There were too many.

He didn't get much further up the hill before he was noticed.

'Ooh looks, it's a shaman, zippety zap!' gnoblars jeered from behind rocks in accented greenskin.

Duffskul waved his staff at them, and they ran away shrieking in terror. 'I dunno, only kind of greeny worse than you lot is the zogging hobgobboes!' he shouted. 'Gnoblars! Hill goblins! No sort of gobbo at all!'

A pair of bored ogres stood guard at the dead-eyed gatehouse to the stunty fort. They stood taller and gripped the handles of their swords as he approached.

'What you want?' one demanded, his voice thick, clogged with fat and anger.

Duffskul leaned on his staff like he didn't have a care in the world and stared up. 'You Golgfag's lot?'

'Yeah, what's it to you?' said the ogre.

'Got a job for him.'

'From who?' said the second ogre. 'We already got employment.'

'So I hear, but I's got an offer for your boss he might find very interesting. Money's a wonderful thing, ain't it?' He leaned forwards and whispered behind his hand, 'And we got lots. Let me in, let me see Golgfag.'

The ogres looked at one another. One shrugged. The other jerked his head into the camp. 'Can't do any harm. Go on then. You'll find him easy enough. He's having his dinner.'

For some reason that made them laugh deeply. Duffskul shook his head. Ogres were such fat idiots.

The place was better organised than a greenskin camp would have been, but only just. Piles of bones, scraps of half-cooked flesh still stuck to them, littered the place, filling the courtyard with the stench of decay even in the cold. Ogres went about their business heedless of everything below gut level, forcing Duffskul to dodge out of the way frequently. Despite the chill, nearly all of them were naked from the waist up. A semicircle of heavy wagons filled the back half of the fort. Giant shaggy draught beasts and mounts were corralled by a fence made of tree trunks nearby.

Golgfag was indeed hard to miss. He sat at the centre of

the camp upon the top half of a broken stunty statue, next to a roaring bonfire. Bigger than every other ogre in the place, his head seemed disproportionately small atop the mountain of fat and muscle that was his body. A maul and sword were propped up next to him, an iron standard depicting a circular, toothed maw thrust into the ground behind. A pair of halfling cooks worked nearby over a smaller fire. Whatever they were cooking smelt much tastier than the gnoblars being roasted over smaller fires.

Golgfag was munching on one such cooked gnoblar. The outside was burned to a crisp, the inside pink.

'When's my stew ready, Boltho? I'm nearly done on my starter!' Golgfag shouted in grumbling Reikspiel.

'Coming right away, gutlord!'

Duffskul licked his lips, at both the halflings' food, and the sight of the halflings themselves.

The ogre tore a mouthful of meat off, white strings of tendon hanging from his mouth.

'Ahem,' said Duffskul.

Golgfag turned round, searching at ogre height for his interlocutor, greasy moustaches flapping. It took him a moment to look down.

'Ah, another course,' said the mercenary brightly. 'Thanks for delivering yourself.'

'Nah, you's not going to eat me,' said Duffskul. 'Got a business offer.' He sat down and began to fill his pipe.

'Oh yeah?' said Golgfag. 'Already got a job. I don't see what a hole-skulking cave runt goblin like you can offer me that the king of Karak Eight Peaks can't. Go on, get out of here, or I will eat you.'

'No you won't,' said Duffskul. He clamped his pipe in his mouth. His eyes glowed green and it ignited. 'Because I'm here from the *real* king of Karak Eight Peaks.'

'I'm not worried by no scrawny goblin magician!' laughed

Golgfag. 'And I'm not too impressed by this Skarsnik either. If he's so great, how comes he's always fighting? He's been at war for half a century! I would've beaten them all by now.'

Duffskul shrugged. He pulled out an object wrapped in oilskin from under his cloak and put it on the ground. He unwrapped it, revealing the lost crown of Karak Eight Peaks. Ogres were greedy for more than food, and Golgfag's eyes widened comically at the sight. He shuffled round on his seat to get a better look.

'Now that's a pretty trinket.'

Duffskul tittered. 'It is, ain't it? From Skarsnik. You like it?'

'What's not to like?' The ogre leaned forwards, face alight with avarice.

'You can have it. Payment. We just need a little favour. Carry on like you is, be all friendly like with the stunties...'

'What, then when the time comes turn on them and give 'em a nasty surprise? That old trick? What do you say I don't just rip your head off and eat you and take that there crown off you right now? I'm getting sick of gnoblar. Goblin's got an altogether gamier flavour. Very nice your lot taste, underground greenies. Hint of mushroom to you. Delicious. I like a nice wizard too, sparkles on the tongue.' A different kind of hunger showed upon the ogre's face. His gut rumbled, twitching behind its horned belly plate.

'Because, fatty, this ain't it, is it?' Duffskul passed his hands and the crown dissolved into a handful of old leaves.

Golgfag sat back and belched out a reek of uncooked meat. 'Right. So in that case, how do I know you have actually got it? Your boss ain't exactly known for his upright nature.'

'Oh, we've got it all right.'

'King Belegar has promised me one tenth of the treasure in his treasure chamber. That's a lot of gold. Now that's a pretty crown. But worst case for me is that you've no crown, and when I pull the old switch on the stunties I get no gold at all. And that is not happening.'

'Lot of gold? Belegar? It ain't a lot of gold,' countered Duffskul – now it was his turn to laugh – 'because he's having you on! Old Belegar ain't got no gold!'

'Nah, he's a dwarf, they've always got gold,' said Golgfag, flapping the shaman's stinking smoke away from his face.

'Not this 'un. Poorer than a snotling, he is. Not much more sense either. Tell you what, do this for us and you can have *half* of Belegar's stunty-hoard. And the crown.'

Golgfag took a bite from the gnoblar's haunch and pondered for a moment. 'Seems fair enough. If you make it three-quarters. Got me overheads – not cheap running a mercenary band like this, and the price of grog is way up. If your lot lose, I'll get only the crown and Belegar's downpayment, nothing else. You understand.'

Duffskul made a sympathetic face. 'Times is hard. That crown is worth a lot, though.'

Golgfag smiled, the gaps in his teeth jammed with bloody meat. 'If you say so.'

'I do says so, and you heard me say it. Now tell me, what do we get for the crown then?'

'The real crown?'

'Course,' said Duffskul.

Golgfag stood up and stretched. He tossed the remains of his first course into the fire. 'See them gutlords marching?' He pointed a greasy finger at heavily armoured ogres sparring with hooked swords as big as an orc. 'You'll get them. And me other lads. The whole lot. I'd throw in a few gnoblars for you as well, but Belegar's messenger was quite insistent on us not bringing them in.' He belched and scratched under his belly plate. 'He didn't want any greenskins in his hold at all. As if gnoblars count! Ain't that the ironic thing? Anyways, we ate all the fighting ones. It doesn't matter, because they're useless at fighting. We only bring 'em along to distract the enemy. No great loss. Still got me pets.'

'They is not gobboes, that's the truth, oh yus.' Duffskul could not agree more on that score. 'Also, you promise no double-double crossing!'

'Hah!' said Golgfag. 'Now that's funny coming from you. Don't you worry, Belegar would never give us more money. Too tight, them dwarfs, especially if he's as skint as you say. It'll be the end of them, if you ask me.'

'And what about the other party?' said Duffskul obliquely.

'The ratmen? Nah, can't stand them myself. Vermin. Always getting into my larder.' He nodded at a couple of spitted skaven roasting on a fire. 'Caught them trying to sneak into the pay wagon three nights ago. When they pay you, half the time they don't pay you, if you know what I mean. If I told you how many of their cash deliveries turned out to be magicked, the chests full of rats in black cloaks that go all maniac on yer with their little stabby knives, you'd be surprised.'

Duffskul hiccupped. 'Nah, I don't think I would.'

Golgfag laughed. 'Right. Your lot's got experience there. Let's shake on it then.' He gobbed a truly impressive mouthful of spit into his palm and held out his hand to shake, humie-style. His fingers were thicker than Duffskul's limbs, and smelt of roast greenskin. 'We got a deal?'

Duffskull took a finger on the proffered hand and shook it carefully. 'We have got a deal.'

'See you around, little greeny. I'm off to finish my dinner. I'll send word to the lads not to eat you on the way out.' The general's vast bulk shifted around. It was like watching a hill move. 'Send us the details later. We'll need some kind of signal. You have a little think about that, all right?'

'All right.'

'Until later, shorty,' said Golgfag.

'Until later, fatty,' giggled Duffskul.

# FOURTEEN

*The Hall of Clan Skalfdon*

Atop a mound of rubble, King Belegar stood at the front of his Iron Brotherhood, Notrigar beside him bearing the clan banner of the Iron Hammers. The dwarf battle line stretched from the eastern side of the hall to the west, the high ground of an ancient rock fall at the north-western end held by Durggan Stoutbelly and the grand battery of Karak Eight Peaks. Past the Iron Brotherhood, the east end of the rubble pile was occupied by the Clan Zhorrak Blue Caps, and beyond that the rubble shelved off. From there to the walls of the hall, the ground was level, the flagstones uncovered by detritus. Two hundred yards behind Belegar's position was the Gate of Skalfdon, one of the last fine things remaining in the derelict hall, a massive portal barred by a rune-carved stone gate five feet thick.

To the south, the Hall of Clan Skalfdon stretched away, the ancestor statues carved into its far walls lost in the gloom. A few lonely glimlights still burned up in the high roof a full twenty centuries after the fall of the city, stars lost in a stone forest of pillars supporting the vaulted sky. Most of the light came from less grand sources – torches and lanterns in the main, held by the dwarf host.

Belegar looked up and down the ranks of his people. Six hundred of them, pretty much all the strength he had, barring Duregar's garrison holding the East Gate at the end of the Great Vale. Clan Skalfdon's hall swallowed them up, built at a time when a thousand times six hundred dwarfs had dwelled within Karak Eight Peaks. That glory was long gone, like the Skalfdon clan itself, the last of whose scions had perished in one of the many attempts to retake the Eight Peaks before Belegar was successful.

Successful. He snorted. This wasn't success. Already the skaven were creeping out of their holes, coming in through the dozen archways at the southern end of the hall.

'Something troubles you, my king?'

'Aye, Notrigar, a great deal,' said Belegar. 'I look at them and my blood boils. This is their domain, not mine. Look at how at home they are in the ruins, skulking about in the graves of better people. Look at them! Look at their dirty feet scrabbling on the faces of our ancestors. Look at the weapons they carry. They value nothing, not hard work, or craft, or skill – all they wish is to tear down and destroy, and disport in the remains. They thrive on blight and decay. They don't build anything to last. They don't build anything fair to look upon. All their kingdoms are but the debris of dying civilisations. It is unfair that such as these should inherit the world while better folk perish.'

'It strikes me as so, my king,' agreed Notrigar. These depressing rants of Belegar's had become more frequent, his moments of humour seldom as the war wore on.

'It strikes me that the gods are a bunch of baruzdaki,' said Belegar, 'by whom our own great ancestors were sorely mocked. Everything's gone, diminished. Look to this battle, one of the great acts of our days, and I see the pale reflections of the Karaz Ankor in pools of blood. Our ancestors battled the lords of misrule themselves, forcing them step by step out of this world and back into their own. What would Grimnir, who holds to this day the hordes of Chaos at bay, think of his descendants smashing rats into the dirt in their own homes?' He shook his head.

Mutters of agreement came from the ranks of the Iron Brotherhood.

'Still, we'll give them a pasting to remember, eh, lads? It ends here! One way or another, or I'm no dawi.' Belegar pointed, past the carpet of giant rats and slaves seeping into the hall like rising floodwaters. Glints of metal could be seen coming through the gateways, blocks of troops forming up behind the wretches in the vanguard.

'See, brave khazukan!' shouted the king, so all could hear. 'See how our great foe comes! See how he marshals all his strength against us! The Headtaker is here!'

A wail of fury went up from the dwarfs. They clashed their axes against their shields and roared. Belegar continued to speak, his anger powering his voice through the clamour raised by his warriors.

'He comes to see us die, to see an end to dawi in the great city of Vala-Azrilungol! Well, I say, let him come. Let him break his vermintide upon the shields and axes of the sons of Grungni. Let him be disappointed! Khazukan! Khazuk-ha!' he bellowed.

'Khazukan! Khazuk-ha! Grungni runk!'

Durggan added the voices of his war machines to the dwarfish war cry. At various points within the hall, range-markers had been secreted, white stones that told Stoutbelly exactly who he could hit from where, and with what. The lead ranks of skavenslaves now passed the first of these.

Cannons boomed thunderously, tearing long holes in the ranks of the slaves. They squealed in terror, and doubtless those nearest the carnage would have turned to flee if it were not for the endless swarms pushing them on. At the back, whips cracked. In reply to the cannons, streaks of green whistled into the dwarf ranks, felling warriors along the length of the line.

'Jezzails!' shouted their officers. 'Shields up!'

'Garrak-ha!' shouted the dwarfs. Triple-forged dwarf steel rippled upwards along the dwarf line, locked together with a clash. Bullets still punched through, but fewer dwarfs fell.

'Belegar! My lord! Get down!'

Belegar stood at the front of the Iron Brotherhood shouting his defiance. Warpstone bullets pinged off his rune-armour and the Shield of Defiance, disintegrating into puffs of nose-searing green smoke. 'Let them try, Notrigar. I am no skulking ratman to hide at the back of his warriors. Let them come! Let them come! Queek, I am here! I am waiting for you!'

Dwarf crossbows twanged as the skaven came into range. Shortly after, the popping reports of handguns joined them. So tightly packed were the skaven that every bullet and bolt found its mark. Those who fell were pulped under the feet of those following. Bolt throwers skewered them in threes and fours, cannons blasted them to pieces. Grudge-stones rained down, sailing between the columns of the roof on perfect trajectories. But there were thousands of skaven, and no matter how many died, there were always more. The tunnels leading back into the lower deeps were thick with them, their red eyes shining in the dark.

At the appropriate time, Durggan unleashed the fiery horror of his only flamecannon, incinerating a wide cone of skaven. They squealed in fear and pain, and the air was thick with the smoke of their burning.

'Here they come, lads!' bellowed Belegar. He gestured forwards with his hammer. 'At them!'

Shouting the war cries of their ancestors, the Iron Brotherhood ran into the mass of skavenslaves.

Queek watched patiently from a broken statue, squeaking orders when he felt his minions were letting him down. These were carried off by rapid scurriers, who forced their way into the ranks to seek out Queek's officers.

'You wait, little warlord, this is good,' hissed a voice only Queek could hear. The shadows cast by a pillar danced with more than the flamelight of battle. Queek's trophies were unusually silent, cowed by the verminlord.

'Pah! Queek hate waiting. Queek want to smash-kill dwarf long-fur and take head! But Queek is no fool, Lurklox-lord,' he said, the honorific unpleasant on his tongue. 'Dwarfs outnumbered ten to one. And this is but the first clawpack! They have no reserves. Queek guess that no dwarfs are anywhere else nearby, except sick, young and old.' He tittered. 'Young very tasty. Not so tough as old long-furs!' He sneered. 'Dwarfs are stupid, slow-thinking – not quick-clever like skaven – but they are strong. Very good armour. Fine weapons. Much singing.' He shuddered; the grinding-stone sound of the dwarfish battlesongs hurt his sensitive ears. 'No matter.' He waved his hand-paw dismissively. 'Under enough pressure, even dwarf-forged steel will snap. Soon will be time. Loyal Ska!'

'Yes, great Queek,' said Ska from the foot of the statue, where he restricted access to the mighty Queek.

'Ready my guard. Tell Grotoose now is time to loose his monsters.'

Queek watched the dwarf line. Having made a space at the front of the king's position, Belegar's Iron Brotherhood were retreating with mechanical precision from their initial foray to the safety of the line. Slaves scattered in the opposite direction, many shot down as they tried to flee. Others surged forwards, drawing themselves right onto the dwarfs' guns, where they died in droves. 'Pah!' said Queek. 'That is what slaves are for, yes-yes, Lurklox?'

There was no reply. The shadows were empty.

'He has scurry-gone,' said Ikit Scratch from his position along the central run of spikes on Queek's trophy rack.

The dead-thing sounded afraid.

From the gates behind Queek came an unpleasant bellow as Grotoose, the Great Packmaster of Clan Moulder, prodded his creatures into the fight. First to come were packs of slavering rat ogres, starved for the battle. They ran at the dwarf lines, barely directed by their packmasters.

Behind them came two gigantic Hell Pit abominations, their naked, maggoty skin rippling as they heaved themselves forwards, their many heads snapping at the air. The creatures, a hideous mix of flesh and machine, moved surprisingly quickly. Cannonballs slammed into the foremost abomination, and it howled in idiot rage. But its unnatural vitality saw its skin knit back together almost instantly, and it continued onwards. They squashed hundreds of slaves as they went towards the dwarf shield wall, but that did not matter. Queek had thousands and thousands more of such weak-meat. Every dwarf killed could never be replaced. He snickered as the first then the second abomination burst into the dwarf line, punching a big hole in it. No slaves followed into the openings, too terrified of the beasts. But the abominations were mighty enough alone. The entire dwarf east flank became bogged down fighting only one, while the other abomination turned at right angles to the beard-thing's battle line and began to work its way up towards the west flank, scattering those dwarfs it did not kill.

The rat ogres, meanwhile, loped forwards, giant hands grasping, swatting aside any slave that did not move away quickly enough. Queek watched as they swiftly arrived at the front of the battle. The largest pack was sent against a weak spot in the dwarf line hard by the king, a group of blue-capped beard-things wielding slow-loading crossbows. Such a pathetic weapon, typical of the dwarf-things: powerful but ponderous. Obsolete and doomed as their owners! The beard-things had time for three shots and no more before the rat ogres went raging into them. These dwarf-things were lightly armoured and did not last, the surviving few breaking and running, allowing the rat ogres to pile into the flank of Belegar's bodyguard.

Queek's eyes narrowed. This was the moment he had been waiting for. He bounded down the side of the statue, towards the front of his Red Guard.

'Now, Ska, now! Sound the advance!'

Skaven gongs rang. The slavemasters ceased cracking their whips, allowing the slaves to flee. They needed little prompting, their ragged remnants trickling away from the hall, leaving space for Queek's advance. The second line of skaven readied themselves, these well armed and armoured. Gongs clashed, bells rang. They started forwards.

At their centre went Queek Headtaker.

Belegar's hammer crushed the skull of his opponent, spattering all those around him with skaven brains. His fellows threw down their arms and ran for it, affording Belegar a moment's respite. From his vantage point, he could see up and down the line of his warriors. All were embattled. In two places his line had been breached by the abominations, and more deadly creatures were coming to attack them. Rat ogres were headed right for Clan Zhorrak. Belegar swore. The Blue Caps were no match for the beasts, and their supporting units were thoroughly occupied with the reeking monstrosity rampaging through his rear echelon.

'Blue Caps, bring them down!' he shouted, gesturing with his hammer.

The dwarfs shot numerous quarrels into the rat ogres, felling several. But there were well over a dozen of them, and most barrelled forwards ignoring the missiles sticking out of their bodies. With a hissing roar, the rat ogres bounded up the rubble pile, right into the Blue Caps. The dwarfs dropped their crossbows to pull out their double-handed axes. Bravery was not enough against the creatures, and the quarrellers were lightly armoured. Sword-long claws ripped the quarrellers apart. The rat ogres pushed through their formation, slaying many. By the time the Blue Caps of Clan Zhorrak broke, there were few left. Without stopping even to feed, the rat ogres pivoted and slammed right into the flank of the Iron Brotherhood. Signal flags fluttered on the opposite side of the cavern. Skaven war-gongs and bells tolled. Seeing the king's guard assailed, and the dwarf line sorely pressed all along its front, the skaven elite pressed forwards.

'Queek.' Belegar pointed towards the approaching skaven.

The rapidly thinning horde of slaves fled. Those who were slow were pushed forwards onto the axes and hammers of the dwarfs by the bigger skaven coming from behind. With horrifying speed, Queek and his Red Guard were upon the Iron Brotherhood.

The dwarf hammerers were holding their own against the rat ogres, smashing skulls, ribcages and knees with typically dwarfish efficiency. But they were pinned in place by the monsters, and could not react effectively to the charge of Queek's favoured.

'Protect the king! Protect the king!' shouted Brok Gandsson. A knot of hammerers hurried forwards, and surrounded Belegar. The Red Guard smashed into the dwarf front, huge ratmen almost umgi-tall, their sleek black fur rippling with muscle. They wore the tokens of their might: the teeth of black orcs and giants, stolen dwarfish talismans, beardscalps and skulls. Tirelessly the Iron Brotherhood fought them back; for every one hammerer who fell, three elite skaven paid with their lives.

Queek had not yet entered the fight, but that was about to change. He scurried up the rubble like it was a set of shallow steps, the hated Dwarf Gouger and his serrated sword held out either side. He launched himself skywards, spinning as he went. Using the momentum of his somersault, he punched the spiked side of Dwarf Gouger through a hammerer's helmet. Queek landed on the shoulders of another, his sword flashing down to end the dwarf's life before he could react, then leapt again. Hammers aimed at him seemed to move through treacled ale, so slow were they in comparison to the Headtaker. He leapt and spun and killed and killed and killed, unhindered by his heavy armour and unwieldy trophy rack. Without gaining so much as a scratch, he was in the middle of the Iron Brotherhood's formation, killing his way towards Belegar.

Belegar roared. 'Now, Notrigar! Now! Sound the horn! Sound the horn!'

The dwarf horn-bearer lifted the Golden Horn of the Iron Brotherhood to his lips. Bejewelled, ancient and honoured, the Golden Horn was among Clan Angrund's most treasured relics.

A bright note lifted over the battle, pure as fresh-cut diamond. The dwarfs took heart at its sounding, singing their songs of grudgement louder and fighting harder. But that was not the purpose of its winding.

A noise like a giant drum came from the Gate of Skalfdon, followed by the rattling of chains so heavy their movement could be heard through the thickness of the gate. The gate slid upwards, the stone moving smoothly over its ancient mechanisms, flooding the hall with golden light.

Roaring out the name of their leader, Golgfag Maneater's mercenary band marched into the hall. The dwarf line near to Durggan Stoutbelly's position opened, and the ogres barged their way into the fight, mournfang cavalry and sabretusks going before them, driving wolf rats away from the artillery battery. Skaven were flung high into the air by the force of the ogres' impact, and the mercenaries penetrated many yards into the seething fur before they were slowed. The ogres were untroubled by the skaven's weaponry, and killed the creatures easily, their cannon-wielding warriors slaughtering whole units with each blast. Golgfag's disciplined force then turned to the left, and began fighting their way down the front of the dwarf line, their cavalry pushing their way deep into the horde. The pressure came off Durggan's position, and the dwarf artillery intensified its fire, blasting, spearing, roasting and squashing hundreds of clanrats.

Belegar smiled. His eyes gleamed. He pointed his hammer at Queek. 'Come on then, Headtaker! Match your skill against mine. There is one head here you will never have!'

'Charge-kill!' screeched Queek. He leapt from rock to rock, then into the dwarfs.

Time slowed in his quick skaven mind. He reacted without thinking, relishing his skill. In battle he was free of scheming lords and underlings and verminlords. Here he was the mightiest, unmatched Queek, the greatest skaven warrior who had ever lived! No more, and no less.

He bounced and slaughtered his way through the clumsy beard-things, killing them with ease. Their hammers moved so slowly! His Red Guard, not so mighty as he, fared less well against the long-face-fur's elite, but it did not matter. All he needed was a little time, and for now the Red Guard were full of courage, scrambling forwards up the piled stone to replace those slain. Ska Bloodtail fought at their fore, knocking down dwarfs with every swing of his mighty paws.

Queek had come up the hill some way from the dwarf king. Once within the packed ranks of the dwarfs he started to kill his way towards Belegar. Jammed together, the beard-things were easy prey and handy stepping stones both.

A horn rang out several yards from Queek, the horrid nature of its tune hurting his ears. There was the sound of a gate lifting, and shortly the music of the battle changed. Queek was too involved in his own melee, too intent on the dwarf king, to take notice of what it betokened.

Belegar turned to face the Headtaker, a triumphant look on his flat, funnily furred face. He shouted a challenge at the warlord. Queek grinned.

He bounded from the shoulders of one of the king's tough-meats, killing him and two others before his paws touched the ground. Queek ducked an arcing hammer, and three more dwarfs died.

Then Queek was before King Belegar. The beard-thing glared at him, his eyes ablaze, the reek of hatred leaking from his body. His long-fur twitched on his patchy-bald face, his hand gripped his hammer tightly.

'So, Belegar beard-thing. You want to fight Queek? Good-good! Queek is here!' said Queek. He always used Khazalid when he spoke with the dwarf-things. It upset them so much.

Queek launched himself at the dwarf king so quickly it was hard to see him move. Belegar was ready, side-stepping the warlord's rush and landing a heavy blow on Queek's shoulder guard. Queek rolled with the hit, saving his shoulder, but his armour split with a shower of glinting, green-black motes of metal. He squealed at the shock. Belegar reeled, blasted back by the magic of Queek's warpshard armour.

The pair circled each other for a moment, Belegar with his guard up, his shield in front of him, hammer at the ready. Queek held both his weapons wide, his sinuous body low. He hissed and giggled, and his tail twitched behind him with excitement.

'So long I have waited for this!' he said; his use of the secret tongue of the dwarfs clearly riled the king.

'I too, filth. Today will be a great day when your entry might be stricken from the Dammaz Kron of Karak Eight Peaks!'

Queek attacked without warning, hammering Belegar with a flurry of blows from both his weapons. But slow and stolid though the beard-thing was, he was always in the right place, always ready with a block when Queek thought he had a killing blow. Queek twisted around Belegar's replying strikes, acrobatically evading blows that would have shattered his body had they connected. Five times Queek was sure he had landed a final blow on the king, five times Belegar deflected them. Queek was quick, Belegar skilled. After two minutes of fighting, all Queek had to show for his efforts were a series of small scratches on Belegar's shield.

Battle raged all around them, the dwarf and skaven ranks now thoroughly intermixed. The din of battle in the hall was amplified by the stone walls. Fire, blood and death were everywhere. Queek boiled with irritation. He hid it behind a wicked smile.

Queek wiped his mouth on the back of the paw holding Dwarf Gouger. 'Belegar-king good warrior! This is most satisfying for mighty Queek. Too many famed killers die too quick-quick. That very boring for Queek.'

Belegar glared back at him.

'But beard-thing king not as good as Queek! He cannot stand against mighty Queek for long. Already, Queek has slain many beard-things. See?' He waggled his back, sending a dried dwarf head's beard swinging atop his trophy rack.

# Belegar Ironhammer

## True King of Karak Eight Peaks

From his earliest days, Belegar knew that he had a great destiny – to reconquer the lost hold of Karak Eight Peaks and atone for the sins of King Lunn, the city's last ruler before its fall. Fifty years ago, he achieved his goal, and ever since, he has struggled to hold the small portion of the city he reconquered against the skaven, orcs and goblins that have long called it home. Recently, a mighty blow was struck as, with the aid of High King Thorgrim Grudgebearer, the orc warlord Gorfang was slain, leaving one less enemy to fight and crossing out many grudges from the Dammaz Kron. But with the goblin Skarsnik and the skaven Queek still at large, Belegar remains embattled, and as time grinds on and tumultuous events engulf the world, even he is forced to admit that the prospect of ever truly reclaiming Karak Eight Peaks looks bleak.

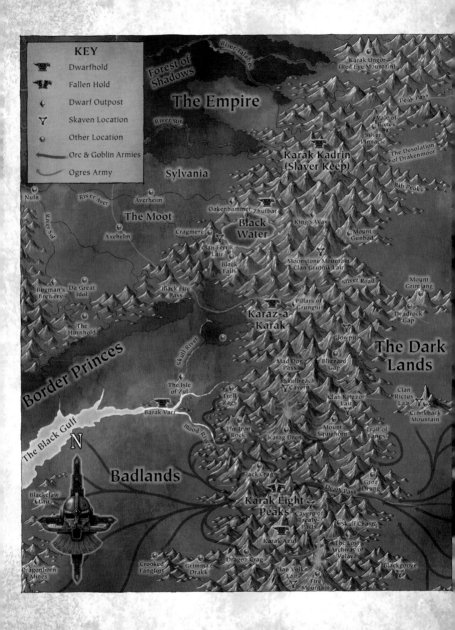

KEY

Dwarfhold

Fallen Hold

Dwarf Outpost

Skaven Location

Other Location

Orc & Goblin Armies

Ogres Army

Forest of Shadows

River Talabec

River Stir

The Empire

Karak Ungor
(Red Eye Mountain)

Peak Pass

Vale of
Bones

Silver
Pinnacle

The Desolation
of Drakenmoor

Karak Kadrin
(Slayer Keep)

Rib Peaks

Nuln

River Aver

Averheim

The Moot

Oakenhammer   Zhufbar

Black
Water

King's Way

Mount
Gunbad

River Sol

Axehelm

Cragmere

Clan Ferrik
Lair

Black
Falls

Moonstone Mountain
Clan Grubnik Lair

Silver Road

Mount
Grimfang

Sylvania

Bugman's
Brewery

Da Great
Idol

Black Fire
Pass

Black Fire
Pass

Karaz-a-
Karak

Pillars of
Grungni

Deadrock
Gap

The Hornhold

Border Princes

Skull River

Glowpit

The Dark
Lands

The Isle
of Zul

Barak Varr

Mad Dog
Pass

Blizzard
Gap

Skullreach
Cavern

Clan
Rictus
Lair

Troll
Zags

Clan Krizzor
Lair

Crookback
Mountain

The Black Gulf

N

Blood River

The Iron
Rock

Karag Dron

Mount
Squighorn

Trail of
Fangs

Badlands

Black Crag

Groz
Drung

Blackclaw
Lair

Death Pass

Karak Eight
Peaks

Cavern of
Treaty Pacts

Skull Chasm

Dragonhorn
Mines

Crooked
Fangfort

Grimmaz
Drakk

Dragon Crag

Karak Azul

Clan Volkn
Lair

Fire
Mountain

The Lost
Archway of
Valaya

Blackgouge

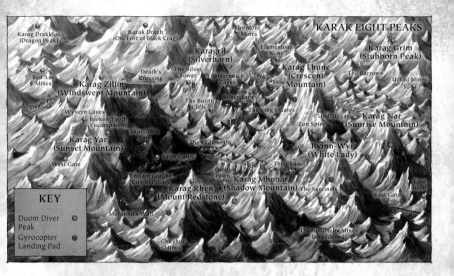

## KARAK EIGHT PEAKS

Karag Drakkloc (Dragon Peak)

Karak Drazh (Orc Fort of Black Crag)

Irontoit Mines

Karagril (Silverhorn)

Flamestone Mine

Karag Lhune (Crescent Mountain)

Karag Grim (Stubborn Peak)

Red Axe Mines

Death's Crossing

The Silver Tower

Spidernotch Caves

Death Pass

The Barrows

Uzkul Mines

Karag Zilfin (Windswept Mountain)

Death Pass

Silver Tarn

Wyvern Caves

The Burnt Cliffs

The King's Gates

Broken Tooth Encampment

Skarsnik's Lair

Und-Uzgar

Zon Spire

Karag Nar (Sunrise Mountain)

Karag Yar (Sunset Mountain)

The Endless Pit

Kvinn-Wyr (White Lady)

West Gate

Grim Gates

Grobi Town

The Citadel

Entrance to the City of Pillars

Karag Mhonar (Shadow Mountain)

Karag Rhyn (Mount Redstone)

The Sentinels

East Horn

Morzund's Wall

East Gate

Diamondhelm Mines (abandoned)

Ghuzhul Mines

### KEY

Doom Diver Peak ◎

Gyrocopter Landing Pad ◉

## THE UNDERGROUND KINGDOM

Karag Zilfin (Windswept Mountain)

Karagril (Silverhorn)

Karag Lhune (Crescent Mountain)

Wyvern Caves

The High Mine

Gyrocopter Landing Area

Grung Zilfin

The Foundries

Skarsnik's Lair

The Hall of the Moon

Zilfin Heart Chamber

Zon Spire

Hall of Oaths

The Grand Urbaz (Trade Hall)

The Grand Irkul

Grim Gates

The Citadel

Hall of Chiselwards

Chamber of Runes

Carven Tomb

The Grand Forge

Entrance to the City of Pillars

The Great Gate of Defiance

The King's Hall

Temple of Grungni

Hall of Pillars

Crossroads

The Vault of Ancestors

Grobi Town

Hall of Pillared Iron

King's Armoury

Treasure Vaults

The Grey Forge

The Great Mines

The Great Gromril Mine

Arch of Kings

Hall of Clan Skaldon

To the East Gates

The Grand Tombs

The Great Staff

Tomb

Fungal Forest

To the West Gates

Squig Cavern

The Grand Avenue of the Ungdrin (The Underway)

The Cavern of Stars

The Hall of Reckoning

Queek's Trophy Den

The Grand Avenue

The Thune Deeps

Hall of Ghosts

The Cavern of Red Eyes

Tombs

Breeder City

Drakk's Rest

The Bone Caves

Zilfin Dum

Worm Pit

The Trench

Skaven Tunnels

Skaven Lairs

The Rift Mine

The Grand Abyss

# QUEEK HEADTAKER

## WARLORD OF CLAN MORS

Respected and feared across
the skaven Under-Empire and
beyond, Queek Headtaker
is utterly deadly, his prowess
in battle legendary amongst
allies and enemies alike. Queek
is also widely considered to
be quite, quite mad, known
for talking to the heads that
adorn his trophy rack. Queek,
however, knows that he's not
mad. After all, if he were,
how could they answer him?
Most recently, Queek has
been ensconced in a three-
way war beneath Karak Eight
Peaks, vying with the dwarf
King Belegar and the goblin
Skarsnik for dominion over that
ancient realm. Queek cares not
for conquest though, nor for
the cataclysmic events in the
outside world – he's only there
because there are plenty of
enemies to slay. Of late, he has
begun to feel himself slow – he
is nearly ten years old, and he
knows that his end is near…
But if Queek is to die, he will
make sure that all his enemies
follow him into the grave.

'Beard-thing king's littermate. He was very poor. Not so good as strong-meat Belegar, but Queek kill him anyway. Now I kill-slay you. I bring him out specially from Queek's trophy room, so he see you die-die. Soon your head will sit next to his. You will have long-ages to discuss how mighty Queek is. Won't that be nice for long-white face-fur?'

To Queek's frustration, Belegar did not react as so many beard-things would at his taunting – with a wild bellow of rage and a foolish attack. Instead, he warily circled the skaven.

And then he made his mistake. The tiniest opening. Belegar's eyes flicked involuntarily up to the head of his brother impaled upon the spike.

Queek reacted instantly. Belegar was ready again, catching the blow of Dwarf Gouger upon his shield, but he was distracted and the block was not as true as his others had been. The shield was slightly too far out; it would take a fraction of a second longer to reposition. Queek made as if he were to make a second swipe. Belegar tensed to react. Queek swept Dwarf Gouger up and away, pirouetting past the king's shield, putting all his weight and momentum into a backhand blow that sent Dwarf Gouger's vicious spike through the king's gromril and into his side. Queek yanked it free, and danced backwards, but too slowly. Belegar slammed him in the face with his shield, denting Queek's helmet. A following blow from his hammer drew sparks from the rock as Queek rolled aside. He was licking dwarf blood from the maul as he regained his feet. He tittered, although his head rang like a screaming bell.

'Mighty Queek!' bellowed Ska. He was throttling a dwarf in ornate armour in one hand. The creature's face went purple, and Ska cast it aside with a clatter. 'We are in much-much danger!'

Queek's eyes darted about. Ska was correct. Big-meat ogres and dwarf-things had pushed back the skaven line. The left flank was melting away. The dwarfs were occupied in containing the Hell Pit abomination there, and that was all that was saving his clanrats from destruction. How long it would hold them back was uncertain; it was surrounded on all sides by angry beard-things and was being hacked into pieces by their axes. The other abomination continued to wreak havoc, but elsewhere ogres pushed deep into the skaven horde with seeming impunity, while the dwarfs' cannons were firing freely into Queek's army. Worse still, the last rat ogre went down as Queek watched, its head smashed into a bloody pulp. The king's guard were now free to concentrate on Queek's Red Guard. Their formation tightened up, they began to push forwards, and the Red Guard were dying quickly, their morale wavering. Queek was in danger of being surrounded, and cut off.

Queek took all this in an instant. He made his decision to retreat just as quickly. He backed up. Belegar screamed at him, charging forwards with his hammer raised. Queek leapt out of the way, landing on the edge of the rubble pile's cliff-like face.

'Run-retreat!' he squeaked. 'Fall back, quick-quick!'

Gratefully, the Red Guard fled, more of them bludgeoned to death as they showed their tails.

'We meet again soon, long-fur,' chittered Queek, dodging hammer blows as dwarfs interposed themselves between him and the king. 'Until then, Queek takes another trophy.'

He jumped from the circle of dwarfs, pushing off with one foot-paw from the helmet of one of Belegar's warriors. He aimed himself at the king's banner bearer, fending off the warrior's hopeless parry. Queek relished the look of surprise and fear in the beard-thing's face as his sword descended, cutting perfectly into the weaker mail at his neck and severing the dwarf's head. The head toppled along with the standard, the metal icon painted red by fountaining blood.

Ska scooped up the fallen prize, and together they fled the stony mound.

'Notrigar! Notrigar!' howled Belegar.

'Oh dear,' said Queek to Ska as they scurried away. 'Look like long-fur beard-thing lose another littermate.'

The dwarfs cheered as the skaven fell back, hurling insults after Queek. Some of the skaven army retreated in good order – Queek's guard and his other stormvermin units held firm – but most did not and scrambled for the exits. Ogres ran them down without mercy, knocking handfuls of them flying with each swing of their massive clubs and swords. Green trails in the air marked out where jezzail teams aimed for the mercenaries, but the toxic bullets seemed not to affect them much, and it took several rounds to bring even a single ogre down.

The battle-dirges of the dwarfs changed. Victory songs erupted along the line at the flight of the skaven.

At the centre, the Iron Brotherhood found themselves unengaged. They yelled insults and banged their hammer hafts on the rock and on their shields.

Brok Gandsson sought out his lord, who stood at the brink of the cliff, looking down upon the scattering of bodies and blood-washed rock.

'A great victory, my king!' said Brok, his eyes bright, the shame of his murder of Douric forgotten for the moment.

Belegar looked with hollow eyes at the headless body of his cousin.

'My lord?' said Brok. He gestured for another to take up the fallen standard.

'It is not a victory, not yet. If we prevail, and I say "if" carefully, Brok Gandsson, a dozen of our finest lie dead around us. Grungni alone knows how many others have fallen.'

'Shall we pursue them? We stand a chance of catching the

Headtaker,' said Brok keenly. 'Many are the grudges that can be stricken from the Book by his death.'

'Pursuing Queek is futile,' said Belegar. 'We will be drawn into the mass of troops waiting for us and killed piecemeal. We have other foes of direr nature, and closer to hand.' He pointed his hammer at the second abomination. The first was dead, but in their fury at the losses of their kin, the dwarfs of the Stoneplaits clan continued to hack at it. The second was dragging its vile bulk through the army, mindlessly unaffected by the general rout of the skaven. A bold unit of miners stood their ground in front of its heaving bulk. They buried their mattocks in its sickly white hide, only for them to be torn out of their hands by the convulsions of its flesh. A cannonball smacked into it, as effectual as a child's marble impacting dough. 'There is yet one more task for our hammers.'

'My king!' Brok bowed. He ordered the Iron Brotherhood to come about face. The king marched with them, his wound concealed by his shield. He gritted his teeth against the pain and told no one of it.

The abomination reared over them, stinking of decayed meat and warpstone-laden chemicals. The weapons of half a dozen clans were embedded in its flabby sides, its underside slick and red with the blood of those it had crushed under its enormous weight.

Upon seeing their king and his guard arrive, the remaining miners fighting the creature took heart and shouted their war cries anew. Those without weapons took up whatever they could find to assail the creature.

'The heads! Destroy the heads,' ordered Belegar.

'They're high up for a killing stroke,' said Brok.

'Then let's get its attention,' said Belegar, 'and make it bring them nearer our hammers.'

He strode forwards. Shouldering his shield, he swung the Ironhammer two-handed, smacking the thing hard on the rump. Waves rippled away from the impact. A second blow shattered a leg, a third a wheel grafted to its rear.

Finally recognising what it felt for pain, the abomination howled and reared up, dragging a pair of dwarf miners off their feet. They hung on to their picks for grim death as it lumbered around to face this new irritation.

'Khazuk! Khazuk! Khazuk-ha!' shouted Brok.

The hammerers advanced. Their numbers had been whittled down by a quarter in their earlier fight, and they had been battling for a good part of the morning without rest or refreshment. Lesser creatures would have been weary, and suffered for it. But these were dawi, many highborn, all warriors of the finest mettle. In their endurance they were indomitable, and they swung their hammers as if taking them up for the first time that day. Like triphammers in the forges of Zhufbar, the hammers of the Iron Brotherhood fell in a wave, pounding upon the skin of the horror, snapping bone and mashing flesh. The creature roared, swiping with one of its many arms. The first rank of hammerers were knocked down like pins in a game of skittles, but thanks to their armour few were hurt. The second rank stepped up to deliver another rippled blow. A grasping hand was shattered, a bloated paw burst. Brok Gandsson bellowed a challenge and ran at the side of the creature, pushing himself up the shattered machinery crudely grafted to its limbs. His feet bounced on its rubbery hide, but he kept his footing, ran to the top and cracked it hard over one of its nine heads. The neck attaching it to the sack of its body cracked, and the head sagged, dead. The abomination flung its upper portion to and fro, sending Gandsson flying.

Shouting mightily, the hammerers followed their champion, surrounding the creature and smashing at it furiously. The abomination thrashed, howling horribly. It killed but a few of the dwarfs, and its lower portion was soon so pulverised that its unnatural vitality could not heal all the tears in its flanks. Crying, it sank low, biting at its tormenters, allowing the hammerers access to its heads by doing so. These the dwarfs smashed to pulp one after another as soon as the snapping jaws came near.

Finally, the last head was split. With a tremendous shudder and a pitiful moan, the abomination breathed its last through pulverised lips and broken jaws.

The hammerers gave a ragged cheer.

'Well done, Brok Gandsson,' said Belegar, as the Iron Brotherhood helped their bruised but otherwise unhurt champion to his feet with many a clap on the back. 'A deed worthy of the ancestors.'

Brok bowed his head. 'My thanks, my king.'

'Now blow the Golden Horn once more. It's time we left this battlefield and retreated to the next defence.' Belegar looked around sadly. To do so meant leaving the deeps completely in the hands of his enemies. From now on, they would be fighting for the citadel's roots alone.

The war for the underhalls was lost, probably forever.

The horn blower lifted the sacred relic to his lips, but did not blow.

'What...?' said Belegar. All dawi eyes looked to the ground.

Through the ground came a rumbling sensation that built steadily until the floor itself vibrated. No dwarf could mistake it for an earthquake. The sensation was too regular, too localised for natural perturbation of the rock.

'Tunnelling machines,' gasped Brok.

'Reform!' bellowed Belegar. 'Reform... ahh.' He gasped, and clutched at his side. Red blood dripped upon the floor. His head swam. A strange, unholy heat radiated from his wound.

'My lord,' said Brok in dismay. 'You are wounded!'

Belegar shouted back, annoyed at himself for betraying his injury. 'It is nothing – a scratch. I gave the Headtaker more to remember me by than this, believe me. I commanded the army to reform. Look to them, not me. Be about it quickly, or all is lost!'

'Yes, my lord.' Brok relayed the order, and his orders were passed on by others. Dwarfs were efficient in all things, and very shortly horns sounded as the dwarfs called back their warriors from the pursuit.

A sound came from behind the Iron Brotherhood's new square.

'My king!' shouted Brok.

Brok pointed at the abomination. Its skin shuddered. Three of its mouths worked. Bones cracked as jaws reset. Eyes grew bright. Flesh knitted together. It vomited freely from all of these mouths, and with a pained squeal, it jerked fully back into life and hauled itself up once more.

# FIFTEEN

*Enter Skarsnik*

Queek's scampering slowed. He looked to the ground and giggled. 'Halt-stop!' he called, holding up his hand-paw.

The Red Guard tittered, recognising the rumbling for what it was – the anticipated arrival of their reinforcements from the third clawpack. They formed up. Other units were slowing, their flight turning. For a moment they stood in a state of stilled disorganisation, before flowing back together, units consolidating almost magically from the chaotic mass of the rout. From the gateways into the hall more skaven issued. This was the remainder of the first clawpack, ordered to join battle by Queek only when the tunnelling machines made their presence known.

'Hehehehe,' snickered Queek. 'Now we see who is the best, Belegar-king. See, loyal Ska, how the dwarf-things have broken their line in their foolishness. Too quickly they are to believe Queek would run-run! They have fallen for mighty Queek's trap! They will all die-die, no matter how fast they stump-run to find their clawpacks again!'

Ska frowned. To his simple mind, it had looked like they were about to lose. Ska wasn't particularly quick, but he was smart enough to know saying so would not be wise. 'Yes, mighty Queek,' he said instead.

The vibrations grew stronger, a bone-shaking grinding joining them. The entire hall rumbled. Just when it seemed they couldn't possibly get any louder, the tone of the noise changed and piles of splintered rock mounded up in various places in the hall.

Queek leapt onto a boulder and brandished his weapons. 'Be ready!' shouted Queek, his voice barely carrying over the noise of the tunnelling machines. 'Third clawpack arrives! Today, mighty Queek take long-fur's head!'

'Queek! Queek! Queek!' squeaked his army.

The snout of a drilling machine appeared from one of the oversized molehills to the north, fifty yards short of the rapidly reforming dwarf army. The drill poked a few feet overground, then withdrew. With nothing to support it, the centre of the hillock collapsed, leaving a gaping hole in the ground.

Queek waited gleefully, his tongue searching out fresh scraps of dwarf flesh and blood in his fur.

Green light issued from the hole. Smoke poured after it. Other machines were poking up out of the floor and walls, and retracting, leaving fresh tunnel mouths behind them. One by one they fell silent and the tremors dwindled.

'Not long now, loyal Ska. Truly is Queek the most cunning of generals.'

'The most cunning of the cunningest,' agreed Ska.

Something emerged from the hole. It was a long way to see for Queek's weak skaven eyesight. He squinted hard and made out a bouncing, round shape headed for the dwarf lines.

'That not third clawpack...' said Ska in dismay.

'Queek can see that!' squeaked Queek loudly. 'Queek know!'

The hole burst outwards as dozens more of the creatures

came boinging out, their powerful hindlegs propelling them at great speed into the air. They slapped into the ground, rolling and bouncing, shoving themselves off with their legs to repeat the process. The mushroom stink of green-things blew from the holes.

'Skarsnik!' chittered Queek, stamping from foot to foot. 'Skarsnik! What is this? How does he know? How does he still *live?*'

As if invoked by the name of their king, the green-things poured in great multitudes from the holes in the ground. Regiments of night goblin archers came first, firing as they ran, the new tunnel mouths wide enough to let them come out four abreast. The skaven, expecting allies to come from the ground, were taken by surprise, and some among the newly rallied army were seized again by panic. Black-fletched arrows fell among them, bringing forth many death-squeaks. The massed skaven retreated from the holes, allowing legions of goblins to flood the hall.

There were many tribes, and many kinds of green-thing. Queek narrowed his eyes and hissed. 'Imp-thing been busy!'

The greenskins wasted no time in attacking both armies. From a hole opened right before the Gate of Skalfdon, ranks of tittering spearmen, drunk on fungus beer, marched out. They jogged into position on the far side of the dwarfs. Staggering fanatics carrying massive iron balls were pushed from their regiments. They blinked and stared around themselves, laughing and drooling. And then they began to spin.

Faster and faster they went, round and round, the drugs coursing through their veins allowing them to drag the huge weapons they carried up and get them airborne. In a blur of metal and spinning pointed hoods, they connected with dwarfs turning to face the goblins behind them.

The fanatics moved quite slowly, but such was their momentum that they smashed the dwarf shield wall apart, caving in the best armour and pulping bodies. If their initial impact was bloody, their lives after were short. Some spun through into the skaven on the far side; others wavered unsteadily along the dwarf line or turned back upon their frantically shrieking comrades. Ultimately, they came variously to throttle themselves on their chains, collapse exhausted or crash into the pillars and rubble piles that made the hall so hazardous for them.

It did not matter, the damage was done. The goblins followed their fanatics quickly, charging the disordered dwarf lines.

Squigs were running amok through the dwarf army, gobbling down a dwarf with every bound. Queek's quick mind followed his quick eyes and nose as he judged the situation. 'Now would be a good time to fall back, lad,' said Krug, from his perch.

'Oh, good time for you to talk now, dead-thing,' muttered Queek. Still, he was of half a mind to follow the dwarf king's advice, retreating while the beard-things were occupied with a new enemy. Let them wipe each other out. Queek would come back for whoever was left later.

He would have done so too, had Skarsnik himself not appeared.

Skarsnik rose from a hole in the ground in the very middle of the hall. Explosions and flashes of magic surrounded him, the indescribable noise of squigpipes played him in, making sure all saw his grand entrance. He walked cockily from the hole, his attendants carrying banners stuck with the heads of the leaders of the third clawpack. He walked to a pile of fallen rock, and climbed unhurriedly to the top, his rotund pet obediently following. Queek squealed in annoyance. The sheer arrogance of Skarsnik enraged him. He behaved like he was the best, when who was the best? Queek was!

'Listen, youse lot!' shouted the green-thing, his voice carried on the magic of the smelly lunatic who always accompanied him. Sure enough, he was there, blowing foul fumes from his pipe not far behind the king's right shoulder. 'I's the king here, so why don't all you furboys and stunties zog off. Give to Skarsnik what belongs to Skarsnik, and we'll call it quits.'

With that inspired piece of oratory, Skarsnik held aloft his prodder and let a stream of violent green energy streak into the roof. Razor-sharp shards of rock blasted out from the impact, slicing into whoever was below. Which was mostly goblins, but Skarsnik, true to form, didn't care about that.

This was altogether too much for Queek.

'Skarsnik! Imp-thing! Kill-kill!' he shrieked. He ran forward, leaving his guard behind. They milled about confused until Ska Bloodtail squeak-ordered, 'After him! After the mighty Queek!'

Seeing their lord and his guard surge ahead, the skaven clan leaders, clawpack masters and other officers decided they had better advance. Their ragged charge became organised as more of them came to the same conclusion and followed.

The skaven were so intent on the goblins that they didn't notice the ogres change sides.

'Keep up the fire to the front there!' shouted Durggan Stoutbelly.

The cannons boomed over the heads of the Axes of Norr, detailed to guard the battery. It was an honourable task, given to them in thanks for their heroic efforts at the door of Bar-Undak.

Borrik ducked as a bolt of green lightning blasted past his face. He snarled in the direction of Skarsnik. The goblin king was stood upon a pile of rock in the centre of the battlefield, capering madly.

'He looks pleased with himself,' muttered Gromley.

'Aye,' said Grunnir, spitting on the floor. 'Little green kruti.'

This is not looking good, not looking good at all, thought Borrik. The goblin ambush had surprised both armies, but the dwarfs suffered the most for it. Their flank, anchored by Durggan's war machines, had become cut off from the bulk of the dwarf throng as a prong of the greenskin ambushers pushed its way through the army. Worse, although Belegar was sounding the orders for retreat, their way from the cavern was blocked by hundreds of grobi and no small number of urk emerging from at least two fresh tunnels.

And there were the ogres as well. This wasn't a very good day.

'Here they come again, honourless fat baruzdaki,' said Borrik. 'Norrgrimlings-ha!' he shouted.

A regiment of swag-bellied Ironguts ran up the slope at the much-depleted battery. Only two cannons remained. The others were silent, destroyed by magic or their crew all slain. Dead goblins, skaven, dwarfs and ogres were intermingled around the battery, their corpses dangling from the earthworks and dry-stone walls erected before the battle.

'Fire!' shouted Durggan. With a deafening bang and gouts of smoke, the cannons unloaded two lots of grapeshot right into the teeth of the ogre charge. The last few Forgefuries added their hand-cannon shots to the fusillade. The front rank, four ogres wide, stumbled and fell.

Gromley cocked his eyebrow. 'Now I don't say it often, but that was impressive.'

'Well I live and breathe, at least for a few moments longer,' said Borrik, shouting over the ogres' deafening war cry. 'Gromley impressed by something! I reckon I can die happy, and maybe not a little surprised.'

Gromley's sour response was lost to the clatter of ogre gutplates hitting gromril. The thin line of the remaining Axes of

Norr, five all told now, bowed but did not break. 'At 'em, lads!' shouted Borrik, and hewed an ogre's foot away with a single blow of his rune axe. The ogre hopped about, crashing down when Gromley took his other leg off at the knee.

'Serves 'em right for being so tall,' he said.

The Axes of Norr hurled back the charge. The remaining ogres broke and fled. The dwarfs let out a small cheer from tired throats.

'I'd kill for some ale right now,' said Borrik.

'You are killing,' said Gromley, 'but I don't see any ale at the end of this.'

'There might have been more, if the rats hadn't done for poor old Yorrik,' said Grunnir. 'Oh, look at that, they got Albok.'

'Grungni curse those treacherous ogres,' spat Gromley.

Albok lay dead, his head open from the crown to his nose, his brains glistening inside his broken helmet. Four Axes of Norr remained standing.

Insane tittering came at them. A pair of fanatics spun into view. Two shots rang out, and both goblins fell with smoking holes between their eyes. Borrik looked up to see Durggan blowing the smoke from his pistols.

'Aye, good lad, Albok,' said Borrik. He lifted his shield. Every sinew and muscle twanged with fatigue. There wasn't much more to say to it than that. They'd grieve properly later, if there was a later.

Goblins milled about just out of grapeshot range, the corpses of the three previous failed charges buried now under dead ogres. 'That's right,' said Gromley. 'You stay down there.'

'Hang on, lads, this might be us,' said Grunnir.

Golgfag was marching up the hill, his maneaters behind him.

'They're a mean crew and no mistake,' said Gromley.

Borrik looked down his meagre line of clansmen, four Axes, three Forgefuries. Where had they all gone? He remembered a time when the Norrgrimlings had been a large and prosperous clan. He was going to have a lot of explaining to do when he got to the Halls of the Ancestors. 'Grunnir, Gromley, Uli, Fregar, Tordrek, Gurt, Vituk... I'd say it's been an honour...'

'Not living, breathing and fighting with this lot of grumbaki!' said Grunnir.

'Hush! The time for jesting's done.' He gave Grunnir one of his sterner looks. 'It's been more than an honour,' continued Borrik. 'A lot more. I could say more, I could wax lyrical, but you know what I mean. We're dawi, aren't we? I'm not an elf to collapse into tears and give everyone a cuddle.'

'Dawr spoken,' said Gromley.

Golgfag's ogres were breaking into a charge.

'Norrgrimling khazuk! Khazuk-ha!' Borrik said. His warriors repeated the words. He wondered what each was thinking here, at the last stand of the Axes of Norr.

He supposed it didn't matter. What mattered was that they stood by him until the end.

Durggan was lining the cannons up to get one last shot on the ogres. One of his crew let out a cry and fell, a black-fletched grobi arrow sticking from his throat. Another died, slumping over the gun with a warpstone bullet embedded in his chest.

'Keep it up! Keep it up!' barked Durggan. 'We'll not fall without one last blast, eh, lads?' He helped the remaining crewman of the cannon to line up the barrel. The second was ready, the last dwarf of its crew grasping the firing string, but Golgfag raised a pistol as big as a dwarf handgun and blasted him off his feet. As he was thrown backwards, the dwarf jerked the cord. An ogre took the ball to his gutplate, sinking to his knees with blood gushing around his hands. The other ogres hurled themselves into the Norrgrimlings. Golgfag singled out the thane, and attacked.

As proud and skilful a warrior as Borrik was, he could not stand against the Maneater. Golgfag quickly put him down with a punishing blow to the head. Through blurring vision, Borrik saw his remaining clans-dwarfs smashed down, barged off balance by fat stomachs, then bludgeoned by umgi-high clubs.

The maneaters wheeled and went for the cannon. Durggan, working on his own now, struggled to get the last piece aligned.

'Not today, stunty,' said Golgfag. He drew another pistol and blew out Durggan's guts with it. So died the chief engineer of Karak Eight Peaks.

The ogres halted. There were none left alive on the high ground except Borrik. He couldn't move.

'Look at this lot,' said Golgfag waving his giant hand out over the battlefield. 'This is madness! Nobody's going to win this. Stunties in the north-east, skaven to the south, gobboes in the middle. It don't make sense.'

'They are not soldiers, not like we are, captain,' said one ogre, almost as massive as his master and dressed in out-sized Imperial finery.

'What now, Captain Golgfag?' said another.

'I reckon we're done here. Fulfilled our side of the contract. We're never going to see that dwarf king's gold if we stick around for the end of this mess. It don't matter whose side we're on. Besides, I got a healthy down payment.' He patted a bulging pouch at his side. A gold object was poking out of it. Even through his near insensibility, Borrik recognised the crown of Vala-Azrilungol, lost for ages. He added that to his growing mental list of grudges.

'Kulak, shout the withdrawal. We're leaving.'

'Captain! What about that one? He's still alive,' said someone Borrik couldn't see.

Golgfag swung around and looked right at Borrik. The ogre chief walked towards him, his boots filling Borrik's vision. A rough hand grabbed his mail and rolled him over. Borrik found himself staring into the lumpen face of the world's foremost mercenary captain.

'Tough little buggers, your lot,' said Golgfag. 'I really hate fighting dwarfs. You take ages to kill. All that armour! Haha! Ha!' he laughed, as if to include Borrik in his joke. A gale of halitosis swept over Borrik, rank with poorly cooked meat. 'It ain't nothing personal, stunty. Business is business.' Golgfag patted Borrik's chest with a massive hand.

'The lads are coming, captain,' said the finely dressed maneater.

'Right then,' said Golgfag, looking away. 'West tunnel, third in. Looks very badly guarded. We'll fight our way out that way. Any objections?'

None came.

'Good.' Golgfag hitched his trousers into a more comfortable position and stood, his gut obscuring Borrik's view of his face.

'What about him?' said an ogre. 'You not going to kill him?'

'The stunty? Nah,' said Golgfag, leering down at Borrik. 'It's your lucky day, shorty. Like I said, I've fulfilled my part of the contract. I've finished here.'

The ogres left Borrik lying in the shattered remnants of his clan.

If I ever get out of this alive, he thought, I'm donating my entire treasury to the priesthood of Valaya, and then I'm taking the Slayer oath.

Queek butchered goblins by the score. Spears of wood and toughened mushroom stalk shattered under the blows of his weapons. He snarled and spat as he slew them, squeaking in frustration as his blades became fouled in their filthy robes. He was attempting to reach the hated imp, Skarsnik, the so-called king. But for every goblin he slew, there seemed to be a dozen more. They tried to retreat from him, and wisely, but could not for they were packed into the hall so tightly. The dwarf artillery had been silenced, but Skarsnik was still blasting skaven and dwarf-things alike with impunity with the prodder. Queek had witnessed Skarsnik's magical trident at work many times in the past, but never like this. It glowed with green light so bright it was nearly white. The glare of it left painful after-images streaking across his vision. The energy bolts it threw seemed many times more powerful, and more numerous, than ever before.

'Let me pass! Get out of Queek's way!' shouted Queek at a group of skaven who found themselves in his path. They were lowly clanrats, scared beyond comprehension. They stared at him stupidly as he yelled at them to move. They did not, so he cut them down where they stood. Skarsnik was now only one hundred and fifty scurries from him. The goblin had seen him and was gesticulating obscenely. A bolt of green light came after his gestures, singeing Queek's whiskers as he threw himself out of the way.

'You wait-wait, green-thing. Today you die-die!'

Queek leapt onto a pile of rubble, and from there threw himself into the melee swirling around its base. He cleared himself a space, slaughtering combatants from both sides. An ogre was close, isolated from his fellows a few yards further on. Queek launched himself at it, slamming his pick's spike into the creature's forehead. He used this to arrest his leap – curving over the ogre's back, he yanked Dwarf Gouger out in a spray of blood and brains. Landing nimbly, he found himself alone on bare rock, as skaven, goblins and the ogre's comrades fled from him.

The way to Skarsnik was clear.

Queek gathered himself for another leap, tittering evilly.

The ground shook. Light blasted around him and he fell to the floor, Dwarf Gouger clattering from his grasp. His ears rang from the blast. When he looked up, goblin and skaven corpses smoked all around him.

At first he thought he had been hit by Skarsnik, but the goblin was gone from his rock pile. Away to the right of where Skarsnik had capered, Queek caught a glimpse of pale grey fur, almost white.

'White-fur!' hissed Queek. 'You pay for this with your head!'

Kranskritt rose from a tunnel in the centre of the cavern, arcane power crackling around him, and came to rest on the side of a toppled pillar. He snarled imperiously and flung out one hand-paw. The ground rumbled. Fissures opened like hungry mouths, swallowing creatures of all kinds indiscriminately. Queek started, meaning to run-scurry at the white-fur and strike him dead. But there was something else with him, a shadow behind him, half hidden by the black glare of Kranskritt's magic.

Verminlord. Queek snarled. At first he thought it the same one as had come to him, but it was not. The horns were different, for one, and it was less hidden in the shadows than the other.

'Two verminlords in the City of Pillars?' he whispered to himself, ill at ease. 'Unprecedented.'

The ground shook regularly as Kranskritt and his master – for the verminlord was almost certainly the weak-willed sorcerer's ruler – unleashed a storm of earthquakes, sending even the agile Queek staggering. Snarling, he ran towards Kranskritt.

'Fool-fool! Stop-stop!' shouted Queek.

To his surprise, Kranskritt heard him and looked down. An expression of pure, malicious calculation crossed his face. His hands rose. Queek tensed, ready to dodge. His warpstone amulet pulsed with protective magics.

The moment passed and Kranskritt performed a deep bow. One without any sign of submission, the sort of acknowledgement given to an equal! Kranskritt was getting too confident. Another reason to kill him.

'Do not despair, mighty Queek!' the sorcerer shouted over the noise of his patron's continuing magical barrage. 'I came from my hunt in the mountains as quick-quick as I could. Clan Scruten will aid mighty Queek and save the day from green-thing treachery!'

The verminlord loomed over Kranskritt. The grey seer's tail swished easily, given confidence by the proximity of the daemon. Queek snarled. His mind worked fast. If he killed Kranskritt now, it would be in front of everyone at a time when the sorcerer was helping turn the battle. Furthermore, he had a verminlord stood right behind him. Queek fleetingly considered matching his blades against it, but wisely decided not to.

He shouted instead. 'Fool weak-meat! You send the green-imp scurrying away from mighty Queek's blade! You will pay for this!'

'And mighty Queek was doing so well without me,' said Kranskritt sarcastically. 'See! The goblin tunnels collapse. They are trapped! You win-win, mighty Queek. You are correct – I should be paid for this. I should be paid many-much warp-tokens, not with unkind bite of steel.'

Queek bared his fangs and held his serrated sword up in challenge to the seer. Then with a swift turn he sprang away, seeking others to vent his anger upon.

He would kill Kranskritt later. He promised himself that he would.

A great tremor ran through the ground as the skaven daemon and his pet sorcerer unleashed another earthquake. The goblins' tunnels fell in, opening long trenches in the floor. Warriors from all sides fell into the gaping pits.

Belegar's plans were in tatters.

'A thousand times a thousand curses on Golgfag and his honourless ogres,' said one of his bodyguards.

'Yes,' said Belegar absently. He watched the skaven sorcerer. He was troubled anew. Daemons were abroad in Vala-Azrilungol.

'They are ogres. It was a gamble, a poor roll of the dice, no more, my lord,' said another.

Belegar shook with anger. 'It's not that. I don't understand,' said Belegar. 'How did Skarsnik know? How did he speak with them?'

Behind his back, the hammerers shared glances. This was an oft-repeated story: bold King Belegar outwitted by a goblin.

The abomination was finally dead, for good this time, but the price had been high. The crushed corpse of Brok Gands-son leaked its life-fluids onto the bare rock, pinned under the bulk of the twice-living monster. Only thirty or so of Belegar's elite hammerers remained.

Belegar looked at the disaster unfolding in the hall. Durg-gan's battery was shattered; all his men and those set to guard him were dead. The sorry remnants of the flank the artillery had anchored were surrounded on all sides, cut off and beyond hope. The horns sounded the retreat time and again, but many of the dwarfs of Karak Eight Peaks were mired in battle with one faction or the other and could not retreat. Either that or they had fallen into all-consuming fits of hatred, desperate to bury their axes in their despised foes. These dawi had lost all reason and did not heed the signals. Worst of all, the path to the doors of Clan Skalfdon was thick with goblins.

'Sire, sire!' said a familiar voice.

'Drakki?' Belegar said flatly. 'Why aren't you with the rear-guard, recording our...' He wanted to say defeat, he should have said defeat, but somehow he couldn't. He was bone weary, not merely from today, but from fifty years of chasing an impossible dream. Defeat was too big a word to fit into his mouth.

'The rearguard *are* with you, my king. The lines have collapsed. We have been pushed together.' He gestured at the shrinking knot of dwarfs, units fighting back to back. 'Bold dawi await your command, my king.'

Belegar was dazed. 'I...'

Drakki grabbed the king's shoulder and squeezed. 'Do something,' he whispered.

It was thanks to the mercy of Valaya, Belegar supposed, that the ogres were leaving the hall, killing anyone of whatever army who got in their way. He blinked. The fuddle of emotion clouding his mind receded.

'Blow the charges,' he said.

'My king?' said Drakki.

'I said, blow the charges,' Belegar repeated, more clearly. He hefted his hammer. His warriors breathed easier seeing their lord return to them.

'Are you sure this is wise?' said Drakki.

'No. But they are rigged to collapse the hall to the south. If Durggan did his work well – and when did he ever not? – we should be able to retreat through the gate.'

'Dawi of Karak Eight Peaks! Dawi of Vala-Azrilungol that was! To arms to arms! Make for the gate!' called their thanes.

Horns blew loudly. The dwarfs checked their aggression, forming up into squares and blocks.

'Do it now,' said Belegar.

A complex tune played from the Golden Horn of the Iron Brotherhood.

'To the fore! To the fore!' shouted Belegar's clan lords.

The dwarfs, now in a broad column, lurched like a train of ore carts beginning their journey. Slowly they gained traction, and then they were away, axes and hammers falling, carving a red path through thaggoraki and grobi alike towards the great doors of Clan Skalfdon.

Three minutes later, long fuses burned their way to the

charges hidden around the bases of the pillars to the southern end of the hall. Twelve explosions followed one another quickly, their reports amplified to deafening levels by the enclosed space.

The pillars ground on shattered bases. Broken at top and bottom, they tumbled with apparent slowness, an illusion created by their great size and weight. They broke into many pieces as their toppling accelerated, falling on the hordes of Belegar's enemies as effectively as bombs and bringing torrents of stone from the ceiling with them, killing hundreds more.

The dwarfs fought on, too occupied to pay much attention to the roof falling in behind them. The collective scream of skaven and goblins being crushed chilled even boiling dwarf blood.

'My king,' shouted Drakki. He pointed upwards. Belegar followed his arthritis-knobbed finger to the ceiling. 'Something has gone wrong!'

A crack was opening across the sky of stone, dislodging glimstones that had shone for five thousand years. The fissure spread with ominous leisure, slowly, as if it were sentient, and choosing for itself the most devastating route. Stones rattled down on the column of embattled dwarfs.

Shouts rose from along the force's length 'Ware! Ware! Cave-in!'

The dwarfs raised their shields over their heads, as the roots of the world fell in upon them.

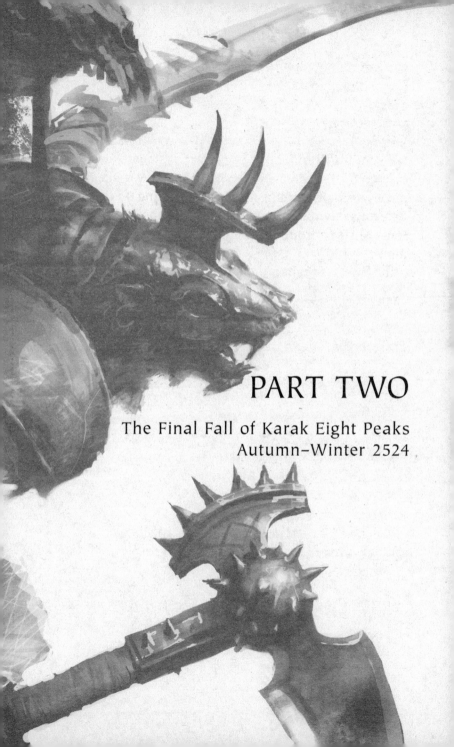

# PART TWO

The Final Fall of Karak Eight Peaks
Autumn–Winter 2524

# SIXTEEN

*Queen Kemma's Oath*

'Tor Rudrum is gone, vala,' said Gromvarl.

Queen Kemma set down her riveting pliers and sagged over her metalwork. She did nothing but thread mail links to one another all day every day, because there was nothing else for her to do. Belegar would not let her out, nor would he see her.

'We are trapped, then,' she said.

'Aye, lass,' said Gromvarl. He reached out awkwardly to pat her back. 'That's about the size of it. A flight of gyrocopters came in yesterday.'

'That's good, isn't it?'

'Only one got through, Kemma,' he said gently. 'The rest were shot down by the thaggoraki. They've overrun all the peaks, those that are not in the hands of the grobi, at any rate.'

Kemma gave a sad nod, staring at the shining hauberk, perfectly crafted although not yet finished, in her lap.

'The last one, pilot by the name of Torin Steamhammer, just got in before the ledges were taken by grobi on spiders.'

'Spider riders? I thought they lived in the forests in the lowlands.'

'They did,' said Gromvarl, wheezing as he sat down on a three-legged stool. He took his pipe out from his jerkin and filled it. He thought to take a half-bowl, for there was precious little tobacco left in the Eight Peaks, just like there was precious little of anything fine remaining. But with things the way they were he figured he probably had scant days left to smoke what small amounts he had, and after a second thought rammed it full with his thumb. 'All sorts of monsters up here now. Things I've never seen in the mountains before. The world's in turmoil, vala.'

'Do you have to call me that?' Kemma said sharply. A booming played under their conversation, deep and monotonous, never stopping – the beat of an orcish battering ram on the great gates of the citadel. The greenskins had been at it ever since they'd driven the dwarfs back from the outer defences. Belegar's warriors did what they could to keep Skarsnik's hordes back, but they were low on everything bar rocks to drop on the besiegers. 'You're my only friend, Gromvarl. My only link with home.'

Gromvarl looked at her fondly. How much she's grown, he thought. Such a pity the way fate falls. 'Aye.'

'He still won't talk to me, will he?'

Gromvarl shook his head, sending his clouds of smoke shifting about his head.

'My son?'

'Thorgrim's fine, my lady. He's fretting about you. Keeps asking his dad to come and talk things through, but Belegar's having none of it.' He didn't tell her that Belegar had precious little time for his heir either. He had become withdrawn, pale. He wasn't sleeping, he was sure of that. Dawi were tough, and Belegar tougher than most, but that wound he was trying so hard to hide from everyone was not only obvious, it was not healing. Gromvarl was worried, very worried, but he did his best to hide it from Kemma behind an air of grave concern.

'My husband is an arrogant, prideful fool, Gromvarl,' said Kemma.

'He's one of the best, if not the best, warrior in all the Karaz Ankor, va– Kemma.'

'He's an idiot, and we'll all die because of him.'

Gromvarl couldn't disagree in all honesty, so he harrumphed and looked around the chamber, searching for the right thing to say. It was austere, cold, lacking a womanly touch. He found it depressing that such a good-hearted rinn as Kemma should have been brought to this. He was glad he did not have daughters. He was glad, in these awful times, he had no children at all. Still, he had not finished imparting his run of bad news. He mulled over how much he would say, but he had promised to keep her up to date.

A promise is a promise, he reminded himself. Without honour, and trust, what did they have left? An oath lasted longer than stone and iron.

'There's more, Kemma,' he said quietly. Kemma fixed him with her eyes, expressionless, waiting patiently. 'The gyrocopter brought a message from Karaz-a-Karak. After he read it, the king sat on his own in the Hall of Pillared Iron all day, bellowing at anyone who came near. He only told us what it said this morning, when he'd calmed down. A bit. Most of the holds are under siege, it can't be much longer before they all are.'

'And?' said Kemma. 'There is more, isn't there, Gromvarl?'

The longbeard sighed. She always was far too clever. 'Karak Azul has fallen.' His heart pained him to speak it aloud. 'King Kazador and Thorek Ironbrow were both killed, an ambush in the high passes some time ago.'

Kemma drew in a sharp breath. Ironbrow in particular was a terrible loss. None had his wisdom and skill with the runes. Much sacred knowledge was lost with him.

'The hold was overrun not long after,' continued Gromvarl. 'The message from the High King was the same as all the others the king has had these last weeks.'

Kemma clutched at the hauberk. The rings tinkled. Gromril, by the look of it. 'This is for Thorgrim,' she said. 'He's outgrown his last.'

'He's getting a good girth on him,' said Gromvarl approvingly. 'He'll be a strong lad, and a good king.'

Much to Gromvarl's dismay, Kemma burst into tears.

'He'll never be king! Can't you see? It's all over. They're coming to kill us all. They'll kill you, and the king, and my son!'

Gromvarl reached out his hand uncertainly. A year on, his arm still pained him. Though it had set true, it had been wasted from weeks of disuse, and half-rations were no aid to building its strength back up. 'Come on now, lass, there's no need for that. It's worse than it was even in the time of King Lunn, I grant you, and yet your husband is holding out. There's not many who could do that. The runes might no longer glow upon the gates...'

'Why?' demanded Kemma. 'The magic of the ancestors deserts us.'

Gromvarl clucked his tongue and rattled his pipe on top and bottom teeth. 'No one knows. No one knows anything any more.' It was a poor answer and did little to satisfy her. He blundered on. 'My point is, they're strong still. They're tall, made of stone, steel and gromril. Made to last forever. They have not fallen yet. Why,' he forced a smile, 'the urk have been at it for days and they've not even dented them.'

'There are many things like that in the dwarf realm, supposedly eternal, and they are failing one by one,' said Kemma. She wiped her eyes, angry at herself for her lapse in control. 'I'm sorry, but this is my son! A curse on dawi heads and the blocks of stone they call their brains. We should have gone months ago. Pride will kill us all.'

'You'll see,' said Gromvarl. 'Things are bad, but we'll prevail. We've less ground to cover now the surface holdings are gone. Duregar's finally been called back from the East Gate. We've some strong warriors here. Good lads, and brave. Most are veterans. I've not seen such a lot of battle-hardened dawi in my life. With them at our backs we've every chance. We've still got our defences. Kromdal's line is the strongest yet. There are only four ways through that: the King's Archgate, the Black-vault Gate, Varya's Stonearch and the Silvergate. Hundreds of dawi wait there, and they're all spoiling for a fight. And if they get through that there's the Khrokk line, and after that...'

'After that they're into the citadel,' said Kemma harshly. 'Belegar is waiting for our enemies to fall on each other, or to wear themselves out. But they won't. Ogres, greenskins and thaggoraki have us under siege. There's never any less of them, and fewer of us every day. We've nowhere left to run. My husband's too set in his ways! He can't see that they're not going to kill themselves on our shield walls – they're going to keep coming until they break through and destroy every last one of us.'

'It's worked all the other times.'

'This isn't like all the other times! Valaya preserve me from the thickheadedness of dawi men!' she said. 'You've already told me there's no help coming. We've not changed, Gromvarl. It's why we are going to fail. Doing the same thing over and over and over... All it has to do is not work once. It didn't work at Karak Azul. Why should it work here? They killed the reckoner. Dawi killing dawi! Do you know why?' She didn't give him a chance to respond but answered for him. 'They killed him because he knew. Because he wasn't a tradition-bound fool.'

'Because he was helping you leave,' said Gromvarl. He deliberately avoided the word escape.

'It could have been you,' she said in a small voice. 'I'm glad it wasn't.'

# SEVENTEEN

*Ikit Claw at the Eight Peaks*

'Patience, Queek, patience. You cannot kill Kranskritt, not any more.'

Queek hissed and gripped the arms of his throne. He didn't like this new advisor of his much. For a start, the dead-things he had so carefully collected over his bloody career would no longer speak with him while Lurklox was around. Secondly, the verminlord showed no deference or fear towards him whatsoever. Kranskritt's daemon ruled him utterly. Queek was determined the same would not be the case with him. He had the sneaking suspicion he wasn't succeeding.

'Pah! What sneaker-squeaker know?'

'I killed many thousands for the Council while I still lived, little warlord,' said Lurklox menacingly. 'Deathmaster Snik-ch's skill is a poor imitation of my glorious ability.'

'What you know of killing in plain view, Queek means! You hide and hide before stab-strike. Too cunning, too cautious. Mighty Queek sees an obstacle, mighty Queek destroys it!

Hidey in the dark is not my way.' Queek grumbled and settled into his throne. 'Why all this pretence-pretending! It boring! Queek bored!' He cast a look at his favourite trophies, arrayed upon a massive rack fanning across the back of the throne. Dwarf Gouger and his sword were in a lacquered weapon stand taken from some Far Eastern place to his right. All down the aisle leading to the throne-burrow mouth were heaped piles of dwarf banners. The right claw of Clan Mors liked to boast he had more dwarf standards than the dwarf king himself. But to have them all on display made him uneasy. These were Queek's private things! Not to be seen or touch-sniffed by any other. Mine.

'You will do as I say, small creature,' said the voice, coming first from near, then from behind and then to his left, 'or I will devour you as surely as the Horned Rat himself devoured Kritislik. Arrogance is a virtue, but too much of a good thing is still too much.'

Queek glanced about. Lurklox had disappeared completely; the twitching shadows that betrayed his presence were not visible. Queek felt the first stirrings of fear. He shifted on the throne, acutely aware of his musk glands for the first time in years.

'You are right to be afraid, O most mighty and invincible Queek,' mocked Lurklox's voice, coming from nowhere in particular. 'I know you are wary of the Deathmaster, and yet perhaps one as talented as you in kill-slaying might best him in open combat. Yes-yes,' the voice turned to musing. 'That would be a good-fine match to watch. But I am not the Deathmaster. I am Lurklox, the greatest assassin ever to have been pupped in Skavendom! In my mortal years my name alone could stop a ratkin's heart. In open battle you would stand no chance against me then, and now I am the immortal chosen of the Horned Rat himself. You could never beat me.'

Queek's ears twitched.

'Oh I know-smell you think of it, and that a part of you wishes to try. Against the lesser verminlords of the Realm of Ruin, you might even triumph.' The voice hissed close to his ear, startling Queek. 'Never against me! And if we were to come to violence-conflict, it would never be face to face. You would die screaming in your sleep, mad-thing Queek, and I would place your head upon your trophy pole to rant at those you killed, for no one else would hear your words. This would be my kindness to you, for the pain would be great but the humiliation worse. Do as I say-command. You are important to my plan-scheme, but no one is indispensable. You should know that. You should understand. Do you understand, Queek?'

Queek stared straight ahead, unblinking. 'Yes-yes,' he said through clenched teeth.

'Good. Now listen-hear to what I say-squeak. You cannot kill Kranskritt. You know why. News of his success has already reached Skavenblight. My brother in darkness aids him. They seek to regain the seers' position on the Council. I suspect this to be the will of the Horned Rat, to test his chosen. The seers of Clan Scruten always were his favourites. I see no reason why they are no longer. My advice is that it would be foolish to disturb this test.'

'Kranskritt is powerful, useful-good,' said Queek. 'You say this Soothgnawer wanted to create good impression with Kranskritt's victory by helping mighty Queek? This is nonsense. He wants Queek dead, to take all glory for his scheming white-furred self. When Kranskritt is no longer useful, he is no longer good. Then Queek slay-kill. If you try stop me, then we will see if mighty-dark Lurklox say-squeaks the truth about supernatural battle-prowess.'

'You are not as mad as they say.'

Queek giggled. 'Mad or not, Queek still mighty.'

'That you are, Queek of Clan Mors, although you have many enemies. Too many for even you.'

'Kranskritt, Skrikk, Gnawdwell, Soothgnawer and Lurklox,' he said rattling the names off quickly. 'Queek does not care.'

Lurklox did not speak, Queek knew he was reading his body language and scent for the lie in his words, probably his mind too, and he knew also that Lurklox would find none.

'I withdraw,' the daemon said presently. 'Ikit Claw comes. Do not reveal my presence! It will be worse for you than would be-is for me.'

Queek chittered his acknowledgement, irritating though it was to be beholden to the verminlord.

The hall fell silent. Lurklox allowed none near Queek while they spoke. Not even the dead-things. Not even loyal Ska!

Queek could hear the clanging iron frame and steam-venting hiss of the approaching Ikit Claw long before he could see him. It was not by accident that the dignitary was forced to walk the lengthy corridor. Queek watched the warlock slowly approach. He did not move fast, being more machine than rat, but there was a solidity to him, a stolidness too, that was lacking in other ratkin. He reminded Queek of a dwarf-thing. Queek suppressed a titter at the thought.

Ikit Claw did not speak until he had finally clanked to a stop before Queek's towering trophy throne. A voice rasped behind his iron mask. 'Greetings, O great Queek, Warlord of the City of Pillars. I bring-carry tidings. Yes-yes, I have slain many beard-things – I have broken Iron-Peak!'

Queek had heard that the rival Clan Rictus had as much to do with bringing Azul-place low as Ikit had, but he was too canny to mention it. What Ikit Claw said was as much provocation as delivery of news; Queek's own failure years ago to destroy Karak Azul was widely known.

Queek squeaked in annoyance as Ikit drew in a long metallic breath, presaging a long flurry of ritual greetings and mock-flattery. Queek went straight for the point.

'Why-tell are you here?'

A menacing green glow emanated from Ikit's iron mask. 'I bring great Queek tribute. The Council bid I gift you Clan Skryre weapons. Very kill-kill, these devices.'

Ikit paused. If he was expecting gratitude, he was disappointed.

'Where-tell are they? Show mighty Queek!'

A grating clunk sounded from Ikit's metal face that might have been a noise of regret. 'Clan Mors will not be granted direct usage of these weapon-gifts. Much work has gone into their creation by Clan Moulder and Clan Skryre, although mostly hard-work thinkings of Clan Skryre. Trained teams of Clan Rictus direct them where Queek needs.'

'I see-smell,' said Queek coldly. 'Is cunning Ikit Claw also to remain, to hold Queek's hand-paw all the way to victory?'

Ikit raised his paw to his chest and bowed slightly. 'Unfortunately not. As mighty Queek doubtless knows in his most labyrinthine and devious mind, the chief servants of the Council must hurry-scurry on and on. I cannot stop-stay,' he said. 'I am bid-go to the mountain of the crested beard-things, there to make much war-killing, and end another infestation of dwarfs for betterment of all skavenkind. Fool-clans besiege Kadrin-place for many months, and cannot break it. I have much fame, much influence. I killer of dwarf-places. They call for me to come here. But mighty Queek does not need much help, does he? Not like weak-meat fighting the orange-beards.'

Without waiting for a reply, the master warlock engineer turned tail and began clanking his way back. 'But I will be back if Queek cannot do the task,' he said. 'So speaks the Council of Thirteen.'

'We shall see-see,' said Queek softly as he watched Ikit painfully clatter his way out again. 'While fool-toys of Clan Skryre face beard-things, Queek will deal with his other enemy, and then we see-smell who is the greater. Tomorrow, Skarsnik imp-thing dies on my sword.'

'Wait, Queek, there is another way...' said Lurklox. The shadows thickened once more, and a rank smell of decay filtered into Queek's nose from behind his throne. Ikit Claw left the throne-burrow and the door slammed shut. Queek levered himself out of his chair and gathered up his things. He felt better once his trophy rack was on his back. He lifted his weapons. 'Yes, there always another way, rat-god servant. There is Queek's sword, and there is Queek's Dwarf Gouger. Two ways is enough choice for Queek! Skarsnik die by one of them. Which, Queek not care.'

'Queek!' said Lurklox warningly. 'We must be cunning...'

But Queek was already scampering away, calling for his guards and the loyal Ska Bloodtail.

At the Arch of Kings, dwarfs waited.

A tributary of the Undak had once run through the cavern, and the arch had been built to bridge it. In its day, the cavern was among the most glorious places in Karak Eight Peaks, a cave of natural beauty enhanced by dwarf craft. The river had gathered itself together from six mountain streams in a wide pool below a small hole some half a mile upstream. The dwarfs had channelled the flow into a square trough five dwarfs deep and sixteen wide, coming into a broad grotto of cascading flowstone. Lesser channels led off from the river to aesthetic and practical purpose, flowing in geometric patterns around stalagmites, before exiting the cavern through various gates and sluices to power the triphammers of the western foundries.

The river was long dry, the streams that fed it blocked by the actions of time or the dwarfs' enemies, the natural columns and peaks of the stone smashed. The trough had become instead a dry ditch, the rusted remains of the machinery that had once tamed the river broken in the bed. But the walls were true, sheer dwarf masonry still flawlessly smooth, affording no purchase to the most skilful of skaven climbers, and so it still presented a formidable obstacle to invaders. For fifty years the Arch of Kings had aided Belegar in keeping the ways open between the citadel and the dwarf holdings in Kvinnwyr. Additionally, it provided an easily defensible choke point to fall back to, should need arise. Now the dwarfs had been driven out of their halls in the White Lady, that need had arisen, and the ditch kept the enemy from coming any closer to the citadel from the mountain. The Arch of Kings was the key defence for the west.

Belegar's enclave had erected a gatehouse on the eastern side of the riverbed, modest by the standards of their ancestors' works, but sturdy enough. As the road descended from the apex of the bridge's curve, it encountered thick gates of iron and steel that barred the way to the citadel. A wide parapet with heavy battlements hung over the road, overlooking the river beyond. The wall-walk was machiolated over the foot of the bridge, to allow objects to be dropped onto the heads of attackers. Similarly, murder holes pierced the stone of the gate's archway before the gate and behind it. A portcullis was set behind the gate, behind that, another gate, and behind that was a regiment of ironbreakers, well versed in the arts of war and irritable with the lack of decent ale.

Ikit Claw's weapons went there first.

'Movement!' called Thaggun Broadbrow, the lookout that fateful day. His fellow quarrellers immediately started on the windlasses of their crossbows, drawing back the strings. They were practised; their bows were drawn quickly and the sound of bolts slipping into firing tracks clacked up the battlement.

'See,' said one to another, 'I always held that crossbows are better than guns. Where are the handgunners, eh? Out of powder, that's where. Whereas me, my lad, will always have a missile to hurl, as long as there's a stick and a knife to sharpen it with to hand.'

'Aye, true that, Gron, too true.' Gron's companion tapped out his pipe on the wall and carefully stowed it before fitting his own bolt into his bowstock. 'Always be able to send a couple of them away, no matter what the situation.'

'Grim. That's what it is, Hengi. Grim.'

'Aye. Grim comments for grim times.'

'Rat ogre!' called the lookout. 'Rat ogre...?' Thaggun's voice trailed away into astonished query.

Gron peered out into the dark. 'Now what by the slave pits of the unmentionable kin is that?'

'Big, that's what,' said Hengi, sighting down his weapon at the beast approaching.

Big didn't cover it. This was the largest rat ogre any of them had ever seen, and being dwarfs oathsworn to defend Karak Eight Peaks to the bitter end, they'd seen more than their fair share of the things. This one was a head higher than the biggest, covered all over in iron and bronze armour. Grafted to each arm was a pair of warpfire throwers, the tanks feeding each thick with plating.

'I don't like the look of that,' said someone. 'Why isn't it charging?'

'Ah, who cares? We'll have it down in a jiffy,' said another.

'Not before it goes crazy and kills half its own!' said someone else.

But the rat ogre plodded forwards, showing none of the snarling, uncontainable antipathy its kind usually evidenced.

'Quarrellers of the Grundtal clan! Ready your weapons!' shouted Gron.

The clansdwarfs rested their weapons' stocks on the battlements, secure in their position behind the thick stone.

'Take aim,' called Gron.

They each chose a point on the rat ogre.

'Loose!' said Gron, who would never be caught dead saying 'fire.'

Artfully crafted steel bows snapped forwards on their stocks, sending bolts of metal and wood winging at the rat ogre, by now halfway across the bridge. A unit of skaven bearing the banners of Clan Rictus ran cautiously behind it.

Not one of the bolts hurt the creature. They hit all right, but clattered off its armour. A couple punched through or encountered weak spots and stuck in the creature's flesh, but it was unaffected.

'Reload! At it again!' cried Gron. 'You lot down there better be ready,' he shouted through a hole to the gate's ironbreaker guards.

Quickly the dwarfs wound back their bows and fitted fresh missiles. Again they fired, to similar effect. Several clanrats fell screaming from the bridge, felled by wayward bolts, but the rat ogre stomped along, blinkered by an eyeless helm. There was a smaller rat riding its back, Gron noted. The rat ogre's arms came up to point brass nozzles at the gates.

'Everyone down!' yelled Gron.

With a whooshing roar more terrifying than dragon-breath, green-tinged fire belched from the rat ogre's weapons. It washed against the gates and melted them like wax. Backwash shot up through the murder holes onto the parapet. Several quarrellers were hit this way, spattered by supernatural flames that would not go out. They screamed as the fire burned its way through cloth, armour, flesh and bone.

The sharp smell of molten metal hit Gron's nose. The Axes of Clan Angrund below were shouting, orders to form up and sally forth echoing up. It did no good.

The warpfire throwers blazed again. The rat ogre held them in position for a long time, melting its way through the portcullis and the second gate. The stones warmed under Gron's feet. Screaming came from below as the ironbreakers were engulfed. A terrible way to die – Gron had seen it before. They would be cooked alive in their armour, if not outright melted.

'Bring it down, lads!' he bellowed. 'Get it away from the bridge!' Doing so was suicidal, but this thing had to be stopped.

His warriors stood up and crossbow bolts rained down. At this close range they had greater penetrative effect, and the rat ogre roared in pain. It took a step back and raised its arms.

'Down!' shouted Gron, and once more the quarrellers hit the stone flags. The battlements could not save them. Green fire washed over and around them, setting the quarrellers ablaze. Gron felt the diabolical heat of it as a patch stuck to him, charring its way into the skin of his left arm. A gobbet of it hit his right thumb. He gritted his teeth; no one suffered like a dwarf. But try as he might, the agony was unbearable and he screamed.

The fire abated. His arm and hand no longer burned, but were useless. His left arm he could not feel at all aside from an awful warmth. His right hand was clawed and blackened. His dawi were all dead or mortally wounded. The stone of the parapets glowed red-hot, the crenels melted back to rotten-toothed stumps.

Hengi rolled onto his back, groaning.

'Hengi! Hengi!'

'My eyes... Gron, my eyes!'

Gron looked out. The rat ogre had moved aside. Skaven waited for the ruined gates to cool. He saw then that the rider of the rat ogre was nothing of the sort, but some hideous homunculus grafted to its flesh.

'Hengi, Hengi, take my bow.' He thrust his weapon at his blinded kinsman as best he could with his ruined limbs. Hengi's hands were sound, but his upper face was a red raw mess, his eyes weeping thick fluids. Lesser creatures would have been howling in agony, but they were dawi. Pain could not master them. 'They've something controlling the rat ogre, some creature of theirs. If we can kill it, we might be able to stop it.'

'Shoot then,' said Hengi, his voice thick with bottled pain.

'I cannot, my arms are ruined. You will have to do it. Let me aim it for you, here!'

Gron guided Hengi to a crenel whose merlons were not red-hot, pushing him with his shoulders into the gap. The pair were hidden by the smoke of stone burning beneath them, allowing Hengi to fumble the crossbow onto the wall. Gron got behind Hengi and sighted down it as best he could.

He squinted. 'Left a touch. Up, up! No, down. Easy, Hengi. Now,' he said.

The last discharge of a dwarf crossbow upon the King's Archgate occurred, sending a bolt fast and true to bury itself in the wizened creature on the back of the rat ogre. The monster reacted immediately, shaking its head as if coming out of a drugged sleep.

It roared. Clanrats squeaked in fear. The warpfire throwers belched again and again, fired by the furious monster without thought. Gron looked on with satisfaction as the rat ogre spun round, setting the regiment alight. Presently its fuel ran out and the skaven brought down their wayward creature eventually, but only after one regiment of thaggoraki had been entirely destroyed, and three more fled.

Gron looked back over the dry river. The darkness was alive with movement and red eyes. As soon as the rat ogre was dead, they were on the move again.

He sank back against Hengi. Soon the skaven would be coming for them.

'Let's not let them take us alive, eh? Lad?' said Gron. 'You'll have to go last, I can't move my hands at all.'

Hengi nodded. His knife slid from his belt.

\* \* \*

All along the third line of defence, similar things were happening. Rat ogres armed with ratling guns, upscaled poisoned wind mortars and other terrible weapons came against the dwarfs. One by one the gates fell, with such speed that the dwarfs of the Khrokk line had no time to prepare, and this too fell the same day.

The way was open to the citadel.

# EIGHTEEN

*A Gathering of Might*

Duffskul hiccupped and waddled along the corridor to Skarsnik's personal chambers in the Howlpeak. He hummed to himself as he went, trailing clouds of stinking shroomsmoke behind him. He was wearing his best wizarding hat – a once very bright yellow, now so grubby it was almost green – and a collection of charms that hummed with Waaagh! magic.

The little big 'uns and moonhats by Skarsnik's chambers scrambled over themselves to open the doors.

'A fine welcome, oh yus. You got the right respects for your betters, grotty boys,' he said. They simpered gratefully at his praise.

In the corridor it was freezing; the constant winds whistling through the windows gave the mountain its goblin name and its hurty-bit biting temperatures. In Skarsnik's rooms it was a different matter, swelteringly hot from the fire blazing in the hearth. Duffskul brought in a gust of sharp-smelling winter with him, but it was swiftly defeated, carried off by the vapours steaming from his robes in the sudden heat.

'Duffskul, me old mate,' said Skarsnik, looking up from his work. As usual papers tottered around him, and on many other desks too, to which he flitted as he worked. He wrinkled his eyes, holding a parchment at arm's length.

'Too much reading's bad for you, boss, oh yus.' Duffskul kicked old bones, rags and bottles out of the way as he made his way over to a sturdy dwarf chair near the fire. Gobbla lay asleep on the filthy rug before the flames, whiffling gently in his sleep.

'Someone's got to keep these zogging idiots in line,' said Skarsnik. 'Can't do it if you's not organised...' His words trailed away as he deciphered whatever it was that he had written there.

'I always said you was a funny little runt. Done us proud you have wiv all that thinking there in the old brain box.' Duffskul rubbed his hands together in front of the fire and sighed contentedly. His heated robes gave off the most noxious smell. 'Ooh, that's nice, ooh, that's very nice!' He smacked his lips and pulled out his gourd of fungus beer. He sloshed it around disappointedly. 'If only I had a little drinky to help meself really enjoy it.'

Skarsnik had gone back to his work, the enormous griffin quill in his hand scratching over his parchment.

'Wanna drink? Help yourself,' he said distractedly.

Duffskul didn't need telling twice. He grabbed up the nearest bottle and uncorked it. 'You is running low.'

'And you is going to have to brew up a lot more fungus beer. And preferably stuff that don't taste of old sock!' said Skarsnik. 'Precious few stunty barrels to nick, and none of the grapey goodstuff coming out the west these days, so don't you go gulping it all. I needs me drinks to thinks,' he said, and giggled quietly.

Duffskul guzzled anyway, glugging priceless Bretonnian wine right from the bottle until it had nearly all gone. 'Ahh! Now that is better. Ooh, that is a lot better.'

'Right. Now you is all nice and comfy, why don't you tell me what you is doing here,' said Skarsnik, finally looking up and laying down his quill. 'I am a very busy goblin.'

'Ain't you just, ain't you!' giggled Duffskul.

'Get to the point, you mad old git,' said Skarsnik affectionately. Duffskul had been with him right from the very start, and had stuck with him when others had wandered off, turned traitor or inconsiderately died.

'Well, we has questioned the ratty scouts.'

'Yeah?'

'And we has kept careful watch on their doings and all that, oh yus.'

'Tolly's boys?'

'Best sneaks in the peaks,' said Duffskul. 'And I has been trying to speak with da Twin Gods! Gork and Mork, what you has visited and who is the mightiest greenies of them all.'

'Right. And? Are the ratboys going to attack, then? They've got them stunties well bottled up. Only a matter of time before they make their move on me. When and where, that's what I want to know, when and where.'

'And you shall know, king of the mountains!' Duffskul swivelled in the armchair, and leaned on its torn, overstuffed arm. 'The rats are going to try and drive us out for good, starting with orctown in the old stunty city and da camps outside the walls.'

'Right,' said Skarsnik, who had expected as much. 'East Gate?'

'Drilla's boys went to kick out the stunties yesterday. Empty. Well, it was – full of black orcs now.'

'Hmm.' Skarsnik drummed his fingers on the table. 'Well, let's ambush the little furry bleeders.'

'They'll be expecting that,' said Duffskul.

'Course they will! That Queek's not an idiot, even if he is as mad as snot on one of your better madcap brews. But what he's not gonna be expecting is a *special* ambush, and so I's going to make it a very special ambush. He'll definitely not expect that!'

'Oh no, oh yus,' said Duffskul.

'The Waaagh!'s building, Duffskul, greenies coming to me from left right and centre.' He paused, and looked down at his lists, running ink-stained fingers down the parchment. 'I reckon I should meet with this Snaggla Grobspit. Drilla's lads have already come over. Time to take that cheese-stealing maniac to task, don't you fink?'

'Oh yes, boss! Oh yes. Oh yus,' said Duffskul, his eyes spinning madly in his face. 'And I've got a cracking idea meself.'

'Have you now?' said Skarsnik. 'Right then, tell me all about it, and we'll figure out exactly what we is going to do...'

The paired skaven warpsteam engines at the gates of the Hall of a Thousand Pillars chuffed madly, whistling as they vented pressure to equalise their efforts. Masked Clan Skryre engineers looked out from the haphazardly armoured embrasures holding their machines, then scuttled back to their charges, fiddling with knobs and tossing levers. Satisfied that their pistons were synchronised, the tinker-rats blew whistles at one another, then set about yanking more levers into the correct positions to open the doors. The tone of the engine's voices deepened as their gearing wheels thunked into position, engaging with the massive cogs that worked the door mechanisms. Huge gear chains twanged as they came under tension. Machinery hidden high in the roof of the Hall of a Thousand Pillars rattled, and the great gates of the underhalls of Karak Eight Peaks creaked open.

The skaven massed behind the doors shrank back in terror of the sunlight. Few of them had ever been overground, and the prospect of a world without a roof sent a chitter of nervousness through their ranks.

'Hold-hold!' their masters ordered, cracking whips and punching the most timid.

The gates crushed rubble and other detritus to powder as they opened. Ponderous but unstoppable, they were one hundred feet tall. The tired sun picked out their decoration as they swung inwards, the runes and clan marks of the beard-things that made them still fresh as the day they had been carved.

'Forward!'

The first claws of skaven scurry-marched up the ramp leading into the surface city.

All around Karak Eight Peaks, skaven emerged blinking and terrified into the sunlight, pale though it had been made by the choking ejecta of the world's volcanoes and the endless, uncanny storm that wracked the skies. At the fore of the warriors emerging from the Hall of a Thousand Pillars into the surface city went Ikk Hackflay, a rising star in Queek's entourage. He was a logical replacement for Thaxx and Skrikk, whose heads now graced the Grand Warlord's trophy room.

From the skaven-held mountains, more warriors emerged. Four of Queek's five clawpacks. Reduced by months of war, they still numbered in the tens of thousands. Over one hundred thousand warriors marched forth. Every column flinched as it walked out into the day, and not just for the frightening lack of a ceiling. They all expected to be ambushed as they came out, no matter how well hidden or supposedly secret their burrows were.

They were not ambushed. The immediate fighting they had planned for never came. They surfaced instead to a ghost town. The thickly packed orc-shacks and tents in the city were empty, as were the encampments in the weed-choked farmland beyond the city walls.

Queek surveyed all this impatiently from the top of part of the rubble slope created by the collapse of Karag Nar.

'Careful, Queek,' said Krug from his trophy rack. 'He's a wily one, that Skarsnik.'

'What news?' he said to his gathered lieutenants. 'Grotoose?'

'Nothing, great Queek.'

'The fifth clawpack has found not one of the green-things, exulted Queek,' fawned Kranskritt. Queek gave him a hard look. He still did not trust the grey seer. Only Lurklox's insistence kept the wizard alive.

Skrak reported the same, as did Gnarlfang and Ikk Hackflay, who had been furiously stomping from place to place in search of something to kill.

'There is no one here,' said Gritch, his assassin's voice pitched just over the wind soughing through the dry winter grasses. There had been precious little snow that year, though it was bitingly cold. 'The siege camp is empty. They have abandoned their attack on the gates. There is a new idol in the main square of the beard-thing city. Stone and iron, it stares-glares with skull-eyes at dwarf-thing fort-place.'

'So good your scouts are. Well done! So skilled to find big stone giant, but not little things,' Queek said. 'What about scouts sent to the mountain halls and peaks? Where is the Skarsnik-thing, where are his armies?'

'Many scouts not scurry back, great Queek,' said Gritch, bowing low.

'Queek very impressed.'

Gritch began to protest, but Queek cut him off. 'Big-meat ogre-things?' said Queek.

'Gone with the gold,' said Skrak.

'Fools,' said Queek. 'Why they so obsessed? Gold soft, useless.' He held up his sword and looked up its length. 'Not hard-sharp like steel. They like to eat, more than a skaven gripped by the black hunger.' He shrugged. 'Maybe they eat it.'

'Skarsnik has gone then,' said Grotoose. 'He has fled the wrath of mighty Queek!'

Queek rounded on him, raising Dwarf Gouger. 'Oh no, do not be mistaken. Little imp watches, little imp waits to see what we will do. Little imp thinks he will beat Queek in very-very cunning-clever trap. But little imp will not trap Queek.'

'Will he attack in the day?'

'Skaven love-like the night. We scurry under the big roof now that is no roof at all. Skaven not like it, pah! But Skarsnik's little soldiers no different.'

Kranskritt glanced nervously up at the sun, shining pale yet still menacing through the thick cloud. 'What do we do then, mighty one?'

Queek wondered if he could strike the seer dead now. He could, he thought. Lurklox was not there, and he did not see Soothgnawer – nor did he think he was near, for his trophies whispered their wisdom to him, something they did not when either verminlord was close by. He refrained from acting upon his whim.

'We clear the city as planned, Queek decrees! Tear it all down, break it to pieces, smash the imp-thing's little empire on the surface as we smashed his town in the Hall of a Thousand Pillars. Then we will see if he can be tempted out or not.'

Orders were given, and the army split into its various components to cover the vast area encompassed by the bowl sheltered by the eight peaks. Clan Skryre engineers set up their war machines near the mostly securely held skaven mountains in case of attack, while the armies subdivided further and began the work of demolishing the greenskins' settlements. In ruined fields covered by scrubby forest, greenskin shelters were kicked down. Clanrats clambered over the crumbling dwarf city, levering stones out of the walls of rough-built huts. Warpfire teams torched entire villages of tents, while wind globadiers tossed their poisons into ruins and caves that might hold monsters. Teams of rat ogres tackled the bigger structures, clawing down idols of stone, wood and dung.

None, however, could bring low the great idol of Gork staring fixedly at the citadel in the centre of the city. Queek followed the line of its gaze. Glints on the battlements of the citadel showed dwarfs powerlessly watching as the skaven rose up to take control of yet more of their ancestral home.

'Soon, Belegar long-fur, it will be your turn,' hissed Queek.

The idol was as tall as a giant, but much more massive, its crude arms and legs made of monoliths stacked on top of each other and chained in place in crude approximation of orcish anatomy. A huge boulder with crude eyeholes hacked into the face topped it off, a separate jaw of wood hanging by more rusty chains from its face. It looked as if it should be pushed over easily, but would not fall. Warpfire splashed off the rock and iron. Warp-lightning crackled across it without effect. More powerful explosives were sent for. All the while the idol hunched there, apish and insolently strong as the day wore on.

Still Skarsnik did not come.

From his position atop the parapets of Howlpeak, Skarsnik watched the skaven go about the business of wrecking orc-town. Fires burned everywhere.

'They is behaving like they own the place, burning our houses down,' said Skarsnik. 'Old Belegar is probably loving every bit of this.'

'Should we go and get them now, boss?' said Kruggler. Crowds of orc and goblin bosses hung around him, the lot of them sheltering under nets and swags of cloth covered with dust and dyed grey to hide them from the skaven's eyes.

Skarsnik snapped his telescope shut; the skaven weren't the only ones to steal from dwarfs. 'In a minute, Kruggs.' He swept his hand out towards the eastern peaks. 'We'll wait until they're nice and spread out, then we'll attack, smash the centre, rout the rest and have a nice big ratty barbecue.'

'I is not for waiting!' grumbled Drilla Gitsmash, king of the Dark Lands black orcs. What with his thick accent, he was almost unintelligible behind his heavy, tusked visor. 'We should get out there and smash 'em good now. I is not for waiting!' he repeated.

'Oh yes you is, if you want to win,' said Skarsnik, looking up at the black orc as if he weren't twice his size and four times his weight, before re-extending his telescope and turning back to the view. 'But if you wants to go out there on your own and get chopped up to little itsy bitsy pieces, then go ahead. I is sure my boys could do with a laugh. No?' Drilla said nothing. 'Good idea that. Best to wait until we're all going out. Is everyone in position?'

'Yes, boss,' said Kruggler.

'Tolly Grin Cheek?' This was not the original supporter of Skarsnik from way back, but the fourth murderous goblin to bear the name, and the facial scars that went with it.

'He's up behind them, boss.'

'And that Snaggla fella? Not sure about him. Tell you, spiders is fer eating, not riding – and what's this nonsense about some spider god? How many gods are there, boys?'

'Gork and Mork,' said one. 'That's four.'

'Five?'

'Definitely more than one!'

'One,' grumbled Drilla. 'Mork don't count.'

'There's two!' said Skarsnik, his voice becoming shrill. 'Two. Gork and Mork. Not three, or lots, or twenty-two thousand.'

Goblin faces creased in pained confusion at the mention of this incomprehensible number.

'I told you, boss, I fought wiv some of them forest boys up north in the Border Princes,' said Kruggler. 'They is real sneaky. Morky as you like. You'll love it.'

'Right,' said Skarsnik. He gave the vista one last pass with his telescope. He squinted at the sun. Noon, as near as he could reckon it. Not good for his night boys, but it couldn't be helped. 'Now or never,' he said. 'Positions, lads. And get the signal to Duffskul sent!'

Skaven passed under Duffskul's nose. From the shoulder of the idol he was looking right down at the top of their pointy little heads, and some of them looked right back at him. He pulled faces at them and laughed at how close they were. They couldn't see him, couldn't smell him, didn't know he was there at all. They milled about, trying one thing after another to destroy his idol, arguing over how it had got there. Duffskul knew the answer to that, of course.

It had walked.

It had taken him ages to ride it back down from old Zargakk the Mad's wizlevard cave, way up over the Black Crag. A risky journey, but funnily enough, he hadn't been bothered by anyone at all on the way back.

A single puff of smoke, black as a night goblin's robes, rolled up into the sky over the tumbled parapets of the Howlpeak's Grimgate. Duffskul laughed. He did a little dance. He whispered horrible things in the general direction of the skaven.

And then he did his magic.

'What-what is that noise?' said the skaven warlock nearest to the idol's foot.

'What noise?'

'Deaf-deaf, you are! A scream-shriek, getting louder.' The pair of them looked left, looked right and all around them, turning in circles to find the source of the rapidly loudening cry.

'I hear now!' said the second, exactly half a second before a goblin smashed itself to paste yards from their position. All that was left was one twitching foot, a shattered pair of canvas wings, and the echoes of its scream.

Only then did the skaven, born and bred in a world with comfortably low skies, think to look upwards.

Goblins were arcing through the heavens in long lazy curves, swishing their wings back and forth like birds. The illusion was impressive. One could almost think a goblin could fly, so at home the doom divers seemed in the clouds.

They were, unfortunately for the goblins, as aerodynamically gifted as boulders, and their flights lasted only marginally longer. Unfortunately for the skaven whose regiments they steered themselves onto, they did about as much damage as boulders too. A goblin's head was uncommonly dense, especially when crammed into a pointed helmet.

'Look-look!' The second skaven tugged upon the sleeve of the first.

'Yes-yes, I see! Flying green-things, very peculiar.'

'Not there,' he said, grabbing hold of his colleague's head and pointing his gas-masked face at the head of the idol, their field of vision being somewhat restricted. 'There!'

The skaven looked up at the idol. The idol, eye-caves glowing a menacing green, stared back.

'*Waaaaaghhhhhh!*' the idol shouted.

The skaven shrieked as a heavy rock foot ground them out of existence.

Atop its shoulders, Duffskul whooped. By way of reply, the mountains and ruins of Karak Eight Peaks resounded to the blaring of horns and the clanging of cymbals, the roll of dwarf-skin drums and the tuneless squeal of the squigpipes.

With a rapid clacking, the Grimgate swung open, splitting the grimacing orc-head glyph painted over the ancestor runes in two.

Out marched legions of greenskins. They headed right for the centre of the city.

'All right, Mini-Gork, I believe we'll be needing to go thata-way!' said Duffskul.

With rumbling strides accompanied by the grinding of rock, the Idol of Gork swung about and set off towards the enemy.

'He is coming! Green-imp shows his hand-paw! Foolish green-thing. Loyal Ska, sound the advance!'

Skaven cymbals clashed, and the entirety of Queek's first clawpack rose up from its hiding places. Forming rapidly into claws, the elite of Queek's army made a wall of strong, armoured ratmen across the widest of the Great Vale's shattered boulevards.

'Forward!' shouted Ska. 'Forward for the glory of Queek! Forward for the glory of Clan Mors! Forward or I'll kill-slay you myself!'

Ikk Hackflay's Ironskins were off first, the fangleader eager to prove himself. Queek had had his eye on the skaven ever since he had raided Belegar's lower armouries months ago, tak-ing enough dwarf armour to equip his entire claw, changing their names from the Rustblades to the Ironskins afterwards. From the speed he set off at, he evidently felt Queek's scru-tiny upon him.

Lightning blasted skywards from the ground, bursting gob-lins apart in the air. Some got through, some of those shattered the scaffolds the lightning cannons were mounted upon, and so the goblin doom divers and the best of Clan Skryre occupied one another.

'That's good, that is,' said the dead dwarf king Krug. 'Stops them from smashing your lads up.'

Queek hissed irritably. 'Of course, Queek knows this. It is all part of Queek's plan!'

Down the slopes of the mountain, innumerable hordes of goblins poured. Queek glanced nervously around the mountain bowl, across the city and out beyond where the lower reaches of the further peaks were hazy. His eyesight was as good as any skaven's, which is to say at distance, not very good at all. But he saw no sign of movement elsewhere, and heard no sound of battle.

'Ska!'

'Yes, masterful Queek.'

'Send messengers. Be sure to warn our lieutenants. This is not the fullness of the green-things' force.'

Ska nodded, detailing his own minions to fulfil the orders.

Meanwhile, Skarsnik's vanguard were jogging forwards to form a broad front. Queek ordered the slaves ahead, and with a terrified chittering, caused as much by the snarling packmasters at their rear as fear of the enemy, they surged across the mounded ruins of the dwarf city towards their greenskin foe. As the slaves neared, the goblins laughed loudly and shoved out whirling fanatics towards them. Queek had seen this so often by now that the tactic no longer held any surprises for him, but he remained wary of them. They spun round and round, laughing madly, hefting giant metal balls at the ends of long chains that should have been impossible for a goblin to lift.

He could not see their connection with his slave legions directly. The bodies of weak-meat tossed high in the air by the goblins' swinging balls informed him of when it happened anyway.

'Pick up speed! Hurry-scurry!' shouted Queek. The Red Guard broke into a jog, their wargear clattering. 'Mad-thing green-things will come through, kill-slay slaves – we must be through before they can turn and chase Queek!'

Queek's elite burst through their screen of slaves, hacking down those who did not get out of the way. The goblins had advanced some three hundred yards from the Grimgate, filling the wide road and spilling into the ruins either side. The city here had been much reduced, piles of rubble with twisted trees poking out from them or greened mounds showed where once workshops and homes had stood. It made for difficult ground to fight over.

The town sloped downwards from Queek's position, following the contours of the Howlpeak. Above was the still-open Grimgate. Ikk Hackflay's Ironskins pushed their way out of the slaves there, slightly ahead of Queek's formation. From his vantage, Queek saw the broad, bloody lanes through the skaven created by the fanatics. These wobbled in uncertain lines, some looping right the way back round towards the goblin lines. The casualty numbers were horrendous, but all were slaves and of little worth. Queek snickered; they had performed their role excellently. The fanatics were falling one by one, smashing into low walls, dropping from exhaustion, or becoming hopelessly tangled with the slaves, their miserable deaths aiding the skaven cause far more than the ratkin ever could in life.

The slaves were thinned by panic, fanatics, bow-fire and doom divers. Clanrats came through them to support their general. Poisoned wind globadiers ran before them, approaching perilously close to the goblin lines before heaving their spheres of gas into their foes' tight-packed ranks.

Queek sniffed the air. The wind was rank with greenskin. Neither his nose nor his eyes could pick out Skarsnik. 'That way!' he shouted, pointing directly at the centre of the greenskin force. 'Come-come, quick!'

With a fierce cry, the Red Guard ran forwards. They burst

through their screen of slaves and into the goblin vanguard, where they hacked their way through two mobs of goblins in short order. Queek's view of the battle became restricted. He heard rather than saw the charge of Hackflay's Ironskins, and the following clanrats. The first line of goblins bowed under pressure, nervous of the stormvermin carving their way through and the masses of clanrats coming next.

Deeper into the greenskin army Queek pushed, spinning and leaping, effortlessly felling the feeble warriors. Another goblin regiment parted before him, throwing down their shields and crooked spears rather than face him. His Red Guard skidded to a halt, momentarily cowed by the massive mob of black orcs they saw on the other side.

'Oi! Squeaker!' shouted their leader, a massive brute of an orc. 'I'm gonna have you!'

The black orcs executed a flawless turn to the left, and charged.

'Kill-slay them all!' squealed Queek. 'Breeding rights to the three who kill most big-meat!'

Spurred on by his generous offer, Queek's Red Guard broke into a run. The two elite units met with a clash of metal that drowned out all else.

These were no goblins, but the ultimate orcs, bred by magic in the slave pits of Zharr-Naggrund. They smashed down the Red Guard with their huge axes. The Red Guard duelled with them, seeking to keep the black orcs at arm's length with their halberds. The skaven felled a good number, but there were many, and they were fearless. The Red Guard's advance ground to a halt. Their leader pushed his way forwards, levelling his massive two-handed axe at Queek.

'Come on then, Headtaker! I've heard a lot about you. Nonsense, I reckon.'

The greenskin's accent was outlandish, but Queek understood. He replied in the beast's own language.

'Come die then – always space for more trophies for Queek!'

The orc roared and charged, bowling over a Red Guard who got in the way and trampling him down into the dirt. Queek spun round, allowing the orc to pass him, then smashed the spike of Dwarf Gouger through its chest. The orc made a noise of surprise. Queek finished it with a thrust through its visor slit with his sword, skewering the orc's small brain. It fell over heavily.

Queek wasted no time, prising off its tusked helmet and sawing its head off. He handed it to one of his guard, who jammed it upon a free spike on Queek's rack. He'd left many empty for today.

Seeing their leader cut down disturbed the black orcs, and the Red Guard pressed their advantage, surrounding them and hewing through their thick mail with their halberds. Clan-rat regiments had cut through the shattered goblin vanguard, joining Queek. They pressed back at greenskins moving to fill this potential gap in the line.

'Ska! Break them!' called Queek, cutting down two more of the black orcs.

Ska nodded, slammed a black orc out of the way, and leapt at their standard bearer.

The black orcs' metal icon wobbled in the air as Ska attacked, then fell.

The orcs, reduced to a knot surrounded by ferocious skaven, broke. Queek and his warriors cut many of them down. Predictably, the greenskin centre collapsed around them. Seeing their toughest regiment destroyed, and well aware that their destroyers lingered still in their midst, a huge tranche of weaker greenskins broke.

'The way to the gates are open!' squealed Queek, forgetting in his exultation exactly who he was dealing with. The clan-rats surged forwards after the fleeing goblins.

Horns sounded from all across the city. The left and right

flanks of the goblin army angled inwards, coming at the mass of skaven from both sides. A fresh wave of doom divers began to rain down from the sky, unsettling the skaven with their shrieks. They plummeted into the horde of ratmen with final wet splats, their broken bones and flying harnesses shattering into spinning shrapnel that cut down many ratkin. Under the ferocity of this suicidal bombardment, the clanrats' advance slowed and began to break up.

'No! No!' shrieked Queek. 'We have them!'

He bounded up onto a ruined wall, the last corner of a building torn down who knew when. The age-worn stones were cold under his bare foot-paws.

Queek hissed at what he saw. Goblins were pouring out of the mountains to the west, encircling his rear. The huge idol they had discovered that morning had come to life, smashing its way through the skaven centre, some sorcerer atop it flinging bolts of green lightning from its shoulder. Queek wished for a screaming bell, or an abomination or two, but the dwarf-things had slain both of his. From caves thought cleared came a stream of squigs, including one big as a giant. It squashed as many skaven as it ate. Lesser round shapes bounded around its feet. A collective squeak of terror drew Queek's attention to the foot of Karag Zilfin, where mangler squigs carved red ruin through his army.

Queek returned his attention to the fleeing goblins. Skarsnik had lured him into a trap, that much was certain, but it was not going to plan. The green-imp's bait force had not rallied and fled still.

Even so, the skaven army was at a disadvantage.

Squeaks from the foot of the wall called to him. His minions had caught up with him. A gaggle of messengers stood there, waiting expectantly to carry fresh orders away.

A final messenger, its fur matted with drying blood, came to a panting stop. 'Great Queek! Much terror-slaughter on the east. Giant spiders attack.'

'How big? Fist-paw big?'

The messenger shook his head and swallowed. 'Wolf-rat big and... Much-much bigger.'

Queek bared his teeth in anger. Away out beyond the outer edges of the city, into the derelict farmland to the east, many death-squeaks were being voiced. He narrowed his eyes. In his blurred distance vision, large shapes lurched against the pale horizon.

Just as he thought he was getting a paw on the situation, a terrifying screech rent the air and there was a snap of leathery wings. A dark shape swooped overhead, bringing with it a carrion stink and a sharp, reptilian smell.

A wyvern bearing an orc warboss landed heavily right in the middle of the clanrat regiments behind Queek.

A fresh wave of panic rippled through the clanrats around his position. This proved too much for them. Predictably, they ran. A huge section of the skaven centre collapsed. There was now a large part of the central battlefield devoid of combatants, each side running from the other. Queek was left alone with his Red Guard, who held fast about the Great Banner of Clan Mors.

'Stand! Stand! Cowards!' squealed Queek. He turned to his messengers with a snarl.

He pointed to one.

'Kranskritt!' he commanded. 'Go to him! It is most important he kill-slay the idol!'

He spared a look for the rampaging rock construct. Warp-lightning crackled around it with no effect.

To another he said, 'To the Burnt Cliffs with you – call out the reserves.' He spoke then directly to Ikk Hackflay and Grotoose. 'Ironskins and rat ogres, pursue green-thing rout.'

'And you, mighty leader?' rasped Ikk.

Queek scanned the sea of black-robed goblins, seeking out the tell-tale splash of red that would reveal the location of

Gobbla, and therefore his master. Queek could not find him! The imp-thing would have to wait. He turned his face to the wyvern flapping about the battle and slaughtering clanrats.

'Queek has other matters to attend to.'

# NINETEEN

*War in the Great Vale*

'Waaagh!' cackled Duffskul madly. He danced a little jig and threw bolts of green lightning from his fingertips, blasting skaven to pieces with every shot. His knees popped as he danced, but he was too excited to care. Swarms of ratmen fled before the feet of the Idol of Gork, squealing in terror. Wherever the stone monster went, skaven units burst apart like ripe puffballs, disintegrating into individual warriors who ran in every direction like mice fleeing an orc. 'That's right, ya little ratties! That's right! Run away!'

Duffskul's eyes glowed with the surfeit of Waaagh! energy washing over the battlefield. From atop his idol he could see right across the Great Vale for miles and miles. The main scrap was right there, in the old dwarf surface city, but smaller skirmishes were going on right the way across the entire bowl. Outside the walls, wolf riders ran down blocks of skaven infantry. Streaks of green whizzed down from on high where jezzail teams discharged their guns. Doom divers plummeted from even higher up. Batteries of goblin artillery duelled with skaven lightning throwers, sneaky gobboes dripping in night-black squig oil fought running battles with groups of skaven assassins. Right at the back, mobs of spider riders ran amok, unopposed by anyone. The ratboys were trying to bring their lightning cannons about, but weren't having much luck. Not long now and they would smash up the skaven artillery. There was a lot more to see than just the big ruck at the centre, oh yus.

Duffskul liked a nice fight, and this was the biggest and best he had ever seen. There were loads of greenies! Lots of lots, boys from every tribe and every kind of greenskin you could think of – except sneaky hobgobboes and stupid gnoblars, naturally – while there were so many ratties on the other side that he couldn't even begin to count them, and Duffskul could count pretty high for a goblin. It was a proper Waaagh!

'Waaagh!' he screeched. 'Waaagh!' The powers of Gork and Mork flooded through him and out his arms and toes and nose, the great idol of mad old Zargakk filling him with power.

What had happened to Zargakk, Duffskul had no idea. No one had seen him in years. He was probably dead. Good thing too, or there'd be no way Duffskul would have got his hands on the idol.

'Come on, Gork!' he called. A phantom foot formed from the magic spilling from Duffskul's skin. With a screech he sent it smashing into a unit of ratties, squashing them flat. He laughed uproariously, so hard he cried. Orc magic that one; Duffskul might be crazy, but he was deeply in favour with the Great Green Twins.

The idol lurched to one side, nearly tipping Duffskul from his perch on its shoulder. With desperately scrabbling hands, he caught himself on the rough stone. Sucking his lacerated fingers, he cast about for his attacker.

A flash of black lightning crackled against the idol, making it moan. It stumped around to face its tormentor, a white-furred skaven sorcerer who was hurling magic of his own at Duffskul's new pet. Unlike the blasts from the skaven cannon, this was hurting it.

'Oi!' he shouted, responding with a crackle of his own destructive magic. He screamed in triumph as it fizzed towards the skaven, but the rattie waved a dismissive hand, and the green light of Waaagh! power dissipated. The sorcerer raised his hands and hurled twin blasts of blacklight at the idol's knee. Duffskul countered, but the magic got through, weakened, but still effective. With a tinkle, the chains binding the menhirs of the idol's left leg burst apart. The idol took another step, reaching out crude hands to grab the sorcerer, but its foot was left behind.

'Watch out! Watch out!' Duffskul said in horror as the foot-less leg descended once more.

The idol let out a moronic bellow as it fell. The ground rushed up at Duffskul.

'Heeeeeelllllp!' he wailed. The idol crashed down, breaking into a dozen pieces of bouncing rock that rolled all over the place, trailing wisps of dying magic.

The sorcerer stood triumphantly, sure of his victory.

Duffskul was having none of that. Bruised but otherwise undamaged, he stood and rolled up his sleeves. 'Oi! Ratty! Who do you think you are?'

The rat snarled, exposing the tiny needle teeth either side of its flat incisors. Its eyes went dead-black. Smoke tinged with purple flares poured from its mouth.

Duffskul threw up his own hands. Giant green fists formed around them. He held out his hand, a hand that had become the magic-wreathed, crackling fist of Gork himself. He swung at the sorcerer, who warded off Duffskul's magic with his dark mist. Duffskul swung again. The skaven responded too late, and Duffskul grabbed him hard.

'How you like that, eh, ratty? Orc magic that. I know it because I is the chosen of Gork and Mork, their teller of fings to Skarsnik, who was raised up high because of me!' He squeezed hard. The skaven squealed.

'We make deal-deal?' it said in mangled greenskin.

'I don't fink so.'

Duffskul sucked in deep, inhaling the winds of magic rushing over the excited orcs and goblins. Power filled him. So much power! He could drink it all in and then he'd be the bestest wizlevard who ever lived, mighty as the gods themselves!

Duffskul's head hurt with the strength of it, a good pain, deep and satisfying, like the kind of itch it is a pleasure to scratch. The magic-light flaring in his eyes bleached out his vision.

Duffskul giggled. The skaven white-fur shrank in his magic fist. 'I'm gonna do this proper, you squeaking cheese-thief,' said Duffskul. Determined to make a show of it, Duffskul fished inside his robes and pulled out a piece of shamanshroom. He taunted the skaven with it.

'You know what this is, ratty? This is a shamanshroom. From da deep caves, where only those in da know can go. An old shaman, taken root, you might say, gone into da great green! But they leaves some of their magic behind, leaves it for the likes of me to eat up and squish ratties like you. Oh yus.'

Duffskul popped the leathery fragment in his mouth and chewed hard with black teeth. Something of the dead shaman's residual power flooded into him, augmenting the magic coursing through Duffskul to catastrophic levels. Everything went far away. He could hear the laughter of the Twin Gods in the distance. Sometimes that was a good sign. But not always, far from it.

'Now I is... Now I is...'

He hiccupped. Something went *pop* deep inside his brain. Duffskul frowned.

'Whoopsie,' he said.

With a wet splotch, his head exploded, fountaining a great deal of blood and a lot less brain all over the remains of the idol and the skaven sorcerer both.

The green fists evaporated into mist, and Kranskritt fell, taking in a deep and welcome breath to his bruised lungs.

'Heh heh, green-thing. Very good. Very interesting. But you dead now.' He frowned and leaned in to check. The green-thing's head had gone, what was left soaking messily into his dirty yellow robes. 'Yes-yes, definitely dead.'

Trying to salvage his dignity, Kranskritt brushed as much brain off his clothes as he could and walked away, checking all the time that no one was looking.

Skarsnik held up his prodder and waved it. Horns sang out all through the fleeing tribes. The regiments immediately stopped and turned around. A few of the more enthusiastic lads carried on going right through the city and up the mountain slopes; others were too far gone in panic to heed the rallying horns, but the majority – and all of these were Skarsnik's own boys, he noted proudly – reformed their ranks. A fresh flood of night goblins poured out from the gates to reinforce his back line.

Skarsnik peered under the black cloth covering Gobbla. 'You all right under there, mate?' he said. Gobbla snuffled back. 'Good.' Skarsnik looked up and down his lines. All in order. 'Let's see what we can see,' he said and unsnapped his telescope.

The skaven army was in total disarray. Split up by Skarsnik's ambushes, large parts of it were isolated into groupings of a few hundred strong. He watched with satisfaction as the foreigner Snaggla Grobspit and his giant spiders tore apart the skaven war machines. But it wasn't over yet. The Head-taker had a strong force about him, and was heading for that cocky big head Krolg Krushelm on top of that big lizard he was always riding about. Well, Skarsnik would wait to see what happened there. Either way, Krolg's loss would be no great one. The orc hadn't been in the Peaks long, and hadn't yet learned to show the proper respect. That was the usual way with the orc bosses, but this one was more uppity than most, and making the other orcs behave badly.

He turned his spyglass elsewhere. In other parts the battle was in balance, not going quite as well as he had hoped. The manglers had run out of steam over by the Burnt Cliffs and been killed, allowing skaven reinforcements to pour out of the rat holes there and strengthen the flank about the base of Silver Mountain. Big Red the giant squig was stomping far from the main fight, chasing down a dwindling pack of ratmen, but was effectively out of the battle. A flare of magical energy drew his attention to the Idol of Gork rampaging around the skaven rear. A sympathetic 'Oooh!' went up from the army as the magically animated statue lost a foot and pitched forwards flat on its face. Skarsnik saw Duffskul fall with it, then lost him amid the ruins. 'He'll be all right,' said Skarsnik to himself, although he was worried – not for Duffskul, but mainly because he had expended his store of secret weapons and the skaven still weren't broken.

Still, neither was his army.

He turned his telescope to the front, where, through the magnified points of goblin hats, he saw Ikk Hackflay's Iron-skins and a bunch of massive ratboys closing with his position. Furry ogre-things came with them, driven on by a fat, mean-looking skaven. Two of Queek's best, he thought. Be good to get rid of them. 'Ready, lads! We've got big furry lads coming in, one mean looking fella leading them, and some ogre-fings with a fatty ratty. We's gonna kill them both. Everybody ready?'

'Waaagh!' they responded.

'I'm glad you said that,' he said, with a crooked smile.

Queek ran at full scurry towards the wyvern and its stupid-meat rider. The wyvern charged about on the ground, smashing prey down with its heavily armoured skull and gulping them down whole. Gore hung from its mouth. The bloody remains of skaven were scattered everywhere, along with piles of the wyvern's dung. As it moved, it toileted, clearing room in its bulging stomach for more meat. Given enough time, it would eat itself into a torpor, but wyverns had big appetites and that time would be too long in coming.

The orc speared a clanrat, dangling the still-squealing creature in front to the mouth of his mount. The wyvern's beady eyes fixed on the morsel, and snapped at it as the orc snatched the skaven out of the way. He laughed uproariously as he teased the beast.

Queek signalled to his guard to halt, and strode out. He banged his weapon hilts on his breastplate to get the orc's attention.

'Big-meat! Queek the Mighty, ruler of City of Pillars, will fight you.'

Hearing this, the orc heaved on the wyvern's reins, pulling it around to face Queek.

'Headtaker,' he spat. Krolg eyed the stormvermin twenty paces behind Queek carefully. They made no move to come forwards, or he might well have flown off. That's why Queek had ordered them to stay where they were. The wyvern spread its wings and bellowed. Its tail arched high over its back, in the manner of a scorpion. Black venom dripped from the point of it sting. The vinegary stench of it made Queek's eyes run.

Krolg dug long spurs into the tender skin under the wyvern's wings. It leapt into the air, gliding the short distance at Queek. The impact of the beast's landing shook the ground. The orc thrust at him overhand with his spear, a clumsy blow that Queek parried easily, riposting with a powerful backhand against the wyvern's head. Queek had never fought one of these creatures before, and its iron-hard scales took him by surprise. The blow jarred his arm so hard his teeth clacked together. The wyvern barely registered it, snapping at him from one side while the orc drove his spear at him from the other. Queek sprang back, only to expose himself to a punishing strike from the wyvern's poisoned tail. Queek barely threw himself aside. He skidded as he landed, vulnerable for a moment, but the orc and his mount were too slow. The stinger plunged into the ground, whipping back almost as quickly.

Queek wiped spatters of burning venom from his muzzle. The orc atop the wyvern chuckled at him and urged his mount on.

The rock here was harder to gnaw than it appeared, so the old saying went.

The goblins stumbled backwards, pushed by the fury of the stormvermin. A massive rat-leader slew a brace of goblins with each sword stroke. Skarsnik levelled his prodder at him and let fly with a blast of raw magic. Some sixth sense caused the rat-leader to leap aside, and Skarsnik burned up half a dozen of his fellows instead.

'I'm going to have to sort this out myself, aren't I?' said Skarsnik. 'Come on, Gobbla.' He pulled on his squig's chain, and the pair of them shoved their way down to the front.

Skarsnik's prodder emerged first, punching through the gap between two goblins and spearing a stormvermin on its triple prongs. Skarsnik grunted as he pushed, shoving the dead rat back off its feet and tripping those in the ranks behind it. The rat was big, but Skarsnik was strong. Under his robes he was a mass of knotted muscle, his success such that he had grown huge for a night goblin – for a goblin of any kind, for that matter. Only Fat Grom had been bigger, but as Skarsnik liked to say, that was all fat and it didn't count.

'Come on, you ratties!' shrilled Skarsnik. Recognising their master's arch nemesis, the stormvermin scrambled over each other to get at him, eager to be the one to take his head. He stabbed and blasted with his prodder. Gobbla fought at his side, snapping the heads off halberds that might have speared his master, snapping the hands off that held the halberds, and snapping off the heads of the vermin that guided the hands. Skarsnik was old and thoughtful, but when roused he was mean as an orc warlord after a heavy night on the fungus brew. With Gobbla by his side, he was well nigh unstoppable. By his own efforts, he opened a wide circle in the front ranks of the stormvermin. 'Go on! Get on at ya!' he shouted, whirling the prodder round his head and whooping with delight. The goblins pushed forwards after him, chanting his name.

Skarsnik brought his prodder in a wide arc, aiming to decapitate three stormvermin with one blow, only to find it intercepted by a black sword. A terrible strength was behind it. He pushed, and a fat, heavily muscled skaven pushed back. Skarsnik did not know his name, but it was Grotoose. A pack of rat ogres moved in and boxed in Gobbla, leaving the King under the Mountains to face Grotoose alone.

The Clan Moulder war-leader leaned in close to Skarsnik, both of them grimacing with hatred and effort. With a flourish, Skarsnik disengaged, flinging Grotoose's sword arm wide. Skarsnik reversed the prodder, sending the weighty ferrule on its base driving into Grotoose's flabby stomach. Air exploded from the skaven's mouth, and he doubled over. Skarsnik stepped in, but Grotoose was shamming. As Skarsnik approached, Grotoose slammed his sword hilt into Skarsnik's head, and again. Driven back, Skarsnik stumbled, his feet fouled in the chain attaching Gobbla to him.

Grotoose loomed over him, blotting out the pale sky.

He raised his sword. 'Now you die-die!'

Grotoose never landed his blow. Gobbla came from the side, a bolt of crimson death, teeth snapping. He swallowed the claw leader of Clan Moulder whole.

Skarsnik got to his feet and patted his pet. 'That was close! That was too close,' he muttered. 'Good boy, Gobbla.'

Gobbla burped.

Skarsnik took a moment. The stormvermin and rat ogres had been driven back, the flow of battle moving away from him. Annoyingly, the stormvermin's boss was still alive and kicking, but he was on the defensive. 'They don't need us no more, come on. We got some strategising to do,' he said. His speech was peppered with bastardised Reikspiel and Khazalid words he used for concepts Orcish lacked the capacity to express. He led his pet back to his vantage point to begin said strategising.

He extended his telescope again. The battle was much as it was before. Then he saw something he had never seen, a blurring shadow that leapt all over the battlefield. One instant it was in one place, in another elsewhere. A disk of metal whirred out from this darkness, curving through air and flesh alike without interrupting its course. It banked around and flew back to its starting point, being snatched out of the air by a huge clawed hand.

'That's weird,' said Skarsnik. 'That looks a bit like one of them...'

Gobbla whined. Skarsnik looked down.

'What's wrong, boy?'

Gobbla's nose snuffled. He looked up into Skarsnik's eyes with his one good one.

'Gobbla?'

A dribble of blood collected at the corner of the squig's mouth. Skarsnik knelt down, concerned. A squelching sound came from Gobbla's innards. Skarsnik put his ear to the squig's side.

Gobbla whined again.

A knife burst through the top of the squig's skull. Gobbla's eye rolled back into his head, and the squig collapsed, deflating. His bulk wobbled and shook, and the knife cut downwards.

'Gobbla!' screamed Skarsnik.

Grotoose hauled himself from a long slit in the squig's side. His skin was blistered from Gobbla's potent stomach acids, fur falling out in clumps. Half his face had been melted off. Groaning in pain, he dragged himself away with fingers whose flesh came away from the bone as he scrabbled at the rock.

Skarsnik looked on in speechless horror. Grotoose raised a head with eyes that had been burned to whiteness.

'I first Clan Moulder beastmaster in Eight Peaks,' he said thickly. 'It take lot more than stupid red-ball, fungus-thing to kill me.'

His face contorting with rage, Skarsnik raised the prodder high and drove it down through Grotoose's back so hard it shattered the stone beneath. Grotoose shuddered, as if he'd still planned on getting up, before he finally realised he was dead.

'Gobbla,' said Skarsnik, in a small voice. The battle forgotten, he dropped his prodder and fell to the squig's side. The squig sagged in on itself, its capacious body pooling like a half-empty wineskin. Skarsnik knelt and hesitated, eyes surveying this most cruel ruin as if he could bring it back to wholeness by wishing it otherwise.

It didn't happen. It couldn't happen. Gobbla was dead, his small, faithful brain leaking out through the hole in the top of his head.

Skarsnik laid both hands on the leathery hide of his closest companion.

'Gobbla,' said the Warlord of Karak Eight Peaks, with a catch in his throat. 'Gobbla!'

Queek dodged another thunderous blow from the wyvern, tripping on a half-buried lump of masonry as he did. He was panting heavily, bleeding down one arm from a lucky spear-thrust.

'Getting tired, incha, little rattie?' rumbled the orc. 'You're a tasty fighter, that's what they all say. Down in the Badlands they say that. That far away. Yeah, that's right. Ain't you proud?' The orc laughed. 'Broken Toofs, my tribe. We heard that all right, we heard all about da Headtaker.' He widened his eyes in mock fright. 'But I reckoned it was all bluster, all talk. Load of nonsense. No rat going to outfight an orc every day of the week like what they say you can, though I see you got a couple of blackies up there on your spikes. Idiots, they are. No fun in them. I ain't one of them snaggle-toothed stunty slaves. I'm a free orc – you'll never beat me.'

Queek kept his distance from the circling wyvern. He spat on the ground. Let the orc talk himself into an early grave. The ones with the big mouths always spoke too much, leaving themselves open to Queek's mightiness.

This fight had gone on too long. If he didn't finish it soon, the green imp might win!

How to end it? How to end it? Queek burned inside.

'My name,' said the orc, 'is Krolg Krushelm! You hear that, now. I wants you to be thinking it when I guts ya! I'm a real greenskin, not like this sneaky little git here. No wonder you ain't been beat yet. As soon as I'm done with you, I'm taking that cave runt down. It's about time the Eight Peaks had a real boss.' Krolg spurred his mount.

The wyvern roared, spraying Queek with foul-smelling spittle. The tail swiped down, jaws coming at him from another angle, Krolg's spear from a third.

Queek had the measure of his opponents. A good fight, a fine challenge. A pity to finish it.

He ducked the sting, batted the spear tip aside with his sword, rolled under the wyvern's head, sprang to his feet and, with a powerful swing, buried Dwarf Gouger in the wyvern's eye. The spike on the pick punched through the soft eyeball and the thin bone at the back of the socket with ease.

The wyvern bellowed in agony and spread its wings. It wrenched its head back from the source of its pain. Queek kept tight hold of Dwarf Gouger's haft, letting go only when the time was right. As he arced through the air, Krolg's mouth formed an 'o' of surprise below his twisting body.

Krolg was still wearing the expression when his head toppled from his shoulders and rolled into the dirt.

Queek landed on his feet in a crouch, a gleeful smile on his lips.

He waited until the wyvern's death throes had ceased before retrieving his favourite weapon.

'Boss! Boss!'

Skarsnik heard the words only dimly. His entire attention was fixed on the dead Gobbla, his hands still pressed into his gradually sinking flesh.

A hand grabbed him. 'Boss!'

Skarsnik whirled round and snarled into the face of Kruggler.

Kruggler took a step backwards, both hands raised. 'Boss! Now ain't the time. Don't let them see you like this, boss. The lads need bossing, boss! What are we going to do?'

Skarsnik shivered. The skin around his eyes felt tight. A

strange emotion he'd not felt before... Nah, nah, that wasn't right. Once before, long ago, when Snotruk had killed Snottie, his loyal companion in his lonely days as a runt. Hollow like, all empty inside, like nothing really mattered any more.

He shook it off, but it clung on, clamping around the quivery bit of meat inside his chest like it would crush it with cold, cold ice.

'Ye're right, ye're right.' He nodded at Gobbla. 'Someone take that away!' he said, trying to sound like he didn't care. The goblins that came forward were wise enough to handle the dead squig very carefully indeed. Kruggler helped the goblin warlord up while one of Skarsnik's little big 'uns smashed the chain with his long axe.

The weight gone from his foot felt weird. He wiggled it around speculatively. Definitely weird.

'Boss!' said Kruggler in exasperation.

'What? Yeah, sorry, the battle, the battle.' Skarsnik raised his hand to his eyes. He couldn't see very well because they kept filling up with water and he didn't know why. He blinked it away and took stock of the battle.

Towards Silver Mountain, a fresh horde of clanrats running down the remainder of the squig teams there.

To the east, the now very distant form of Big Red trumpeting his way towards the evening. To the south, a mighty arachnarok spider being dismembered by the mysterious shadow.

To the centre, the broken Idol of Gork – or was it Mork? He really couldn't be sure – and an additional item: one slaughtered wyvern, topped with a headless orc. The Headtaker's troops were forming up, gathering stragglers back into solid formations. The formation that Skarsnik's little big 'uns had broken was being bullied back into shape by its leader.

'I've seen enough,' said Skarsnik.

'What?' said Kruggler.

'It's a bust. We've lost. A good scrap, but we couldn't pull it off, because there really is a lot of them, ain't there?' said Skarsnik to himself. 'Farsands, and farsands.' He did a quick mental calculation, the kind that would make a normal goblin die of a brain infarction. 'That's actually a lot more of them than there is of us...' He looked to the citadel. 'Old Belegar's next. We need to scarper.'

'What?!' repeated Kruggler.

'Kruggs, mate, we have lost! Can I make it any simpler for you? If we don't shift, Queek'll have our heads on that poncy bedstead he wears on his back quicker than he'll have Belegar's. I don't think I want to stick around for that. Sound the retreat!' he shouted.

'What about the rest of the boys?'

'What? Out-of-towners, weird scrawny runts wot smell of old leaves and ride about on spiders, and deadbeats? Nah, they played their part. Leave 'em. Besides, if we all go at once, then the rats might attack us before we can get away, mightn't they?' Skarsnik tapped his grubby forehead with a bloody finger. 'Always thinking me. That's why I is king and you is not.' He addressed his signallers again, before they commenced their flag-waving and horn-blowing. 'And by retreat, I mean walking back inside carefully with your weapons ready, not running for the hills so we's can all get out of breath, run down, chopped up and et by ratsies! Got that?' he bawled.

His horn-blowers and flag-wavers nodded. At least some of them understood. They relayed his orders as best they could. Some of the greenskins even obeyed them. All in all, thought Skarsnik, as he watched his tired tribe and its allies about face and march up to the gates of the Howlpeak, things could have been a whole lot worse.

Once he'd regained the gates himself, he went up to the broken battlements atop it. Through his telescope he watched the skaven break into a desperate run as the last of the Crooked Moon tribe withdrew to the safety of the Howlpeak. For a long time, he kept his spyglass trained on Queek's furious, furry face and watched it get madder and madder. He kept watching, in fact, until the gates clanged shut.

Now that was funny.

'Gobbla,' he said, meaning to share the moment with his pet. 'Gobbla, look at that, eh? Boy? Boy?' Skarsnik looked down at his side.

But, of course, there was nobody there.

# TWENTY

*Lurklox's Deal*

Skarsnik went into his private rooms as quickly as he was able. That was not very quickly. He had to patrol the borders of his much-reduced kingdom to make sure the lads were watching out properly, and that there were units ready to see off an attack, and that the outsiders who had come into the Howlpeak didn't cause any bother. That went double for any who were orcs. He had a few challenges now Gobbla was gone, but that was not such a bad thing. He needed to put a couple of orcs down to keep the rest in line. Without Gobbla, they found him still extremely dangerous, and the fact that he could still break an orc with his bare hands without his giant pet had quietened them down real quick. But Gobbla's loss was telling on him in other ways. Without the squig, he'd lost his skaven assassin early warning system. He might as well leave the door unlocked, dismiss all his guard and go to sleep with a knife conveniently laid out next to his bed.

Once inside, he locked the door and commenced pacing,

the butt of his prodder clashing on the floor. He banged it harder and harder as he got more and more worried. Skarsnik was no stranger to dilemmas, but this one was a real pickle and no mistake.

'Got to get organised, got to get organised!' he muttered to himself. 'Where is I if I don't gets organised?' He glanced to his papers, but this time they didn't hold the answer. 'Gotta fink!' he said, and worried at his fingers with sharp goblin teeth. 'Item one,' he said to himself. 'Old Queek's going for conquest. Item two, there's loads more of them than there is of us. Item three, them stunties aren't going to be there much longer, and when they is not, old squeaky Queeky's gonna come knockin' on me door with all his monsters and such. So what to do? Need Duffskul, yeah.' He made to call the sha-man, but remembered he was dead too. Who else could he call on? No one had seen Mad Zargakk in years, Kruggler was the brightest of the gobboes to hand but still very thick, and there was no point at all in asking an orc...

He caught something from the corner of his eye, a flicker in the room where one shouldn't be.

'Oh, come on. Not again!' he groaned. He levelled his prod-der at the globe of black lightning crackling into being. 'I'm not in the mood today, ratboy! Buzz off or get a face full of Morky magic!'

But as the visitor manifested, Skarsnik's expression of defi-ance turned to a gape. His intention to zap the rat dissipated. This wasn't your usual rat with horns, magicking himself in to have a pop – although it did, he supposed, have horns. And it did look like a rat, only not that much. Bigger, it was. Everywhere.

'Rats,' he said, 'aren't usually that big.'

Skarsnik took a step back as an immense shape stepped out of the shadows. Although, that wasn't right, because the shad-ows came with it. They writhed over the thing, whatever it was, stopping Skarsnik from getting a good look at it. He got an impression, nothing more – long, hairy arms lined with thick tendons, black claws, and a head crowned with an impressive rack of horns above a masked face where terrible eyes burned.

For the first time in a long time, Skarsnik gulped fearfully. The thing! The weird thing from the battle that had taken out Grobspit's spider monsters, right there in his bedroom! The creature was huge, bigger than a troll, all wiry muscle and patches of fur. It had claws bigger than Gobbla's teeth. Then Skarsnik recognised it for what it was, and recovered his wits. Better the daemon you know, and he knew this kind well enough.

'Oh. Right. It's one of *those*.' The stink of rodent and glowy green rock was unmistakeable. 'Ratfing daemon, one wiv lots of extra shadow, but a ratfing daemon you is. Well, ain't I honoured,' he said archly. 'Oi, back off,' he shouted, holding his ground. His prodder crackled with power. 'I ain't no snotty to be pushed about.'

'I am a lord of the Thirteen in Shadow!' scoffed the rat-daemon. 'I am master-assassin! That cannot hurt me. You cannot hurt me!'

'Yeah, right. Shall we give it a little try? I reckon a blast of Mork magic'd put a very big hole in you, you... you... ratfing. Don't you?'

'This is no stand-off, green-thing. I mighty-powerful. I show you mercy. If I wanted you dead, tiny and most vexing imp, dead you would be.'

'Who's showing who mercy? You want to test?' He jiggled the prodder. 'Fzapp!' it went, very quietly but menacingly. Skarsnik sniffed at the sharp smell of discharged magic. 'What is it you want, anyhow? Not seen one of your like for a while.'

'I am verminlord! Master of skaven. You have glimpsed-seen my kind?' said Lurklox, catching his surprise just a moment too late.

Skarnsik nodded the tip of his pointy hat to a large skull mounted over the fireplace. 'Yeah. You could say that. Bagged that one about fifteen winters back.'

Lurklox looked at the yellowing skull then back at the prodder. Skarsnik grinned evilly.

'So now we got that out of the way, what do you want, then? Get on with it, I haven't got all day. Just lost a battle, and I need to do something about it.'

Skarsnik's bravado rather put Lurklox off his stride, and spoiled his grand entrance. He stood taller, but the goblin would not be intimidated.

'Green-thing!' said Lurklox portentously. 'You are beaten-defeated. The indefatigable Queek has smashed your army for the last time.'

Skarsnik looked off at his heaped stuff, disinterested. 'Has he now? There's a lot more where those boys came from.'

'Lie-lie! Green-things like strength. You beaten, you not strong. They leave soon, and you die-die.'

'Right,' said Skarsnik. 'I'm no quitter though, and I've won a lot more battles than I have lost.'

'Already your large and bouncing beast-thing is no more.' Lurklox pointed at the broken chain still manacled to Skarsnik's ankle. 'We kill-slay it, we kill-slay you.'

'You wait a minute,' said Skarsnik with sudden and dangerous anger. 'The fight ain't gone out of me yet, you big horned rat... rat... What was it you said you was?'

'I great verminlord!' shrieked Lurklox.

'I don't care what you are, you're in my bedroom and I'm not happy about it!'

Lurklox sniffed the air and made a disgusted noise. 'Neither of us are. To business, then! I come offer-give with mighty gift-offer for green-thing Skarsnik! In possession of Ikit Claw, arch-tinker rat, is a very powerful bomb.'

'A bomb?' said Skarsnik.

'A bomb! The greatest bomb ever made by rat-paw and skaven ingenuity.'

Lurklox waved a paw, and a scene wreathed in warpstone-green smoke shimmered in the air before Skarsnik. It showed a vast and busy workshop. Skaven in strange armour worked at cluttered benches. Atop one of these was an intricate brass device the size of a troll's head.

'Yeah?' said Skarsnik, careful to hide his surprise at the workshop, the likes of which he'd never seen before. He rapidly factored its existence into his calculations, allowing for it being an illusion, but he reckoned it probably wasn't. 'So what? Why are you telling me this? Gloating, are we? Going to blow me up? Didn't work last time, did it?' He decided the towering rat god wasn't going to kill him just yet, and he sat down on his filthy bed with a groan. It had been a testing day.

'No-no! I give-bring to goblin warlord! A fitting gift-prize for worthy foe.'

'And what the zog exactly am I supposed to do with this giant metal egg, eh?'

'There are many dwarf-places left. See!' Lurklox brandished his shadowed claws again. An image of a strong dwarf citadel surrounded by a siege camp. 'Zhufbar-place! Impregnable, undefeated. Many skaven die here. Perhaps you could win great glory for yourself by bringing it low?'

'Looks like you've got plenty of furboys there right now. What do you need me for? And come to think of it, why not just get one of your sneaky pink-nosed little pals to do it? You don't need me at all.' Skarsnik's eyes narrowed. 'Why not just off me now? I'm not buying this at all.' Skarsnik emphasised his words with the prodder.

'You are as much boon-thing as problem-trouble, green-thing. Many pieces on the board-game. I prefer to keep you alive. The skaven at Zhufbar-place are weak. You are strong. Dependable.'

'That's nice to know,' said Skarsnik.

'You do as I squeak-say, green-thing?'

Some of the defiance went out of Skarsnik. He felt older than ever. He was tired. Outside a sea of rats awaited him, Queek wanted his head and might just get it this time, he'd lost his only useful advisor, and then there was Gobbla. The next time this big rat paid him a visit, he might not survive. Skarsnik slumped a little, it was time to face facts. 'I don't see I got much choice,' he said quietly. 'But it's going to cost you more than the big boom boom,' he added sharply.

'Yes-yes?'

'If I can't kill Queek,' he spat the name, 'I'll not be happy leaving both them gits alive. Bring me Belegar's head for me collection, and I'll do as you say. Skarsnik will leave the Eight Peaks,' he smiled. 'Although it's more like six and a half peaks now, ain't it?'

'You swear-swear, and you go to Zhufbar? Lead your mighty armies there?'

'And then I'll never come back. I swear it. Although you know that means nothing, right?'

Lurklox's masked face appeared for a moment in the swirling green-black fog surrounding his form. Something like a smile wrinkled the skin visible around his eyes.

'I see why we have not beaten you yet. You are almost like a skaven.'

'Oi!' said Skarsnik. 'There's no need to be rude.'

There was much to be done upon the surface. Queek's desire to see the green-things' shanty totally demolished and their burrows stopped up bested his patience, and it was growing dark before Queek, still besmirched and begrimed with the filth of battle, marched back towards the comforting darkness of the underworld. His troops lined every street on his route, squeaking out his name. He went slowly, letting them see him, his head held high and chest puffed out, his trophy rack bloody with new heads. Ska went behind him, his Red Guard marching in perfect step after Ska.

'Another victory!' Queek said. 'Another victory for mighty Queek! Queek brings Clan Mors only victory!'

'All hail mighty Queek!' shouted Ska.

His guard clashed their halberds on their shields and shouted. The army cheered, bowing and fawning over their leader as he walked past them.

Once inside, Queek made straight for the burrows he had requisitioned as his base for this war on the surface. His servants awaited his coming. Blind, weak and castrated, they were feeble examples of the skaven breed, and that suited Queek perfectly.

He went to be cleaned, allowing the quaking slaves to unstrap his armour. They licked blood from his fur, bit out tangles and scabs, and gingerly cleaned his few scratches. His armour was given the same attention. Once upon a time, Queek had been lax in his hygiene, allowing the muck of battle to cake his armour for weeks at a time until he stank. Not any longer. He had resolved not to go abroad filthy as a plague monk. He told himself it was all about appearances, but deeper down, and as Sleek Sharpwit's head kept telling him, it was because the smell of death reminded him that he was getting old.

As his servants worked on him, he relaxed. Some of the murderous tension went from his muscles. To his followers he had delivered a great victory, but all he could think about was the green-thing retreating back through his gates to the safety of the Howlpeak. Queek's lip curled, his fists clenched. Belegar was easy-meat now, dead-meat weak-meat, but his extermination of the dwarfs would give the imp time to retrench, and Queek had not slain as many of his goblins as he had hoped.

If he were truthful, he was lucky to have won at all.

The torches in Queek's chamber flickered. In the corner he had a pile of looted glimstones, their cold light forever constant, but these too stuttered. The presence of his dead-thing trophies, always tentative of late, receded entirely. A shadow gathered. It would be behind Queek. It always was. He did not give Lurklox the pleasure of turning to greet him.

'Little warlord preening, good-good. Sleekness is stealthiness,' said the verminlord's voice, as Queek had predicted, from behind him.

Even blinded, the thralls felt the powerful presence and scurried to get out. The shadow grew around Queek, making everything black. Queek alone remained illuminated, alone in the dark.

Lurklox stepped through into the bounds of this world, gracefully uncoiling himself from nothing into something. Although he had seen it many times now, Queek was unnerved by the way the towering verminlord stepped out from the shadow.

Queek did not care for the way Lurklox spoke to him, nor did he like the way his fur stood on end in the rat-daemon's presence.

'What have you found out?' demanded Queek.

'Impudence, haste-haste. Always the same. Either too much greeting, or none at all. The warlord clans never change.'

Sensing that Queek had steeled himself against such provocations, the verminlord got to the point.

'The grey seer needs you as an ally. Your Lord of Decay Gnawdwell moves to ally with Clan Skryre. It is he that makes the attempts upon your life. It was he that bid-told Thaxx to delay. It was he that called upon Ikit Claw to shame you. You are being used, Headtaker. Gnawdwell grooms many replacements for you.'

Queek burst into laughter. Lurklox's anger grew thick, a palpable, dangerous thing, but Queek did not care. 'Great and stealthy Lurklox talk as if this not known to Queek!' He dissolved again into giggles. 'None of this news to Queek. Every lord tests his lieutenants. So what? Most die, some live to be tested tomorrow. And Queek has lived to see many tomorrows! Gnawdwell will not be disappointed by Queek disappointing him.'

Lurklox loomed, growing bigger. Queek stared defiantly up at the shadowy patch he judged the verminlord's face to occupy.

'Then what of Gnawdwell's prize, long life and forever battle?' said Lurklox, and Queek's blood ran cold. 'Does it still stand, or was Gnawdwell only lying to Queek? Queek is a fool-thing, mad-thing. Queek does not know everything, but I do.'

Lurklox let his words hang, making sure he had asserted dominance over the warlord before continuing. Queek wanted to know if the offer was real; Lurklox could taste his incipient fear at his growing age. Good. Let him be afraid.

'Time runs on,' said Lurklox, hammering the sentiment home. 'Time Queek no longer has. I have come from council with Skarsnik. I have struck a deal with the goblin-thing for you. The war here will soon be over. Queek is needed elsewhere.'

The shock on Queek's face was a further reward for the verminlord.

'Yes-yes!' said Lurklox, encouraged. 'Deliver the dwarf-king's head by sunset tomorrow and Skarsnik will leave the City of Pillars.'

Queek snorted and licked at a patch of fur his slaves had missed. 'What else did you give-promise Skarsnik? Queek's lieutenants make uncountable bargains with the goblin king, and he breaks every single one. What make Lurklox think this time will be any different?'

'Queek guesses well. Clever warlord. There was something else. The promise of that head... and something Ikit Claw does not yet know is missing. A threat-gift. If the imp-thing not take, then we use it against him.'

'Why not use this thing-thing against him in first place, mysterious Lurklox? Simple way best. Skaven too stupid to see.'

Lurklox did not answer.

'Very well,' said Queek. 'I will slay the beard-thing and hand over his head to the imp. Queek has-owns many dwarf-thing trophies already. What does Queek want one more for?'

On rickety shelves, nearly two dozen trophy heads looked at him with empty eyes.

Queek refrained from explaining to Lurklox just how tricksy the goblin was. It would give him a great deal of amusement to see the verminlord upstaged by the imp. There was no way that the so-called king would give up the kingdom he had been fighting over for his entire life. And when he broke his deal, Queek would kill him and take back Belegar's head and Skarsnik's into the bargain. Queek tittered.

'A great-good deal, clever high one, most impressive.'

# TWENTY-ONE

*The Final Saga of Clan Angrund*

In an out-of-the-way cellar of the citadel, Gromvarl stood in a pit in the floor and tugged at an iron ring set into a flagstone. Unprepossessing, lacking the adornment of most dwarf creations, a slab of rock hiding a secret. There was a finality to it.

'Someone give me a hand here!' grumbled the longbeard. 'It's stuck.'

'It's the differentiation in air pressure – sometimes does that, sucks it closed. It's murder to get open,' said Garvik, one of Duregar's personal retainers. 'Come here. Ho ho, Frediar! Hand me a lever.'

Garvik's nonchalant manner turned to swearing. Soon there were four of them in there, arguing over the best way to prise the door open. Finally, after much effort, it budged. Air whistled around the broken seal. They tugged hard, and a fierce draught set up, building to a shrieking wind that settled into an eerie moan once the stone had been set aside.

Gromvarl looked down the narrow shaft the trapdoor

covered: big enough for a dwarf, no more. He held his lamp over it. Red iron rungs stretched down into the blackness. The shaft descended thousands of feet. That it had not been uncovered by the thaggoraki or the grobi was a wonder. Only weeks ago, a handful of rangers had set out from this place to guard the refugees fleeing the sack of Karak Azul. There had been hopeful talk of their numbers swelling those of the dwarfs of Karak Eight Peaks, but Karak Eight Peaks had become a place of wild hopes. None of the dwarfs of Iron-peak had ever arrived, and the warriors sent out to help them were lost.

A double-or-nothing gamble for the king, and the dice had come up poorly once more. The dice these days were always loaded. Douric could have told him that. The king rolled now in desperation, a dawi down to his last coin.

'Gromvarl! Get yourself out of there. The king's coming.'

Gromvarl disdainfully allowed himself to be helped up out of the pit, like he was doing those who helped him a favour, and not the reverse. Truth was, he was not so spry any more, but he hid it under a barrage of complaints.

Once out, he stood among a group of fifty dawi gathered in the cellar, three dozen of them dressed for hard travelling, all armed. The room was crowded, the damp air fogged by their breath and the heat of their bodies. Longer than it was broad, with a tapering roof of close-fit stone, the cellar was flawless work, but all unembellished as the escape door. No such place of shame should be decorated. No carven ancestor face should look upon the backs of dwarfs as they fled. That was the reasoning. A shame that ordinarily ale barrels and cabbage boxes hid.

Several of those present were proper warriors, rangers and ironbreakers. They stared at the floor, humiliated beyond tolerance by the king ordering them to leave. They understood that what they had to do was important, all right, but Gromvarl would bet his last pouch of tobacco – and he was down to the very last – that every one of them wished some other dawi had been selected and told to go in his place. They chewed their lips and moustache ends and fulminated. Gromvarl could see at least three potential Slayers among their number.

A dwarf matron rocked a babe in arms. The child, its downy chin buried in its mother's bosom, snuffled in its sleep. Gromvarl smiled sorrowfully at the sight. There were too few unkhazali in these dark days, and there was no guarantee this one would survive. His expression clouded. Dwarf babies were as stoic as their elders, but they still cried from time to time. One misplaced call for milk and ale from the bairn could spell the end for the lot of them.

Better out there than in here. His thoughts turned to others, whose parents could not be swayed to leave. He thought too of Queen Kemma, shut up in her tower. As merciful as Belegar had been in permitting, and in some cases ordering, others out, he could not be swayed to release his queen and his prince. Oaths, said the king. Sadness gripped Gromvarl. Some oaths were made to be broken.

With that in mind, he clutched the key in his pocket.

Torchlight glinted from artful wargear. The king and his two bodyguards entered the small cellar where the dwarfs waited to flee.

The king was wan, his eyes heavily pouched and bloodshot. He tried to hide the stiffness in his side, but Gromvarl was too old to be fooled. The rumours of the king's injury told of a sad truth. That was far from the worst of it, however. Gromvarl could tell from the look on Belegar's face; he had finally given up on the slender hope of aid from elsewhere. He was prepared to die.

'I'll not make a meal of this,' said Belegar softly. 'I know none of you made this decision lightly, and some of you didn't want to go at all. Let it be known that I release you all from your oaths to me. Find some other king, a better king. Under his protection and in his service, may you live out more peaceful lives.

'Warriors,' he said to those handful of such. 'I have not chosen you to go because I can spare you. I cannot. I have chosen you because you are among the finest dawi left alive in Karak Eight Peaks. These are your charges. They need you more than I do. I release you also from all your oaths to me, and consider them fulfilled two and a half times over. Had I gold to give, you would have it by the cartload and in great gratitude. Instead, I place upon you one final burden – guard these last few of the clans of Karak Eight Peaks with your lives and your honour. Do not let the bloodlines of our city die forever.'

At these words dwarf resolve stiffened. Gazes were no longer downcast. Lips trembled with new emotions, and spines straightened.

'Aye, my king,' said Garvik, then the others repeated this one after another, some of the shame at their departure leaving through their mouths with the words. Belegar held the eye of each one and nodded to them.

'Now go, go and never return. This was a glorious dream, but it is over. We wake to the darkest of mornings. May you all see the light of a better morrow.'

Gromvarl stood back. Garvik wordlessly indicated that they should begin. A ranger went first, the group's guide, spitting on his hands before he reversed into the dark hole and took grip of the first of the iron rungs. The moan of the wind changed tone as he blocked the shaft.

'Four thousand feet,' he said, his words bearing the soft accent of the hill dwarfs who had once ranged above the ground of the Eight Peaks. 'Your arms will hurt, dawi or not. Keep on. After me, leave ten rungs, then ten rungs between each that follows after. Anyone thinks they're going to fall, call a halt. Pride will kill everyone beneath you should you slip. Remember that. Don't talk otherwise. This way is as yet undiscovered by our enemies, let us keep it that way.'

His head disappeared into the shaft. They counted ten ringing steps.

'Next!' whispered the ranger from the ladderway.

The first went, then the next. As they disappeared into the dark, wives bid farewell to husbands, children to fathers, warriors to their master. Then they were all gone, swallowed up by the ground as if they had never been.

Gromvarl watched them all go into the hole, one after the other, his heart heavy and a lump in his throat. So went the last sorry inhabitants of Karak Eight Peaks, to a doom none within would ever know.

When the last had gone, the king nodded. Gromvarl beckoned to two others. With their help, the trapdoor was replaced. Runes of concealment flared upon it. As the marks faded back into plain stone, the trapdoor went with them. The inset iron ring disappeared, as did any sign of a join with the pit floor. Then the dwarfs levered the flagstone that concealed the pit wherein the trapdoor nestled back into place. Masons hurried forwards, swiftly mortaring it back into place. Within a couple of hours, it would look like any other slab in the floor of the cellar.

Barrels were rolled back in, filling up the room.

The escape route disguised, the dwarfs filed out in silence.

'And here we come to the end of it all,' said Belegar. 'Fifty years of dashed hopes and broken honour. Was it all worth it?'

Never numerous, there remained only two hundred fighting dwarfs left in all of Karak Eight Peaks, a sum that included those untried warriors previously restricted to garrison duty, and those elders honourably retired from the front lines. A shattered people remained, drawn in to this last toehold from every part of the kingdom that had been so painfully retaken. Too few to adequately defend the doors into the Hall of Pillared Iron, Belegar had ordered them into a square at the centre of the room.

'Do not lament cracked stone, cousin,' said Duregar. 'If you swing the hammer so clumsily, the chisel slips. Best learn to swing it better.'

Belegar laughed blackly. 'There has to be a next time for the learning to take, Duregar.'

Duregar shrugged, working his mail into a slightly more comfortable position. 'Then others will learn from our errors, if errors they were. There's no harm to be found in trying to do something right and failing. Better to chance your arm than never risk failure at all.'

'Your words are a comfort to me.'

'They are intended to be, my king.'

'To the end, then, Duregar?'

'As I swore, to the end. For the Angrund clan, and for the chance at a more glorious future.'

Duregar gripped his cousin's hand tightly. The king squeezed back.

'Whatever it is I have achieved here,' said Belegar, 'I could not have done it without you, Duregar.'

A black masked face appeared around the main doors at the far end, and quickly withdrew.

'A scout, lord!' shouted one of the lookouts.

'Leave it be. Get back into formation. At least we know they'll be here soon. A small surprise seeing us stood here rather than behind more barred doors, eh?' Belegar paused. 'I'd make a speech, say words of encouragement to you all, but you need none of that. You know what is coming, and will fight boldly all the same. I could not be prouder of you all. I...' He stopped. 'This is something better said with ale rather than speech.'

The hogshead of ale at the centre of their formation was cracked open. To the last the dwarfs were fastidious in all they did, carefully tapping the barrel with a spigot, lest any go to waste. Foaming tankards were passed around, each dwarf given as much as he desired. The days of rationing were ending along with all else.

They drank quickly, wiping suds from their beards with satisfied gasps. This was the king's ale, the best and last. In quiet ones and twos they clasped arms and said their farewells, toasted kinsmen fallen in battle or treacherously murdered by the thaggoraki and grobi. Fond reminiscences were aired, and particular grudges recounted.

Belegar counted his men again. Of the Iron Brotherhood, fourteen remained. Duregar's bodyguard swelled their ranks to twenty-nine. They had only three cannons pointed at the two main gates, precious few guns or other machines, and just a smattering of crossbows.

'Like the last days of King Lunn,' said Belegar. 'Traditional weapons, tried and tested – none of your new fangled gear. Iron and gromril and dwarfish muscle.'

'Personally, I'd be glad of a flamecannon,' said Duregar.

'Aye,' admitted Belegar. 'So would I.'

Noise echoed up the corridors leading from the lower levels of the citadel.

'Here they come! Dawi, to arms!' shouted Belegar. His wound twinged as he climbed atop his oath stone and took his shield and hammer from his retainers. He tried not to wince.

Explosions rippled out, their distant rumbles carrying billows of dust into the hall. Worthless slave troops, sent to their deaths in the dwarfish traps. That was always the skaven way. Belegar wished that Queek would get on with it.

The battle was short by recent standards. Four waves of skaven came in and were thrown back, broken upon the unyielding steel of the shield walls. Poisoned wind globadiers scurried in the wake of the clanrats to be shot down by dwarf quarrellers with tense trigger fingers. This last time the skaven's poisons choked their own. Ratling guns and warpfire thrower teams met the same fate, every one felled by pinpoint shots. The dwarf cannons fired until their barrels glowed.

But the dwarfs were few, and the skaven many. In ones and twos the final brave defenders of Karak Eight Peaks fell. The defensive ring around Belegar grew smaller and smaller. The skaven pressed their attack. The cannons fell silent. The number of dwarfs shrank steadily from two hundred, to a hundred, to fifty. The fewer they were, the harder they fought, no matter how tired they were, no matter how thirsty for ale. Each kinsman dragged down fired the dwarfs with righteous anger, driving every one on to acts of martial skill that would have been retold in the sagas and noted in books of remembrance, if only there were survivors to carry their stories away.

It was clear there would be none.

The latest skaven attack flowed back from the dwarfs, but there was no rest. A flood of red-armoured skaven bearing heavy halberds came streaming into the room.

'Queek Headtaker's personal guard,' said Belegar. 'He is coming.'

'This is it, then,' said Duregar, who stood side by side with his cousin still. 'You and he will meet for the final time. Strike him down, Belegar. Send him back to whatever hell sired him.'

Belegar set his face and hefted his hammer. The crust on his wound opened again. Blood dampened his side under his armour.

The stormvermin of Queek's Red Guard crashed into the remaining two-score dwarfs. The stormvermin were fresh and fired with vengeance. Long had the Iron Brotherhood been a ratbane. They hacked down the dwarfs, although the folk of the mountain gave good account of themselves. The last dozen dawi crowded round their lords, sending the Red Guard back time and again. Belegar and Duregar fought back to back, hammers crushing limbs and heads.

One by one the last of the dawi were dragged down, until only Belegar and Duregar remained. All round the kinsmen, skaven fell upon the fallen, tearing at dwarf flesh in their feeding frenzy, or wrenching trophies from the corpses. Duregar was attacked by six of the creatures at once and pulled down, his last words in that life a defiant war-shout to Grimnir.

'Come on! Come on!' bellowed Belegar. 'Take me too, then, you miserable vermin!' He brandished his hammer, sweeping it about him, but the skaven withdrew to a safe distance, imprisoning him in a circle of spearpoints. 'Where is the Headtaker? I would show him my hammer!' Belegar wept freely, tears of sorrow mingled with tears of anger.

The ring opened, and in stepped Queek.

'Here I am, dwarf-thing. Eager-keen to die?' he said in high-pitched Khazalid. This was too much for Belegar. To be confronted with this theft of the innermost mysteries of the Karaz Ankor at the very end was one insult too many.

'Still your tongue! The language of our ancestors is not for you to profane! Bring your head here so that I may crack the secret of our speech from your skull. Attack me, Headtaker, and let us see how well you fare against a king!' roared Belegar.

Queek hefted Dwarf Gouger and his sword. 'Queek kill many kings, beard-thing. Your head joins theirs today, yes-yes.' He tittered, then sprang into a spinning leap, the infamous Dwarf Gouger and sword whirling with deadly speed.

Belegar parried them with stolid economy. Queek curled over a hammer strike that would have flattened a troll and landed behind the king. Belegar faced him.

'And I thought the Headtaker a master of combat,' said Belegar quietly. All emotion save hatred and defiance had bled from his face. He stood on legs weakened by his wound and battle fatigue, but he stood nonetheless. 'If you are the finest warrior your kind has to offer, no wonder you must resort to cheap tricks to bring your enemies low.'

Queek snarled and ran at Belegar. He punched forwards with the head of Dwarf Gouger, intending to make Belegar sidestep onto the point of his sword. But Belegar moved aside a fraction of an inch, evading the maul. He stamped down on Queek's sword, though it moved almost too quickly to be seen, wrenching it from Queek's grasp. A hammer blow of his own caught Queek by surprise. The skaven warlord moved aside awkwardly, holding only Dwarf Gouger. The hammer grazed him nonetheless, bruising his sword arm and driving his own armour into his flesh. Queek jumped back, swordless, blood matting his fur.

'Pathetic,' said Belegar. 'Flea-ridden vermin, swift and twitchy. There's not a dwarf alive who isn't worth twenty of you.'

'Queek has killed many hundred beard-things,' said Queek. He shook his arm. Agonising pins and needles ran from his shoulder to his hand, jangling the nerves of his fingers. His shoulder was numb. 'Queek kill one more very soon.'

'Probably. I am tired, and I am beaten, and the memory of our last encounter festers still in my flesh. But even as you hack the head from my neck, Queek, you will know that you could never best me in more honourable circumstances.'

Few skaven gave a dropping for honour, but Queek was one of this unusual breed. His honour was not as a dwarf would see it, but it was there, built of arrogance though it was. Queek became enraged at this slur upon it.

The duel that followed was swift, its outcome inevitable, but Belegar was not done yet. Queek spun and ducked, casting a deadly net of steel about the dwarf with his terrible maul. Belegar smashed it aside several times with his shield, but with each swipe he became weaker. Queek hooked the king's shield with the spike of his weapon, yanking it free from Belegar's arm with a squeak of triumph. A following blow smashed into Belegar's side, causing the king to cry out as his wound burst wider, but Queek overreached himself and the dwarf's hammer hit his left side, rending apart his warpstone armour and cracking his ribs. Agonised, Queek staggered, only at the last turning his stumble into a spin that had him facing the long-fur again.

He and Belegar panted hard. Belegar bled freely from the wound Queek had given him in their last encounter. Blood pooled about his feet. He had other wounds, some small, others graver. He could not see it himself, but his face was ghostly white.

Queek smiled in spite of his pain. The end approached.

'Greet-hail your ancestors when you meet them, beard-thing. Queek will come for them next. Death is no refuge from the mighty Queek!'

Again Queek charged, putting all his cunning into a complicated swipe reversed at the last moment to send Belegar's hammer spinning away from him. Another blow took the dwarf king in the knee, shattering it, and sending the dwarf down. But to Queek's amazement, the king arrested his fall. Holding himself in a kneel, his weight on his undamaged leg, he glared at the skaven, his eyes poison.

Queek swung Dwarf Gouger a final time. The spike connected with the side of the king's helmet, punching through the gromril. Queek squealed at his victory, but his cries turned to pain. He looked down. The dwarf had somehow got Queek's own sword up, and now it pierced him at the weak shoulder joint of his armour. He stepped back, and Belegar fell over with a crash, his eyes never leaving Queek's face.

Queek screamed as he pulled out his sword from his armpit, the weapon's square teeth dragging lumps of his own flesh with it. Ska rushed out from the ranks of the Red Guard, but Queek shoved at his massive chest with his unwounded hand.

On shaking legs, Queek walked over to the dwarf king. He plucked Dwarf Gouger free, casting it onto the carpet of dwarf bodies. With a yell, he swung his sword over his head, severing the king's head with one blow.

He dropped his sword and bent over, then held aloft Belegar's head with his good arm. He stepped up onto the dwarf king's oath stone.

'The City of Pillars is ours, from deepest deep to loftiest peak! Queek brings you this greatest of victories, only Queek!'

His guard squeaked out their praises, and Queek showed them all the lifeless head of Belegar. Such a fine trophy. Such a shame he had to give it up.

# TWENTY-TWO

*The Last King of Karak Eight Peaks*

Gromvarl staggered up the stairs. Black spots swam in front of his eyes, crowding out what little light there was left in the citadel. The poisoned wound in his back throbbed a strange sort of pain, at once unbearable yet simultaneously numb. He fought against it with all his dwarfish will, forcing himself on in the fulfilment of his first, last and most important oath.

The protection of Vala Kemma.

The sound of fighting still sounded from below, but it was that of desperate, lonely struggles fought in dark corners against impossible odds, and not the regimented clash of two battle lines. Screams came with it, and the stink of burning. There were only the old, the sick, and the young in the upper levels. The skaven were coming for Karak Eight Peaks's small population of children.

Gromvarl stumbled on the steps, his feet failing to find them. He broke a tooth on the stone. Five thousand years old, and still a sharp corner on the step edge. Now that, he thought, was proper craftsmanship.

Kemma was up above, locked in her room and forbidden to fight. Gromvarl had one of the only keys, but had been forced by the king to swear he would not use it.

The king was dead. As far as he was concerned, the oath died with him.

He staggered his way upwards, his progress growing slower and slower as he went. The fiery numbness had taken hold of his limbs. He had to rest often, his unfeeling hand pressing against the stone. He knew that if he sat down he would never reach his destination.

Finally, he arrived, one hundred and thirty-two steps that had taken a lifetime to climb behind him.

The door wavered ahead of him, its black wutroth shimmering as if seen through a heat haze. He fell to his knees and crawled towards it, the poison in his blood overcoming his sturdy dwarf constitution at the last.

With a titanic effort of will, Gromvarl slid the key home in the lock. Only his falling against the door enabled him to twist it at all.

The door banged open and he fell within. He moaned as he hit the floor. He slid into blackness. To his surprise, it went away again, and he managed to heave himself up to his knees. His head spun with the effort.

'Kemma!' he said. 'Kemma!' His throat was dry. A fire raged in it, consuming his words so they came out as insubstantial as smoke.

The queen was not there. The room was too small for her to hide. There were sounds coming from her garderobe, smashing, a frantic scrabbling.

A black-clad skaven came out, a scarf wrapped around its muzzle. It was a wonder it hadn't heard the door; then Gromvarl realised that the sounds of battle were very close behind.

Upon seeing him, the skaven assassin leapt over him, and pulled back his head sharply by the hair. A blackened dagger slid against his throat, the venom that coated it burning his skin.

'Where dwarf-thing breeder-queen?' asked the skaven. Like all of its kind, its voice was surprisingly soft and breathy. Not a hint of a squeak to it when they spoke the languages of others. Gromvarl found this rather funny and laughed.

The skaven twitched behind him, agitated.

'What so amusing, dwarf-thing? You want to die?'

'Not particularly, you thieving thaggoraki.' He burst out laughing again.

'Very good. You die-die just the same.'

A loud bang filled the room. The skaven slid backwards, its poisoned knife clattering to the floor. Gromvarl tossed the smoking pistol away.

'Never did like guns,' he grumbled, 'but I suppose they have their uses.' He fell onto his hands and knees. 'Not long now, eh, Grungni, eh, Grimnir? Soon I'll be able to look you in the eye and ask how I did. Appallingly, I'll bet.' He coughed, and bloody froth spattered from his mouth. Before he fell face down onto the floor, he smiled broadly.

Vala Kemma had always been as particular as any dwarf. Even in this prison in all but name, she'd kept her mail well oiled and her armour shining.

The mannequin that it had sat upon was empty.

Kemma had got away.

'That's my lass,' he said into the stones of the floor. They were cool, welcoming. His breath dampened them with condensation. 'That's my lass,' he whispered, and the stones were damp no more.

Kemma ran through the upper storeys of the citadel, her secret key clutched in her hand, not that she needed it now.

Poor Belegar, he always underestimated her. Leaving her shut up behind a simple lock? She felt a moment of anger; it was almost like he didn't think her a proper dwarf, probably because she was a woman.

But she was a dwarf, with all that entailed. Dawi rinn, and a vala too. More the fool him for not realising. He had always been so blinkered! Look where that had got him. Look where that had got them all.

People were running, those few warriors stationed in the top floors of the tower towards the sounds of fighting coming from the stairs, the remainder away to the final refuge with as much dignity as they could muster.

Only now, at the very end, were some of the dwarfs succumbing to panic, and not very many of them at that. Most were shouted down and shamed by their more level-headed elders, and there were plenty of them up there to do the shouting.

She caught sight of a familiar figure, bent almost double by the weighty book she had chained about her neck. Magda Freyasdottir, the hold's ancient priestess of Valaya. Even at the end she was dressed up in the lavender finery of her office, her ankle-length, silk-fine hair bound in heavy clasps of jet.

'Magda! Magda!'

The priestess turned, her face surprised. Kemma ran right into her arms.

'Steady, my queen,' she said ironically, and rightly so, for Kemma's kingdom was by now much circumscribed. 'I am not so steady on my feet as I was. I have someone here who might better appreciate your hugs. My king!' she called. 'Here he comes,' she said to Kemma. 'The last king of Karak Eight Peaks.'

Thorgrim came through the door, fully armed and armoured, his wispy beard hidden behind a chin-skirt of gromril plates. The sight of it made Kemma's heart swell. Next month he would have been eleven years old, nineteen years until the majority he would never attain. In his boy's armour he looked ridiculously young. In the visor of his helmet, his soft brown eyes, so like his father's in particular, were wide with fear but hard with duty. My son, thought Kemma. He would have been a fine king.

'Mother!' he shouted with undwarf-like emotion. The others looked away at the boy-king's unseemly display. They embraced. Someone tutted.

'I thought you were dead.'

'I too,' said Kemma. She looked him deep in the eyes. His return look said he knew it too, that soon they would be.

'Where are your Valkyrinn?' said Kemma to Magda, looking about for the priestess's bodyguards.

'Gone. Gone to fight, and now doubtless dead.'

'The king is dead?' she asked, although she knew the answer.

'Fallen. We are the last few dawi of Karak Eight Peaks. Thorgrim is our lord now.'

'Whatever you say, mistress Magda,' said Thorgim.

Magda chuckled. 'You're the king! You don't have to defer to me.'

'I think I will,' said Thorgrim gracefully. 'If it's all the same to you.'

The last few dwarfs were running down the hall towards the room, heavy boots banging sparks from once fine mosaics. Worryingly, this included the last few warriors. Bloodcurdling screams and a horrible squeaking pursued them.

'We better get in, and quickly,' said Magda. She produced from under her robes a heavy object wrapped in oilcloth and offered it to the queen. 'You'll be wanting this.'

'My hammer?' guessed Kemma.

'Of course. No queen should stand her last without her weapon. Are we dawi, or are we umgi females to go screaming into the night?'

Kemma nodded and took the oilcloth from the priestess; there indeed was the hammer.

'Thank you.'

'I took it from the armoury. I had no doubt you would need it at the end. Valaya provides for her champions.' She gave a weary sigh, and steadied herself on Kemma's shoulder. 'I fear she has one final task for you before the end.'

Freya beckoned her through the door. The few dwarf warriors outside nodded their heads grimly and slammed it shut. A key turned in the lock from outside, and those inside barred the door as best they could, nailing planks across the door and frame that had been left there for that purpose.

What a last stand. Here were the young and infirm, the very, very old. Those beardlings old enough to fight or who flat out refused to leave, those young unkhazali who were too young to chance the journey. Their parents' choice, not theirs. Kemma wished Belegar had ordered them all to go.

A room mostly full of those who never would or could no longer swing an axe. But all of those strong enough to lift them held one. Cooks, merchants, beardlings and rinn. All dwarfs had warrior in them, but some were more warlike than others, and the dwarfs in that room were among the least. They were down to the very last. She and Thorgrim were the champions of the room, the last heroes of this failing land.

She looked out of the room's small window. Snow swirled around the tower, but it could not obscure the hordes of greenskins camped outside, insolently within gunshot of the walls. It made her sick to see them. Within hours, she reckoned, they would be fighting with the skaven over her bones.

The door shook. The beardlings tried their best to be brave, the younger children were openly terrified, the unkhazali cried in their mothers' arms. There were not many children there; Karak Eight Peaks had never been a kind environment to raise beardlings. And here they all were, Karak Eight

Peaks's hopes for the future, trapped like rats and waiting to die.

The warriors in the corridor called out their battle-cries. From beyond the door a clashing of blades and the squealing of dying skaven set up. Thorgrim looked to his mother.

'Don't hold your axe so tightly,' she scolded gently. 'It will jar from your hand, and then where will you be?'

'Sorry, mother,' said Thorgrim.

Kemma smiled at him sadly. 'Don't be sorry. You have never done a wrong to dawi or umgi or anyone or anything else.' She reached up to pat his face as she always had, a mother's gesture for her child. But, she realised, he was not a child any more, despite his years. He was a king. She grasped his arm instead, a safe warrior's gesture. 'You would have been a very great king, my boy.'

The sound of arms abruptly ceased. There was a thump on the wood and a dying gurgle. Blood pooled under the door. Queekish squeaked outside. Silence. Then the door began to shake.

The door bounced in its frame. The wood splintered. The nails in the planks worked loose, and the first of them clattered to the floor.

'They're coming!' screamed Kemma. 'They're coming!'

The fight was short and bloody. Kemma barred the way, keeping her son behind her, but he was singled out, and he was among the first to die. Kemma held back her grief and fought them as long as she could, a succession of untried warriors taking the position at her side. The skaven were stormvermin, strong and cunning warriors, but she was a queen, her hammer driven by a mother's grief. They stood no chance. Ten she slew, then twenty. Time blurred along with her tear-streaked vision.

Kemma felt relief when the poisoned wind globe sailed into the room over the stormvermins' heads, and shattered on the stone walls behind her. The choking gas poured with supernatural alacrity to fill every corner. The skaven in front of her died, white sputum bubbled at its lips, eyes bulging. Kemma held her breath, though her head spun and eyes stung and blurred. She ran forwards, hoping to buy time enough for the dwarfish young to die. Better a quick death by gas than the lingering torment of enslavement that would await them should they be taken alive.

'Dreng! Dreng thaggoraki! Dreng! Dreng! Dreng!' she shouted, swinging her hammer wildly. Her lungs burned, she could feel them filling with fluid. She was drowning in her own blood. Still she fought, sending the skaven breaching party reeling. Behind her, the cries and coughs subsided. Good, she thought. Good.

'Za Vala-Azrilungol!' she cried, holding her runic hammer aloft. The runes on it were losing their gleam, the magic leaching away, becoming nought but cut marks in steel. 'Khazuk-ha! Vala-Azrilungol-ha! Valaya! Valaya! Valaya!' She swung her hammer for one final swing, bloodying a stormvermin's muzzle, but she was dying, her strength fleeing her body, and they brought her down. They pinned her to the floor, and she spat bloody mouthfuls at them. She panted shallowly, but could draw no sustenance from the air. The world and all its cruelties and disappointments receded. A golden light shone behind her as the halls of her ancestors opened their doors. Before she passed through, she flung one last, panting curse at her murderers.

'Enjoy your victory. I hope you live to regret it.'

The column of greenskins toiled up the slopes of the mountains, into the bitter chill of the unnatural winter. They were led by a toothless, wrinkled old orc clad in nothing but a pair of filthy trousers and a stunty-skin cloak with the face still attached. The head of the stunty sat on the orc's scalp, moustaches hanging either side of the orc's face, beard tied under his chin. Consequently the dangling arm and leg skin of the dead dwarf only came halfway down the orc's back. He had on no shoes, no shirt, no nothing, and it was freezing cold.

'This way, this way!' said Zargakk the Mad, for that was who the orc was. 'No it ain't!' he scolded himself. 'Oh yes it is!' he replied.

'Just where have you been these last years, Zargakk?' said Skarsnik. 'Funny you just turning up this morning like that. We could've used you in da fight.'

'Yep, yep,' yipped Zargakk. 'Could have, could have. But I's been busy. Yep, very busy. Part of it I was, er, dead. Yeah. I forget, um, the rest. But you got me Idol of Gork, dincha? That was a help! And I'm here now. Whoop!' His eyes blazed green. Smoke puffed from his ears. Duffskul had been nutty, but Zargakk was totally crazy.

'Funny, ain't it,' said Skarsnik, half to himself, 'in an ironical kind of way, that we is using the same little hidden ways to gets out that them stunties used to get in.'

'Suppose,' said Zargakk. The goblin and orc chiefs marching with them shared perplexed looks.

'But there's no stunties there now, boss, none at all. They's all gone!' said one, who was either braver or even thicker than the rest.

Skarsnik shut his eyes tight and shuddered.

They had marched out in the morning, after a nervous-looking skaven had delivered the king's head. Zargakk had been sitting on a toppled stunty statue in front of the Howlpeak, the citadel burning behind him. All across the skies were clouds of blackest black, so black the night goblins didn't really notice it was day at all. In the east, south and north they were lit red by the fires of the earth. Only to the west was there a hint of blue, and that was pale and scalloped by roils of ash.

Up, up onto the slopes they went, chancing the high passes. The main road out of the Eight Peaks to the west was buried in rubble from the skaven's detonation of the mountains. Although large numbers of skaven had departed to the north, some remained, and the East Gate was most likely in the hands of the ratmen by now. Skarsnik wasn't banking on them keeping their word, so up into the cold they went.

From high above the Great Vale, Skarsnik turned to take one last look at his former domain. His entire army stopped with him. Most of it did, anyway, those elements that did not tripping over the ones that had, and no small number of them slipping to their deaths as a result.

'Garn! Get on! Get on!' yelled Skarsnik, planting his boot in the breeches of a mountain goblin. 'Blow the zogging horns, you halfwits. Do it! Get 'em moving! Just cos I is stopping don't mean *everyone* should!'

Horns blared, the mountains answering sorrowfully. Drums rolled like distant thunder in the forgotten summers of the world. Skarsnik thought there might never be a summer again.

'Look at that. Would you look at that,' said Kruggler, peering out from under his dirty bandages. He'd been wounded across the forehead during the battle, but his skull was particularly dense and he seemed unharmed. 'Seems such a waste, leaving it all behind.'

'Yeah,' said Skarsnik. 'Don't it just? All them zogging rats just upped and left an' all. Ridiculous. It's empty. Empty after all this time.'

'The greatest stunty-house in all the world!'

'Second greatest,' corrected Skarsnik, holding up a grubby finger. 'Second greatest. And it was all mine.'

'Why they going?' said Kruggler.

'Search me,' shrugged Skarsnik. 'Don't make no sense.'

'Why don't we just go back then?' said someone.

'Nah,' said Skarsnik. 'We do that, they'll come back. Besides, new vistas, new worlds to conquer. All that.'

'Stupid rats,' grumbled Dork the orc, current boss of Skarsnik's bigger greenies. Skarsnik had lost so many of his chieftains he wasn't sure who was who any more, and he couldn't exactly stop to check his lists.

'Mark my words, it'll be full of trolls soon enough,' said Tolly Grin Cheek the Fourth.

'Maybe,' said Skarsnik, raising his eyebrows. 'Wouldn't be the first time, except, it won't happen.'

'How you know that, boss?' said Dork.

Skarsnik plucked a human-made watch from his pocket and screwed up his eyes to peer at it. 'I just do. Should be about now.'

'What, boss?' said Tolly Grin Cheek.

'You don't think I'd let those ratboys have the place, did you? You don't think I'm beat do you? Eh? Eh?'

The goblins and orcs looked at each other searchingly. No one wanted to hazard a guess at the right answer to that one.

'Course not!' said Skarsnik. 'Y'see, those ratboys are too zogging clever by half.'

'Not like us, eh, boss!' said Dork. The others laughed at their own cleverness.

'No. No. Definitely not,' replied Skarsnik flatly. 'Anyways, that big ratfing promised me two things. Old Belegar here.' Skarsnik patted his dwarf-hide pouch, wherein languished the severed head of the king. 'And one of them fancy machines the ratties are always meddling with. I had a mob put it down there, set it off to go, then run away.'

'What was it, boss? What was it?' they shouted excitedly.

Skarsnik pulled a pained expression and shuddered. 'Can't one of you zogging morons have a guess, just one guess?'

'A super trap!' said one.

'A big axe?' said Dork hopefully.

'A troll!'

'A dragon!'

'Two dragons!'

'Lots of dragons!' someone else shouted, getting carried away with the whole dragon idea.

'It's a bomb, you snotlings-for-brains. Our boss here got a big bomb off them, didn't he?' Zargakk the Mad said. 'He did, he did!' he added, nodding in enthusiastic agreement with himself.

'That's the truth, right there,' said Skarsnik. 'A bomb. Apparently, they was going to blow up the big dwarf mountain up north where the king of all stunties live. Well, not now they ain't!'

They all shared a good laugh at that.

'This big rat god fing showed up, and offered it to me. Tried to talk me into blowing up Zhufbar with it! So I said yes.'

'But we ain't at Zhufbar, boss!'

'Yeah, Zhufbar's, like, miles away.'

'It's at least three.'

'More like loads.'

'Will you just let me finish?' shouted Skarsnik. 'Zhufbar's one thousand and eighty-four miles away, if you must know. So I thoughts to meself,' he continued at normal volume again, 'I ain't walking all that way on the say-so of a ratboy! Then I finks, well, if I ain't going to have the Eight Peaks, and the stunties aren't going to have the Eight Peaks, then the zogging ratboys certainly aren't going to have it. I'm going to be the last king of the Eight Peaks. Me,' he said, low and growly. 'Not some mange-furred rat git with cheesy breath! I tells you, it's the biggest bomb what ever there was. Huge! All brass and iron and wyrdstone.' He had to exaggerate its size. The goblins would never have believed something small as a troll's head could do so much damage.

'Weeds toe what?'

'He means the glowy green rock what the ratties likes so much,' said Dork, glowing almost as much as said rock himself with self-satisfaction.

'Yeah, that's right. The green glowy. About a ton of it, I'd say, all packed about with black powder.'

'What's an "aton"?'

'Lots! A ton is lots! Very heavy! It's lots, all right?' said Skarsnik, his hood vibrating with irritation. 'So lots it'll make them little bangs what the ratties brought down Red Sun Mountain with look like squigs popping on a fire. And I made 'em give it to me! Me!'

A tinny chime sounded from out of the watch, strange music to play out the destruction of their home, accompanied by the slap-tramp of goblin feet as the tribes wound their way upwards.

'And that's the timer,' said Skarsnik. He chuckled evilly.

They all stared expectantly at the city. Big 'uns and bosses had to lash the lads to stop them from gawping at what their betters were looking at.

Nothing happened. Nothing at all.

'Was that it? Has it gone?' asked a particularly thick underling, who was staring right at Karak Eight Peaks's desolate ruins.

'No. No. No! That wasn't it, you zogging git!' Skarsnik roared. He spun round and blasted the gobbo with a bright green zap of Waaagh! energy. The goblin exploded all over everybody else.

An uncomfortable silence fell, punctuated by the drip of goblin blood. Karak Eight Peaks remained resolutely, undemolishedly there.

'Er,' said Kruggler, tentatively tapping Skarsnik's shoulder. 'You know them skaven gizmos, they don't always work, do they, boss?'

'Mork's 'urty bits,' said Skarsnik. He sniffed. He spat. He shuffled about a bit. The chain that Gobbla used to be attached to clanked sadly. He couldn't bring himself to take it off. 'Not with a bang, but with a whimper,' he muttered to himself.

'Sorry, boss?'

'Nothing, Krugs,' said Skarsnik with forced bonhomie. 'Nothing. Just something I read in a humie book once.' Skarsnik shook his head and waved his sorry band onwards. 'Come on, boys. Nothing left to see here. Nothing left at all.'

''Ere, boss,' called someone. 'I got a question.'

'Yes?' said Skarsnik. 'Dazzle me with your piercing insight, Krugdok.'

'Just where exactly are we going?'

'And I remain undazzled,' said Skarsnik with such sharp sarcasm you could have trimmed a troll's nose hair with it. Besides Zargakk, not one of the goblins or orcs, excepting perhaps Kruggler – and then only perhaps – noticed. 'To tell you the truth, and I really mean it this time...' The goblins dutifully tittered. The orcs scowled. '...I haven't got a bleedin' clue.'

And with those eternal words, the last king of Karak Eight Peaks turned from his kingdom for the final time, and trudged over the mountain shoulder. Ahead of him the lowering volcanic skies hid an uncertain future.

# TWENTY-THREE

*Twelve in One*

Thanquol splashed through shallow puddles on the walk-way by the sewer channel. He had given up trying to keep his robes clean. They were roughly made anyway, not like the finery he was used to.

'This not good-good,' he grumbled. 'Grey seers fall low, Thanquol lowest of all.'

He scurried along, head constantly twitching to look behind him. He missed the comfort of Boneripper's presence. He got more done when he wasn't constantly watching his own back.

Not very far over him were the warrens of the man-things, the city-place they called Nuln. He was here to take it for Clan Skryre, and things were not going very well at all.

If he'd known how much the clan would expect of him, then he probably wouldn't have thrown himself on their mercy.

Probably.

Not so long ago, Thanquol and his fellow seer Gribikk – how annoying to find him here too! No doubt he had already reported Thanquol's presence back to Thaumkrittle – would have been in charge of the expedition, and it would all have been over some time ago. But it was Skribolt of Clan Skryre who was in charge, his large contingent of warlocks supposedly fighting alongside Clans Vrrtkin, Carrion, Kryxx and Gristlecrack. Naturally, the entire expedition was unravelling.

It was all Skribolt's fault, not his. The Great Warlock was a fine inventor, Thanquol could see that, but he lacked vision, and his strategies lacked scope. How was it Thanquol's fault that Clan Vrrtkin and Clan Carrion had turned on each other? How was it his doing that they could not even take a warehouse full of gunpowder without fighting among themselves?

Of course, he was being blamed. Poor Thanquol, once the darling of the Council, now a scapegoat for a tinker-rat of limited vision. He gnashed his teeth at the terrible injustice of it all. He was desperate. The plans to raid the man-thing's city for gunpowder and a working steam engine had come to nought. The Council of Thirteen had made it very clear the mission would succeed, or heads would be forfeit. As things stood, that meant *his* head, and that would not do at all. The emissary from the Council had been quite specific, in a roundabout way. Thanquol still could not believe that the grey seers had fallen so far. The shame of having to explain himself for something that patently was not his fault made his ears burn. Worst of all, it had been a lowly warlock who had come all puffed up and guarded by the Council's elite Albino Guard to deliver the ultimatum. That was a grey seer's task.

Skribolt was close to ridding himself of Thanquol. He was in league with Gribikk – it was the only explanation. They'd taken Boneripper from him not long afterwards, ostensibly for repairs, but Thanquol knew the truth of it. Another attack on the surface failed shortly afterwards, again due to the treachery of Clan Vrrtkin. Ordered to report his own 'failure' by farsqueaker, he had sabotaged the machine and fled to the sewers. The uprising was going wrong all over the Empire, and they couldn't blame him for all of it. But they didn't have to. He was at last resorts. He didn't know whether to be more angry than afraid, or more afraid than angry. If this didn't work...

Thanquol reached the door he sought and glanced about himself, nose twitching with nerves. The bundle he carried mewled, and he shushed and patted at it. A splash sounded up the river of filth flowing sluggishly past him. He stayed deathly still, ears pricked for any sound, but nothing came to him but the steady drip of water, and a far-off rushing sound from where the sewer discharged into the river.

He unfroze, tail moving first and then his whole body melting into nervy activity. With his free hand he drew forth the key for the door, stolen from the city sewerjacks many years ago.

They hadn't missed the key. The lock was so clogged with rust it was patently obvious no one had been here since his last visit. He had to place the squirming bundle on the floor to turn it. The squealing it made set his heart pumping and glands clenching. The door groaned louder still when he pushed it open. He paused again, holding his breath until he was satisfied.

He scooped up the bundle and scurried in, pushing the door slowly to behind him.

As he suspected, the chamber was undisturbed. The man-things definitely hadn't been there, and he breathed a little easier. Cobwebs thick with dust festooned the domed ceiling. A lesser drain ran diagonally through the circular room, cutting off a third of it from the rest before disappearing through a culvert in the walls. Thanquol absently patted the bundle again, and set it down in the corner as far away from the stream of human waste as he could. To summon the vermin-lord, it was important his offering was as pure as possible.

He flexed his right hand-paw. The grafting scar around

his wrist itched. He held both of them, regarding their mismatched nature. 'Gotrek!' he hissed, recalling the moment his hated nemesis had severed the paw. He clapped his left hand over his muzzle. Who knew if the dwarf-thing were here, lurking in the shadows and ready to foil him yet again?

Thanquol took a generous pinch of warpstone snuff to calm his nerves. His head pounded at the effect, his brain strained against his skull. His chest rose and fell expansively. His vision cleared, and he saw revealed the straining tendrils of magic crossing the room. So much of it in the world!

Enough perhaps for success. His eyes narrowed, and he allowed himself his most diabolical chuckle.

Thanquol set to work.

First, he brushed as much dust away from the centre of the room with his foot-paws as he could, revealing the stone beneath. Though segments of the walls dripped with moisture, and filth ran through it, the room was otherwise wholesome, and surprisingly dry. With a shard of sharpened warpstone, he scratched out a double circle and filled the band between inner and outer layers with intricate symbols. He fought the urge to nibble on the warpstone shard, at least until he was done. When he had, he munched on the blunt end as he scrutinised his work. He nodded, and turned to the bundle.

He unwrapped it quickly.

'So ugly!' he hissed. 'Not like skaven pups. Come-come! You sing for Thanquol now.'

Thanquol drew his knife and placed the squealing bundle in the centre of the circle.

When he was done, Thanquol carefully dripped the blood into the gouges in the floor. His usual frenetic movement became measured as he carefully filled in each. This had to be done precisely. Messing it up didn't bear thinking of. He whispered words of summoning under his breath, hoping it wouldn't be like the last time, hoping that...

Skarbrand...

Do not think-recall the name! he told himself. It was probably still listening. He calmed himself, waited until the memories of the bloodthirster he'd accidentally called up the last time faded, then continued.

He placed the pup's remains and its bloodied rags outside the circle, and held up his hand-paws.

Although his past efforts had ended in disaster, once more the white-furred sorcerer attempted to slice the veil between realms. Once more he attempted to bring forth a vermin-lord. He spoke-squeaked the words of power, calling upon the Horned Rat and the mightiest daemons of his court. Green fire crackled from his eyes and between his upraised paws.

'Come-skitter! Join me in the realm of the mortal! I command you! I, Grey Seer Thanquol so squeak-say!' he said. There was a blast of power and the fabric of reality rippled.

He stood there exulted, hands still upraised. It was working! Nothing happened.

He let his arms drop, and looked around. The room was unchanged. He was alone.

Once more Thanquol had failed. This time, at least, he had not done so with the same disastrous consequences as his previous attempt. He groaned. His paws clenched.

'Why-why?' he said. The temptation was to storm out, destroy the circle, and find someone else to blame. But he could not. He was the one being blamed – entirely unjustly – by others. He had to succeed.

Tail swishing, the grey seer paced out of the circle, careful not to scuff the marks. He went around and inspected them all.

'Perfect! Perfect! They are all perfect! The Horned Rat himself could not have drawn them better. Why-why does it not work?!' he squealed angrily. The bloody rags caught his eyes. Maybe *two...?*

It was then that Thanquol perceived a shadowy hand reaching out of the blackness gathered in the chamber's vaulted ceiling. The claws ripped through reality with a screech that sent pain running down his spine. The enormous hand headed unerringly for him. He found that he could not move, not even when the hand grabbed him by the ankles and lifted him upright, dangling him upside down as its owner stepped out of a black abyss of shadows. Remembering the fate of Kritislik, Thanquol liberally vented the musk of fear.

But he was not consumed. The entity stepped through into the realm of the mortal, casually bestriding Thanquol's protective circle. It examined him with curiosity, peering at him this way and that.

Thanquol could do nothing but squeak in wide-eyed wonder. He had seen verminlords before, of course, but never anything like this. No horns had ever sprouted so majestically as the ones upon its head. Multiple sets curved and entwined the daemon's face. They seemed to sinuously curve and move as Thanquol watched them. Beneath the horns one eye was missing. In its place was not an empty socket, but a warpshard, or if the angle was correct, a black hole of endless nothing. Thanquol's head throbbed as he looked into it.

'Ahhh, Thanquol, you took your time. Perhaps you are not so gifted as I thought?' it purred. 'I have waited for you to call me. Yes-yes, we have much to do.'

'Who-what are you, O great master?' shrilled Thanquol.

The creature placed him gently alongside the channel. Only then did the grey seer notice that one of the verminlord's foot-paws was in the drain. It did not sink into the river of filth but hovered above it.

The ancient being stooped to Thanquol's level.

'Our name is Lord Skreech Verminking,' said the verminlord. 'There are many of us, and one.' As he spoke, Thanquol saw before him – or perhaps he imagined it – the verminlord's visage flicker, revealing many ghostly aspects that together somehow made the face the creature wore: the contagion-ridden body of a plague priest, the shadowy assassin, the hungry hordes, the tinkering weaponsmith, the future-gazing seer. 'The ruins, the decay, they give me power. I was called here by blight and destruction. There is much in the world in this time, and it is good,' it said, sniffing the air and craning its neck. 'And by you, Thanquol.'

Thanquol swallowed in awe. Could it be? The grey seers had long spoken in whispers of 'the One', a Rat King – a conglomerate evil. As mortal skaven had their hierarchies of clan, caste, and rank, so too did the verminlords above them. There was one, an entire Council of Thirteen elevated by the Horned Rat in the past to daemonhood as one creature. He was their ruler, the lord of the supposed Shadow Council of Thirteen. Had Thanquol really just summoned forth the most powerful of all verminlords? He had always known he was special, but this was pleasing confirmation. Pleasing indeed. He smiled.

The grey seer looked up into that strange face staring back at, and possibly through, him. It seemed to have read his thoughts, for it looked down upon him indulgently, its enormous claw reaching out to ever so gently stroke his horns. 'I am who you think I am, yes-yes, little seer. You have a purpose. I have need of your singular talents. Together we shall conquer.'

Thanquol's heart soared. With this creature at his side, none could stand before him! He couldn't wait to see Skribolt's face, or to smell him squirt the musk of fear.

'Nuln-place first?'

The verminlord nodded its head, pleased with the seer, or so it seemed to the conceited Thanquol. 'And much more besides. We have many tasks ahead of us. But first, gifts!'

Impossibly, a huge shape was in the corner of the room, half shadowed, like it had been there all the time and was patiently waiting for its cue. Thanquol's eyes widened. The largest rat ogre he had ever seen stepped out of the shadows.

Thanquol's whiskers twitched with glee.

'Many thanks-gratitudes for such beneficent generosities, O great and unplumbably wise Lord Verminking!' Thanquol's eyes narrowed, his imagination alive with much smashing and kill-slaying. 'I shall call him Boneripper,' he said.

In the war council of the Nuln-place clawpack, all was not well. For hours the skaven assailing the city had hurled accusations at each other by the dimly flickering light of warp-braziers. The room the council occupied was a small one, built and forgotten by humans long ago, and pitifully insufficient in size to contain so many over-weaning egos.

'I say-squeak you are a worthless weak-meat, and all Clan Vrrtkin are puny-small and shifty!' squeaked Warlord Throttlespine of Clan Kryxx. He had drawn his sword and pointed it at Warlord Trikstab Gribnode of Clan Vrrtkin. 'You are at fault for our lack of success, tricking and lying and attacking when we should fight together.'

'Lies, lies! Not good lies either,' squealed Gribnode. He pulled his own sword. The other members of the war council stood hurriedly from the table, upsetting their chairs. 'All knows Thanquol-seer is weak link in rusty chain here, and you are next weakest, Throttlespine. Banish Thanquol, great and cunning Warlock Skribolt! Banish him, so we not have to suffer the stink of his slack musk-hole! It is this that foils our efforts! Then let us banish Throttlespine. He is in league with Thanquol! His cowardice too is legendary.'

Throttlespine growled and jumped onto the table. 'Coward, am I? I lead from the back of my ratkin as every true warrior should-must, whereas you, where are you? Skulking and hiding off the battlefield! You are to blame, and seek to smear my good-true name with ordure of failure. I am a loyal servant of the council!'

'No, I am the loyallest servant of the council!' retorted Gribnode.

'Stop-cease, halt!' squeaked Skribolt. 'This is too much!' Unable to get anyone to listen to him, he began to crank the handle of his warp-lightning generator.

Throttlespine was tensed for a leap when the sound of fighting came from outside.

'Stop-stop!' squeaked a stormvermin beyond the door. 'Many-much council leaders exercise deep and important thinkings. Go aw–' The guard's order was cut short. The sound of armoured bodies clattering off the walls took its place. A terrifying roar had them all looking at each other, and struggling to control their fear glands.

A single blow felled the plank door so hard it hit the flagged floor with a bang like a cannon shot. On the other side was the largest rat ogre any of the council members had ever seen, even Grand Packmaster Paxrot of Clan Moulder, and he knew his rat ogres very well. The four-armed behemoth doubled over to squeeze its bulk through the doorway. Following the monster came Grey Seer Thanquol.

'Thanquol?' said Skribolt, his hand slowing on the warp-lightning crank, then speeding up again. 'You are banished!'

'Good-good, all still here? I bring news from the Council,' said Thanquol, who was puffed up and obviously very pleased with himself.

This proclamation was most stunning to Great Warlock Skribolt, whose claw still churned the handcrank on his warp-energy generator. His muzzle twitched as he grasped for what to say.

'Yes-yes, after so much incompetence,' and here the grey seer paused to look at Skribolt, 'I am to be in charge. Any disputes can be directed to my bodyguard, Boneripper.' At this, Thanquol nodded at the hulking beast stood snarling behind him, surveying the gathering with hate-filled eyes.

'But that is not...' Skribolt started to say, but the grey seer cut him off.

'My *new* bodyguard, Boneripper,' said Thanquol. 'The old one was mostly dead,' he added dismissively. 'This one better. Now that the element of surprise is gone-lost,' Thanquol continued, 'I feel it is time to switch tactics. My plan is to–'

At last Skribolt found his tongue. 'Enough! No more! Halt-stop!' said the Great Warlock, the last words coming out perhaps more shrilly than he had wished. 'On whose orders were you gift-granted authority? Why-tell was I not informed?'

Skribolt was standing, lightning wreathing him as his whir-ring contraption sucked in the winds of magic. All the other skaven – warlords, a top assassin, and a master moulder – took a step backwards away from the two.

When a voice spoke from the shadows all turned, finding a terrible sight. The blackness strained with life, and an awful shape moved there. Such was the power inherent in it that several of the lesser warlords let their musk glands loose.

'On our authority, Great Warlock!' said the shadow. The room went black, lit only by dancing chains of lightning. A long, elegant claw reached out, snuffing out the sparks between Skribolt's backpack conductors. In the blackness a single terrifyingly evil eye radiated green over them, hold-ing them each in its turn, leaving none in any doubt that his most treasured schemes had been exposed, digested and dis-missed as the work of fools.

As suddenly as it appeared, the blackness was gone. The war council was alone again.

'What do you bid-command, O great and exalted leader Thanquol?' intoned Warlord Throttlespine, bowing low. The rest of the skaven followed suit, although they did subconsciously shuffle away from those who had befouled themselves.

Thanquol had already surmised that Throttlespine was the smart one, yet it was gratifying to be proven correct. Nodding his head slightly in acceptance, Thanquol began again. 'As I was squeal-saying, my plan...'

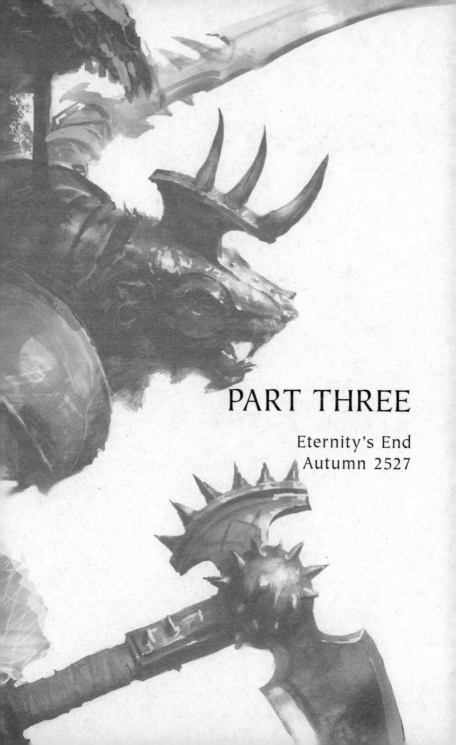

# PART THREE

Eternity's End
Autumn 2527

# TWENTY-FOUR

*The King's Head*

The world had changed.

No longer could the dawi count the mountains as their own. They teetered on the brink of extinction.

Thorgrim Grudgebearer ground his teeth together. The Dammaz Kron lay under his hand. It had glutted itself on woes, growing thicker faster than at any other time in the High King's remarkable reign.

He stared at the Granite Gate two hundred feet away. Massive twin doors of stone, imposing despite being only half – and it was exactly, precisely half – the height of the tall, vaulted corridor they barred. The gates shuddered under an impact from the far side: a quiver in the stone so small that only a dwarf, stone born and stone master, could see. Bands of runes carved into the gates glowed intensely with inner blue light, their magic striving to keep the gates whole and closed.

The skaven were coming. As sure as Thorgim's chin wore a beard, they would get through. The ratkin had burst every defence, arcane and otherwise, that the dawi of Karaz-a-Karak had thrown up.

Thorgrim thought on the horrors that afflicted his people.

Karak Azul overthrown.

Karak Eight Peaks lost a second time.

Zhufbar swarmed by an endless tide of vermin.

Barak Varr pouring smoke from its great dock gates, the pride of the dwarf fleet broken in the sea before it.

The holds of the Grey Mountains overcome and lost in three horrific nights of bloodshed.

Karak Kadrin poisoned.

Karaz-a-Karak besieged for years now, cut off on all sides above and below. The streams of refugees pouring into the dwarf capital from other kingdoms had given Thorgrim much anguish. At a time when he thought his dream might be fulfilled, that the lost realms of the Karaz Ankor would be reclaimed, it had all come to nothing. The fleeing dwarfs brought with them tales of proud strongholds cast down, and not only in dwarf lands. Many dwarfs of the diaspora had fled back to their ancestral homeland from human cities – their habits and speech strange; some of them even trimmed their beards! – telling of similar woes beyond the mountains. But what was more horrifying than the incoming flood and the dire tidings they brought was that it had stopped. No dwarf had come into Everpeak for months.

Tilea, Estalia and Bretonnia ashes. The Empire devastated. The moon cracked in the sky, invasion from the north, and ratmen swarming from everywhere.

'We stand alone,' he said into his beard, his unblinking stare locked upon the door. It shuddered again.

'The runes will not last, my liege,' muttered Hrosta Copperling. A runesmith, but a mere beardling compared to the likes of Kragg the Grimm and Thorek Ironbrow. Their kind would never come again into this world. Hrosta was loyal and dedicated to his task, but his store of knowledge was paltry.

Thorgrim did not grace Hrosta's obvious statement with a reply, but continued to stare at the Granite Gate.

Forty feet wide, fifty tall, the gate was a lesser portal of Everpeak. Leading onto a once-safe and well-travelled section of the Ungdrin Ankor, it had become, like all the other many gates into the mountain, yet another way for the skaven to attack them.

'Thaggoraki,' Thorgrim growled. He thought of what he had seen from the Rikund, the King's Porch at the summit of Karaz-a-Karak. The endless seas of enemies, whose bodies stained the roads leading to his kingdom brown. There were so many of them, more than there had ever been before.

'My king, I implore you to return to the Hall of Kings,' said Gavun Tork, the most venerable of his living ancestors.

'You leave, my friend, we have lost too many heads full of wisdom. Go back and be safe. My duty is here. The time for counsel and talk is done. The Axe of Grimnir will speak for me.'

'Thorgrim, please!'

Thorgrim jerked his head at the living ancestor. Two of his hammerers broke from the ranks of the Everguard. 'Escort Loremaster Tork back to the eighteenth deep. Keep him safe.'

'Aye, my king,' said his warriors.

Tork gave the king a helpless look, his rheumy blue eyes brimmed with concern that threatened to spill into the deep lines on his face. 'If I were but two hundred years younger...'

'You have swung many axes for the glory of Karaz Ankor, my friend,' said Thorgrim. 'Let those younger take your place. Yours is a different burden.'

'I...'

'Go!' said the king.

The living ancestor shook off the hands of the hammerers. 'Very well. But stay safe! This is foolishness. You should not risk yourself.'

'You are wrong, loremaster,' said Thorgrim, his flinty eyes

returning to regard the door. 'It is exactly what I should do.'

The clink of the Everguard's armour receded. Silence regained its hold over the throng. One hundred ironbreakers, irondrakes in support, and three score of his Everguard.

It should be enough, thought Thorgrim.

The doors' runes flickered and went out. The rock at their centre glowed bright orange, a pinprick at first that spread out in a perfect circle. The stone of the Granite Gate had been chosen well; there was not a flaw in it.

'Close secondary portcullises!' bellowed the gatewarden of the Granite Gate.

Three sets of heavy iron portcullises descended simultaneously from slots in the roof, their machinery noiseless. Only when they met the ground, and their heavy-toothed bottoms slid into matching holes in the floor, did they make the faintest clink.

The glow in the doors spread to engulf their middle, top to bottom. The light of it glowed redly from the ceiling and polished floor, catching in the eyes of ancestor statues, whose faces, changed by shadowplay, took on horrified expressions. A dribble of molten rock ran from the gate's centre, creating a hole that grew as the rock collapsed outwards, a hole that guttered a plume of fire.

'Irondrakes!' called the gatewarden. 'Airshaft doors ready!'

Fifty runic handcannons were levelled at the door.

The Granite Gate sagged all at once, its perfection lost in a pool of cooling slag.

'Fire!' bellowed the gatewarden. Tongues of flame burst from the irondrakes' guns, aimed at the centre of the hole. Whatever was on the other side exploded noisily before it could withdraw. Green-tinged fire rolled out, licking at the irondrakes' enchanted armour without effect. Squeals of dismay came from the other side of the doors. The stink of skaven fear and burning rock washed over the throng, and the air became stuffy and difficult to breathe.

The stone skinned over and cooled to a dull, ugly grey. A thick vapour obscured whatever lay on the far side of the broken gate.

Next came a hissing noise, as a green mist issued from the breach.

'Gas! Gas! Gas!' shouted the gatewarden. 'Airshafts open!'

The noxious fog rolled towards the dwarfs, sinking low to the floor. The clink of rolling glass and its shattering followed. Lesser plumes of poison sprouted as short-lived mushroom clouds around the front of the dwarf line.

The gatewarden's orders were quickly obeyed. Dwarfs cranked open large steel flaps, revealing shafts that stretched far up the mountain. Steam engines churned on levels above, creating a ferocious wind that blew downwards, exiting from angled horns to blow the gas back towards the door. More squeaking came.

Thorgrim smiled to hear them panic. The dwarfs were slow to embrace the new, but when they did, you could be sure it would be perfect.

The gas dissipated, misting the air. It was in danger of choking the dwarfs, and so the doorwarden ordered the steam engines disengaged. The pumped wind ceased, and the natural pressure difference between the low halls and the high mountain sucked the gas away, venting it harmlessly high above the tree line many thousands of feet above their heads.

Only then did the skaven come. As usual, the frantic squealing of slaves being driven at the dwarfs preceded the main assault. These were shot down without mercy, the blasts of the irondrakes' handcannons immolating them by the handful.

'No matter what they do, they are not coming through this tunnel,' said Thorgrim.

In that, the High King was wrong.

What should have come next was more slaves, thousands of them, sent to die solely for the wasting of the dwarfs' ammunition.

Through the reek of battle came no slaves. Instead the smoke curled around a great shape, horned and tall as a giant. Light warped around it, as if recoiling from the unnatural beast, shrouding it in a flickering darkness.

'Verminlord,' called out Thorgrim. 'This one is mine!'

The rat-daemon strode forwards. Jabbering in some unholy tongue, it swept its glaive in a wide arc, allowing its hand to slip far towards the counterweight at the bottom, and extending its reach to well over fifteen feet. Trailing green fire, the weapon impacted the first portcullis with a thunderous clash. The steel was sundered, deadly shrapnel from its destruction slicing into the ranks of irondrakes. 'Fire!' called the gatewarden. Handgun fire from embrasures in the walls joined the shorter-ranged bursts of the irondrakes. All were stopped by the cloak of shadow that wreathed the daemon. The second portcullis was broken. Thorgrim ordered his thronebearers forward. They obeyed instantly, bearing the great weight of the High King's throne without complaint. The ironbreakers parted ranks to allow their king passage.

'Shield wall!' roared the gatewarden. A line of overlapped steel formed to the front of the ironbreakers. The irondrakes withdrew, leaving the ironbreakers facing the monster before them. The third portcullis was thrown down, its refuse clattering off the ironbreakers' shields. The verminlord threw back its head and squealed.

Then the skaven attack began in earnest, a rush of clanrat warriors pouring through the ruined gateway. As they reached the heels of their demigod, the daemon broke into a run, glaive thrumming around its head.

Thorgrim raised up his axe, and roared out a challenge. The creature came right at him. It brought its weapon down in an overhead sweep that would have slain a rhinox. But the mystic energies of the Throne of Kings responded and a flaring shield of magic stopped the blow three feet above Thorgrim's head. He shouted his war cries, voicing the unyielding defiance of the dwarfs, and struck back. The Axe of Grimnir clove through the shadow protecting the creature and into its evil flesh. Blackness like ink spilled in water escaped from the wound, bringing with it the scent of rot. Thorgrim's beard prickled at his proximity to the thing. He bellowed again, and swung again, and the creature blocked, spinning its glaive around the axe, nearly tearing it from Thorgrim's grasp.

The skaven were upon his warriors. Driven to a great fervour of war by the presence of their god's avatar, they slashed with their weapons with strength beyond their feeble bodies, and bit so hard they broke their teeth. But they did not care. Thorgrim's bearers hewed about them, keeping the creatures from their lord while he duelled with the daemon.

The verminlord struck again, thrusting with the point of its glaive, spear fashion. The rune of eternity blazed again, but the warpmetal – greenish black and as unearthly as its owner – slid through the protective magic. The great strength of the verminlord punched it through the Armour of Skaldour, ripping open Thorgrim's side. The poisonous pain of warp contamination burned in his blood, but his roar was one of anger for the damage done to his panoply, for the skills to repair it had long been lost. The verminlord regarded him with amusement glittering in its red eyes. It assumed a guard posture, ready to strike again.

A fey feeling came upon the dwarf king. The settling of some great power about him. He felt it first as one feels the breath of another upon the cheek, perhaps unexpected, often welcome. His beard crackled with energy. This was magic, or he was umgdawi, but it was a clean sort, heavy with age, and if dwarfs respected anything at all, age was foremost. His doughty mind rebelled against it, yet against his will his heart welcomed it, and it came into him without resistance.

The world glowed golden. The metal of his throne gleamed in

a way he thought impossible. The gold took on a most amazing lustre, a warmth pooled about his wounded side, and he felt the metal move there.

Infused with this glamour, Thorgrim lurched to his feet, his bearers expertly accommodating the movement of the king in combat as they fought themselves. He ran to the prow of his throne, and it felt as if the stuff of his wargear helped him – the metals that made it lending power and purpose to him above and beyond the already mighty measures he had of both. He came up level with the beast's head. Before the power upon the king, the dark magic that pinned the rat-daemon to the fabric of the earth unravelled, the glow going from its glaive blade, the shadow wafting back as surely as the gas attack had been dispersed by the ingenuity of the dwarfs. The verminlord understood what was coming at it and recoiled. The thing was slowed somehow, and the king brought the axe down hard, splitting the skull of the creature before it could move out of reach. It died with a shriek that had warriors of both sides clutching their ears in agony. A jet of noxious black spewed from its shattered head as it fell backwards. The glaive dropped and vanished, while the body collapsed into its own shadows, boiling away to nothing before it could crush the ratmen scurrying at its feet.

Seeing their godling so decisively bested, the thaggoraki wavered, even though they were hundreds deep and outnumbered the dwarfs many times over. Their cowardice had ensured the dwarfs' survival time and again.

'Forward!' shouted Thorgrim. 'Retake the gate. Allow not one of them to set paw upon the sacred stones of the inner mountain!'

With a great shout the ironbreakers pushed forwards. Thorgrim's Everguard led the charge, bludgeoning skaven with looks of murderous determination. The waver turned into panic, then into rout.

Almost as one, the skaven turned tail and fled, many dying on the axes and hammers of the vengeful dwarfs as they scurried to escape, and leaving their wounded to their fate.

'Victory!' shouted Thorgrim. 'Victory!'

'My king, of course the traps are primed,' said Chief Engineer of the Cogwheel brethren, Bukki 'Buk' Ironside, 'but we are...'

Buk was not an easily intimidated dwarf, not by a long measure of beard, but he wilted nonetheless under Thorgrim's furious stare. Not the boldest dawi, nor the oldest, nor the wisest, could weather the king's glare. His advisors stood in a semicircle before the Great Throne, all of them deeply interested in their beard ends.

'There is no place for "but" in my kingdom!' said the king. His eyes were red with unexpressed emotion and lack of sleep.

'We stand ready at your command, my king,' said Buk hurriedly, bowing several times as he shuffled from the king's displeasure back into the safety offered by his engineering peers.

'Good!' snapped Thorgrim.

'My king,' began Gavun Tork. He stood at the head of a dozen other living ancestors, all grim and uncomfortable-looking in their gold-thick finery and elaborate beard plaits. 'We have advised you several times on this matter. We counsel that we should weather this storm as we always have...'

'As I have heard your counsel!' said Thorgrim. He patted the Dammaz Kron. 'So we sit and we sit and we wait, while our defences are weakened and our numbers dwindle.'

Nockkim Grumsbyn, a short but headstrong dwarf, tired of Tork's moderate attitude and pushed his way forward. 'Defence has guaranteed our continued existence for many millennia, what you propose is suicide.'

'Hiding behind our walls has all but doomed us!' roared Thorgrim, all deference to the ancestors' age and wisdom burned away by his furious despair. 'For the entirety of my reign I have desired to march out with the axe-hosts of the dawi kingdoms and exterminate the skaven. Time and again I argued that this alone would save our kind. But you counselled against it, you and your like, Nockkim. And so we find ourselves skulking like trapped badgers in our hole, while our enemy, allowed to grow unchecked to uncountable numbers, plots our final demise. No more!' he roared again. He stood. 'Get out! Get out, all of you! I am king of the dawi nations. Your advice is flawed. For too long have you filled my ears with the whispers of caution, keeping me from reclaiming the glory of our ancestors, dwelling instead upon their dwindling legacy. Well now it dwindles to the point of extinguishment. Get out, I say!'

The entire gaggle of king's councillors stepped back in horror. Never had they seen Thorgrim fly so brashly in the face of traditional respect.

'Sire, there is something amiss.' Tork gestured at Thorgrim's throne. 'The throne, your words – there was an odd light upon you in the battle and although it may have gone...'

'Out! Get out! All of you!' Thorgrim slammed his fist down on the Dammaz Kron. 'Out,' he said, his voice subsiding. 'Get out.'

Thorgrim's Everguard stepped forward. 'Clear the throne room! By order of the High King of the Karaz Ankor! Clear the throne room!'

The Everguard, all fifty of them on honour duty at that moment, formed a line in front of their king and marched out slowly, shepherding the king's council out before them.

All around the mighty hall, whisperings and rustlings spoke of servants and other attendants withdrawing.

It took a full five minutes for the scandalised court, its servants and Thorgrim's bodyguards to leave the room. The great doors swung to with a soft boom.

Thorgrim stared down the aisle between the columns for a while. When he was completely sure he was alone, he stood up, gasping at the pain from his wound.

Whatever the strange power was that had settled on him had healed his armour, but not his flesh. Many dawi had seen him struck, but none had seen his armour rent. Consequently, none knew of his wound but a select few of his closest retainers and the priestesses of Valaya who had treated him. From all of them he had extracted oaths of silence on the matter. Among this select few, only the priestesses knew that it was not healing, poisoned by warp metal. He would let no one else know. If he began griping about every scratch, then how were his people to feel? Dwarfs were of adamant; nothing could break them. They needed to see that quality exemplified in him.

He gritted his teeth against the pain as he stepped from the Throne of Power, steadying himself on its dragon-head decorations for a moment before going on. He had already been weak before the wound. Writing so many grudges into the great book had demanded too much of his blood.

He went to the back of the throne and bent down. Agony stabbed him afresh and he choked back a cry. It was partly to deny the others the sight of their king in pain that he had sent them away, but mainly because Tork had been wrong. The light in the throne had not gone.

It had faded. The gold gleamed still, but only as bright as dwarf gold should. The magic had hidden itself away, that was all. Thorgrim could feel it all about him, and the king knew where it might be.

Sure enough, the Rune of Azamar was glowing with a steady light, more brightly than it had for centuries. The rune of eternity had been carved, it was said, by the ancestor god Grungni himself at the dawn of time. So powerful was it that only one of its type could exist at a time. It was also said that so long as it was whole, the realm of the dwarfs would endure. Thorgrim placed his hand upon it, and the rune's pulsing could be felt through the metal of his gauntlets. He let his hand drop. This magic was alien to him, not of the dawi at all. But it was not malevolent. Cautious though he was in most matters, he somehow knew this for an unassailable fact.

He missed his runesmiths more than anything then. Kragg the Grim had died months ago during the Battle of the Undermines there at Karaz-a-Karak. The only other who had exceeded his knowledge had been Thorek Ironbrow, and he was also dead, slain years before. No other had their knowledge. He considered asking the younger runesmiths, or the runepriests of Valaya, or the priests of the ancestor gods, but that was a risky course of action. They would likely be as baffled as he, and the tidings would get out. In that time of threat and upheaval, there was only so much more the dwarfs could take. The last thing Thorgrim wanted were whisperings of fell powers in their king's throne, or, perhaps more damaging, wild hopes of the ancestor gods' return. Was this not Grungni's own rune? Did it not guarantee the persistence of the dawi race while it was still whole? Thorgrim felt the first stirrings of such hope himself.

No one was coming. He could not risk the crash in morale that could follow the revelation of this hope being false.

He would wait and see. That was the proper dwarf way. Only when he was satisfied would he reveal this new development.

His mind made up, he wearily got into the throne. He sighed. He supposed he had better apologise to the longbeards. Tork at least needed to know what was happening.

Before he could summon his servants, a long, mournful blaring filtered down sounding shafts into the hall. Thorgrim sat forwards, listening intently. Up on the tops of Everpeak's great ramparts, the karak horns were sounding. The immense tusks of some ancient monster, the twinned horns were blown whenever danger threatened. From the notes played by the hornmasters, the entire city could be informed of the nature and size of the enemy force.

They played ominously long and low.

The doors at the end of the hall cracked open. A messenger huffed his way up the long granite pavement to the foot of the throne. Red-faced, he executed a quick bow and began to speak.

'My king, a fresh force of thaggoraki is moving to reinforce the besieging ratkin outside the gates.'

'Who brings this news?'

'Gyrocopter patrols, my liege. They report a massive horde on its way.' The messenger's face creased with worry. 'They fill the Silver Road with their numbers for twenty miles and more. Clans Mors is here, Queek Headtaker at their head. Banners of the warlock clans and their beastmasters also. Clan Rictus too. They have many hundreds of war engines, my lord. Also in the deeps, my king. Traps give forewarning. Mining teams report much stealthy movement.'

'This is it,' said Thorgrim, clenching his hand. 'This is it! Bring me my axe! Thronebearers! Everguard! Marshal of the Throngs, call out the dawi of Karaz-a-Karak! We skulk no longer behind our gates! Open the Great Armoury. Take out the weapons of our ancestors. Let them sit in prideful peace no longer! Dawi and treasures both to war! To war!'

As the king lifted his voice, more horns played out their alarms from the many galleries of the Hall of Kings. Within minutes, the entire city was abustle, called to the final battle.

The electric flea-prickle of the skitterleap tormented Thanquol from horn curl to tail tip, and then the sensation was gone. He clutched his robes about him with the sudden chill.

From Nuln to Lustria to the man-thing place of Midden-heim, Thanquol had followed Lord Verminking. He had been dragged about the world only half willingly, skitterleaping unimaginable distances. He did not trust the verminlord, because he was not a fool. Thanquol knew he was being used. He was arrogant enough to think initially that he was the master in his relationship with the Verminking, but wise enough to quickly reach the correct conclusion. Thanquol was merely a pawn in the mighty daemon's game.

Once he had accepted that, everything did not seem so bad. Surely it was no bad thing to serve the most powerful rat in existence after the Great Horned One? And he was learning a great deal from the creature. More, perhaps, than Verminking intended to teach.

He examined their new location. It was an unusual place for a meeting, thought Thanquol, but the symbolism was hard to miss.

Even with its head blasted to rubble, the statue of the ancient dwarf-thing was enormous. Once this great stone king would have watched over the Silver Road Pass, an image of the strength of the dwarf kingdom. Now, in its ruin, it made rather the opposite statement.

'They come,' hissed Verminking. 'Be silent, be deferential, or even I will not be able to protect-keep you!'

Clouds of shadows blossomed all around Thanquol and Lord Skreech. Ten more verminlords towered over him, gazing down, their ancient eyes gleaming with malice.

'Why-tell the little horned one here?' asked one of two diseased Lords of Contagion among their number.

Not knowing what to do, Thanquol gave the sign of the Horned Rat and bowed low before each. This seemed well received by the entities. Only the two foulest-looking of them gave tail flicks of displeasure.

'You know why, Throxstraggle,' answered Verminking, his

own twin tails flickering menacingly. He glared intently at the greasy rat-daemon for a long moment before continuing, addressing the circle of verminlords. 'We asked-bid you here so that we all agree. The Council of Thirteen decree is that the clan that delivers the dwarf-king's head name-picks the last Lord of Decay. We are as one on this agreement, yes-yes?'

This was news to Thanquol. From Verminking's feet he tried to gauge the reaction around the circle. Most of the verminlords bowed their heads in assent. A few of them looked irritated and abstained. It was with some pride that he noticed that none of the verminlords had horns as twisted or as magnificent as did the mighty Lord Skreech.

'We are but eleven in number – where-tell is Lurklox?' asked one, a grossly inflated parody of a skaven warlord.

'Here,' said a voice from behind them. Thanquol startled, but was pleased not to have leaked out anything regrettable.

A black-shaded Lord of Deception joined the circle, its face masked and body hidden in curling shadows. 'As we anticipated,' it said in a whispering voice, 'the end of the dwarf-things approaches.'

'All goes to plan-intention?' asked Verminking.

'What plan-intention?' said a white-furred verminlord of inconstant appearance. 'We agree-pledge that Clan Scruten will be reselected to the Council. This is our plan.'

Again, general indications of assent from the circle, with some dissension.

'Quite right, we all declared it to be so. Why fret-fear?' said Verminking reasonably.

'My candidate is ready. Tell-inform me how the head will be won, and how it will be delivered to Kranskritt.'

'You doubt our purpose?' said Lurklox.

'Lord Skreech takes new-pet Thanquol with him everywhere. He is a grey seer. I suspect-think Lord Skreech intends to gift-give the head of the long-face-fur to him.'

Verminking bristled. 'You doubt my word, Soothgnawer?'

Soothgnawer laughed. 'I would be a fool weak-meat to give any credence to your words at all.'

Verminking dipped his head in appreciation of the compliment. 'Be easy. Thanquol has been very useful, very cunning. He will win great reward for his efforts, but...' He looked down. 'His place is not to be on the Council. We need his many talents elsewhere.'

Thanquol inwardly shrank. Until the fateful words were said, he had felt privileged; now he felt like a serving-rat. He kept up his outside appearance of interested confidence, behaving as if he often attended gatherings of such august personages, but inside he seethed.

'Is this true, little grey-fur? Tell me the truth! I will know otherwise.'

Several of the giants crowded over him. Thanquol's glands twitched. 'Mighty lords! The fine and most infernal Lord Skreech Verminking has not told me of any plans to gift-grant me the fine and high most honourable exalted station of a seat among the Thirteen.' This was exactly the truth. Verminking told Thanquol very little, only revealing his intentions when the outcome was already unfolding.

Soothgnawer sniffed the air as Thanquol spoke, then stood straight.

'He speaks the truth, the precise truth, although he is very much disappointed to hear he will not sit beside the other little Lords of Decay. Very wise, very clever not to tell the little one of your plans, Skreech.'

'The wise and cunning Thanquol knows everything he needs to know,' said Verminking.

Thanquol looked up to the verminlords talking around him. That they could smell untruth and knew the mind of any skaven was an established fact. But it suddenly dawned on him that these gifts did not work upon each other. To all intents, in their own company they were as reliant on bluff and double-dealing as any other skaven. He wondered how. He wondered if he could possibly replicate their methods...

Thanquol remembered this for later use. Already ideas were forming. He wasn't yet decided on how he could wring an advantage out of this information, but he would. He was certain of that.

# TWENTY-FIVE

*Queek's Glory*

Queek was old. He felt it in his stiffening limbs. He saw it in the grey that grizzled the blackness of his coat all over, a coat once sleek and now broken with dry patches, whose coarsening fur revealed pink skin crusted with scurf.

Decrepitude surprised him suddenly, coming on swift as an ambush. He had thought to suffer a slow decline, nothing like this. Only three years after his great victory at Eight Peaks, and look at him. Beyond the limits of his arms' reach, his sight grew dim and unreliable. Through the mists of age, the marching lines of his army blurred into one mass, losing colour around the edges. His smell and hearing remained sharp, but into his limbs a weakness had set, one that made itself more apparent with every passing day in the numbness of his fingers and the stiffness of his joints. The cold made it worse, driving him into frequent murderous rages that his troops had learned to fear.

It was always cold now, no matter where they went. It had

been since the night the Chaos moon had burst, circling the world with glittering rings that obscured the stars. In the mountains it snowed all year round.

So much had happened. The swift victory Gnawdwell had wanted had not come. In many places the Great Uprising had not gone to plan, and the Great War against the dwarfs dragged on and on. The land of the frog-things and lizard-things had been annihilated, most of Clan Pestilens along with it, while in the lowlands in the ruins of the man-thing's lands, the skaven conquered, only to fracture along clan lines. Such was the way of skaven. Alliance with the followers of Chaos had come, a move that made many on the Council, Gnawdwell included, deeply uneasy.

That was politics, and it was not for Queek. During that time Queek had fought the length of the Worlds Edge Mountains, destroying dwarf strongholds one by one, and exterminating their inhabitants wherever they were to be found. Clan Mors had grown rich on the plunder.

Finally, Queek had been ordered to Beard-Thing Mountain-place, where all attempts to take the dwarf capital had failed. Gnawdwell, inscrutable as always, continued his attempts on Queek's life, simultaneously releasing the full might of Clan Mors and ordering it to go to Queek. Queek had not been back to Skavenblight in the years since their last meeting, wary of Gnawdwell's intentions, but for the time being Queek seemed to be in his lord's favour. All Clan Mors's allies and thralls, from the Grey Mountains, Skavenblight and beyond, came with the Great Banner of Mors. Karak Eight Peaks had been emptied, leaving it an empty tomb for the many warriors who had fallen there in the long years of war.

The dwarf realms had been reduced to but one, the mightiest, the greatest. Karaz-a-Karak, Everpeak, as dwarfs and men respectively called it. Beard-Thing Mountain, as the skaven called it. A name supposed to convey their contempt, but uttered always with fear. Under skies perpetually darkened and striated with the sickly colours of wild magic, the skaven marched to bring their four thousand-year war with the Karaz Ankor to its end.

'This whole pass stinks-reeks of dwarf-thing,' said Queek, sniffing tentatively. His tail twitched. The scent of the dwarfs had become inextricably linked with bloodshed in Queek's mind, and thus with excitement. It never failed to arouse his sluggish pulse, to excite his aged heart.

'What does the mighty warlord expect it to smell of?' said Kranskritt haughtily. The presence of Ikit Claw made the grey seer arrogant. Despite the long enmity between their clans, the two of them were knot-tailed much of the time, constantly tittering and squeak-whispering just out of Queek's earshot, or so they thought. Queek's hearing was better than he let on.

Queek growled by way of reply. He was in no mood to bandy insults with the seer. Kranskritt still smelt youthful to Queek, granted unnaturally long life by the Horned Rat. Even those grey seers without alchemical or mechanical aid could be known to reach the ridiculously advanced age of sixty. Not like Queek. Queek was old, he felt it. Kranskritt could smell it. Weakness.

'It will smell of burrow and home soon enough,' said Ikit. 'We will smash the beard-things and take their heads. No more dwarf-things! All done. All ours.'

'This is true. Once enough failures accrue, they call for Queek. No one is better than Queek at killing dwarf-things. Queek will end this siege. Queek will win this war!'

The dead things on his back wailed and gibbered. What they said now made little sense. When their utterances became intelligible, what they said made Queek's fur crawl. Their voices never ceased. The long periods of quiet he had once enjoyed were no more. Even when the verminlords were close, which had been rarely of late, they did not stop their racket.

'Not without my help,' said Ikit. He too, under his mask of iron, had aged better than Queek. Queek could smell the long-life elixir on him. 'I am the pre-eminent slaughterer of dwarf-things. They call me here to finish it – you are only to help.'

'Yes-yes,' said Queek sarcastically. 'Queek hear many times of great Ikit Claw's impressive victory over orange-furs of Kadrin-place. I hear the flesh of the dead so poisonous after Ikit Claw's masterful plan not even trolls would eat it, and even now, three cold-times since big death there, the air is still deadly to breathe. Very good plan, making such a fine mountain-holdfast uninhabitable to skaven clan-packs. Very clever way of denying living space to Clan Skryre's enemies.'

'And the dwarf-things,' said Ikit, his voice ringing inside his iron mask. How Queek had grown to loathe that voice.

Queek found the warlock engineer even more irksome than the grey seer, although he was secretly relieved that the warlock's clanking pace allowed him to walk more slowly. Ikit's war engines were impressive, even if it annoyed him to admit it to himself. A lesser clan might scrape together enough warp-tokens to buy one or two lightning cannons from Clan Skryre. A greater clan might have a dozen. In the siege train of their army there were hundreds, dragged painstakingly through tunnels and mountains to assail this last enduring rock of the dwarf-things. No other warlord clan could access such mate-riel. As a result of Gnawdwell's manoeuvring, Skryre and Mors were open allies. The supply of sorcerous machines had been cut off to all other clans. Clan Eshin had not been drawn into the pact, but provided Queek's army with their warriors any-way. Clan Moulder backed all sides, so consequently many of their creatures, and specifically the newer rat ogre weapon-beasts bred in conjunction with Clan Skryre, supported his troops. With Skryre came the larger part of Clan Rictus's clanrats. From Rictus, Ikit Claw had his own bodyguard, the

Clawguard, war-scarred stormvermin as large and imposing as Queek's own Red Guard. At Queek's back went one of the largest skaven armies ever to brave the surface.

'The fate of more than the dwarfs depends upon this war,' said Kranskritt. 'Remember, O ignoble and most devious warlords, whoever takes Thorgrim-Whitebeard's head will win the seat on the Council of Thirteen. Most assuredly it will be I, and Clan Scruten will regain its rightful place.'

Queek snorted. Poor-fool Kranskritt. He was naive to the point of idiocy, not like mighty Queek! Gnawdwell had forged a pact with the other Lords of Decay, stipulating this final condition for victory in the struggle for the seat. Tired of the long years of instability the empty seat had provoked, the other clans had agreed. Clan Mors and Clan Skryre had steered events masterfully so far. Together they would claim the head of Thorgrim and break the power of the grey seers forever.

Queek wondered how long Clan Skryre had been working themselves into this position. He had no doubt that the head of the dwarf king, once he took it, would find its way into the paws of Clan Skryre, who would at the last cheat Gnawdwell. Who would stop them? Clan Pestilens were mostly destroyed in the war for Lustria.

Mighty Queek, that was who. He recalled the scratch marks on the order scroll that had arrived six weeks ago, and which he had swiftly eaten. Gnawdwell would allow Queek some of the long-life elixir, if he brought the head of the long-fur to him.

Finally, finally. Queek could not wait. He had tasted infirmity and had no liking for it.

Kranskritt was being cossetted and fooled. Even the verminlords were being played off against each other. Or were they deceiving the Council? The interminable power plays of the skaven court made Queek's teeth ache. Ever dismissive of politics, he had grown careless over the last few years, openly provocative. He set out to deliberately antagonise the heads of other clan clawpacks. Only his reputation, his distance from Skavenblight, and his own skill at arms kept him alive.

He bites his own tail, just to see it bleed, others said of him. 'Doom, doom, doom! Death, death, death!' wailed the chorus of his victims.

Only when he had a battle to fight did the ailments of mind and body recede.

The endless column of skaven crested a rise in the Silver Road Pass, and the capital of dwarf-kind came into view.

Queek was chief general of the most powerful warlord clan in all Skavendom. As such, he had seen Karaz-a-Karak many times before, but never so close. The mountain was colossal, one of the tallest in the world. Soaring above the pass and into the bruised clouds, its peak was lost to the boiling skies, its flanks dappled by the polychrome strangeness of magical winds. The raw stone had been shaped by generations of the dwarf-things, so that giant faces, hundreds of feet tall, glared challengingly at Queek. The main gate was yet many miles away, but even Queek's failing eyesight could see the dark smudge of its apex reaching high up into the cliff face that held it, surrounded on all sides by soaring bastions. The skaven leaders and their bodyguards left the road and mounted a hillock that blistered the side of the mountain. They clambered onto the rubble atop it. The beard-thing watchtower that had occupied the mound had been melted into bubbled slag. Streaks of metal in the contorted stone hinted at the fate of its garrison.

Kranskritt hissed, daunted by the sight of Everpeak. In contrast, Queek felt the confidence only those gifted with supreme arrogance can. Behind Queek stretched more clawpacks than had ever been assembled in one place. Millions of skaven were his to command. They marched by in an endless stream, their fur carpeting the road as far as the eye could see, from one end of the pass to the other. More moved underground, ready to attack from below.

'How will we take-cast down such a place?' said Kranskritt. 'There must be so many beard-things within.'

Ikit Claw laughed, his machinery venting green-tinged steam into the chill noon, as if it shared his amusement. 'The dwarf-things breed slowly. Many breeders produce no young. They were dying even before we challenged them for their burrows,' said Ikit. 'Surely you must know these things, wise one?'

Kranskritt shook his hand at the warlock. The bells on his wrist conveyed his irritation in tinkles. 'The will of the Horned Rat is my interest, not the breeding habits of lesser races.'

Ikit sniggered again.

'Are you sure this plan of yours will work, Queek?' said Kranskritt. He had stopped using the insincere flattery of their kind some time ago when speaking with the Headtaker. This social nicety had always annoyed Queek, but it annoyed him more that Kranskritt had ceased its use. 'It is rather simplistic, attacking directly.'

'Queek's plan is sound. We come on all fronts. Every shaft and hole will be assaulted at once, white-fur. And what does white-fur know of strategy? Thorgrim beard-king will not know where to defend. His forces will be scattered and easily worn down. This is the way of the dwarf-things – to stay behind their walls and fight, fool-meat that they are. We have the numbers, and they have no time. So declares mighty Queek.'

'It is still simple,' said Kranskritt. 'A pup-plan.'

Queek shrugged. 'The simpler the better, white-fur. How many grand schemes fail-wither due to incompetence and stupidity, or treachery? Treachery is so much the harder when there are fewer folds to hide in. Simple plan, Queek's plan, is best.'

'For this once, the mighty Queek speaks wisdom,' said Ikit Claw. 'All weak points are already known. This fortress has been attacked a hundred times, a thousand. There is nothing we do not know about it. Why waste time with cunning ruses to learn what we already know?'

'We have a long wait,' said Queek. 'We must meet-greet the clan warlords here and take command. Too long they have besieged the great beard-king. Thorgrim-dwarf-thing must be very sad at all this. He need not worry, for soon it will all be over. Mighty Queek is here!'

A day later Queek ordered the attack. Alone atop a newly broken statue, he watched the advance through brass looking glasses – made for him by a foolish warlock, who was dead as soon as he completed the commission. Let not know of Queek's weaknesses!

The slave legions went in first, if for no other reason than Queek had them, and they went in first by tradition. From their thousand gunports, the dwarfs gave fire.

He saw the light flashes of cannons long before he heard the sound. Rolling thunder filled the pass. The vast numbers of skaven looked puny in front of the great gates of Karaz-a-Karak.

The hundreds of lightning cannons in the skaven train were pushed into range and set up under fire. Warlocks squealed frantic orders. The guns elevated and replied.

Soon the vale at the doors of Karaz-a-Karak was thick with gunsmoke lit by discharges of greenish lightning. The skies overhead were dark, polluted by magic seeping into the world from the north. The thunders of the battle vied with those ripping the heavens apart. The imaginings of the most deranged flagellant of the Empire could not outmatch the scene. This was the end of the world, beating its apocalypse upon the stone doors of the dwarfs.

The skaven died in howling masses at the gate, the machines

they dragged with them to penetrate it smashed to pieces before they ever reached the stone and steel. Slaves surged back and forth, waves on a beach capped by froths of blood as they were cut down by dwarf and skaven alike.

So it went. So Queek expected it to go, until one of the many attacks he had ordered from the underworld broke through and skaven got into the soft underbelly of Beard-Thing Mountain-place, silenced the guns one by one, and allowed his siege engines to approach unmolested. Queek had killed many examples of the myriad creatures that crowded the world, but his greatest pleasure, and his greatest skill, lay in killing dwarfs. He knew their minds well. They would sit behind their stout walls until nearly dead, and then likely as not they would march out, determined to kill as many of the enemy as they could before they themselves were killed.

'It will cost you many lives,' said the voice of Krug. Queek's ears stiffened. The voices had been constant yet incoherent for a very long time. Krug spoke clearly, without the respect he once had. Queek glanced behind him. From a spike on Queek's rack, Krug's eye sockets glimmered with wild magic.

'Yes-yes, but I have meat to spend. The dwarf-things do not,' said Queek.

'They will make you pay,' said Krug, and there was a note of pride and defiance in his voice.

'Do not be so sure, dead-thing!' Queek snapped. Krug's voice melted into gruff laughter, before rejoining the howling chorus of the others.

Queek scratched at his head; it was bloody from his constantly doing so. The voices receded eventually.

The battle did not proceed as he expected.

The dwarf bombardment ceased. The last thunder of their discharge rolled and died. Queek watched, fascinated, as smoke puffed from the gunports and blew away. The lightning cannons went on firing unchallenged, blasting showers of rock from the mountain and its fortifications. Surely his infiltrators had not succeeded so quickly?

The great horns mounted high up the mountain blared: first one, then the other, their mournful, bovine hooting joined by hundreds of others from every covered walkway and battlement carved into the mountain. The noise of it was dreadful, and Queek flinched from it. Under it there came a great groaning creak.

'The gates! The gates!' he said excitedly, moving his field glasses from the gunports to the doors.

He fiddled with the focusing wheels, cursing their maker as the vista became a blur. He pulled the view back into focus in time to see a gleaming host emerge from the gates of Karaz-a-Karak.

The king went at the fore upon his throne. He looked as if he rode a ship of gold upon a sea of steel.

From out of the gates, the last great throng of the dwarfs marched to meet their doom.

Queek lowered his glasses for a moment. His nose twitched in disbelief. His fading eyes did not deceive him. From the vale, the sounds of gruff beard-thing voices in song drowned out the crack of lightning cannons, and the clash of arms was louder still. Loudest of all was the voice of the king. Queek raised the glasses again. Thorgrim stood upon his throne platform, one finger tracing the pages of his open book. His words, though faint, were heard clearly by Queek even from so far away.

'For the death of Hengo Baldusson and the loss of ninety-seven ore carts of gromril, five hundred thaggoraki heads. For the loss of the lower deeps of Karak Varn, two thousand thaggoraki hides. For the cruel slaying of the last kinsfolk of Karak Azgal, nine hundred tails and hides. For the...'

His recitation of his grudges roared from him, the atrocities of four thousand years of war driving his warriors onwards.

Queek watched in disbelief. For the dwarf-things to sally out so early was unheard of! He panned across the column. There were hundreds of beard-things. Thousands! He gave a wicked smile.

'The whole army of Beard-Thing Mountain comes to make war on Queek!' he tittered. 'Very kind, oh very considerate, of Thorgrim dwarf-king to bring his head to Queek's sword!'

As the dwarfs advanced into the seething mass of skaven, the guns of the walls spoke all at once. Cones of fire immolated hundreds of slaves, while cannon balls streaked overhead, the guns' aim recalibrated, to shatter dozens of the lightning cannons.

A good loss, thought Queek. He laughed as he watched Clan Skryre's pride battered by the vastly superior dwarfish artillery force. No matter how many war engines they dragged up here, the dwarf-things would always have more. Open space before the gates became a killing field, a zone of destruction advancing in front of the dwarfs in a devastating creeping bombardment.

The skavenslaves predictably broke. They fled away from the vengeful dwarf-things only to be slaughtered by the skaven stationed behind them. They went into a panicked frenzy, tearing each other apart, gnawing on anything to escape. This was a fine exploitation of the explosive violence of the skaven's survival instinct, and had won many battles on its own. But every dwarf was armed and armoured in fine gear. The weapons they carried glowed with runes, Thorgrim's dread axe brightest of all. The Axe of Grimnir shone as if sensing the rising tide of war, emitting a radiance that could be seen far down the gloomy pass. The throng of armoured bodies shone blue in its reflected effulgence.

The dwarfs waded through the frenzied slaves regardless of their snapping mouths and their insensate fighting. Weapon-light pushed back the twilight of the dying world.

Queek had never seen so many magical weapons deployed in one place. He would not have thought there so many in the world. Queek's triumphal squeaking quieted as the dwarfs cleaved their way relentlessly through the slave legion and into the clawpacks waiting behind. Skaven died in droves. Soon enough, the dwarfs were through the slaves and trampling Clan Rictus and Clan Mors banners underfoot.

A titanic boom rumbled from a few miles up the pass. Queek swung his glasses around, catching sight of the sides of the pass collapsing along a good mile of the road. The rocks peeled away either side to bury thousands of his troops, and his better ones at that, in deadly avalanches. Pale new cliffs shone in the war-choked gloom, menacing as bared fangs.

No, this was not quite as good as he first thought. Still, the inevitable was happening. The dwarfs drove forward. Caught up in their hatred, they were moving further and further away from the gates. The guns would soon stop for fear of killing their own. Something Queek himself had no qualms about.

Making his decision, Queek secreted his seeing aid within his robes.

'Loyal Ska!' he called.

The great skaven limped around a boulder that had until recently been the nose of a dwarf king.

'Coming, O mighty one,' he said. Ska too was old and slow, but his arm was still stronger than that of any other.

'Order up the next clawpack! Make the dwarf-things rage. Soon-soon they go out of range of their guns, fool-things. Ready Queek's Red Guard. When the beard-things are tired, when they are alone, then Queek will attack and add the head of the last king to his collection!'

'Yes, great one,' said Ska with a curt bow.

'Ska?'

'Yes, O mightiest and bloodiest of warlords?'

Queek looked back into the valley, the battle a shifting blur without his glasses. The noise from below told him all he needed to know. He had seen many dwarf armies at bay before, fighting to their last out of sheer, stubborn vindictiveness. A sight that was as glorious as it was terrifying. 'The long war is nearly over.'

'For the slaughter of the miners of Karak Akrar, fifty thaggoraki hides!' roared Thorgrim. The power of the throne was in him, the pain of his wound dulled by his hatred. The stink of the rat creatures surrounding him angered him further. Only their blood could slake the terrible thirst for vengeance he felt. 'For the deaths of Runelord Kranig and his seven apprentices, and the loss of the rune of persistence, nine hundred tails!' The Axe of Grimnir hummed with power as it bit into worthless furry hides.

'Onward, onward! Crush them all! Queek is impudent – we shall meet him head on and take his head!'

His army, initially reluctant, were overcome with their loathing. Every dwarf fought remorselessly.

Thorgrim spoke of Karak Azul, and Zhufbar, and the sack of Barak Varr, and the endless litany of unpaid-for wrongs that stretched back to the Time of Woes. The orders he gave were few and barked impatiently. Always he read from the Great Book of Grudges. He became a conduit for grudgement; millennia of pain and resentment flowed out from its hallowed pages through him.

The slaves were all dead. By now the dwarfs had pierced deep into the skaven army, moving away from the gates to where the vale was wider. The outlying elements reached the thaggoraki weapon positions. At the vanguard went the Kazadgate Guardians. These well-armed veterans had pushed into the war machines and were cutting their crews down. Their irondrake contingent, the Drakewardens, drove off reinforcements coming to save the machines with volleys from their guns. Their handcannons crippled the war machines, and warp generators exploded one after another in green balls of fire. The surviving warlocks squealed in anguish to see their machines destroyed.

A clashing of cymbals heralded a counter-charge led by a skaven in an armoured suit that hissed steam. Thorgrim, up on his throne, had a fine vantage point and recognised him as Ikit Claw.

'For the warpstone poisoning of the Drak River, the life of Ikit Claw!' he said, pointing out the warlock.

Claw came with a thick mob of stormvermin, but these were cut down easily by axe and forge-blast. Ikit Claw attempted to rally his followers, casting fire and lightning from his strange devices at the ironbreakers and irondrakes. But the Drakewardens walked through the fire unscathed. Their return fire blasted the stormvermin around Claw to bits. He wavered, Thorgrim thought, but a terrific racket drowned out the battlechants of the dwarfs as a dozen doomwheels came barrelling over a rise. Too late to save their cannon, the doomwheels exacted revenge for their loss, running down a good portion of the Kazadgate Guardians.

At this insult, Thorgrim took pause. He had come right out in front – too far in front. In the wider vale, the dwarfs had no way of protecting their flanks, and his army was being encircled, broken up into separate islands of defiance. They were gleaming redoubts in a universe of filth. Thorgrim could count the warriors remaining to him, and their numbers dwindled. The skaven were effectively infinite.

Thorgrim looked from side to side. His Everguard and throne stood alone, one of the smallest of these islands. His fury was the greatest and had carried him furthest.

The Great Banner of Clan Mors, festooned with obscene

trophies, was approaching him at the head of Queek's Red Guard. Alongside it came rat ogres of a new and vicious kind, bearing whirring blades instead of fists, smoke belching from the engines upon their backs.

The High King and his bodyguard were cut off. The nearest group of his army had noted the peril he was in and were fighting desperately to come to him. They hewed down skaven by the hundred, but there were always more to fill the gap. They might as well fight quicksand. By the time the other dwarfs reached the High King, it would be too late.

'Bold dawi,' said Thorgrim. 'Queek comes. We shall meet their charge.'

His Everguard reformed into a square, clearing space in the skaven horde for their manoeuvre with their hammers. Thorgrim spied Queek's back banner at the front of the formation moving to attack them.

'Stand firm!' he called. 'In our defiance, eternity is assured!'

Queek broke into a run, coming ahead of his followers, his yellow teeth bared, the pick that had taken the lives of so many dwarfs raised high.

Queek vaulted over the front line of the Everguard, cutting one of them down. Before he landed, the lines of dwarf and skaven met with a noise that shook the mountain.

Queek had not waited for the best time, thought Thorgrim; he would have been better served holding off for a few more minutes. But it was still a good time, he thought ruefully.

The Everguard were the elite of the dwarf elite, warriors bred to battle, whose fathers' fathers had served the kings of Karaz-a-Karak since the dawn of the Eternal Realm. The Red Guard could not hope to match them.

Queek, however, could. Thorgrim was chilled at how easily the skaven seemed to slaughter his warriors, spinning and leaping. Every thrust and swipe of his weapons spelled death for another dwarf, while their own hammers thunked harmlessly into the spot the skaven lord had been a moment before. There were still many ranks of Everguard between Thorgrim and Queek, but time was not on their side.

'I'll not wait to be challenged by that monster! Forward, thronebearers. Forward! Everguard, you shall let me pass as your oaths to me demand!'

In dismay, the Everguard parted, fearing for the life of their king. They were beset on all sides, the rat ogres chewing through their right flank. The dwarfs killed far more skaven than died themselves, but they fought the same battle every dwarfhold had fought and lost: a hopeless war of attrition.

'Forward! Forward! Bring me to him so that he might feel the kiss of Grimnir's axe!'

The shouts of dwarfs were becoming more insistent. They were far out of the range of their guns. The cannons spoke still, slaughtering every skaven that came close to the gates, but the greater part of the throng of Karaz-a-Karak was isolated, and surely doomed.

Thorgrim reached the front line. His axe sent the head of a rat ogre spinning away. His Everguard cheered as it died. He would not allow that he had doomed his hold and the Eternal Realm. Only victory was on his mind; it was the only possible outcome. The magic in the throne reached up, lending strength to him through the metal of his armour and weapons. Queek changed course. He was twenty feet away, then ten. The square of dwarfs shrank as more of their number fell, Thorgrim's thronebearers stepping back in unison with them.

The end was coming.

'For Karaz-a-Karak! For the Karaz Ankor!' Thorgrim shouted, and prepared himself for his ancestors' censure for his foolishness.

Horns sang close at hand. Dwarf horns.

Thorgrim eviscerated a rat ogre. It went down, teeth still clashing. He lifted his eyes upwards. Against the glow of the shrouded sun, he picked out figures. The silhouette of a banner emerged over a bluff, as down an almost invisible game trail, dwarfs came.

Atop the banner gleamed a winged ale tankard.

'Bugman is here! Bugman comes!' shouted the dwarfs, and swung their tired arms harder.

Bugman's rangers were few in number, no more than a hundred. Vagabonds who roamed the wastelands behind their vengeful leader, survivors of the sacking of Bugman's famous brewery, they were scruffy and ill-kempt. But each and every one was an implacable warrior, as skilled in the arts of death as he was in brewing. Crossbow bolts hissed into the Red Guard's rear. Surefooted dwarfs ran down the steep slope, tossing axes at the greater beasts and bringing them down. A brighter light shone, that of fire, and what Thorgrim saw next burned itself into his memory.

Ungrim of Karak Kadrin was with Bugman's rangers. On him too was a strange, magical glow. His eyes burned with the heat of the forge. The Axe of Dargo trailed flame, the crest on his helmet elongated by tongues of fire. With a desolate roar of rage and loss, the last Slayer King launched himself twenty feet from a cliff top straight into the skaven ranks. Burning bodies were hurled skywards with every swipe of his axe. Behind him came many Slayers, the last of his kin and his subjects, each one orange-crested and bare-chested. They scrambled down rocks and set about their bloody work. Night runners detached themselves from the shadows, hurrying to intercept the reinforcements, but they were slaughtered, flung back, their remnants scurrying away back into obscurity.

'Bugman! Ungrim!' laughed Thorgrim. His face changed. 'Queek,' he said quietly. He ordered his thronebearers to set down his throne. 'Headtaker! I call you! Queek! My axe thirsts for vengeance. Come to me and with your blood we shall strike many grudges from the Dammaz Kron!'

# TWENTY-SIX

*The Death of a Warlord*

His troops were letting him down again! Queek smelt the fear-stink, heard the calling of beard-thing instruments and the change of pitch in their shouts from despair to excitement.

'Must finish this quick-fast,' he muttered.

The Horned Rat must have heard Queek. Thorgrim approached him, stepping down off his land-boat, bellowing Queek's name.

'Good-good,' snickered Queek. 'Very good! Here dwarf-thing, a spike is waiting, much company for the long face-fur!'

Queek flicked his wrist, spinning Dwarf Gouger, and took up his battle stance. With one finger he beckoned Thorgrim onwards.

Thorgrim shouted at him, his voice deeper than the pits of Fester Spike. 'Queek! Queek! For the death of Krug Ironhand! The head of Queek!'

Queek laughed at his petty grievances.

'Queek flattered that mighty beard-thing not need his special book to recount Queek's fame!'

'For the illegal occupation of Karak Eight Peaks! The head of Queek!' shouted Thorgrim. The dwarf-thing's eyes were glazed and spittle coated his beard. Quite mad, thought Queek. Good.

'Queek is coming!' trilled Queek, and laughed. 'Queek killed many dwarf-things – soon there will be no more left to kill. This makes Queek sad. Maybe Queek take a few of High King Thorgrim-thing's littermates back to Skavenblight for fighting practice? Truly Queek is merciful.'

Roaring his hatred, Thorgrim charged, just as Queek had anticipated. Dwarfs were a weak race; their affection for their pups and littermates made them easy to goad. Such a pity, Queek had wanted this duel to be one to savour in the long years ahead, when he grew young on Gnawdwell's elixirs and there were no more dwarf-things in the world to slay.

Queek waited until Thorgrim was so close he could see the red veins threading his tired eyes before launching his rightly famed attack. Queek leapt, his age forgotten, his body spinning. He drew his sword and simultaneously swung the weighted spike of Dwarf Gouger at Thorgrim's helmet. Queek's mind worked quickly, so fast the world appeared to move more slowly to him than to those of longer-lived races. He did not know it, but it was a blessing in some ways, this rapid life cycle. Queek could enjoy the sight of his weapon spike hurtling towards the dwarf's face in unhurried slowness.

Queek blinked. Thorgrim swept up his axe. Impossible! The runes on the axe shone as bright as the hidden sun, searing their image onto Queek's eyes. He could not read the scratch marks, but in one terrible moment of understanding their meaning became clear: Death. Death to the enemies of the dwarfs!

Dwarf Gouger met the axe. The rune-shine whited out his vision, and he knew if he survived his eyes would never recover. Dwarf Gouger shattered on the edge of the blade with a bang and discharge of freed magic. Queek landed, panicked. He thrust at Thorgrim with his sword, seeking to make him dodge aside so that Queek could put distance between them. But the snarl nested in the thing's long face-fur grew more ferocious. He grabbed Queek's sword in his armoured fist and yanked him forwards. Queek scrambled to get back, but could not. So unusual was the situation that he did not think to release his sword's hilt until it was too late. Thorgrim dropped his axe and grabbed Queek by the throat, lifting him high into the air. Only then did Queek let his sword go, and Thorgrim flipped it around, using it to cut loose Queek's treasured back banner. The dead things' heads fell, screaming in exultation, free at last.

'For the Battle of Karak Azul, the head of Queek,' rasped Thorgrim, his voice ruined by his screaming.

Queek squirmed and thrashed, his teeth clashing in panic. He braced his legs against Thorgrim, trying to flip backwards. His world turned black around the edges. Queek scrabbled with his hand-paws, raking at the king's face.

'For the killing of Belegar Angrund, rightful king of Karak Eight Peaks, the head of Queek,' spat Thorgrim.

Queek's struggles weakened. His frantic gouging became more precise. He gave up trying to hurt Thorgrim and desperately attempted to pry the dwarf's granite grip loose. The fingers would not shift, and Queek's own bled as his claws tore loose on the king's impenetrable armour. Thorgrim tightened his grip. Queek's choking became wet, feeble as the death croaks of a dying slave-rat.

The king pulled Queek level with his bearded face. 'For the death of many thousand dawi, the head of Queek. Now die, you miserable son of the sewers.'

The last thing Queek ever saw were the eyes of Thorgrim Grudgebearer, burning with vengeance.

\* \* \*

Thorgrim shook the skaven. Queek's neck snapped. His body went limp, but Thorgrim continued to squeeze, the litany of woes he shouted at Queek transforming into a long, inchoate roar.

At last, he dropped the body at his feet and stamped upon it with ironshod boots, shattering Queek's bones. He spat on it with disdain.

'You can keep your head upon its neck, thaggoraki. I'll not have it sully my halls.'

Thorgrim retrieved the Axe of Grimnir and gestured to his thronebearers. The skaven were in full flight, mad panic radiating out from the points where Thorgrim stood and where Ungrim slaughtered them. Queek's Red Guard were smashed down as they broke.

'That's right! Flee, you worthless, honourless cowards!' shouted Thorgrim. The sun had sunk below the level of the boiling clouds, and a golden light shone on the battlefield, as if the strange aura of his throne had expanded to take in the whole of the vale.

Satisfied at what he saw, he turned and walked back towards his throne, his bearers kneeling in anticipation. He looked forward to striking out many grudges today.

Unseen by the king, a black-clad skaven flitted from the churning mass of fleeing ratmen and ran at him. Too late, one of his thronebearers called a warning, dropping the throne and raising his axe to protect his lord. His bodyguard were too far away to intercept it, caught up in the merciless slaughter the battle had become. Thorgrim was exposed and alone, surrounded by bodies.

The assassin leapt as Thorgrim began to turn, drawing two long daggers that wept black poisons. It drove them down, putting all its momentum into the strike with a victorious squeal. The blades shattered upon the Armour of Skaldour, and Thorgrim dispatched the creature, opening its body from collarbone to crotch with the Axe of Grimnir.

Thorgrim flicked the blood from his rune axe and remounted his throne as a ragged cheer went up. All around the skaven were fleeing. Trapped by the avalanches unleashed by the dwarfs, they had nowhere to run, only a few making it over the broken mountainside blocking the road back to the safety of their tunnels. They still outnumbered the dwarfs five hundred times, but their flight was unstoppable. Only Queek could have halted them, and Queek was dead.

'Destroy them all! Destroy them!' shouted Thorgrim. 'Let none escape!' Cannon and gunfire slew those who attempted to run towards Karaz-a-Karak in the confusion. Ungrim and his Slayers cut down the warlock engineers, Ungrim's axe blasted fire over their leader. Thorgrim saw Ikit Claw fall. He watched to see him rise again, but he did not. Another grudge answered.

A roaring filled the vale as gyrobombers flew over the king, stirring his beard hair with their progress. They swooped low, bomb racks rattling, blasting the skaven apart. Ungrim's fire consumed those few ratkin who tried to reform.

The battle was over. Thorgrim saw the greatest victory of his time play out around him, and it felt good. But the strange power had left him and his throne. It gleamed only as much as gold could gleam, and his armour felt heavy upon him again. He sent a silent prayer to Grungni for his aid, if that was indeed who had sent it.

'My king!' said a thronebearer. Thorgrim glanced down to the ashen face of Garomdok Grobkul.

Thorgrim felt ice in his heart. Somehow, he knew what Garomdok was about to say before he said it.

'The Rune of Azamar, my king, it is broken!'

# TWENTY-SEVEN

*Eternity's End*

At the edge of the battlefield, three dwarf lords watched their kin go about their sorrowful work.

'I could not save them,' said Ungrim Ironfist. Fire still flickered around him, on his axe and in his eyes, but it could not hide his despair. 'I marched too far from my gates, filled with thoughts of vengeance. They sprang their trap. Three of their abominations breached the gates. They had within them bombs full of gas...' His face contorted. He could not understand why anyone would do such a thing. 'Everyone, everything... It is all gone, gone!'

'Rest easy, lad,' said Josef Bugman, who had a particularly disrespectful way with kings. 'Here, let me get you something for your nerves.'

Bugman beckoned over one of his warriors, a young dwarf already scarred and grim-eyed from many battles. Bugman took a tankard from him and offered it to Ungrim. 'Fit for a king,' he said encouragingly.

The Slayer King stared at him, deep in shock. 'I am not a king any more. I have failed in one oath. Only by fulfilling the other can I make amends.'

All over the battlefield dwarfs worked, retrieving their lamentable number of dead. There were many runic items scattered amid the gore. These were attended to even before the slain, while a large block of troops stood ready, in case the skaven mounted another attack, took them unawares and armed themselves with the treasures of their ancestors. Dusk had fallen. Night came quickly, abetted by the fumes that clogged the sky and kept the sun away.

'Drink,' said Bugman encouragingly.

'No, no, I will not,' said Ungrim. 'I cannot rest, I will not rest. My Slayers and I will go to the Empire, to lend what aid we can to the Emperor, if he still lives.'

'All need light in dark days,' said Bugman.

'Grimnir is with me,' said Ungrim.

'At least let me give you a few casks of ale for your warriors. They'll march further and fight harder with a little of my XXXXXX in their bellies.'

Ungrim nodded, and Bugman gave the necessary orders. The last dwarfs of Karak Kadrin, unsmiling though they were, were nevertheless grateful.

Thorgrim and Bugman watched them go into the fast-falling night, Ungrim's fiery aura making of him a living torch to light the way.

'A kingly gift, Master Brewer,' said Thorgrim.

'I am not a king either, High King,' said Bugman affably. 'But I do what I can.' He sighed. 'A bad business this. A bad, bad time.'

'It is a time we cannot recover from,' said Thorgrim quietly. 'Look at Ungrim. Karak Kadrin fell three years ago and he behaves as if it were yesterday. If we prevail, shall we all be the same? Broken-minded, fit only to roam the lands of our ancestors?'

'Steady now, that's not like you to say so, king.'

'The Rune of Azamar is broken,' said Thorgrim.

To them both, the mountain breeze blew a little more chill. Silently, Thorgrim led Bugman round the back of the throne and pointed out the awful truth. There was no light to the rune, and a long, fine crack ran across it from top to bottom.

Bugman tamped down tobacco into the bowl of his pipe and sat down upon a rock. Behind them, dwarfs shouted and chisels clattered as the stonemasons' guild repaired what damage they could to the walls. Bugman blew out a long plume of smoke. 'Aye,' he said at last. 'I am not surprised.'

'The Karaz Ankor will fall.'

'What about Ungrim? The light of Grungni was on him. Surely that's worth something.'

Thorgrim eased himself down next to the old brewer. 'It's not the light of Grungni. Something similar affected me too, filling my armour and weapons with might. Ungrim is possessed by some fire spirit, and I think something rooted in the spirit of metal came to me.'

'Is it gone now?'

Thorgrim nodded.

'Well,' said Bugman, 'Grungni or not, there's still good in this world, that's for sure.' He gave the king a penetrating stare. 'Will you drink with me, High King? You'll not refuse my brew too, will you now?'

Thorgrim was taken aback. 'A king can refuse many things, Master Brewer, but never a sup from Bugman's own barrels.'

'Good for you,' said Bugman. 'But I can do better than my own barrel. I reckon you could do with a bit of pepping up. Here, drink from my own tankard. You'll never taste its like, I promise.' The dwarf passed over a battered pewter tankard. Once finely worked, it seemed to have taken much hard use and its decorations were worn smooth where they were not tarnished.

The High King took the tankard from Bugman. It brimmed with frothy ale, although the cup had been but moments before hanging empty at the brewer's belt. The colour was perfect: a deep, golden brown, as pure as a young rinn's eyes. And its bouquet... Thorgrim lacked the words to describe it. Just smelling the beer made him lightheaded. He immersed himself in the sensation. It brought back memories of happier days, and he forgot all his woes.

Bugman chuckled. 'Go on then, don't just stare at it! Drink up, I swear by Grungni's long beard you'll feel better for it.'

Thorgrim did as he was told, even though part of him did not want the moment of expectation to pass. He put the pewter to his lips and drank deeply of the ale. Warmed to perfection, it tasted finer than anything he had ever partaken of before, and he'd enjoyed plenty of Bugman's ales in the past.

As he drank it down, a glow as golden and clean as the colour of the beer seeped into his limbs. There was a brief, vicious stab in his side as the wound seemed to fight back, but it was overwhelmed, and the warmth pushed aside the dirty, itching pain the injury caused him. He drank half the tankard down, of that he was sure, before pulling it away. His gasp of satisfaction turned to one of amazement. The tankard was still full.

'Take another pull, O king,' said Bugman.

The king did. When he finished, he patted his side, then prodded it, then poked hard. Nothing.

'The wound is not healed, I'm afraid,' said Bugman. 'It's too far gone for even my old great-granddad's tankard to fix with a couple of draughts. But you won't feel it for a while, and it might just tip it onto the right road to be mended. The curative powers of the mug and my ancestor's best brew. You'll not get that anywhere else now but from my own pot. Count yourself privileged.'

Thorgrim, usually so stern, was wide-eyed. 'It is the greatest honour I have enjoyed in a long time, Master Brewer.'

'Isn't it just?' said Bugman. He looked the king dead in the eye. For all his power and honourable ancestry, Thorgrim felt the battered ranger, born from the dwarf exodus, little better than city-dwelling umgdawi, to be far more than an equal to him. 'When my old dad's brewery burned to the ground, and my folk were all killed, I thought it was the end of the world.' He sighed, a spill of smoke twisting its way from his mouth. 'And it was the end of one. Another began. I am still here. Don't scratch out the dawi yet, High King. There's fight in us all still.'

Bugman hung his magic pint pot, now mysteriously empty again, from his belt. He stood up and offered his hand to the king, like they were two merchants in a bar and not a dispossessed brewer and the lord of all dwarfs. Thorgrim shook it.

'I'll be away now.' He looked into the night, broken only by the dwarfs' lamps and torches and the light streaming from the high windows of the forts. 'There are other dwarfs out there as need me.'

'Still?' said Thorgrim.

Bugman smiled down at the king. 'Aye, and there always will be. Whatever happens next, king of kings, don't ever forget that. We've lost a lot, that's for sure, but there's no use crying over spilt ale. As long as the mountains are made of stone, there'll be dwarfs in them, of that I've no doubt.'

Bugman lifted up his head, and let out a long trilling whistle. The call of the high mountain chough, not heard for years in those parts. It brought a tear to the king's eye.

Dark, solid shapes moved from out of the rocks. Thorgrim rubbed his eyes. He felt quite drunk. Bugman, seconds ago alone, was surrounded by his warriors.

'Look after those of my lads that fell here, king.'

Thorgrim nodded. Bugman winked and vanished into the dark.

Blearily Thorgrim got into his throne. From the vantage it offered, he looked about, but Bugman was nowhere to be seen. He suddenly felt very tired.

'I shall rest a moment,' he said. 'Just a moment.' He sat down, closed his eyes, and drifted off to the sound of dwarfs hard at work repairing the damage others had done.

Thanquol was nauseous. No matter how he held himself, he felt like he was about to fall over. The walls of the tower – he assumed it was a tower, but who knew if it was or if it was not – did not look right. He felt like he was standing at an angle even when he was quite straight. Wherever Lord Verminking had brought him was not of his world.

'Now we show you, as promised,' said the verminlord.

'What should I see?' asked Thanquol. He stared into the swirling scrye-orb Verminking produced out of nowhere.

'Doom, yes-yes. Doom which will lead to your ascension,' said Skitzlegion.

This did not exactly answer Thanquol. He had no idea how the swirling clouds within the orb amounted to doom, and how was he going to ascend? The grey seer was about to question the verminlord further when the mists of the globe coalesced into faintly glowing images. He was watching a dwarf-thing.

'The king of all dwarfs!' he whispered. 'How do you do-accomplish this? Dwarf scratch-magic makes see-scrying impossible.'

'Not to us,' said Verminking, tittering. 'We know things you shall never know. Concentrate. Think yourself inside his head. You will know all. You will know his thoughts, his heart, his mind. Breath-breath! Yes, yes, that is right. In, we skaven can steal into anything, why not another's soul? Listen to me, Thanquol, and you learn much, plenty-good magic...'

Thanquol's vision swam. And then he wasn't there any more.

\* \* \*

Thorgrim Grudgebearer looked up the first curl of the spiral Stair of Remembrance. The walk to the King's High Porch atop Karaz-a-Karak was always an arduous climb, but right then the stairs were as daunting as a steep mountain slope. He was bone tired. He'd woken a few hours before dawn to find himself exhausted. A clean tiredness, that of the purged, but heavy upon him. He suspected his whole body ached, but could only feel the renewed throb of his wound. Bugman had been right, though. The returned pain was less than it had been before he drank from the fabled tankard. He supposed he should rest more, and he would, but this had to be done first. With his jaw set in determination, the High King began the journey up the spiral stair. Although he longed for sleep, this personal ritual, a way to both commemorate the fallen and ultimately to clear his head, had to be performed.

Despite his victory, his mind was awhirl. Ungrim – grown stranger than ever – had given the High King much to muse over, but that would have to wait. And Bugman, with his never-empty cup and unquenchable hope. Could it be the dwarfs would persist? Now the ale glow was gone, Thorgrim was not so sure, and his oaths to retake their ancient realm seemed laughable.

The stairs demanded his attention, and he turned it upon them. Up and up he wound, each step bringing him pain.

No one but the High King might use these stairs. The lookout at the top and its King's View was his privilege alone. It was High King Alriksson, Thorgrim's predecessor, who had shown Thorgrim the way, and even then he had not been permitted to look out, not until Alriksson was dead, and he had made the journey alone.

With each clumping step, Thorgrim remembered one of the slain from the day's battle. He recalled each dwarf, his name and clan. The journey took hours, yet Thorgrim always ran out of stairs before he ran out of names. The rest of the fallen must await his return trip.

Towards the top, the air grew very thin, and Thorgrim's lungs laboured hard, aggravating the pain in his side. Dwarf blood was thick, but the air was too sparse here even for them. His progress slowed. The last quarter took longer than the rest. He saved the names of the greatest of warriors for this difficult part of the climb.

At last he reached the top, a high dome carved right inside the very tip of the mountain, adorned with carvings unseen by any other eyes and lit with a king's ransom of ancient runic glimlights. The sight always awed him slightly, a reminder of the power and glory of the old dwarf kingdom. Coming here was like ascending into the heavens themselves.

Outside, there were no longer any stars. Thorgrim pushed open the rune-heavy door to the porch. The stone slid outwards soundlessly.

Wind whistled around the edges. The air this high was icy and incredibly thin. Thorgrim took deep, panting breaths to stave off dizziness and stepped onto the shallow balcony of the King's High Porch. Twelve paces across, seven deep, a small balcony, whose balustrade pillars were fashioned in the shape of dwarf warriors. Cut from a natural bay in the mountain, the porch was invisible from below. When shut, the door behind Thorgrim blended seamlessly with the stone. Below him the high snowfields of Karaz-a-Karak plunged downwards. The horizon to the east was a dull silver, the rising sun fighting against the murk. In the few clear patches of the night-gripped sky overhead, only rings of black-green could be seen, the whirling remnants of the cursed Chaos moon.

From the top of the world, Thorgrim looked down upon the lesser peaks. They marched away to every horizon, untroubled by the wars of the creatures who lived among them. Only now in this private spot did the High King begin to open and examine the chambers of his mind. Karaz-a-Karak had resisted, but for how long? And how much stock could he put in the legend of the Rune of Azamar? He wished Ungrim had remained behind – he had never expected Bugman to – but perhaps he could do something to aid the realms of men. In some of the few accounts Thorgrim had received, the Emperor was dead; in others he was alive, but his nation was a ravaged ruin. If he still lived, he would need all the help he could get.

Deep in thought, Thorgrim never saw the black shadow unfold from the rocky peak. Spider-like, it crawled down a cliff face before letting go.

'Assassin!' squealed Thanquol in his nowhere place.

'Hsst!' warned Verminking. 'Do not let your excitement alert the king to our presence. We are in his mind!' Then, more gently, he continued, 'This is the culmination of many scheme-plans. Deathmaster Snikch delivers the final blow to the dwarf-thing's empire. It has taken him long-long to work his way to the top of Beard-Thing Mountain-place. No other but he and Lurklox could have achieved it.'

'The king's armour...' began Thanquol doubtfully.

'He bears new knives, they are warpforged, each triple blessed by the retchings of the Verminlord Lurklox, Master of All Deceptions. They can slice through gromril as easily as incisors sink into a corpse. He will not fail, now hush, and watch!'

In mid-air, the dark shape somersaulted and drew forth its three blades – one in each hand and a third in its tail. With all the momentum of his fall, Snikch drove all three blades into his target.

Thorgrim staggered forwards, great stabs of pain coursing through him. Thanquol gasped, sharing a sliver of his agony. As the king fell to his knees, Thanquol fell to his. Through Thorgrim's eyes he could see the points of three blades jutting out of his chest, and for a gut-churning second, Thanquol thought it his own.

Thorgrim's last thoughts were for his people. Like a damned fool beardling he had left the door open behind him. There were so many grudges left unanswered. His last thought crystallised with painful clarity – of course, the hateful cowards had stabbed him in the back.

Thanquol's consciousness retreated from the dead king, and he observed the scene once again through the scrying-orb.

Tail lashing with excitement, Thanquol watched Snikch saw off the king's head with his tailblade. The Deathmaster kept watch on the open runic door, his tail performing the grisly deed by its own volition.

'That head will come to you, little horned one,' purred Verminking behind him. 'You must take-show it before the Council of Thirteen, Reclaim the grey seers' rightful place.'

'But... but... you told Verminlord Soothgnawer, many praises be upon him, that...'

Verminking chittered, half in amusement, half in exasperation. 'I had not expected such naivete from you, little seer.'

Thanquol, who had long anticipated himself on the Council of Thirteen, let his mind race with possibilities.

In the orb, the asssassin was scrawling runes upon the stone.

Verminking explained. 'He is summoning Lurklox. Dwarf scratch-magic prevents skitterleaping, but his scratch-markings will overcome them. Soon an army of gutter runners will be inside Karaz-a-Karak. They will open the gates for our rabble army. Clan Mors has been all but destroyed, but the lesser warlord clans wait in the deep tunnels, and they will be inside before the dwarf-things know. The dwarf realm will be utterly broken!'

'Then we have won, yes-yes?' asked Thanquol in surprise. The thought of it seemed... odd.

Verminking shook his head solemnly, his majestic horns swaying. 'We have won much, but not all. The lizard-things and their lands are dead-gone – but Clan Pestilens is broken. I sense Vermalanx and Throxstraggle's fury. Although,' he mused, 'we must not forget Skrolk, or the Seventh Plaguelord, for he is hidden within the Under-Empire even from my eyes. Clan Skryre has been humbled, but Ikit Claw just survived and will be dangerous. While more goes on in the minds of the Moulders than you know.'

Verminking looked down upon the grey seer, his enormous claw-hand patting Thanquol's head.

'And our new allies – the Everchosen, Chaos. They are most powerful of all, yes-yes. We need-must not tell you. Yet we, you and us, we will bide our time. One day it will all be ours.'

Thanquol smiled faithfully up at Verminking. The answer to how to conceal his true thoughts had been simple, when it came to him. As he guarded his words, he must guard his thoughts. All day he had been practising at obscuring his intentions from the verminlord behind a wall of sycophantic loyalty he built across his mind. Once he was certain of the method, he had thought the most treacherous thoughts he could. And Verminking did not hear! All through the battle he had done so without repercussion. He was growing in power.

Shielded by this mental redoubt, Thanquol plotted how he would rid himself of the verminlord for good, and use what he had learned to his greater advantage. He was Thanquol! The most cunning skaven who had ever lived. Lord Skreech Verminking would come to regret forgetting that.

'Yes-yes, O great one,' said Thanquol. His eyes narrowed. Soon he would be the master. Soon he would sit upon the Council of Thirteen in the mortal world. But why should he stop there? Unwittingly, the verminlord had opened endless worlds of opportunity to him.

Thanquol's face betrayed even less than his mind did. 'Your wishes are my commands,' he said, and meant not a word of it.

## ABOUT THE AUTHOR

A prolific freelance author and journalist, **Guy Haley** is the author of Space Marine Battles: *Death of Integrity*, the Warhammer 40,000 novels *Valedor* and *Baneblade*, and the novellas *The Eternal Crusader, The Last Days of Ector* and *Broken Sword*, for Damocles. His enthusiasm for all things greenskin has also led him to pen the eponymous Warhammer novel *Skarsnik*. He lives in Yorkshire with his wife and son.

WARHAMMER®
THE END TIMES

THE LORD OF THE
END TIMES

JOSH REYNOLDS

*An extract from* The Lord of the End Times,
Book V of Warhammer: The End Times
*by Josh Reynolds*

Archaon glared about him, his breath rasping from within his helmet. 'Face me, damn you. I will not be denied now – not now! I have broken your army, I have gutted your city... *Where are you?*'

Canto jerked on his mount's reins, bringing it to a halt behind Archaon. The latter glanced at him. 'Where is he, Unsworn? Where is he?' he demanded, and Canto felt a moment of uncertainty as he noted the pleading tone of Archaon's words.

'I am here,' a voice said, and each word struck the air like a hammer-blow. Canto shuddered as the echo of that voice rose over the square, and the sounds of battle faded. A wind rose, carrying smoke with it, isolating them from the madness that still consumed the world around them. 'I am here, Diederick Kastner,' Valten said. His words were punctuated by the slow *clop-clop-clop* of his horse's hooves.

'Do not say that name,' Archaon said, his voice calmer than it had been a moment ago. 'You have not earned the right to say that name. You are not *him*.'

'No, I am not. I thought, once, that I might be... But that is not my fate,' Valten said. 'And I am thankful for it. I am thankful that my part in this... farce, as you call it, is almost done. And that I will not have to see the horror that comes next.'

'Coward,' Archaon said.

'No. Cowardice is not acceptance. Cowardice is tearing down the foundations of heaven because you cannot bear its light. Cowardice is blaming gods for the vagaries of men. Cowardice is choosing damnation over death, and casting a people on the fire to assuage your wounded soul.' Valten looked up, and heaved a long, sad sigh. 'I see so much now. I see all of the roads not taken, and I see how small your masters are.' He looked at Archaon. 'They drove their greatest heroes and warriors into my path like sheep, all to spare you this moment. Because even now... they doubt you. They doubt, and you can feel it. Why else would you be so determined to face me?'

'You do not deserve to bear that hammer,' Archaon said. 'You do not deserve *any of it.*'

'No.' Valten smiled gently. 'But you did.' He lifted Ghal Maraz. 'Once, I think, this was meant for you. But the claws of Chaos pluck even the thinnest strands of fate. And so it has come to this.' His smile shifted, becoming harder. 'Two sons of many fathers, forgotten mothers and a shared moment.' He extended the hammer. 'The gods are watching, Everchosen. Let us give them a show.'

'What do you know of gods?' Archaon snarled. 'You know nothing.'

'I know that if you want this city, this world, you must earn it.' Valten urged his horse forwards and Archaon did the same. Both animals seemed almost as eager for the fray as their riders, and the shrieks and snarls of the one were matched by the whinnying challenge of the other. Canto tried to follow, but found himself unable to move. He was not here to participate, but to watch. The Swords of Chaos spread out around him, a silent audience for the contest to come. He felt no relief, and wanted nothing more than to be elsewhere, anywhere other than here.

Archaon leaned forward, and raised his sword. Valten swung his hammer, and Archaon's shield buckled under the impact. The Everchosen rocked in his saddle. He parried a blow that would have taken off his head, and his sword wailed like a lost soul as its blade crashed against the flat of the hammer's head. As they broke apart, Archaon's steed lunged and sank its fangs into the throat of Valten's horse. With a wet wrench, the daemon steed tore out the other animal's throat.

Valten hurled himself from the saddle even as his horse collapsed. He crashed down on the steps of the Temple of Ulric. Archaon spurred his horse on and leaned out to skewer the fallen Herald. Valten, reacting with superhuman speed, caught the blow on Ghal Maraz's haft. He twisted the hammer, shoving the blade aside. The daemon-horse reared up, and Valten surged to his feet. His hammer thudded into the animal's scarred flank. The beast cried out in pain, and it stumbled away. Archaon snarled in rage and chopped down at Valten again and again. One of the blows caught Valten, opening a bloody gash in his shoulder.

The Herald of Sigmar staggered back. Archaon wheeled his steed about, intent on finishing what he'd started. His mount slammed into Valten, and sent the latter sprawling. As Valten tried to get to his feet, Archaon's sword tore through his cuirass.

Valten sank back down, and for a moment, Canto thought the fight was done. But, then Valten heaved himself to his feet, and he seemed suffused with a golden, painful light. Canto raised a hand protectively in front of his eyes, and he heard a rattling, hollow moan rise from the stiff shapes of the Swords of Chaos.

Archaon's steed retreated, shying from the light. It gibbered and shrieked, and no amount of cursing from Archaon could bring the beast under control. The Everchosen swung himself down from the saddle and started towards his opponent. As he entered the glow of the light, steam rose from his armour, and he seemed to shrink into himself. But he pressed forward nonetheless. Valten strode to meet him.

They met with a sound like thunder. Ghal Maraz connected with the Slayer of Kings, and Canto was nearly knocked from his saddle by the echo of the impact. Windows shattered across the plaza, and the Ulricsmund shook. The two warriors traded blows, moving back and forth in an intricate waltz of destruction. Archaon stepped aside as Ghal Maraz drove down, and cobbles exploded into fragments. Valten leaned away from the Slayer of Kings's bite, and a wall or statue earned a new scar. When the weapons connected the air shuddered and twisted, and each time the Swords of Chaos groaned as if in pain.

Their fight took them up the steps of the Temple of Ulric. First one had the advantage, and then the other. Neither gave ground. Canto watched, unable to tear his eyes away, though the power that swirled and snarled about the two figures threatened to blind him. Two destinies were at war, and the skeins of fate strained to contain their struggle. The rest of the battle faded into the background... heroes lived, fought and died in their dozens, but this was the only battle that mattered. The future would be decided by either the Skull-Splitter or the Slayer of Kings.

Or, perhaps not.

A figure, reeking of blood and ice, clad in scorched furs, darted suddenly through the smoke. For an instant, Canto thought it was a wolf. Then he saw it was a man, and felt something tense within him. The man radiated power – dark, brooding and wild. He sprang up the steps of the temple, bounding towards the duellists. 'Stay your hand, servant of

ruin,' he howled, in a voice which was at once human and something greater. 'This is my city, and you will despoil it no more!'

'Gregor – no!' Valten cried, flinging out a hand. The newcomer froze, half-crouched, like a wolf ready to spring. Magic bled from him, and the air about him was thick with snow and frost. 'This is my fight. This is the moment I was born for, and you well know it, Gregor Martak. And even if its outcome is not to your liking, neither you nor Ulric shall interfere.'

The air vibrated with a growl that came from everywhere and nowhere at once. To Canto, it was as if the city itself were a slumbering beast now stirring. Archaon hefted his blade in both hands and said, 'Growl all you like, old god. You are dead, and your city with you. And that shell you cower in is soon to join you, Supreme Patriarch or no.'

'Maybe so, spawn of damnation,' the newcomer growled, 'but even dead, a wolf can bite. And when it does, it does not let go.'

'Bite away and break your teeth, beast-god. My time is now,' Archaon snapped.

'No,' Valten said. 'Our time is now.'

Available from *blacklibrary.com*
and

GAMES WORKSHOP®

Hobby Centres.